Praise for

THE FINAL REVIVAL OF OPAL & NEV

"A lively take on the music industry's commercialism, racism, and sexism, and also a commentary on how history and memory are refracted through changing cultural currents."

—THE NEW YORKER

"Heavy subjects don't weigh down this hugely entertaining novel...A testament to Walton's deftness and skill."

—OPRAHMAG.COM

"Easy to read, and yet layered in both its organization and its impact."

—VOGUE

"*The Final Revival of Opal & Nev* features an ambitious literary structure that is rarely seen in contemporary writing. On the surface, it is a complex oral history conducted by a music journalist about her beloved rock 'n' roll duo. But as the interview touches deeper, we see more unexpected layers of the story that will threaten to reverse any established narratives. The unique storytelling matches the depth of the theme that the novel aspires to explore: Black women who dare to tell the truth but whose voices are too often repressed."

—THE MILLIONS

"[A] showstopper . . . Unsparing and raw in its exploration of the personal and political complications these characters face, the novel explodes with color, style, and music as it explores the challenges of love and art, racism and gender inequality in a story that doesn't leave a single note out of place."

—THE DAILY BEAST

"In her powerful debut novel, Walton sews a fictional rock duo so seamlessly into the fabric of music history you'll be tempted to google as you read to hear Opal and Nev's nascent Afro-Punk sound, to see their pictures, to share shaky footage of their provocative live shows."

— *THE PHILADELPHIA INQUIRER*

"A delightful and intriguing investigation into pop culture, American history, and race. It makes you question why you're drawn to the music that you like, forces you to reflect on important moments in pop culture, and makes you think about who gets forgotten over time."

— **MINNESOTA PUBLIC RADIO**

"A true feat of creativity—and a book that uses history to help contextualize what is going on in the here and now. Racism, feminism, and capitalism are all addressed and subverted in Walton's debut novel."

— *SHE READS*

"Walton handles even the most serious issues with a gloriously light, wise touch."

— *COLUMBUS DISPATCH*

"An intelligently executed love letter to Black female empowerment and the world of rock music."

— *KIRKUS REVIEWS*

"A poignant and relevant reckoning for two captivating women . . . An utterly absorbing addition to contemporary fiction."

— *BUST*

"Walton has crafted a rock 'n' roll novel for the ages."

— *LIT HUB*

"Buckle up when you sit down to follow Opal on her journey from a young girl in Detroit trying to find her voice to a confident woman who travels the world speaking her own truth, even when it gets her in trouble. An intoxicating blend of pop culture and politics, feminist power and fun."

— **BEVERLY BOND**, author of *BLACK GIRLS ROCK!: OWNING OUR MAGIC, ROCKING OUR TRUTH.*, and creator and executive producer of *BLACK GIRLS ROCK!*

"Fantastic. I so desperately wanted Opal Jewel to have existed; I wanted to have experienced her music firsthand. What I love most of all about this book, though, is the way Walton quite literally inserts a strong, bold Black rock musician into a history that's often discouraged us from shining, or from even entering at all. Magical."

—**ZAKIYA DALILA HARRIS**, author of the
New York Times bestseller
The Other Black Girl

"What girl who has had to march to the beat of her own drummer can't relate to Opal? Or to the things she says, such as one of my favorite lines: 'Looking the way I did, and as poor as we were, how did I not let life run me over?' Opal's search for herself, for love, for acceptance is infinitely relatable. *The Final Revival of Opal & Nev* is a jewel!"

—**PAT CLEVELAND**, author of
Walking with the Muses

"Voices are marshaled from across America, and then across the Atlantic, and blended seamlessly into a tale about Black culture, Black women, and American capitalism. "

—**TA-NEHISI COATES**,
New York Times bestselling author of
The Water Dancer and *Between the World and Me*

"It delves into the complexities of the creative life, specifically as it pertains to Black women . . . and instead of shying away or egg-shelling, it does what every good book does: tells the truth. A truth that bangs. That shrieks. A siren song to shatter what we've known of the novel. Things won't ever be the same after this. And I'm so happy Dawnie Walton has arrived."

—**JASON REYNOLDS**,
New York Times bestselling author of
A Long Way Down

"*The Final Revival of Opal & Nev* is lovely and lyrical; a warm and wonderful intersection between journalism and fiction."

—**KILEY REID**,
New York Times bestselling author of
Such a Fun Age

"'Bold' doesn't even begin to describe it. Dawnie Walton's exhilarating debut is a thrill ride into the Afro-Punk 1970s complete with a central character so unforgettable, you'll almost believe you've heard her name before."

—**AYANA MATHIS** , author of
The Twelve Tribes of Hattie

"By turns playful and serious, and always wonderfully entertaining . . . the immensely gifted Dawnie Walton creates a vivid chorus of voices as she tells the story of Opal's journey from a dive in Detroit to the stage in New York where everything changes. This novel rocks."

—**MARGOT LIVESEY**, author of
The Boy in the Field

The

Final Revival

of

OPAL
& NEV

★ *a novel* ★

Dawnie Walton

37INK

SIMON & SCHUSTER

New York London Toronto Sydney New Delhi

37 INK

SIMON &
SCHUSTER

An Imprint of Simon & Schuster, Inc.
1230 Avenue of the Americas
New York, NY 10020

This book is a work of fiction. Any references to historical events, real people, or real places are used fictitiously. Other names, characters, places, and events are products of the author's imagination, and any resemblance to actual events or places or persons, living or dead, is entirely coincidental.

First 37 INK/Simon & Schuster paperback edition March 2022

37 INK/SIMON & SCHUSTER and colophon are
trademarks of Simon & Schuster, Inc.

For information about special discounts for bulk purchases, please contact Simon & Schuster Special Sales at 1-866-506-1949 or business@simonandschuster.com.

The Simon & Schuster Speakers Bureau can bring authors to your live event. For more information or to book an event, contact the Simon & Schuster Speakers Bureau at 1-866-248-3049 or visit our website at www.simonspeakers.com.

Interior design by Lewelin Polanco

Cover design by Anthony C. Santagati

Manufactured in the United States of America

3 5 7 9 10 8 6 4 2

The Library of Congress has cataloged the hardcover edition as follows:
Names: Walton, Dawnie, author.
Title: The final revival of Opal & Nev : a novel / Dawnie Walton.
Description: First 37 Ink/Simon & Schuster hardcover edition. |
New York : 37 Ink/Simon & Schuster, 2021.
Identifiers: LCCN 2020046657 | ISBN 9781982140168 (hardback) |
ISBN 9781982140175 (trade paperback) | ISBN 9781982140182 (ebook)
Subjects: LCSH: Women rock musicians—Fiction. |
Rock musicians—Fiction. |Rock groups—Fiction.
Classification: LCC PS3623.A4544 F56 2021 | DDC 813/.6—dc23
LC record available at https://lccn.loc.gov/2020046657

ISBN 978-1-9821-4016-8
ISBN 978-1-9821-4017-5 (pbk)
ISBN 978-1-9821-4018-2 (ebook)

For my parents,
and for Anthony

EDITOR'S NOTE

Disclosure: My father, a drummer named Jimmy Curtis, fell in love with Opal Jewel in the summer of 1970. For the duration of their affair he was married to my mother, who in '71 got pregnant with me. Before my birth, before the world had a chance to know much about my father beyond these facts, he was beaten to death by a racist gang during the riot at Rivington Showcase. And before my mother could bury his broken body, his mistress blazed to stardom.

This is a personal history that, throughout my life, I have taken significant pains to conceal. In my twenty-five years as a journalist, I've never needed to lean on it. I got here under my own steam—toured the world's most dazzling arenas with U2; won awards for following funny money raised by benefit concerts; even interviewed artists who, oblivious of my connections, cited Opal Jewel and Nev Charles, together and solo, as their heroes: Santigold, the White Stripes, and the Yeah Yeah Yeahs, to name just a few. All this work I've compiled as S. Sunny Shelton, the name I put to legal papers on my eighteenth birthday. My chosen name—this hard-earned byline—cobbles together the first initial of my birth name, my favorite word as a child, and the Philadelphia street where the umber facade of my maternal grandmother's row house decays, flake by flake. You could say that every decision I've made to divorce myself from the violent birth of Opal & Nev has been like this: intentional, and a touch paranoid.

So, you ask, what the hell am I doing now, writing the foreword for a story I swore I'd never tell? I could justify my involvement in this project by explaining that the internet and cable news have changed the game for journalists, stretching the boundaries of what's possible and upending all the rules we thought we knew. I could tell you that in this new era, readers and television audiences now accept, even *expect*, a flavoring of bias.

But I wouldn't want to bullshit you.

This book exists because in March 2015, when I was named *Aural*'s editor in chief—the first African American and first woman to win the gig since the magazine launched in 1965—I gave myself permission to write it.

Understand that before my big come-up, I had been playing a game familiar to many women of color outnumbered in our industries. I worked hard, kept my head down, and made a meticulous, watertight case, supported by data-stuffed PowerPoints, for every idea I ever pitched. And still I worried that the reasons for my success would be questioned by even my most progressive white colleagues. I imagined that at cocktail parties, the bane of my socially anxious existence, they would gossip about me after I left their huddles—roll their eyes and snark to each other, between bites of crab cake, "Isn't diversity *wonderful*?"

After our young new publisher offered me the promotion, I nonetheless closed the door of my office on the fourteenth floor, opened the window that looked down onto Liberty Street, and screamed victory to the poor tourists below. I felt pride, of course, but something more, something better: freedom. Freedom to trust my tastes, take my own counsel, make bold moves. Here was a chance, or so I'd assumed, to pursue every fascination I had ever wanted to follow but didn't feel that I could. I looked up at the 1972 *Vogue* photo of Opal Jewel that I'd pinned to a corkboard, its significance to me carefully shrouded among all the other rock memorabilia I kept there, and I thought, *Maybe it's finally time.*

As if on cue, like the supernatural force I'd always imagined her to be, Opal Jewel appeared in my life not long after that reverie. At the April 2015 taping of a Netflix music special honoring studio wizards, the first high-profile event I'd attended since taking *Aural*'s reins, I ran into her—*literally* ran into her, as in both of our clutches fell to the floor, her bullet of lipstick and my cell phone clattering across the marble.

This happened inside the ladies' lounge at New York's Gotham Hall, minutes before the event was scheduled to start. Nev was on the bill, set to play a couple of his old solo hits in tribute to Rivington Records' super-producer, Bob Hize, and Nev's presence had made me skittish enough. But even considering the honoree, no one had expected Opal would show up. (Ironic, considering shock was once her forte.)

She hadn't made the scene in decades, and that night her attire was subdued—she wore a simple black shirtdress, with a yellow paisley turban hugging her scalp instead of one of the old, wild wigs. Still, I knew instantly who she was. I know her the same ways that you do, as Nev Charles's onetime partner-in-strange: the ebony-skinned provocateur, the fashion rebel, the singer/screecher/Afro-Punk ancestor, the unapologetically Black feminist resurrected via GIFs and Instagram quotes for these intense political times. Of course, through my lens, so many other identities were superimposed: *Here was my father's crazy girlfriend. The one he'd got himself killed for. The source of my mother's pain and, by extension, her frustrations with me. My most complicated idol.*

At first when we collided—her gliding in through the door, me stalking out in the treacherous high heels I'd worn to walk the red carpet—Opal Jewel shot me the side-eye of life, the "Honey, *please!*" expression to launch a million new memes. And then she squinted as I scrambled to pick up her handbag. She raised my lowered head with a finger under my chin, and she called me by the first name I ever had. The name that my father, I would later learn, had intended for me, improvised from a dream:

"SarahLena," she said, and it wasn't even a question. "Jimmy's girl."

It was a moment I had dreaded and fantasized about since I was nine. That was the year an older cousin, angry that I had beaten him in a tight game of Chinese checkers on our grandmother's front porch, said that my daddy had got his head kicked in over some "ugly bald-headed bitch." After I called him a liar he snuck into Gran-D's bedroom and pulled the old *New York Times* clipping from her cedar chest. Before I read the story on the melee at Rivington Showcase—featuring Marion Jacobie's iconic photograph of Opal and Nev, and reporting my father as the "1 Dead"—I hadn't known any of it.

All this seemed too much to blurt, standing face-to-face with Opal in the ladies' lounge. I wasn't a child. I was forty-three years old, a top professional at one of my industry's starriest events. The lights in the lounge flickered to signal the start of the program, so I excused myself and hustled out. Thanks to my new gig, I had the privilege of being seated at one of the best tables in the house, right in front of the stage with the *Times* critics and the Netflix executives, but I could barely pay attention to the show. If you ever happen to stream it, there's a moment when the camera pans over the audience, and that's when you'll see me: a grave-faced Black woman wearing a choker necklace and a pile of locs atop her head. Everyone around me is smiling and singing along with Bruce Springsteen and Chrissie Hynde, but I'm staring off somewhere. Studying the monitors, on guard for the past.

That night I didn't see Opal buddying up with Nev and his team, and she wasn't seated anywhere near Hize's table, either. From what I could tell, she wasn't even in the front half of the room that the cameras could catch. I was gulping water by that point, thinking that maybe the stress of the day and three glasses of champagne had made me dream the whole encounter, when the waiter came around again. In front of me he dropped a puck of cheesecake, drizzled over with chocolate ganache, and a note on yellow paper. I unfolded it. In red Sharpie was a phone number, followed by that famous autograph: the OPAL in wide-stance all caps, followed by the cut-diamond shape.

————

We met where Opal was staying in Harlem, in the same brownstone where she had lived with Virgil LaFleur when she first arrived in New York in 1970. LaFleur, her best friend and principal stylist, hovered around us on the parlor level, protective of Opal and skeptical of me. "*Off* the record, *chère*," he chimed every two minutes. Eventually she sent him out, on a hunt for an elusive flavor of gelato conveniently found "somewhere downtown." For more than an hour, then, Opal Jewel and I were alone, and during that time she confirmed something I think I had known, deep down, since I was a teenager growing up in a single-income apartment and yet shuttling off every morning to the toniest private school in greater Philadelphia: Opal was the one who gave my mother the money for my education, straight through to my master's in journalism from Medill. During my visit she was blunt and funny, edge-snatching as always, and when Virgil returned she sent me away but told me I could see her in Los Angeles, if I were so inclined.

On my next trip west, with my first cover as editor of *Aural* off to the printers, I pulled up to the Baldwin Hills address she'd given me. A note on the door pointed me to the back of the house, where Opal, bald as you please, was smoking a joint in a rocking chair and directing an assistant gardener in the care of her tomato, okra, and basil plants. In the daylight her dark skin glowed, still unlined despite her sixty-six years, and the high angle of her cheekbones, sitting above the deep-V chin, gave her an ethereal, almost alien aspect. We talked for another two hours as the dusk came down and the air grew thick with gnats. Although our chats would eventually turn more fraught as we circled the details of her fateful dalliance with my father, these early off-the-record moments were a dream: We touched on her childhood years, the development of her brash political philosophies and style, and how, forty-five years ago now, she, an outcast Black girl from Detroit, and Nev, a goofy white English boy, had decided to take a chance on each other. No, these stories weren't totally new. But even skimming them at surface level, I could see a potential for something deeper. An opportunity to hear anecdotes and revelations I had never read in any of the old interviews with Opal, or even in the relative mountain of press and biography that exists today on Nev.

At some point, the conversation turned toward me. Under the glow of tall citronella torches, Opal showed me an astonishing scrapbook she'd kept featuring my clips and columns, even tiny, terrible concert reviews of forgotten early-nineties acts that had run in the *Daily Northwestern*. As we flipped toward the back of this scrapbook, we lingered on a tribute to the Ramones I'd written, following the death of the last surviving original member, Tommy Ramone, and the exclusive excerpt I'd landed from a new book of Joni Mitchell interviews. Then finally the news, announced in *Billboard* complete with my headshot, of my promotion. It dawned on me she was leading me somewhere.

"So you know I'm a professional busybody," I said. "Is there a reason you wanted to meet with me?"

That's when she dropped an incredible scoop: Nev had broached the idea of a North American reunion tour, starting with a headlining show at summer 2016's Derringdo Festival. And though she had not performed live in more than twenty-five years, Opal was giving it serious thought.

I struggled to keep my head from popping clean off. "You want me to break this news?"

"There's nothing to break yet," she said, still looking down at my picture instead of at me. "I haven't decided to do a damn thing. Him and me, we just talking so far. But I wanted to know what you might . . . think about that."

"What do you mean, 'talking'?" Already I was seeing this tour in my mind: live, wild bits of what I'd only witnessed in fuzzy YouTube clips, a rock-and-roll fantasy I'd assumed it impossible to fulfill. A flash of my mother's face, pained in the glow of televised highlights.

Opal Jewel looked up at me finally, the scrapbook still open on the table in front of us. "I'm trying to figure out if I'm up to it. I'm getting old." She swatted a hand in the air, as if the idea were another gnat.

Yet instantly I knew that this timing was smart. A tour had the potential to excite not only the Mercurials, as Opal & Nev's old cult of fans call themselves, but a new generation—crowds ready to scream along, with these crazy progenitors of dissidence and dissonance, that Black lives matter, that love is love, that the future is female. Ready to embrace Opal Jewel not as ahead of her time, but as *now now now*.

"I was thinking," she said, "that you might get something out of this too. You know how these business types do—they got my head spinning crazy talking about . . ."

". . . promotions," I said, my heart pounding. "They want a book?"

She nodded, squinting. She seemed to be searching my face for something. "If I'm gonna go back to that music, to me and to Nev and your daddy, to doing interviews again and whatnot, it seems like a decent place to start."

And so on that pleasant night in Opal Jewel's garden, I charted in my head the book I would write—the definitive unpacking of the whos, hows, and whys surrounding the riot that killed my father and shot his weird friends and bandmates into our consciousness. I would report it as the latest volume in our Aural History series, chronicling the origins of rock stars, and I'd dispense just enough controlled emotion to make it more salable, more morning-show-ready. Little did I know that these plans would get waylaid. This end product, with its painful revisions of history (both my subjects' and my own), is what follows. You might find it at times untamed and unwieldy, and find that it contains no easy answers. But as I write these words now, embracing the funny, humbling way hindsight works, I promise my fellow Mercurials this: Though in moments it might break your heart, as it surely did mine, this story is the closest I could get to true.

—*S. Sunny Shelton*
February 20, 2017

PART ONE

chapter one

"ALL US RUG RATS"

★　★

OPAL JEWEL:

My sister, Pearl, and I grew up in Detroit. Our mother was Ruby Robinson. That's right—she was Ruby, and she named her daughters Pearl and Opal. Since I was old enough to remember, Mama worked at the GM plant on Clark Street, but not on the assembly line; she was in the cafeteria. Slopping it out to the men as fast as she could when that bell rang for lunch. If one or the other of us was sick and couldn't go to school, Mama would sneak us in and stack up potato sacks to make a pallet on the floor of the pantry, and she'd leave the door cracked so we could see out and so she could keep an eye on us too.

On those sick days, if I managed to doze off I'd wake right on up at noontime. The stampede, darling! From where I was, watching out the sliver of that cracked pantry door, I could only see feet: the backs of Mama's white nursing shoes—I don't know why the hell she wore those white shoes; every night she had to use a chewed-up old toothbrush to scrub the drops of gravy and sauce and whatever else off them—and then, facing Mama and lined up to get their grub, those rowdy men in their steel-toe boots. That's all I could see. But I could hear all kinds of stuff. Even then I could pick out a sound and tune out the rest. If I wanted to, I could focus and hear the forks scraping against the plates, or the wet noises of mouths opening and closing. When they were all lined up I could hear the men rapping to Mama—you know, flirting—and then I'd hear the craziest thing: Mama laughing and flirting right back.

PEARL WELMONT, OPAL JEWEL'S HALF SISTER:*

Opal and I were born two years apart and we had different fathers. You see how we look so different. We never were blessed to meet them, but if we asked nicely Mama would tell us whatever stories she could remember. Mine was a war hero they called Poker Joe—he got killed over in Korea, and oh, he just loved her butter beans. Opal's daddy, I think his name was Paul, he was a much older gentleman who got sick and died when we were too young to remember. Poor Mama, having to deal with all that. Widowed twice with two babies to raise in a broke-down building on the East Side.

OPAL JEWEL:

We had different daddies, yeah. But both of them worked right there at that GM plant, I'd bet you money on that. I wouldn't have judged my mother if she'd just come clean. Everybody deserves to know where they come from. But Mama never even gave us viable names to work with—just dumb stories Pearl could eat right up. What you gonna do? My sister loves to believe.

PEARL WELMONT:

A teacher from our elementary school lived the next street over, Mrs. Dennis, and in the summers when school was out she kept a bunch of us

---

* Pearl, 69, and her husband entertained us over bear claws and apple cider in the living room of their large colonial in Pontiac, Michigan. During the course of the interview, even while discussing her often strained relationship with Opal, Pearl proudly showed off old childhood photos of her sister, as well as promotional materials she's collected over the years related to Opal's career.

kids for a little extra money. And I mean, it must've been a *little* little—for one, because if I'm being honest Mrs. Dennis didn't put a whole lot of effort into it, she just let us run kinda wild. And for two, because our mother really didn't have much to give and neither did the others. All us rug rats had holes in the armpits of our T-shirts. Got oatmeal every day for breakfast, summer or winter, and had the shoes that could talk. You know what I'm talking about? Sneakers so cheap and worn down that the sole comes unglued and flaps around?

PASTOR LAWRENCE WELMONT, PEARL'S HUSBAND:

Amen! And your mama would just wrap some duct tape around the toes to shut them up. [*Laughs*]

PEARL WELMONT:

Mama would drop us off at Mrs. Dennis's place before she caught the bus to work in the mornings, and then at night she'd pick us up after her shift. Those hours in between . . . Well, all I'll say is, they were *long*. [*Laughs*] Mrs. Dennis didn't like us to go outside. She kept all kinds of toys, but we about killed each other fighting over them in that hot old apartment. On any given day there would be about twelve of us, and if the boys were feeling generous they'd let us play with their green army men or with the set of checkers or jacks. If they were feeling stingy, that meant playing house or Mother May I? with the other girls, and, well, you know how girls can be.

OPAL JEWEL:

I started losing my hair when I was nine. First a dime-size patch of it just gone in the crown. Then the edges near my right ear started rolling back. At first I was furious with Mama, because she used to rake the comb through my hair so mean, and I just knew she was ripping it out by the roots. She washed my hair once a week, every Sunday afternoon, and then she'd sit on the sofa while I'd take the position of doom on the floor between her legs. And she'd yank my head back and cleave a part down the middle, and she'd wrestle all that thick hair into two of the tightest, fattest plaits you ever saw. My neck muscles got real strong from all that pulling, honey! And the whole time I'd just be wincing and stewing, you know, because if I even said one "ouch" I got a good smack on the head and a warning to stop acting like a baby. Pearl would go back to our bedroom terrified, because her turn was coming up next. But it was inevitable—Mama was always chasing after you with that damn red comb on a Sunday. If we don't have much else in common, my sister and me, we bonded over that. We were both very tenderheaded.

So at first I thought my bald patches were because Mama was so rough, and I guess she assumed that too because suddenly on wash days she was gentler with me. The plaits got much looser, so loose they would barely last the week, and every night she rubbed extra Blue Magic into the spots where my hair was gone. That big tub of grease . . . I'll never forget the sweet smell of it. Too bad it never could work a miracle.

PEARL WELMONT:

After a while it got hard to hide Opal losing her hair, and the kids at Mrs. Dennis's wouldn't let her play with them—they'd treat anything she touched like it was dirty. Hard to be dark-skinned *and* have a problem like that back in those days, if I'm being honest. At first Opal would get so mad. She'd be crying these furious tears, swelled up from the depths of her little soul, and I'd try to comfort her but she'd squall like the devil and shove me away.

OPAL JEWEL:

Oh, those hooligans called me out my name, honey. It was "Baldy-Scaldy," "Patches". . . . When Mama finally stopped sitting vigil for whatever strands I had left on my head, she'd send me to Mrs. Dennis's with this bright red scarf on, so then I was "Pickaninny." That's the nasty little name that traveled with me back to school that fall and all the way through Eastern High. My sister tried her best to protect me but I was kinda feisty, if you can imagine. [*Laughs*]

I liked Mrs. Dennis, though. She never really refereed all that mess; she probably had enough of it during the school year, and who could blame her. But I was the only one she'd invite up on her sofa, and every afternoon while all the other kids were acting like ingrates, we'd sit together while she watched *As the World Turns* and *The Guiding Light* on her tiny black-and-white TV. Mrs. Dennis loved her stories, honey, and she made sure to hustle along our lunches—bologna sandwiches, always bologna sandwiches on white bread with yellow mustard—so she wouldn't be bothered once they came on. And while she watched, she let me flip through the magazines she kept laid out on her coffee table. *Ebony*, of course, and *Look*, and some trash ones too, the throwaway movie magazines—you remember those. She'd switch them out a lot, but there was one Mrs. Dennis always kept on the table, and that was an old issue of *Life* that had Miss Dorothy Dandridge on the cover. Miss Dorothy had on her *Carmen Jones* outfit, the black and the red, with bare shoulders and a rose tucked into her curls and a look at the camera like . . . *whew*. Brow cocked up just so, and a flash in the eyes. I really liked her attitude. Her style. Maybe that was the first time I ever noticed anybody's style, that the way you looked could make you into a different person, a character. So Dorothy was my favorite. But I also loved Lauren Bacall, because she always looked like she knew something juicy that you didn't, and also like she didn't take no stuff. You could say that I first learned about showmanship and mystique sitting on that couch in the summer, a balding little Black outcast.

By 1961, Berry Gordy's Motown was making Americans notice Detroit for more than automobiles, with big hits by the Miracles and the Marvelettes. That same year, Ruby Robinson sent her two daughters, then fourteen and twelve, on a Trailways bus heading south, to spend the first of three summers with relatives from whom she had been estranged.

OPAL JEWEL:

We were terrified to go. We're talking about the South in 1961, baby! And not just any South. *Alabama* South. *Bull Connor* South. Mama had our plans all set, tickets bought, letters written. And then that May, not long before school let out, we saw all the news about the Freedom Riders. Pictures of buses burning, smoke pouring out the windows. Those kids were not much older than Pearl and me. I would glance at Mama's face when the reports were on, and her jaw would be clenched, her brow scrunched up. I worked up the nerve one night to ask her, "Are the white folks gonna kill us?"

PEARL WELMONT:

"If you don't bother them, they won't bother you." That's what she kept telling us, and in that last week or so before we left she would make us repeat it after her. That might have been the first prayer I ever learned. [*Laughs*]

OPAL JEWEL:

At the bus station she pushed brown bags full of peanut-butter-and-jelly sandwiches into our hands and ordered us to never step foot off that bus. She handed our one suitcase to an attendant, who put it under the coach, and then she watched as we boarded and sat our behinds in the back, just like she'd told us to do.

The whole thing felt like we were being drafted for some war, and on the other end of it were people who were complete foreigners to us. We had never met them, our own family.

PEARL WELMONT:

Opal and I didn't piece it together till years later, when Mama was dying and the doctor was asking questions about her medical history, but that summer she had to have a hysterectomy. We found out it happened two days after we got on that bus. Bless her soul. She didn't have a choice but to make arrangements for us.

At the end of the eleven-hour trip from Detroit to Birmingham, the Robinson girls were met by their aunt Rose Broadnax, Ruby's younger sister, and her husband, William, a minister.

PEARL WELMONT:

We stepped off that bus exhausted, and I guess you could say a little bit wary. Inside the station we saw this fine-looking Negro couple walking toward us. The woman had beautiful pressed hair with a neat bang across her forehead and a flipped-up curl on the ends. It was hot as blazes but she wore a cream blouse with delicate pearly buttons at the wrists and a royal-blue skirt with stockings. Heels too. Butter-leather kittens that clicked across the floor. And the man hung back behind her a couple steps, wearing a full suit and tie and shoes so shined I 'bout went blind looking at them. *Clean.* I looked at Opal and she was looking back at me like, *Is this really* them*?*

OPAL JEWEL:

We just assumed the Negroes down South wore overalls and picked cotton all day. Isn't that terrible? But here come Auntie Rose looking like a bona fide *lady*, honey, like she had a walk-on spot on *The Guiding Light.* She gave us hugs and the next thing she did after that was run her hand over my patchy scalp. "Lord ha' mercy, what is your mama doing with this head?" And don't you know, the next day she took me to a Negro doctor who finally diagnosed it, and I had an answer.*

PEARL WELMONT:

They had a house in Titusville, a pretty neighborhood where all the other Black folks as fine as them lived too. No more dark apartments, amen!

---

* Opal Jewel has a form of alopecia areata, an autoimmune skin condition in which sufferers lose hair from the scalp and sometimes other parts of the body. Though there are some treatments that may promote hair regrowth, there is no cure.

Aunt Rose and Uncle Bill's house was redbrick, with a sidewalk leading up to the front door that split the lawn in two. Plus a garage where Uncle Bill parked their Cadillac—forest green and big as a boat. Aunt Rose had planted azaleas on either side of the walk, and we weren't allowed to play anywhere near them. But we made their backyard ours. I remember us running and laughing, throwing our heads back—just breathing in that soft, sweet air.

OPAL JEWEL:

For whatever sad reason, they couldn't have kids of their own, but you could tell Auntie Rose wanted them bad by the way she treated us like babydolls. She didn't waste no time taking us into town for new clothes. Next to her I guess we looked like real charity cases, true ghetto kids, but after an hour me and Pearl were brand-new. New underthings, new patent leather Mary Janes, those dainty ankle socks with the ribbon of lace around the cuff, a straw hat for me to cover up my head, and two nice dresses apiece—one of them she even let me wear out the store.

We were heading back to the Cadillac with all this loot, and I was feeling mighty happy in my hat and my yellow dress—yellow was my favorite color, still is—and I started skipping ahead down the sidewalk and singing "Shop Around" at the top of my lungs. I saw this tall white woman sashay down the sidewalk from the other direction, but I wasn't paying her no mind. Not till I felt Auntie Rose's hand on my arm, snatching me back so hard my pretty new hat flew off. She whirled me around to look at her. "Watch where you *going*," she said, and she leaned down, real quiet but scary. Then she fixed her face and looked up at that white lady as if to say she was sorry, and she picked up my hat and hustled me and Pearl to the edge of the sidewalk, and her grip stayed tight on our shoulders till that woman strolled her ass on by. And even at that young age I understood. *Oh. Okay, then.* That's *why Mama left.*

That's what the South was like for me. Sweet on the first taste, but something gone sour underneath. It'll try to trick you, now—the sugarberries and the quiet and those lovely spread-out houses. But after that day with Auntie Rose, I could smell the rotten too.

PEARL WELMONT:

Uncle Bill was the pastor at New Baptist Church in Birmingham, and so of course me and Opal started going to service every Sunday and to youth Bible study too. One night me and Opal were washing dishes after supper, and Uncle Bill heard us singing along with the radio—oh, I don't know, probably something from Motown—and he brought us to the choir director.

OPAL JEWEL:

After this life I've led, I know it's hard to imagine my ass in a church. [*Laughs*] But listen, church back then could be a different thing—a political thing, a place of organization and action, real philosophy. You had men in Birmingham like the Reverend Shuttlesworth, who gave shelter to the Freedom Riders over at Bethel Baptist, and, yeah, men like my Uncle Bill. Sometimes he would write his sermon on whatever was happening in the news and in the Movement, and those were the services I liked best. It wasn't just about folks falling out on the floor and writhing, or pastors screaming out nonsense and threats from the pulpit. You had concerned citizens and educated leaders and a good number of them were *about that business*. To make it so that my pretty Auntie Rose didn't have to use dirty facilities, you know, or move out the way of anybody coming down the sidewalk. I wanted to be part of that. *Baaaaaby*, let me tell you, I was a revolutionary at twelve years old! I wanted to join SNCC, CORE, SCLC, all of it! I even started reading Uncle Bill's copy of *Stride Toward Freedom* [the first book by Dr. Martin Luther King Jr.], until Auntie Rose took it away and told me I needed to just enjoy being a girl.

PEARL WELMONT:

That first summer, I got saved. Uncle Bill dipped me in an aluminum tub of water right at the front of the church, everybody a witness, and my relationship with the Lord was born. It felt good and right to have faith, and from that day on I carried it with me no matter what my situation happened to be, no matter what some folks in my own family thought about it. People ask me all the time, you know, "Weren't you upset over everything that happened with Opal? Weren't you passed over?" And I just say right back, "A tranquil heart gives life to the flesh, but envy makes the bones rot." That's Proverbs 14:30, the Good Book. My faith still gives me joy, gives me *life*, and I take comfort in that, amen! I was blessed to have found my voice, literally, in that church—and it was a voice so strong I surprised myself.

PASTOR LAWRENCE WELMONT:

I met Pearl and her sister one Sunday service in the middle of that summer, when I was seventeen. My family's church home was being rebuilt after a bad storm, and so in the meantime we visited over at New Baptist. I played football back then. I was swole so big I was practically busting out my suit, and with the extra people squeezing into the pews . . . Well, you can imagine how hot it could get. So I was getting drowsy, my head lolling around. [*Laughs*] But then I heard this voice that snapped me wide awake. I looked up toward the pulpit and there she was, Pearl Robinson, singing the lead on "Take My Hand, Precious Lord." Mmmm! She had her eyes squeezed shut and stood still as a rock, just rooted to the music, with a voice that blew the roof *entirely* off and sent a chill down my neck in that sweltering room. I went back the next Sunday, and the one after that. All the Sundays till she and Opal went back to Detroit for the school year.

PEARL WELMONT, *SMILING*:

I could sing, now. I could sing.

OPAL JEWEL:

I'm not gonna lie—Pearl shocked the hell outta me. We used to sing together to the pop songs on the radio, just for fun, and the harmonizing sounded decent—nothing too special. But honey, once Pearl got in that choir? Once she learned how to press on her diaphragm and work that alto? The girl opened her mouth and the angels flew out.

PASTOR LAWRENCE WELMONT:

That type of singing cannot be learned. That was the spirit hitting her, and that's what I saw that first Sunday.

OPAL JEWEL:

The voice was there, but Pearl didn't have any presence. She'd just be standing there, closed up like a fist. Even with that stacked body of hers. It was *weird*. You heard the rapture but you couldn't see it.

PASTOR LAWRENCE WELMONT:

While Pearl was out in front of the choir, filling up the whole house, here come something moving to her left. Tiny wisp of a thing, real chocolate-skinned and swaying side to side with a straw hat perched on top of her head. She looked so funny with that hat on in the choir. Little Miss Showboat. That was Opal. That *is* Opal.

EDITOR'S NOTE

It's hard not to be charmed by Nev Charles. When he sings, obviously—that versatile instrument that switches from a sweet and high plaint to a low, cozy rumble—but especially when he laughs. You must have seen this before, in late-night skits or in concert footage or maybe in last year's surreal Doritos commercial: He throws his head back, his green eyes and ginger hair disappearing momentarily from view, until all you see is chin and tongue and uvula and nostrils. The sound that erupts is boisterous and contagious, a blast of distinct "HA HA!s" often accompanied by a single sharp clap of the hands.

I triggered this delightful response when we finally met, as we were getting settled on his private plane, its dingy seats and the peeling adhesive tint over the windows evidence that the money, while still enough to cover jet fuel, wasn't quite what it used to be. Our tête-à-tête was the result of a long negotiation—one that had irked Lizzie Harris, the PR maven who has plotted the direction of Nev's public life for literally as long as I've been alive, through crises including Rivington Showcase, addiction, failed marriages, and, in recent years, the collective shrug with which his new music has been received. Lizzie made it plain that this book was proceeding under duress—*No offense, doll*, she'd said, *I'd just planned to arrange the writer myself*. But since Opal had floated the offer to me—an independent journalist who couldn't be bankrolled, who could spill the possible reunion of Opal & Nev at any moment—she was backed somewhat into a corner.

I made concessions, and she made concessions, and our dance involved a loose agreement that I might be granted some time with Nev so long as

I kept under embargo this talk of a reunion tour. The final step toward yes had been to get Opal & Nev's producer, Bob Hize, whose health by then was seriously ailing, to agree to an on-the-record chat with me—touchingly easy, once I put in writing an interview request that revealed who I was. (When I visited him at his bedside, despite his late-stage cancer his eyes lit up and he called me "dear girl," and I understood why his artists love and respect him so.) Once Bob came onboard for what would likely be the last formal interviews of his life, Lizzie sighed and gave the okay. I thanked her profusely, nearly teary with relief at getting the green light, but, like the toughest, most impressive women with whom I've ever worked, Lizzie skipped sentimentality and launched into logistics.

The best way to get several hours with Nev, she advised, was to do them consecutively and in a confined, non-distracting space. And so we planned that I'd join Nev on a twelve-hour flight from London to Kyoto, where he was due to perform the old solo hits (plus float a few new songs) at a jazz and folk festival. I'd brought along a file of clips about Nev from *Aural*'s archives, including a portrait from 1976, the year America celebrated its bicentennial (and Nev, coincidentally, got naturalized). In it, Nev's head pops out of a gigantic apple pie. Glops of filling and bits of crust cling to his skin and muck up his mullet; wild-eyed and grimacing, he clenches his teeth around the stem of a miniature American flag.

Sitting across from him on the plane, looking for a way to break the ice as we rumbled down the runway, I showed this old photo to him. "First question," I said, mock-serious. "Did you consider *rescinding* your citizenship after this?"

That's when he gave it to me like a gift: that air-gobbler of a cackle. Which startled our flight attendant so badly that she nearly spilled the club soda she was pouring straight into Nev's lap, which led Nev to joke about how such a spill would actually leave his blue jeans *cleaner* than before, which set him off on a recitation of limericks he'd once written in response to Alanis Morrissette's "Ironic" . . . all of which, I confess, had the effect of mesmerizing me dumb. Ten minutes later, he ended the riff with an "Ah, well." And before I could ask a single real question, Nev Charles reclined his seat for what he said would be a power nap. "My left eye'll go twitchy if I don't," he explained, yawning. He proceeded to plunge into a deep sleep, laid out on his back.

I spent the first hour of his snoring organizing my questions and feeling quite competent. Even glancing about with a bit of fondness. The wrinkles around Nev's eyes made him look smart and distinguished. Better than on television. The kind of older man referred to as a fox. Did he look a bit like an older, redder Benedict Cumberbatch? He did, I thought; he did. In the seat next to him was a tote that had fallen onto its side to reveal what he was consuming these days: *The New Jim Crow*; a recent issue of *The Atlantic*; a slim book of poetry that, by some miracle, had just cracked the *New York Times*' best sellers list.

When one hour became two became three, when the flight attendant draped a blanket over Nev's prone body, pure panic surged through me. Time was ticking past, and I'd been told this would be my only shot to interview him. I glanced at the time on my phone, at the books and magazines again: Were these props set up for me to notice them? Would I ruin our rapport if I waggled his foot in order to wake him? Might he think such a move was admirably assertive, or just plain rude? Good lord, had he taken a *pill*? I asked the pretty young flight attendant how long he normally slept on these flights. "It's the only time he gets to," she chided me.

Thankfully, shortly after this, a sudden drop in our plane's elevation jolted Nev awake. His eyes landed on me and he jerked again, as if surprised I hadn't parachuted out the back.

"Sorry about the turbulence, Mr. Charles," the pilot's voice said over the intercom. "We'll take her up a little higher."

Nev returned to an upright position and jostled a pinkie in his ear. Jerked his head toward each shoulder, as if forcing water out. "I'm told you're Jimmy Curtis's daughter, is that right?" he asked.

"Yes," I said, "but I'm not in the business of dropping his name." I scrambled to open the recording app on my phone while Nev was still alert and somewhat focused. "Shall we start?"

"Straight to the chase, then," he said. "Good! A real journalist. A little like your father too. Not much for idle chitchat, that one."

Now Nev was going too fast, getting ahead of himself. As with Opal Jewel, I wanted to start our formal interview at the beginning. I felt that I *needed* to start there, although initially, with a megastar like Nev, I wasn't sure why. Certainly there's been enough ink spilled on the facts of his childhood, enough to comprise two paragraphs of his impressively long Wikipedia page. At first he unspooled it for me with great wit and verve, the way any crowd-pleaser spins through the old repertoire: He burst into snippets of melody when remembering the evolution of a riff or chorus, and his warm English accent modulated high or low with the mood of whatever tale he was spinning. Yes, of course, I was entertained.

But whenever he let loose that silly, spectacular laugh, I couldn't help but wonder how most of what I'd read about Nev failed to answer these core questions: How does a laugh like this—so unselfconscious and assured in its obnoxiousness, so made for a good-natured mocking on *SNL*—square with the image of the lonely, bookish boy he used to be? What was the distance crossed? And what got lost along the way?

This journey begins circa 1962—the year Nev turned fourteen, and his musical life began in another Birmingham.

chapter two

"THE THINGS
LONELY BOYS DO"

★ ★

NEVILLE "NEV" CHARLES:

I was an only child, and I wanted for nothing but company. Someone to kick the football round with, or even better, a girl who'd let me kiss her. Ah, such tragic cliché! My dad [Morris Charles] owned a chain of chip shops called Charlie's across Birmingham, a couple of them in Coventry, and when I was in primary school it was a splendid thing, because at his shops the cod came wrapped in white paper and then underneath that, lining the baskets, he would put the newspaper comics. And the lads got a kick out of that, reading what Buck Ryan was up to between the splashes of vinegar. After school I'd walk to the closest location in Hagley Road, and Dad would be behind the counter, his shirtsleeves rolled up, his hands covered in flour, and the boys from class would stop in. They'd see me in the back booth, with my nose stuck in my notebook as per usual, and when they were leaving they'd wave and shout [*affecting child's voice*], "All right, Nev!" and I'd shout right back, "All right, then! Tomorrow!"

At secondary, it was a different story. All of a sudden everyone cared about how people made their money, and my old mates' fathers were bankers and solicitors and mine made his life standing over crocks of spattering grease. Hooray for the British class system! [*Laughs*]

In her early twenties, Mum [Helen Charles] had a job at a green-grocer's, stacking the produce and helping to check the customers' ration books, but she wanted to act and sing and model—that's actually how she met my dad. When he was expanding the shops, he had the idea to take out an advertisement in the newspaper, and so he went to an agency to hire a good-looking girl he could put in it. I have that old ad framed in one of my homes. Mum is wearing a flowery dress and holding up a chip and smiling, and there's a word bubble over her head and she says [*imitating woman's voice*], "Choose Charlie's!" and underneath her the new locations are printed along the bottom.

Some people, especially you Americans, you look at photographs of my mum and my dad and you make a face and you wonder how the two of them got together, him being so much older and stodgy. Funny how people said the same thing about Opal & Nev—"odd couple" and that bit. But I say my parents made a very smart pair. When her mood was up, my mum was delightful and so talented, and I wish people knew that—how the smallest things she did were sunshine. How sometimes, on weekends when I was little, she'd turn on Radio Luxembourg and make me dance with her. And my dad gave my mum a stable home, which is what everyone needed, wasn't it, coming out of the war? And she had the freedom to pursue all those pleasures that she still had an interest in. Their marriage, I'd say, was a feminist model.

When I was younger I would go with her on auditions for all kinds of things, not just for advertisements but these godawful theater productions. She was a looker, a ginger like me except with blue eyes, but for whatever reason it never really happened for her. Nothing beyond small parts in the panto every Christmas. My dad and I would be in the audience wearing our finest, and everyone in the theater would be laughing and singing along except for him—because he would get choked up, my dad, watching my mum in the chorus in her silly makeup and petticoats. He thought it was the most magical thing in the world, her on the stage, *any* stage, really. But she always dreamed of the bigger roles.

This is a long way round to me telling you how I started songwriting, isn't it? It's a bit like I'm in therapy, yeah? [*Laughs*] The point of it is, my mother stopped trying when the Christmas shows stopped being enough, when she aged out of the chance to play the principal girl. And then she got depressed, although of course we weren't calling it that then, but in any case she wasn't in a mood much to bother with me. Dad was a dear but always gone, tending the shops. So I was alone much of the time, and did the things lonely boys do, I suppose. Yes, that's right, wanking every possible moment. [*Laughs*] No, well, I mean imaginary friends and all that. And then when I was older, that transitioned to making up stories about people I wanted to know, boys I wanted to be. I always had a composition notebook filled with pieces of stories, and companion drawings too. I went on a tear once, three notebooks full about this character I kept coming back to, a poor outcast boy named Thomas who had fits, and during his fits he'd travel to different times and realms. One time he's climbed Mount Kilimanjaro, and at the top he meets a girl his age who has fits too, and they fall in love. Another time he's on a rocket ship visiting the aliens who live on the different rings of Saturn. And every one of his adventures would end with him coming out of his fit and back to the present, and reflecting on everything he's learned while eating a tin of his favorite hazelnut biscuits. That's from an absolutely deranged mind, I tell you!

My mother never paid attention to my crazy stories, until one day she overheard me trying to work out a theme song. Because I thought my stories would be good for telly, you know, and you need a good theme song for telly! But I knew nothing about music, and so I was just testing lyrics to classic melodies, figuring out the notes and pecking them out on her upright piano—"Baa Baa Black Sheep," "Frère Jacques," "London Bridge Is Falling Down," stuff like that. [*Singing to the tune of "London Bridge"*] "Thomas Chapman writhes and shakes / Pulls up stakes, goodness sakes! / Thomas Chapman, trips he takes / Come home, Thomas." Not exactly "When I'm Sixty-Four," is it? [*Laughs*]

But Mum heard me plunking away and it seemed to brighten her up, the idea of me being into music. She started coming out of her bedroom and she'd sit on the piano bench with me, try to show me some chords and play some of the old songs she used to do. "Dream a Little Dream of Me," that was her favorite. One day she asked me if I wanted to take lessons, and the look on her face was so hopeful, so changed toward the better, that I couldn't say no.

And so I started with the piano, and my first teacher was George.

GEORGE RISEHART:*

I was twenty-two, just out of a program at Birmingham City University, when I started coming round to give him lessons. Mrs. Charles was a pretty woman—beautiful, really, with that fiery hair—and she'd hover when I was there, trying to make herself look busy but really keeping an ear out. I think Nev could feel that anxiousness. So he gave it a good try, he did, but at the piano, at least at first, he was shit.

NEV CHARLES:

I thought George was brilliant—coolest person I'd ever met. During the day he taught pathetic sods like me, but by his sideburns and the scuff on his loafers you could tell he had a whole different story going at night. At first he'd wear a cheap-looking black blazer and his hair slicked back very neat, trying to make an impression—but then Mum increased his visits to twice a week, and he relaxed enough to let his curls loose and put on the corduroy. Dad raised an eyebrow but he didn't say much, as long as Mum was happy.

---

* Interviewed by telephone in Birmingham, England, George Risehart, 76, still manages a piano shop and gives lessons out of its cramped back room. "Rosy," he tells me, remains the most popular sheet-music request among his new students.

GEORGE RISEHART:

Oh, you know, I was playing in a band like everybody else at the time. We were a quintet: lead and rhythm guitars, bass, drums, and me banging away on piano. We called ourselves the Boys from Birmingham. We worshiped the trinity: Elvis, Chuck Berry, Jerry Lee Lewis. In another universe maybe we were the Beatles. Maybe even slightly tighter, though, because we had formal training—although to our parents' horror we had no interest at all in playing classically.

The other lads and I shared an infested flat that cost entirely too much, more than we could scrape together from our pitiful club shows, so the lessons were necessary and among the least dreaded ways I could make a few quid. Most of the kids I taught were brats, very entitled—I didn't care as long as their parents were paying me to babysit. But there was something about Nev that just broke my heart, this kid so eager to please but simply not connecting in a traditional way to the music. I felt I was robbing his lovely mother.

One afternoon I was considering quitting after watching Nev wrestle for the hundredth time with something simple—"Yankee Doodle" or something like that—and Mrs. Charles invited me to stay for lunch. When you're young and poor, you don't turn down free food. So I sat at the table with her and Nev, who was so bashful he kept his head down in his notebook, scribbling away. I asked him, "What's that you're writing, Nev-o?" That's how he started telling me his Thomas stories, on and on about the boy with epilepsy and the travels to Kilimanjaro and the hazelnut biscuits. What he wrote was so bizarre and delightful, it got me thinking that there might be a different way, a different mode entirely, of teaching him.

NEV CHARLES:

George asked me if he could borrow a couple of my notebooks because he wanted to read the stories, and of course I was chuffed—it was an honor to get the attention of someone so with-it, someone who had friends and girls and a life filled with all sorts of debauchery! The next time he came round, he brought the notebooks as well as Jerry [Cardinal, the Boys' lead guitarist and singer]. Instead of going into another dreadful lesson, he and Jerry began to play music they'd done based on my stories. There were no lyrics, just the instrumentation, but in the music I could *feel* Thomas: He was twitching between George's sharp notes, he was lifting away during a transcendental bit of guitar, he was calm and reflective at the close. It told a beginning, middle, and end in a way I'd never understood before.

When they finished playing Jerry said, "Well, go on, mate. . . . What do you think?"

GEORGE RISEHART:

And he's looking at me with those green saucer eyes and he says, almost in a whisper, "Show me how to do that. But with the words this time."

Newly passionate about the possibilities of music, Nev continued studying under George Risehart and wrote the lyrics for a handful of Boys from Birmingham tunes—including 1963's "Rosy," the first Nev Charles song captured on record. Although the band was never signed, they found enthusiastic patrons in Nev's parents, who paid for studio time and allowed their son to join in their raucous nightclub concerts.

GEORGE RISEHART:

I never met anyone with a creative mind like Nev's. We were good musicians, the Boys and I, but we weren't so good at the lyrics. "I'm in love with you, doo-doo-doo, ooh-ooh-ooh. . . ." It's difficult to break through the noise like that.

But Nev was a sponge. He'd come to our practices with his notebook and watch Jerry working through a new melody, all of us straining to string together something that we wouldn't be embarrassed to sing in a room full of people. And one day he felt bold enough to chime in with his suggestions.

NEV CHARLES:

With "Rosy," Jerry and the bassist were playing these call-and-response riffs in the chorus—the guitar was *"wah-wah-WAH-la-la-la, wah-WAH-la-la-la-la"* and then the bass was *"dum-dum-doo, dum-doo-doo-doo"* — so I wanted to play off that, write a conversation between two people, the guitar being the woman called Rosy and the bass the man who wanted to know her. "'I like afternoon skies, lit up in every hue' / 'Yes, Rosy, and I do too.' / 'Would you walk by my side, forever staying true?' / 'Well, Rosy, that's up to you.'"

GEORGE RISEHART:

Of course we didn't have a girl in the band, so in our rehearsals we'd have Nev sing the girl part because his voice hadn't fully dropped yet. He'd exaggerate and put on a posh accent, and I'd do the deep man's voice. Eventually, I asked another student from my university days, a singer I knew called Carrie, to sing the part of Rosy for the recording, so that's who you see credited for the vocal.

CARRIE JOHNSTONE:

At the time, I couldn't have known it was going to be anything even close to rock music history—the first recorded song written by Nev Charles! I simply did it as a favor to George . . . well, because I'd fancied him since uni, in the fawning way girls that age tend to fancy boys.

The day we recorded, Nev was there in the studio with his parents. His mum was very pretty and, what's the word . . . poised. I don't remember much about his dad, except that he was balding and older and sort of pleasantly confused by everything. I remember wondering why they were there, and the Boys seemed annoyed as well. Then I realized they were footing the bill for the studio time.

As for Nev, he was quite serious about his song, you know, which was amusing. He kept telling me how he thought I should sing it, how to emphasize certain syllables—my "motivation" and all that. He had a lot of nervous energy. I remember asking George, "Is he meant to be a member of the band?" and George said, "No, darling, but he makes a good mascot." Certainly that hurt Nev's feelings, by the look in his eyes the rest of the session, and I felt bad about that. But maybe it also gave him ideas, because not long after that weekend, during the time George and I were having our moment, I noticed he began hanging round more and dressing in the style of the Boys—the long hair and loafers, the corduroy jacket and gray T-shirt. I'll admit it did look adorable on him, such a tough look on a sweet, nervous kid. I told him as much, and he'd blush and blush.

GEORGE RISEHART:

The Charleses paid for a small pressing of "Rosy," and we sold a few copies here and there out of some local record stores. We had Carrie come do it for some of our gigs, with me singing the male part, but then she and I had an enormous row because she'd caught me with another girl. God forgive me, Carrie, if you're out there! [*Laughs*] We couldn't afford to pay a girl singer for what Carrie had been doing for free, so we thought we'd just scrap doing "Rosy" at the gigs. Then Nev volunteered to sing the girl part, since he used to do it at the early rehearsals, and we figured why not. Nobody came to our shows much anyway.

So Nev started coming up onstage, acting out the part as well in a funny way. The audience got a kick out of it, and it became sort of a novelty thing, a signature of our shows. Suddenly Nev's shyness started melting away, and one day the other Boys and I looked up and thought, you know, *Bloody hell, what's happening here?* Our shows had got more popular, but we weren't all that thrilled because it wasn't down to us. It was because of this little lad who was charming the knickers off everyone.

When he switched from the piano to the guitar, that was the last straw; we'd all got fed up. Especially Jerry, who felt very threatened because Nev was catching on fast. The Charleses were floating us by then—everything we'd done that was worth anything was subsidized by them—and because of that we felt obligated to keep Nev in the mix. But he was clearly eager to break out. At the shows the crowd would clamor for him, and he'd make his way to the front, standing next to Jerry like it was his rightful place. He made us look like the backing band, the accompaniment. At which point, as kindly as I could, I told Mrs. Charles we could no longer accept her money.

NEV CHARLES:

They kicked me out. Actually, no, they didn't, because they never truly decided I was in. [*Laughs*] Ah, can't blame them, really. It all worked out, you could say.

Encouraged by his mother, Helen, who was stung by the Boys' rejection but more determined than ever to push him to success, Nev continued writing songs, teaching himself guitar, and performing on any stage that would have him. During holidays from school—and sometimes even when school was in session, depending on Helen's mood—the two took a train to London in the hopes of stumbling into a break.

NEV CHARLES:

Mum wanted it as much as I did—more, maybe. We'd still listen to the radio, yeah, but watching television together is what really sticks: It was *Top of the Pops* on Thursday nights, *Juke Box Jury* on Saturdays.* At the same time, she was writing letters to the people at the labels and putting them in manila envelopes along with the "Rosy" single, and before she dropped each package in the box she'd close her eyes and whisper a prayer and kiss the back of the envelope for good luck. Not one letter back, not even a "Thanks but no thanks." Still, she never did give up on me.

---

* *Top of the Pops* featured live performances by the day's chart-climbers, while *Juke Box Jury*, an adaptation of an American show, had a panel of musicians, actors, sports figures, popular DJs, and other notable types critiquing new releases and declaring each a "hit" or a "miss." As a solo artist, Nev Charles appeared on *Pops* several times, and on the other BBC series once, during a 1990 reincarnation hosted by Jools Holland.

chapter three

"COPY THE RIGHT PEOPLE, AND THE REST FALLS IN PLACE"

★ ★

Opal Jewel and Pearl Welmont both described their relationship as closer in early childhood. As the siblings matured, their outlooks on life diverged, and each sought to form meaningful connections outside the home.

PEARL WELMONT:

We went back to Birmingham two more summers after that first one, but after the bombing, Mama said "Never again."* And it was like a big hole was blown in my heart. Over the news, yes, but also because I missed Lawrence, and I missed my connection to the church.

---

* On September 15, 1963, white supremacists set dynamite outside the basement of the Sixteenth Street Baptist Church. That Sunday morning it detonated, murdering four Black girls—three of them the same age as Opal that year.

OPAL JEWEL:

Every week Sister Pearl turned it up a notch. Driving us up the wall. Mama didn't mess with religion—who knows what abominations she'd seen holy people do, growing up down there—and by that summer I was old enough to have my own mind and my own interests. My patience with Pearl quoting verses and looking cross-eyed at me on Sundays had worn entirely out. I would've understood it more if all that passion she supposedly felt for Jesus didn't wax and wane, depending on whether she'd heard from that man. If she'd mustered some real gumption, maybe she could've become a preacher herself, instead of a preacher's wife.

PEARL WELMONT:

After a while my yearning got to be too great. And a few months before I turned sixteen I took it upon myself to find a church in Detroit that would welcome me. Got on the bus and rode to a different one every Sunday, until I sat inside Emanuel Cross and my spirit just soared. The pastor welcomed visitors to testify that day, and I drifted up to the microphone and felt moved to sing. The church was packed but they encouraged me—"Take your time, honey!" [*Laughs*]—and the next Sunday I was wearing the choir robes. . . .

PASTOR LAWRENCE WELMONT:

You were the featured soloist before too long, weren't you? Don't forget to mention that.

PEARL WELMONT:

And all these years later, of course, I'm the first lady of that church. Won't He do it?

PASTOR LAWRENCE WELMONT:

By and by!

PEARL WELMONT:

This is all I have ever wanted to do with my life: spread the Good Word any way I knew how. And we have a blessed marriage, equally yoked, because we do that together. The pastor is a shepherd, and I am his rib.

Now, people today have turned *evangelical* into a dirty word, something political, but at the root of it is a deeper love than a lot of folks will ever know. I get that my sister likes to joke about me preaching to her— *at* her, she likes to say—but what I've really been trying to do all these years is save her life. We're sinners, each and every one of us, but we can be forgiven. And when she seeks the Lord's forgiveness, she'll have the peace I've always wanted for her. An unshakable rock.

OPAL JEWEL:

Let me stop you before you ask the inevitable question. Because even with you, I know it's close—it's right there dancing a damn polka on the tip of your tongue—so I might as well answer it now. You journalists would say this to me all the time: "Opal Jewel, what gave you such extra- *ordinary* confidence?" Listen, I may not be as witty as the great Nev Charles, but for sure I'm not an idiot. I understand that what people are really trying to ask me is this: "How in the world did a woman so black and so ugly manage to believe she could be somebody?"

No, no, baby, it's true. I'm not such a phony as to ignore what most people thought when they looked at me before 1971, before I became [*using air quotes*] "unique" or "special" or "striking." I was dark-skinned, and I was bald-headed, and I caught pure-D hell at Eastern High School. "Pickaninny, Pickaninny, Pickaninny." That was the name they yelled at me in the cafeteria, and the name they whispered behind the teachers' backs in class, and the name on that heifer [name redacted for privacy]'s lips before I finally got up the nerve to sock her a good one dead in her mouth.

So. Let's get to the root of this question. Looking the way I did, and as poor as we were, how did I not just let life run me over? I'm sorry, I don't usually use this word, but it's because *fuck* that.

I believe in *myself* above all. [*Pointing to her heart*] I believe I have always had a song, right here, to perform. I had an inner voice, and for a good portion of my life that voice was a lot smarter than me. It was more mature, and it was patient, and it was brave enough to tell me that despite what anybody else was saying, there was more for me out in the world and I deserved every single drop of it. I was just fine knowing that there existed, at some unknown time and in some unknown place, a pretty, dangling ring. And one day I was gonna reach up to grab hold of that ring, and I'd be lifted away.

Survival skills. Some of us have them; some of us don't. Now hold on, wait a minute—don't go taking me out of context like the rest of these fools in your business used to! I'm not talking about blaming victims. I'm just saying that some of us are naturally stronger, better equipped to deal with the bullshit than others, and that's the same as saying that some people are taller than others. Just fact, no judgment. And for those who are going through the tough times and don't have that kind of strength inside them already? Well, that's all right, because trust me: It can be learned. You just have to copy the right people, and the rest falls in place.

EARL CALVERT, ENGLISH TEACHER, EASTERN HIGH SCHOOL, 1962–73:

Eastern High didn't have an official drama program, but because I was a young teacher and the students liked me I got paid a little extra for helping coordinate a production every year. We didn't have a lot of money to stage it, but the school would make some cash selling tickets, and beforehand there'd be popcorn and peanuts you could buy and bring into the auditorium. We'd let the student council vote on what each year's show would be, and it would always be a musical so that the kids who were interested in acting could participate but so could the chorus and the band. It's funny looking back on it now, but we weren't working with material that made logical sense at Eastern. The students said no to *Carmen Jones* and *Cabin in the Sky*—they looked sideways at some of those roles, you know, and this was in the years before *The Wiz* and *Dreamgirls*. What we ended up with was a school full of inner-city Black kids doing *South Pacific*, singing 'bout "Bali Ha'i." [*Laughs*]

A group of us faculty, including the principal and the choir and band directors—and the football coach too, I don't know why—we would hold auditions and decide who got what parts. Now, Opal's sister, Pearl, she was a star in the chorus, and she would blow us away on the singing. It was just a shame that she couldn't act. We couldn't count on her to carry the whole show, but we'd usually try to find a big number for her to do somewhere in the middle, so she could have a minute to do her thing.

Then Opal would come out for her audition, and we'd get to arguing. Technically the singing was not as excellent, but to me she was a shining star on that stage. I believed every word out of her mouth. The best time I remember, and I think this was after Pearl had graduated and Opal was a senior and it was her last shot to get cast, she told us she had prepared her own reading. The principal said that wasn't allowed, said she had to audition using the material that was given to everybody, but for some reason I felt of a mind to speak up for her. So I said, "Go on ahead, Miss Robinson," and she handed me some lines to read along with her. She pulled a plastic cup out of this knapsack she was carrying— she had clearly swiped it from the school cafeteria—and she snatched the scarf off her head and ruffled up whatever little hair she had, and she stumbled around on the stage like a drunk. And then, I swear to my Lord in heaven, she launched into one of the wild Liz Taylor parts from *Who's Afraid of Virginia Woolf?* I mean, can you imagine? "So anyway, I married the SOB. . . ." That's exactly how she started; I'll never forget it as long as I live! [*Laughing*] I could hear Constance Davis, the chorus director, take this giant gasp next to me.

Although she declined to walk in her class's commencement ceremony, Opal Robinson graduated from Eastern High in June 1967. A little more than a month later, Detroit exploded in five days of violence following a police raid on a party at an unlicensed bar. The eighty-two revelers arrested in the raid had gathered at the Twelfth Street speakeasy to celebrate two young soldiers home from Vietnam. Anger over the arrests translated into looting, arson, and worse after the National Guard arrived: Forty-three people, most of them Black men, were killed in street skirmishes.

OPAL JEWEL:

I wasn't throwing rocks in the Twelfth Street riot, but I could have been. Just like I could have been one of those four little girls blown up in Birmingham a few years before. Being a nigger in this country during the 1960s meant that you constantly lived with the possibility of violence. When you look back on how the '67 riot got started, it almost seems silly—the pigs busted up another party, so what? But many of us young people, we were just filled with anger. Justifiable *rage*. We were over-policed and underemployed. Our young men were being shipped across oceans, the first time most of them had ever been outside of Detroit, and because they didn't have any other viable options they were fighting on the front lines of a war nobody could explain. I wouldn't wish that fate on my worst enemies—and that includes several of those tacky, tacky hoodlums from Eastern who went on to be Uncle Sam's henchmen soon as the diplomas hit their hands. So when those kids saw the powers that be stomping all over our joy, on our happiness for the sparing of two Black boys back from Vietnam, boys who had served their country even though it had never served them . . . Well, that becomes the moment when the first pebble strikes the cop car, right? And that's all it takes for everything to bust loose.

That summer I was biding time. I was just a month out of high school, still living at home and dreaming about the miracle that I knew was gonna come my way. Pearl was working some shifts at GM, some secretarial work she was proud of for some reason, and both she and Mama were breathing down my neck about getting a job of my own. But during those days of the riot we were all cooped up in the apartment together glued to the news, the same way we had been years earlier when the Freedom Rides were happening. Pearl was praying constantly—"Lord Jesus" this and "Lord Jesus" that. Mama was making noise about transferring to a new plant in the suburbs, and maybe buying a nice house nearby. Then Pearl would start up about marrying that man and moving down to Alabama, where she could get a Cadillac and have a safe place to park it. I looked at both of them like they were crazy, because they didn't get it. There was no escape to be had, anywhere, by being so damn *regular*.

That's when I decided it was time for me to start cooking up some luck—meeting that miracle halfway. But in order to do that I needed to figure out what direction to go, and in order to do *that* I needed some scratch.

PEARL WELMONT:

You know, my sister has never worked a real job, with structure and hours. And I think that's what makes her so . . . so . . . I don't know . . .

PASTOR LAWRENCE WELMONT:

Obstinate.

PEARL WELMONT:

Yes, that too, but I mean more like . . . impatient, when it comes to looking at me and my life and my choices. She can't relate to normal things, like a marriage and a family, and the sacrifices we make every day out of love.

PASTOR LAWRENCE WELMONT:

Didn't she work at the phone company, though?

PEARL WELMONT:

Well, right, she spent about five minutes at Michigan Bell. But she complained every second, so I'm not counting it.

OPAL JEWEL:

I was one of the girls they paid to bug folks about their bills. The ones who call you during dinner and get cussed the hell out. Seemed like half the people I had to call I knew from around the East Side, and I didn't give a good goddamn whether they mailed in a check. All I cared about was getting *my* check every payday. Because Michigan Bell owned my ass Monday to Friday, but the weekends were mine. Yeah, I sang with Pearl sometimes, I'd set up gigs for us here and there, but singing was just one of the things I could do. I could cook for you, dance you dizzy, whatever you like. Anything I could see, I tried to know at least a little something about it. They call that a *dilettante*, and that's supposed to be a bad thing—but in my mind, I was versatile! Multitalented! Twice as good at everything, as we aspirational Negroes had to be back then. So, you know, I watched Miss Julia Child come on TV, and after that I was going to the white folks' markets to find things like fresh parsley and thyme, and on Sundays, when Pearl was back from whatever marathon church session she was wailing at that day, I'd serve up the prettiest roast chicken you ever saw. Kitchen would be a mess, but the dinner would be delicious. So maybe I was going to be a chef; maybe I was gonna open my own restaurant. Or sometimes I would study the sewing patterns in women's magazines—I'd spend my check at the fabric store and make pretty skirts in all kinds of prints. Yeah, I could have been a fashion designer too. But you already know that.

I'm just saying I was interested in anything that would let me express myself, and get me out of being stuck. I was gonna find a way, honey.

chapter four

"JUST ON THE BRINK, DARLING"

★ ★

At seventeen, due to complete his secondary education and A levels, Nev Charles reached a crossroads. The two paths before him: push on with music despite his failure to attract sponsors besides his parents, or enter university, where he could tweak his talents—namely, writing—to fit a practical, paid trade. In front of his wife, Morris Charles said he'd be happy with whatever Nev decided, but frequently he pulled his son aside to lobby for university. Helen argued fiercely for the riskier path.

NEV CHARLES:

"You're just on the brink, darling"—that was her mantra. She told me I was destined to be more special than university boys. But I wasn't so confident. Well, I should clarify that: I had grown *very* confident—some might say unreasonably cocky—about my talent and my uniqueness. What I was iffy about was the ability of the wider world to get it. There was a lot coming out of the UK at the time, and you'd think the giant success stories would be encouraging, but for me it broke somewhat the opposite. I had no band of mates. I wasn't cute like Paul [McCartney], I wasn't sexy like Mick [Jagger]. . . . My guitar playing was improved but

still not what one might call "good," and offstage, in person, I wasn't terribly witty or charming. Anyone would have been taking a risk, putting
a camera in front of my face.

So I ended up choosing university, and it was an incredible botch. I
was trying to cut it both ways—I figured I could do practical studies to
please Dad, and do gigs on the side around London to please Mum. I
chose to study journalism, but I realized very quickly a problem: [*whispering*] Real people aren't as cooperative as the ones in our heads. Overall it made the writing much less fun and inspired. And it was dangerous,
really, to have me attempting to capture fact! It's shocking to say, but I
often felt a strong urge to punch up the things people said and did—big
journalism no-no, that. [*Laughs*] It was a disaster and I knew it, and in
the face of that failure the balance of my time began to shift toward
songwriting all day, and then playing whatever gigs I managed to get at
night. There weren't many—without Mum it was difficult to get myself
booked.

And let's not forget I was free in London for the first time in my life.
The city distracted me to a massive degree. I don't know how students
there manage it, getting up early every morning when there's the night
before to contend with. The pubs and the excitement and oh, God, the
girls! The beautiful, brilliant, enchanting girls . . .

SANDRA COKIE, NEV'S UNIVERSITY GIRLFRIEND:
We took a class together called Introduction to British Media. We never
spoke then but I did take notice of him because of his red hair, very
shaggy, and the way he'd arrive late and then fall asleep three-quarters
through the lecture. Everything about him intrigued me. I wondered
who he was, especially after he stopped coming to class at all.

A popular pub near campus—that's where we first had a chat. He'd
walked in with this guitar round his neck, and he was haggling with the
man behind the bar about playing a few songs, but the man was firmly
telling him that this was not a concert hall: "We have a jukebox for that."
I'd had a bit to drink with my mates but I recognized Nev straightaway,

so I went up to him and I said, "You're a naughty boy, skipping school." I suppose that was cheeky enough—he stopped arguing with the man, and he turned toward me.

We dated on and off for about a year, during which time he was barely managing passing marks. At times it was lovely between us, especially in the beginning because I think he was . . . well, yes, he was a virgin. He was so sweet and appreciative the first few times, you know, and then for a while he was very attached. I was young, and obviously there were things I found irresistible about him. His talent, of course; he was quite clever for a Brummie boy. I'd make him a ham sandwich in the kitchenette at my hall of residence—he was scrawny, incredibly underfed—and by the time I was trimming off the crusts he'd have made up a funny ditty just to make me laugh, about the mustard being jealous of the mayo, or whatever.

Things began to change a few months in, when his parents came to visit and treated us to dinner at a posh restaurant. I dressed us like proper grown-ups—I trimmed his hair back and put a temporary curl in mine. Mr. Charles was kind and pleasant, a very modest and quiet man, but the entire meal nothing seemed to please Mrs. Charles. As pretty as she was, she couldn't manage a single smile that night, neither for me nor for her son. I remember she ordered a steak, bloody, and as she cut into it she harangued Nev with a thousand questions while he stammered and actually *apologized*: Why wasn't he playing more, writing more? Had he tried to get into the labels for auditions? Didn't he know how lucky he was; didn't he see the other English boys with lesser talent making a name? And couldn't he see now, finally, that university was wasting his time? On that last one she paused and glanced over to me.

It was never the same with us after that. I don't think Nev meant to be mean, but oh, I would cry and cry over the things he'd say. Any music I liked, he'd savage. Joking, or so he'd say, while flipping through my Beatles or my Righteous Brothers, about what a sheep I was turning out to be. But, funny thing: He'd sulk sometimes if I didn't do what the other girls did. Miniskirts were popular then, but I felt self-conscious about my knees—they sat like onion bulbs in the middle of my legs—so I was more conservative and covered-up than the other girls, and he'd criticize me over that. I'm trying to remember exactly how he put it, but . . .The last time he broke up with me, he said something like we weren't a fit because he wanted more than a boring life. Then I'd see him out gallivanting with one pretty, disposable bird after the next—they adored him, flocking and flitting about.

He'd figured it all out by then, but it would still take me a while. I'm not ashamed to admit I was heartbroken.

Near the end of his second year, nineteen-year-old Nev Charles received devastating news that abruptly stopped his hedging. On March 24, 1968, during a sudden storm in Birmingham, Helen Charles was struck by a hydroplaning motorist while crossing a road near her home. She died instantly.

NEV CHARLES:

Dad was in shock. He rang the school to tell me, and before I could finish packing a bag to come home he rang back, as if he hadn't just, and broke the news to me all over again. This went on for some time with him, the amnesia of his grief, and I was very worried. On top of that, of course, I was suffering through my own sorrow and guilt. Total darkness.

The story about the accident made several of the papers, so all kinds of people turned up to the memorial—workers from the Charlie's shops who tried to prop up Dad, and these amateur actors and singers and dancers I couldn't recall, from Mum's early life. They all approached me in the church, with their sad smiles and handshakes, to tell me how beautiful and talented Mum had been, to tell me how proud she would be. I'm looking at them, at these faces wobbling through my tears, and I'm thinking, *Who are you people? How come you didn't come visit when she was alive?*

Dad had asked me to sing at the service because my making music had meant everything to her, had been the thing that could pull her out of her fog and bring her back to herself. I thought about writing something new as a tribute. But the idea of forever connecting her death, which was so bloody unfair and agonizing, with my own creative work, which had given us both such pleasure and pride . . . It just was not possible. And so I did "Dream a Little Dream of Me," her old favorite, with my acoustic guitar. One of the only times in my life I've done a cover, and I barely made it through. I couldn't steady my voice, couldn't bear to look at Dad in the front pew. I did it with my eyes closed and thought of what Mum might say if she were standing right there behind me, if it were an audition for Decca instead of her bloody goddamned funeral.

I'm sorry—it still makes me so angry to think about. My mother was far from perfect but she was lovely, and for better or worse she was a force—pushed me to get where I am, and I still hear her voice in my ear every day.

I stayed in Birmingham awhile, to help my father regroup. I took some shifts at the Charlie's in Hagley Road, and reminisced about the times I'd spent there as a boy. I think I even wrote a couple more installments about my old friend Thomas, just to see what it felt like. Then one day Dad and I were in the kitchen—he was flouring up the cod, and I was lining the baskets—and he said it was time for me to get back to London, to stop worrying about him and get on with my life. I told him on the spot that I didn't plan to go back to school, that it only felt right to do what Mum would have wanted. I asked him for his support, and he wiped his gunky hands down the front of his apron and pulled me in for a hug. "You have it, lad," he said.

Late in the summer of 1968, Morris Charles sold his interest in the Charlie's outposts in Coventry, and gave a portion of the profits to his son. With enough money to cover living expenses for a year, Nev Charles left England bound for New York City.

NEV CHARLES:

America fascinated me, so full of potential and characters. It also had a progressive spirit that I found appealing. Pete Seeger, Bob Dylan, and before them Woody Guthrie: I liked the idea of them, the image of the wandering observer, the songwriter as respected and important. Plus none of them was the most brilliant vocalist or instrumentalist, and that let me know there might be room for my talents.

I was deciding between New York and San Francisco, and New York won simply because the fare was cheaper out of London. I'm glad for that, because ultimately I needed the toughness and edge of New York. Had I been among the hippies in California, I strongly doubt that I would be on this jet chatting to you today; I'd be nodding off in a drum circle somewhere with a needle up the arm. Not saying there haven't been times I found myself *adjacent* to that predicament [*laughs*], but it's the New York inside you that helps you kick.

I didn't know anything when I first came, so I took a flat on the Upper West Side, a tiny one-bedroom with a tub in the kitchen. Ninety-Sixth and Amsterdam. Today that area is Equinox and bloody Starbucks, but back then it was thieves and rent boys and worse, and at night it was an apocalypse, dodgy being an understatement. When I wasn't watching my pocket, all my time was spent on the subway getting downtown.

The Village, that's the New York I had pictured from England. At night I hit as many open mics down there as I could; during the day, I played in coffeehouses, if they'd have me, or around the benches in Washington Square. My mum had always stressed to me, "You have to perform as much as you can—grab any opportunity, no matter how small. You never know who's got eyes on you, Nev." So anytime I was in the Village, whether I was looking for another stage or chatting up buskers or just taking a stroll down Bleecker Street, I made sure everyone saw my guitar in my hands. I'm not sure what I was expecting, trying constantly to be seen, to have some talent inside me recognized by someone, by *anyone*. But I did sense that my shot could very well be improvised, and come at any given moment.

I was stuck in the lease uptown, but it wasn't long before I hustled and found a few temporary living situations that were better suited to my new life. American women, nice, accommodating women—they were wild for the accent, and if I tossed off a tune incorporating their name I might have had a place to stay for weeks.

ROSEMARY SALDUCCI, RECEPTIONIST, RIVINGTON RECORDS, 1965–81:*

There were three of us girls on First Avenue between Eighth and Ninth. One of my roommates met Nev at this café on MacDougal where she was waitressing at the time. So she brings him home along with a couple bottles of wine she'd made off with, and she says to him, "Hey, you gotta play that funny song for my friends!" He picks up his guitar and does an early version of "Chemist Kismet," right there in our living room.

He camped out on our couch for a month and a half. We were very modern girls, so I'm sure Nev got upgraded from that couch a few of those nights. But maybe I'm only speaking for myself.

NEV CHARLES:

"Chemist Kismet" I'd written during winter in London, probably when I was supposed to be in a lecture. I'd had this horrid head cold that I couldn't put up with any longer, so I popped over to the chemist nearest my hall of residence, and in the back running the shop was one of the saddest-looking men I'd ever seen. Mid-sixties and jowly and completely overwhelmed by his customers come to pick up their prescriptions. But he soothed each one of them, answering their questions

---

* As is the case with most support staffers, Salducci, now 70, was privy to the most top-secret shenanigans of her higher-ups. With her red-framed glasses, big barrel-rolled hair, and strong New York accent, she was the breakout star of *Emergency on Line 1*, a 2007 Sundance documentary about showbiz assistants, in which she described herself as a "tough bitch with a long memory." When we met at her rent-controlled apartment in Astoria, Queens, and I congratulated her on the success of that film, she promised that she had "tons of other color" up her sleeve. To my delight, and occasionally my horror, she did not disappoint.

and wishing them to feel better. I went back to my room, downed my medicine, and wrote about him from what I imagined to be his perspective. I gave it a jangly sound, very up-tempo, for irony but also to please a crowd. In the verses I go through his customers and their ailments— [*singing*] "Mr. Trout / Has the gout / Vitamin C will knock it out"— and in the chorus it's about how he can't mend his own broken heart. I never say it expressly in the song, but I had imagined the chemist to be a widower. Later it made me think of Dad, obviously, but it was written before. Anyway, I always played that one for American women, because it's probably the most stereotypically English thing in my repertoire, and they loved it.

ROSEMARY SALDUCCI:

My main job was at Rivington Records as a receptionist for Howie Kelly, who was such an asshole but paid me all right. Artistically, Howie had no clue what he was doing, no ear whatsoever—the company started as cheap rental studios, just these pay-by-the-hour holes that any hack with a guitar could use, as long as they paid up front. But Howie had family loot and a law degree, and he liked to believe he was this master dealmaker—he could see people coming in with big dreams and figured he could bully his way into whatever he wanted.

HOWIE KELLY, FOUNDER, RIVINGTON RECORDS, *GESTURING AROUND RIVINGTON'S OFFICES:**

This place was my dream, and now it's my legacy. Everybody wants a piece of the Rivington catalog, I'm telling you—in the nineties we

---

* Kelly, 82, held court in the New York offices of the label, now run by his son Mark. Joining us was his attorney, Stephen Rowe of the firm Abbott & Deane, with whom *Aural* negotiated the terms of this interview. However, Kelly himself frequently violated those terms; over Rowe's objections, he spoke freely about Opal Jewel despite their earlier legal spats over her contract and use of her image.

made lots of money from rappers, these hippety-hop idiots looking for stuff to sample, and now more than ever we get requests from the TV and movie and advertising people. And that archive, that gold mine, it's all ours—ironclad! It's amazing to think how wide open things were back then and how somebody like me could sign a struggling talent off the street and give him a chance, and he'd actually be grateful and we'd work well together. Today you couldn't think of starting a record label from scratch because, you know, first of all there are no records anymore—no more physical product to sell! Added to that, you've got a million Johnny Fucktards on the internet whining and giving every-thing away for free. It's not a business model that makes sense to me, and I was glad to give it to my son to worry about. It's his pain in the ass now.

When I started the company, Rivington was just half of this floor, including my office and a couple studios, but over the years I built it up. At the beginning we had a few bands and singers that I was managing. I kept my ear to the ground and went to shows to see who the kids liked. We had the How Now early on, and they did very well when they were under me. My memory is not the best, so I have a hard time recalling how I brought Nev in.

NEV CHARLES:

It happened so fast. I was sleeping on a couch one morning when lovely Rosemary, bless her, jostled me awake and ordered me to get dressed and come with her to Rivington. She was very bossy, that one—you've spoken to her? She still has that bray to her, yeah? The most alarming alarm clock ever designed! [*Laughs*] "Wake up, wake up, asshole, let's go!"

ROSEMARY SALDUCCI, *SHRUGGING*:

I just thought he was interesting and different and deserved a chance. Plus my infatuation was over—I had a new boyfriend who was begin-ning to feel funny about Nev always being around. I needed him to get off our couch.

NEV CHARLES:

In half an hour, I was in Howie Kelly's office, doing some of my best tunes. And a couple of hours after that, he'd put a contract in my hand. It turned out to be a *crap* contract . . . but *sha*, it was a *contract*!* Imagine: Somebody was going to give me money, finally, to do the one thing I was dying to do. The thing my mum had wanted for me.

---

* Early Rivington deals varied in the amount paid to artists upon signing, but all of them—including Nev's and, later, his contract with Opal—had one thing in common: The label would manage and thus reap a percentage of everything the artist did, from albums to concert tours and other lucrative appearances. Today, such agreements, called 360 deals, are frowned upon by artists as over-reaching ınd exploitative.

chapter five

"THE SLAB OF QUALITY MARBLE"

★   ★

Howie Kelly had high hopes for his British singer/songwriter's debut, an eponymous collection of ten quirky, acoustic originals (including "Chemist Kismet"), but the album only got a brief mention in a music roundup deep inside the pages of the Village Voice *(whose critic deemed it, vaguely, "interesting"). Shortly after, another blow: Columbia Records poached Rivington's then buzziest band, the How Now, after Kelly botched a deal for them to play Woodstock. By late 1969, with his venture flailing, he was of a mind to cut deadweight—and his focus turned to Nev, who gave him visa headaches and was struggling for an audience.*

NEV CHARLES:

At some point he started turning up at my gigs. He would literally count the pathetic number in the room, minus the bartenders and waitresses, of course, and whatever that number was he'd subtract it from the total capacity of the venue, and he'd dock me that dollar amount from the door. Most often that meant that I, in fact, owed *him* money; oh, yes, he kept a running tab.

HOWIE KELLY:

Obviously the kid had talent—I predicted he could be huge someday. But at some point he had to be set on the right path. Patience isn't usually my strong suit, so he was lucky that the money I got for the How Now bought him just enough to keep him around. And I was also remembering that the best businessmen think outside the box. All the greats have their "no risk, no reward" period, and you could say this was mine. I took a gamble and stole this guy from those fucks over at Columbia, to see what he could do with Nev. And the guy I brought on turned out to be Bob Hize.

[*Tapping his temple*] How do you like them apples?

BOB HIZE, PRODUCER, OPAL & NEV; FORMER PARTNER, RIVINGTON RECORDS:*

My wife, Claudia, was American, a former model, and we were expecting our first child. She was very nervous to be a mother and she missed her sisters, who all had kids by then. Since we weren't terribly close with my own family in England, Claudia insisted that we move to New York, even though I worried about my prospects. My career was still so young. In London I'd been hired to produce a couple jazzy yule records, but I hadn't yet formed the kind of relationships that are required in this business to make a name. Much less a name that could travel an ocean.

So I was feeling a lot of pressure when we turned up here with the baby on the way, and I was grateful indeed to get any employment at all, especially in music. I went to talk to Columbia about producing opportunities, but somehow I walked out with a job in A&R. I suppose technically

---

* I interviewed Bob Hize on a series of afternoons at his apartment in New York City, as he neared the end of a long battle with pancreatic cancer. Despite his physical decline, Hize remained surprisingly lucid and expressed more concern over my comfort than his own during our chats. He smiled while pointing out floral arrangements and cards from both Opal and Nev, and reported that Nev had even called with a special encouragement to get well, as there would be VIP accommodations made for him at the Derringdo reunion show with Opal.

I was qualified, as a musician myself, and my bosses seemed to believe that my being English gave me a different ear and a talent for coaxing someone special out of the masses. But I'm sorry to say I didn't like the scouting much. It required that I drag myself out nearly every night to see live music, most of which was rather hackneyed, and I loathed the club scene. I was thirty, which of course sounds very young now, but back then seemed ancient to just be starting out. I only wanted to go home and rub my wife's swollen ankles. Instead, more often than not, I'd fall into bed at two in the morning, reeking of ganja and drained after having killed someone's dreams by telling them, "I'm sorry, you just aren't ready yet."

A couple months had ticked past and I hadn't found anybody I believed to be a good prospect. I got desperate for someone, anyone, to discover. I remember thinking, *This is not what I pictured for myself.* I much preferred to dig in with an artist who was already squared away, to know them inside out and accentuate the best qualities of who they were. That kind of magic happens in the studio, but I hadn't been inside one for quite some time. I knew I needed to get back, and figured that Rivington, which had become a laughingstock among my colleagues at Columbia after they lost the How Now, might be desperate enough to take me on for cheap.

ROSEMARY SALDUCCI:

He just called the office out of the blue one day. Because of the accent I thought it was Nev at first, Nev with a cold, and I cracked some joke about a chubby girl I heard he'd been going around with, and why wasn't she feeding him chicken noodle soup? But then the voice on the other end stuttered an apology and asked if he could make an appointment with Mr. Kelly, please and thank you.

BOB HIZE:

I figured maybe there was freelance work, overseeing studio sessions and developing the talent. But then I arrived at the offices, and just by looking round I could see that Rivington wasn't even a proper label. There was nothing behind it except this small and pompous man, full of air and

ambition, and the girl who answered the phones to make him appear
legitimate. There was no A&R, no business or legal affairs, no publicity
person to deal with the radio and the newspapers. . . . Each one of the
so-called studios was a closet that I was surprised could fit a full band.

I was always good at dealing with big egos and difficult personalities;
I was born to it, as my own father was a vicious drunk. The key is that you
never take the piss out of them. You approach them with *overwhelming*
respect, and then you do what you need to get done, and then you must
be humble enough to say it was their brilliant idea all along. Understand:
This has been half my talent working with rock stars. [*Laughs*]

With Howie, I oozed flattery. I told him how strong Rivington's roster was, which was halfway true, and how he had everyone at Columbia
atwitter, which was true but not for the reasons I was insinuating. I told
him they were cross over having paid so much for the How Now—that
one was rubbish; I knew Columbia had got that band for a steal. And I
put a shocked look on my face when I asked him who was doing all the
work, and he said it was only him. You know, the full "Bollocks!" routine. The longer I talked and the more deferential I appeared, the more
comfortable he became. He was sitting behind his oversize wooden desk
in a swivel chair, and at the beginning of our meeting he was rather
aggressive, leaned forward like a charging bull and drumming his pen
on the desktop. By the time I had him properly inflated, when I got to
the part where I said something like, *Wow, you could really do damage
to those wankers at Columbia with just a bit more help* . . . Well, he was
leaning back with his feet propped up, and he had that funny look that
people get just before the penny drops.

*The deal Hize negotiated to join Rivington Records was highly unorthodox:
He agreed to help Kelly with roster development and promotions, retaining
creative control in the studio, and in exchange he would make a tiny salary,
plus a 10 percent royalty on album sales. After a year, if nothing hit, Hize
would walk away with no claim. But if a Rivington album did make the charts,
he'd get a 50 percent increase over his old salary, plus a stake in the company.*

BOB HIZE:

Any fool will tell you that from an economic standpoint, this deal was 100 percent risk on my end. It meant that for a full year, my family would subsist on crumbs, and then afterward there was a chance I'd be out of a job full stop. It also meant there was a lot of pressure on me to deliver popular albums, which are rare in the grand scheme. When I confessed to my poor wife what I wanted to do, she put on a brave face and said she'd support me no matter what. But one night early in that first year, when she thought I was asleep, I heard her crying on the line with her sister: "Oh, what has he done? What has he *done*?"

Here's the thing, though, that remained in my head and on my heart: Before I shook Howie's hand and signed the papers, I got a copy of the *Nev Charles* LP. It was amateur. But immediately I could sense the bones of something. And I desperately wanted to be the one to shape it, to chisel the masterpiece from the slab of quality marble.

Those first few days I played *Nev Charles* over and over again, really let it burrow into my brain. I was meant to be meeting with the other acts on the label—back then we had Mary Sharp, who was a Joan Baez type, and a blue-eyed soul duo called the Refreshers, and a handful of others—but something in Nev's record was highly distracting. Or rather, it wasn't something *in* the record that was niggling at me, but something *not* in it. Yes, yes, the music itself was lacking, but that was an obvious fix—I could already hear in my head all the other instruments that should have been behind Nev's guitar, filling up his sound. And it certainly wasn't the songwriting, which was absolutely charming—you know "Chemist Kismet" but there are so many other, better gems on there, bizarre concepts and nuggets that still make me chuckle today. Even after imagining all those things in place and working in tandem, though, there was still something missing.

NEV CHARLES:

Hizey called me up to come round to the studio with my guitar, and I arrived about two hours late with a black cloud over my head. Since everything went wonky with the Boys from Birmingham, I was used to working on my own and pleasing no one else but myself, and I hated the idea of an artistic overlord, especially one who looked the part of an epic square.

But from the start Hizey was so kind in the face of my hideousness. . . . He quoted back to me his favorite bits from the first record, which no one had bothered to listen to, and he confessed that I was, to his mind, the most promising artist at Rivington. *Sha!* This was *me* he was talking about! He also reassured me straightaway that he would take promotions and press and bookings off my list of worries so that I could focus on the music. Having a shield from all the tedium appealed to me.

We went into the studio then and he watched me play a few tunes from his perch inside the control room. And he was doing this rather curious thing that made me uneasy and had me missing chords: He held my album cover in his hand, that dreadful, corny cover, and he kept looking from it to me and back again.

BOB HIZE:

The original cover was this photograph of Nev sitting on a stoop outdoors in winter. In the picture he's got the blond-wood acoustic guitar and he's wearing a goofy sweater and scarf and corduroy pants, with tufts of that ginger hair poking from beneath a newsboy hat. A perfectly docile smile, perfectly nice lad. In studio that first time, he sang and played with his eyebrows knit and this painfully serious look on his face. It was just so unbelievably *earnest*.

I love Nev like he is my own blood. But sometimes I think it's difficult for him to truly see outside of himself. He likes to think that he is not influenced by others, that he is his own unique and strange creation. And yet we all pick up tics, don't we? I discovered that the ones Nev had picked up while living in New York, hanging about in this singer/songwriter scene, had drained him of anything exciting and different. His lyrics were offbeat and imaginative, often wry; by contrast, the image he was mimicking felt trite and predictable, and that weighed down the entire package. He needed to be pushed, needed to be surrounded by fresh sorts of influences that would take him unfamiliar places.

HOWIE KELLY:

"I don't think he'll work as a solo act." This is what Hize says to me after one session with Nev. One! I'm incredulous! I say to him, "What, are you thinking I should drop him, after all this?" And Hize says, "Howie, this kid just needs some change in direction and he can be a real star."

BOB HIZE:

I liked the thought of a feminine energy, and Mary Sharp was a lovely blonde with blue eyes, but she was only going to drag him deeper into this folky style that didn't suit. I didn't know specifically what it was that Nev needed, but I didn't see it within Rivington's existing roster or anywhere in the Village.

I suggested to Howie that we give Nev a budget for a small tour, so that he could look for someone new and dynamic. I didn't know how Nev was going to react to that, but if we gave him the autonomy to select exactly who he wanted, I suspected that he'd eventually warm to the idea and also feel like he had some control.

Ideally, I would have accompanied him, and that would have been a good time for us to learn each other, producer to artist. But I didn't dare, because Claudia was inching up on her due date. So it ended up being Howie, of all people, who played chaperone.

HOWIE KELLY:

At the time, "Gimme Shelter" was the biggest hit out there, and it featured Merry Clayton just wailing away about God knows what. What was that chorus . . . About murder, about *rape*? Who ever heard of such a thing in a song? But she was raw, and she had grit, and she was a real soul sister with lots of attitude—*you* know what I'm saying. Her whole vibe just married with that guitar, and she's going back and forth with Mick in a way that knocked everybody out. And as a business guy, if I see something working very well, of course I want to imitate it! Why wouldn't I? It sounds good, it makes money, win-win.

So I got this British singer, he makes weird rock-and-roll songs, and I'm told he needs a shot of energy, some wake-the-fuck-up. What am I gonna look for? A Black chick with a giant voice, that's what.

NEV CHARLES:

For three months we were on the road. My own shows were forgettable, 7 p.m. gigs in half-empty places, and the people who did turn up were brutish and rude, talking through my entire set. And after those soul-crushing hours, we'd drive across to the Black parts of town—there always *was* a Black part of town, you understand, the segregation in the States is so endemic. You've read about the redlining, yeah? Shameful, shameful . . . Anyway, we'd visit these establishments and we'd be the only white people in the room. Can you imagine? Silly, awkward me traipsing behind Howie, who was like a ball of offensiveness barreling through every single venue. The saving grace was that the patrons liked to drink with us, and for obvious reasons they found us amusing.

HOWIE KELLY:

I must've shown Nev thirty different girls who sang in juke joints around the country. Atlanta, Memphis, Chicago . . . Most of them could sing big and loud, and a few of them were very sexy, you know, and could do the cooing thing like Diana Ross. There was one in Chicago who looked like Diahann Carroll, whom I personally always liked. Sweet as pie too—I bought her a drink after her set and she sat with us for a while. At the end of every night I'd ask Nev, "You like her?" and every night he'd shake his head no. It got to the point where I started making him pick up the tab. We were wasting money.

NEV CHARLES:

And then we got to Detroit.

chapter six

"THOMAS'S GIRL ON KILIMANJARO"

★ ★

On April 11, 1970, Nev Charles and Howie Kelly visited amateur night at a popular nightclub on Detroit's Near East Side, where the Robinson sisters were set to perform.

OPAL JEWEL:

Pearl was sanctified, but I take credit for bringing out the devil in her. She was in church every Sunday, singing it up to Jesus, but on Saturday nights I'd twist her arm to come out with me to this joint called the Gemini. I'd play on her guilt by telling her I was going with or without her, and didn't she want to keep her only sister out of trouble? Worked every time. Mostly because deep down I think she *wanted* it to work. But Sister Pearl would never admit that.

The Gemini had an open-mic hour with a live backing band and that's how we got on. Pearl would refuse to sing anything fun—for some reason she hated the word *baby*, she thought it was too worldly or some nonsense—so that knocked out a lot of the Motown hits right there. And honey, this was 1969, 1970 Detroit! I was trying to meet Mr. Berry Gordy! It was very reasonable that one day he would walk into the Gemini looking for his next starlets, and we're up there singing Christmas carols?

But I always meant for it to be Pearl, I really did. She had the voice; I was just the backup. What I brought to it was the style. I tried to make her stand out, tried to teach her to sway a little with the beat. And I did our outfits. Mine was always the shorter, tighter, lower-cut version of hers. Even though, to tell you the truth, Pearl had a lot more to work with, if you know what I'm saying.

HOWIE KELLY:

Christ, that one had a rack. You didn't know whether you were hypnotized by the voice or the tits.

PEARL WELMONT:

During the time we were singing at the Gemini I was still in touch with Lawrence back in Alabama, and we had already promised ourselves to each other. I had no interest in getting ogled by the men in that filthy place. Most of them were married anyway. But I was working and saving money till it seemed right to move to Birmingham for good, and to be honest, I was also trying to keep Opal out of trouble. And by *trouble*, that's exactly the kind of trouble I mean. You would not believe how many of our old classmates, the girls from Mrs. Dennis's apartment, ended up in that situation, with no husband. Opal never did have any friends, and she looked more mature than she was. Without me to look out for her, she might have been susceptible to a certain kind of wicked attention. That sinning lifestyle can be seductive.

So I tried to keep up with her as much as she'd let me. And if that meant wearing those outfits she made for Saturday nights, well, I'd humor it, long as I was covered enough.

NEV CHARLES:

Howie and I were sitting at a table right in front—it wasn't a big place, and every other inconspicuous spot was taken. We sat through a couple

of ho-hum acts, a guy struggling his way through Sam & Dave . . . And
then the bassist and the drummer kicked in with "To Sir with Love," of
all songs, and the Robinson girls came out.

HOWIE KELLY:

The Coca-Cola bottle and the straw. [*Laughs*]

OPAL JEWEL:

That night Pearl and I were wearing crushed velvet. Gold crushed velvet. Or maybe velour . . . Honey, I don't know, whichever one of those is
the cheaper fabric. I'd made Pearl a jumpsuit out of it with a top that I
tried to keep fitted, so the people could see she had something. And out
of the same material I'd cut myself a halter and shorts, and I took a brass
chain from an old pocket watch I found at the Goodwill and I shined it
up nice and wrapped it around my skinny little waist like a belt, trying to
create some kind of effect. Now, "To Sir with Love" was midtempo, but
me being me, I'd still find a way to shake it, you know, so that right on
beat that chain would jingle like mad, as Nev would say.

HOWIE KELLY:

She had this deep ebony skin, so any colors looked dramatic on her, I'll
give her that. And it was like music every time she moved—you just
wanted to stick a tambourine in her hand and watch her go.

OPAL JEWEL:

For years Pearl had adored "To Sir with Love"—I mean, everybody
was crazy about the movie because Sidney Poitier was so damn fine,
and the sentiment of it was very sweet and chaste. But don't let the
sweetness fool you—that's a belter's song, a big chance to show out,
and Pearl used to beat it dead. You remember, though, that on the
original track Lulu doesn't have any backing vocals, so I had to make
up my own part. Get in where I fit in. And when I listened to that record, I realized that a big part of it, what gave it emotion and light and

air, was the strings. At the Gemini, there was obviously nobody with a damn violin in the house band. I figured, *Well, then that's my part. I'm the strings.* Pearl would go loud and broad, just like Lulu, and I'd fill in high above her, floating real soft and pretty. Like painting those letters in the sky.

NEV CHARLES:

It's really a sappy tune, but by the chorus I was riveted. My God. And the thing besides her singing that I remember the most was her hair. It was blue-black and shiny and obviously fake, and it fell down to her midriff. She was very energetic and moved a lot, and it would sort of shift around on her head.

OPAL JEWEL, *STUDYING AN OLD FAMILY PHOTO*:

Ooh, chile, those early days of me and the wigs! Looking like a vinyl record had melted on top of my head.

NEV CHARLES:

I remember watching her, absolutely gobsmacked, and thinking how mysterious and scrappy she was, this girl in the gold shorts and the bad wig making up her own part. This girl with the voice that flew over and through and around her sister's so strangely.

HOWIE KELLY:

At the end of it I go through the whole rigamarole with Nev, me asking him, "Did you like her?" This time his face looked different, though, all lit up and excited. He didn't have to say a word. I was already gesturing toward the Coke bottle when Nev slapped my hand down. And pointed to the straw.

NEV CHARLES:

She was alien and outcast. She was the difference I wanted. She was Thomas's girl on Kilimanjaro, and she was the one. Opal was the one.

OPAL JEWEL:

After the set Pearl and I went backstage to this tiny greenroom they had at the Gemini—literally, a green room; it had dingy green carpet and olive-green walls, and the air was funky green with a bad old-man smell. I had just taken off my high heels and about seventy-five pounds of makeup when the manager of the place came in, and right behind him was this troll in a suit. Howie Kelly. He was so damn short he was eye level with Pearl's chest, and don't you know he kept his eyes locked there for those first couple minutes he started running his mouth?

He was going on and on about how we were very special, we knocked his socks off, blah blah blah. I thanked him and told Pearl to put on her jacket and cover up, because who knows what kind of freaky thing he was after. Then he managed to get himself together and peel his eyes away from my sister's chest, and he looked dead at me and he said something that made my heart jump: "Do you have representation, sweetheart?"

PEARL WELMONT:

We didn't know this man from Adam—he just came waltzing into the back of the house like he owned the place. And not to be prideful about it, but at the time it seemed suspicious to me that Mr. Kelly was telling *us*, as in the *two* of us, how good we sounded together on the song, but then he kept trying to get my sister alone. He could have been some kind of deviant, you know, a devil, a demon. And Opal was just standing there dumbstruck with her mouth dropped open, not saying a thing.

I was compelled to speak up, on behalf of our family. Now, I have read all my sister's interviews—I have them all here in these scrapbooks, because despite our differences I am proud of her—and I understand that she was hurt by what it was that I said to the man. I have tried to explain to her so many times over the years that I didn't mean it in a *bad* way. I just wanted to know if he was on the up-and-up, because people could be so cruel to Opal. In the moment, it seemed reasonable for me to make sure this wasn't some kind of sick joke. I just asked him, you know . . . "Are you kidding?"

OPAL JEWEL:

Five words that changed my whole life: "Do you have representation, sweetheart?" Obviously, all these years later Howie Kelly is not among my favorite people on this earth. But that night, when he asked me that question? And then fished out that official business card that said RIV-INGTON RECORDS, NEW YORK CITY? Darling, in my mind I was *losing it*. On the inside I was screaming, I was doing cartwheels down the center of the street, I was grabbing Howie by that beady cue-ball head and pressing it into my own pitiful chest.

All that goodness and joy was happening in my head, and then Pearl almost ruined it—"You must be kidding me!" is what she said. I guess that was to ensure that all was right with the world—that she was always going to be the main attraction and that I was the freak at the sideshow. I'm grateful for what she said, really, because otherwise I would have had my nose too open. It was an ugly moment but it brought my feet back down to the ground, and got me ready and focused on grabbing that ring.

I told my sister to shut the hell up. And I repeated those delicious words, real slow, to hear how they sounded rolling around in my mouth. "Do I have representation?" I said, and then, calm as you please, "Who wants to know?"

HOWIE KELLY:

It killed me to be going after Opal and not her sister. The sister had the big pipes and the sexier look, and she woulda been a hell of a lot easier to work with over the years, I tell you that. Obviously she was shocked too, considering the confused expression on her face when I started laying it all out.

NEV CHARLES:

God, I was so nervous to meet Opal that first time! It was like waiting for the headmaster to come and decide what's to be done with you. Howie had gone back to introduce himself and tiptoe around the business part, but I was still sitting at that front table. The next act was up, an enormously fat comedian who was making me even more jumpy because of the awful jokes he was cracking, and I remember drinking this swill of an American beer that I'd paid for out of my own pocket and wondering what Opal, this crazy and strange goddess, was going to make of me. I say *goddess*, mind, because already I worshipped her, truly I did.

Howie was meant to invite her out to have a drink and a chat, but instead he poked his head out the door by the stage and waved me back. When I got up my chair made this horrible screeching noise and the fat comedian started taking the piss—"Cracker looking like a damn carrot," that whole bit, mixed metaphors—and the people were having a good hearty laugh. Of course I was mortified and possibly even redder by the time I entered her room, her realm, her orbit.

OPAL JEWEL:

I think he said hello. I said hello back. My first impression? Hell, I don't remember. Nev looked like Nev. Pale, skinny. That hair, those eyes.

We talked a little. What I remember liking about him most was that he was British. Because I could at least respect the British rock and rollers—they were clear on their influences, clear that what they were doing was just a riff on Black folks singing the blues, and better than that, at that moment in time they appreciated what freshness we could bring to the sound. Billy Preston was practically another one of the Beatles by then, you know, that organ on "Get Back" and "Don't Let Me Down" holding everybody together at the end. And of course Merry had that moment to shine—*outshine* Mick, matter of fact, and that was A-OK by Mick. So if I was going to get into any creative partnership with a white person, I just automatically trusted a Brit to be better.

Howie was a different story.

NEV CHARLES:

When I came in she was sitting on a sofa, leaned back, legs crossed, barefoot. Her toes were varnished crimson. I stood in the door almost the entire time, except when I leaned in to shake her hand. I talked a lot more than she did, out of nervousness. I tried to explain that I liked her sense of musicality, that I could tell straightaway how unique and creative a presence she was, and I said I thought we might do something good together.

Her sister was clutching at her coat and full of interrogations: "What kind of music do you make? How do you earn a living off this? What kind of establishments do you play? Why have I never heard of you?" Opal didn't say a word, just glanced back at her sister and the questions stopped.

The next afternoon, while her sister was in church, Opal agreed to meet with Howie at the Robinson family apartment to discuss her signing a deal to join Rivington Records. Still, Opal refused to accept Rivington's first offer.

OPAL JEWEL:

You know how you get suspicious in a restaurant when the waiter is coming with all your food two minutes after you ordered it? And you sniff at the plate and you wonder, *How in the hell . . . ?* That's how I felt about that contract Howie stuck up under my nose. It's rotten, it's been sitting out too long, I need it fresh. He kept telling me this was the exact same deal that Nev had signed, and I said to him, "Do I look like my name is Nev?"

Mama was in the kitchen making Sunday dinner—she had invited Howie to stay, in her gruff way—and every time I said something she didn't like she made a whole big clatter with the pots. [*Laughs*] See, my mother had told me that I would be a fool not to take this white man up on his offer, leave home and make something of myself. But I understood my worth, even when everybody else thought I came cheap. I have never been one of those okey-doke, "just happy to be here" Negroes, you see what I'm saying? So I'm looking down at that contract and reading words like *perpetuity* and *likeness*, words and clauses that I'm too familiar with now but back then had me thinking, *How can I sign this if I don't understand what it is?*

My heart was falling through the floor, but I told him that I would need to have my lawyer look at it. Now, did I have a lawyer? Nah! [*Laughs*] But I had my gut and my hustle.

NEV CHARLES:

After that first meeting with Opal, Howie came back to the motor inn in a state. I asked him, "Well, come on, then, what's happened?" and he muttered a series of profanities—some terrible racial language as well, I'm afraid—and he said that hell would freeze before he'd see Opal in his lineup. He ordered me to pack my things and said that we were leaving the next morning, that we were going back to Chicago to sign this other girl who he liked and that was that.

As you can imagine, I panicked. I was awake all night figuring how to buy more time so that I could go make a pitch myself. Howie was outside warming up the Camaro, all our things were in the boot, and something told me to call Hizey.

BOB HIZE:

They'd ring every few days from wherever they were on the road, and it typically went the same way: Nev would report that he hadn't yet found the proper match, and Howie would snatch the receiver and say he was this close to making the decision himself. Honestly, I was also beginning to question this process—they'd been gone ages and the whole thing was becoming a unicorn hunt. But if it was ever going to work out, we needed to trust Nev's artistic vision, instead of going down a path of resistance and guaranteed disaster. So I did the best I could to keep Howie on an even keel.

Then one morning I'd just got to the office and Nev rang, talking fast and bright. And he said, "I've found her but Howie's trying to ruin it." He said he had to have this girl, he just had to. It seemed incredibly urgent.

NEV CHARLES:

When pressed I couldn't say why, exactly, although I'm sure she will offer you many theories, perhaps some of them Freudian. [*Laughs; long pause*] I suppose that, first, I thought Opal was interesting, in her music and in herself, and then to my surprise she was quite strong-willed, and those two things together signaled to me that she could back me up in making odd and creative things and then be willing to fight for them.

BOB HIZE:

I told Nev to put Howie on the line, which he did, and my ear nearly burned to a crisp as I listened to him talk about this girl from Detroit. [*Imitating Kelly*] *"She's a real money-grubber"*—yes, that's rich, isn't it?—*"and she's disrespectful and Jesus Christ, she's black as tar!"* I let him wear himself out and when he was done shouting I said the thing I knew would work:

"Well, then, Howie, if you can't do it, you just can't do it."

"Can't!? Who said anything about can't? I'm telling you, the girl won't sign! She's stubborn as a goddamn mule!"

"All right, Howie, it does seem like you can't convince her. . . . And if you can't get her to sign, then you may as well come on back. . . ."

"Well, goddammit, Hizey, I can! No Negro so-and-so from the god-damn ghetto is going to dictate to ME what I can't do, what I can't have!"

So you see, Howie Kelly is the most difficult man, and also the easiest.

NEV CHARLES:

After he talked to Hizey, I convinced him to let me have a go, and then he could come in again with the business. I went to the front desk of the motor inn and prepaid for two more nights out of my pocket.

OPAL JEWEL:

I really thought I had ruined my shot. But then Nev came to see me alone, in the early evening. I had just got off another miserable day working for the overseers at Michigan Bell—I remember in that short time that the weather had started to change, so I was hot and sweaty under a new bouffant wig I had put on to fake that I was all right. . . . And when I rounded the corner and saw Nev's awkward ass hanging around my building, I just about collapsed with relief to know that the thing was still in play.

I wondered how long he'd been there waiting. I was the first one home that day, and I remember feeling embarrassed when I let us inside the apartment because it was that time of the afternoon when the sun is strong coming in through the curtains—a million specks of dust exposed and floating in the light, telling stories on you.

He'd brought me his album to listen to but our record player was broke—the rubber piece that made the turntable spin had just snapped, between Pearl playing her holy-roller records and me with my Family Stone. "Everyday People" . . . Ooh, Rose Stone was the baddest on that track, leaned-back and *cold*, and the bubbles in the dishwater would go flat because I'd be stopping to sing all her parts. Washing the dishes and dusting—those were my chores, honey, and I was clearly not that dedicated to either of them.

Anyway, I asked Nev did he want something cool to drink, and he said that a beer would be nice. I told him we didn't keep any liquor in Sister Pearl Robinson's sanctified home but I could hook him up with some strawberry Quik. [*Laughs*] I meant that as a joke but he said yeah, he wanted some, so I mixed us two big glasses full and we sat at the kitchen table sucking it down through straws, like little kids, and it tasted sweet and good.

Because the record player was broke, I told him he could go ahead and sing me something right then. He said he couldn't because he didn't have his guitar. I said forget the guitar. I said that if you sing like you talk, all high and reedy like that, you mostly need some bottom, and I can give you that, no problem. So he started singing, and I slapped my thighs to make the beat.

NEV CHARLES:

Everything on the album by that point made me absolutely ill, so first I launched into this new thing I was still working out—I was calling it "The A Crowd," tentative title, just bits and bobs about people I'd observed up and down that metro line. It was fascinating to me that if you stay on the A long enough—or any line in New York, really—you meet so many of the people the city has to offer. Rich and poor, stylish and stuffy, Black and white, young and old.

"Eh, it's kind of boring," is what she said. And she may have also used the word *clichéd*. Or maybe I've added that to my memory over the years, but you get the gist: It was horrifying, humiliating, a host of other horrendous h-words. [*Laughs*] I'd done all this arguing on her behalf, on behalf of an imagined partnership in which I was already insanely invested, and then when it came down to the show-and-tell she apparently thought that *I* was the one on audition. I was so taken aback I forgot to be cross.

I wondered if I should go, but she just glossed over my complete mortification and asked me to please sing her something else. I managed to gather up the pieces of my shattered ego and was Johnny-on-the-spot with "Girl in Gold."

OPAL JEWEL, *SINGING*:

"Borrowed time on the stage, but she acts like she owns it / She has my heart and she don't even know it / My mouth is dry, my senses have gone / Wrapped up in the girl with the gold dress on . . ."

Nev claims he made that up right then at my kitchen table, but I've never believed it. Ain't nobody that quick. He had to have put some thought into it. Had to have put some thought into *me*. I was . . . well, I was all in my feelings about that, and I was already sweaty and hot; I was wilting under that bouffant. I put my hand up to my head and before I knew what I was doing I'd whipped the damn wig off.

NEV CHARLES:

Her mouth made this perfectly round O. She looked so beautiful and vulnerable then, she might as well've doffed her top. A glimpse of that vulnerability locked inside Opal—wow, it's rare, but when it hits you? It'll knock you flat. She kept her gaze on mine, and it was like she was questioning me, or maybe fearful of my reaction. Of course, I was curious as to her condition—was she ill? What had caused her hair to go patchy like that? And then I realized in a flash the thing that made her face so fascinating to look at: She scarcely had any eyebrows. But I didn't say a word, I didn't ask any questions, I kept as still as I possibly could. We sat in silence a few moments staring at each other, and then I tried singing the lyric again, testing it in different keys, different rhythms. [*Singing*] "Wrapped up in the girl with the gold dress on . . ."

Just then, her sister came home—the sound of that key in the lock was a jolt. And Opal shot up and scrambled to put the wig back in place, as if we'd been caught at something indecent. The moment was gone. I exchanged some how-do-you-dos with her sister and then Opal was hurrying me off. On my way out the door I asked her what she thought of the song, what she thought of coming to New York now, and she said, "I liked it fine, but I was wearing shorts. Not a dress." I laughed and told her I was taking poetic license. And do you know what she said to me then, the clever girl? She said, "You tell your boss to take some poetic license with that contract, and maybe I'll think about it."

OPAL JEWEL:

I was running a little game, I was acting real tough. But I knew at that moment that I would go, whether the contract improved or not. Nev had a hint of all my stuff, my full-on attitude and ugly. He saw me as I was, and still he seemed to be *choosing* me. It's a basic thing, but I had never in my life been chosen before. You understand what that means? I'm saying here was this stranger, clearly as crazy as I was, this person who dropped into my life out of nowhere, and he was reaching out his hand. What could I do but take it? What could I do but choose him back?

Opal Robinson's first Rivington contract was good for just one year, but stipulated she would be paid in weekly installments of $85 (which, even after taxes, would total a few dollars more than the lump cash sum Kelly traditionally gifted his artists). Awaiting her arrival, Nev spent a lonely couple months *holed up in the Ninety-Sixth Street flat, stuffing cotton balls in his ears to dull the racket of sirens and revelry outside his window. During this period he filled a notebook with new compositions, many of which would make up their first album together,* Polychrome. *Nearly insolvent and reluctant to ask his father to wire more money, he recalls, he subsisted primarily on lunch meat and saltine crackers sprinkled with grated Parmesan cheese.*

NEV CHARLES:

I was gaunt and probably close to developing scurvy, but I was twenty-one years old and "suffering for my art," as they say. I *wanted* to feel morose and romantic; I *wanted* to do penance at the altar of greatness. How bloody pretentious, but . . . in my mind I would push through it and when I came out the other side—when Opal got in place and it was time to record—I would be shining and brilliant and ready, and sporting a lean, craggy face that maybe looked like it had been some places. A face that would make for a better album cover, at least.

I had a lot of work in front of me, because "Rosy" was the only tune I'd ever done with two people in mind. Now I had to dedicate myself to considering everything in that way, coming up with different permutations that would make for something dynamic as the needle moved from track to track. At first I wasn't thinking about lyrics and themes—I was focused on tempos, and on trying to hear the actual sound, what the vocal flow of the album might be. Maybe on one song Opal would sing just the bridge; maybe on another we're trading verses; maybe the album was going to alternate, one song mine and one song hers. The guitar was useful in attempting to figure that out, but I also remember suddenly wishing for a piano as a countering sound. And a drum kit too, to give propulsion, and maybe strings . . . Factoring in a different person meant I was thinking bigger about the possibilities of the music. Two people needed more than what my meager acoustic guitar could offer, especially when one of those people was Opal.

I didn't see any girls; I stopped hanging round the Village. I took an occasional call from Hizey, who was doing his own preparations, and I would ring Opal in Detroit, partly to feel assured that she was indeed coming and partly to remember the cadence of her voice. Sometimes she would speak to me and sometimes she wouldn't.

OPAL JEWEL:

The phone would ring at two, three o'clock in the morning and give us all a heart attack. Pearl and I didn't have a phone in our bedroom, and when the calls first started coming, we'd be sitting straight up in our beds looking at each other with big scary eyes, waiting for Mama to pick up the line in her room and get whatever awful news was coming. Because that's the time of the morning when you find out somebody's dead or needs some bail money. But it would just be Nev wanting to chitchat with me. At three in the damn morning! After a while I learned to run to the wall phone in the kitchen before the second ring, before Mama even turned over. Honey, I was faster than Flo-Jo.

He never seemed to know what time it was, even though I reminded him that regular folk all across America were knocked the hell out. I'd pick up with the sleep thick in my voice and he'd say [*imitating Nev's accent*], "Opal, good!" and ask me to say particular words, sing lines of stuff he'd just written, that kind of thing. Sometimes he'd ask me to sing louder into the phone so he could try to record it, but one time Mama screamed at me to hush, so after that I kept the calls as short and quiet as I could.

Pearl swore he was a drug fiend, hooked on uppers, and that's why he kept the Dracula hours. I'd tell her, "Don't you worry about my business"—but honestly, I was worried too because I couldn't see what I was getting into. On one hand there was this pressure, this feeling that Nev was relying on me to be some kind of muse on demand. And then on the other hand there was Pearl, who was mad and wanting it to fail so she could say she told me so.

NEV CHARLES:

We'd agreed that I would meet her at the airport on a certain date, and Rosemary had arranged the ticket, and we had talked about all of this in minute detail. Three weeks before she was due to arrive, I rang her at home in Detroit and the phone kept going and going, which was odd, and then her sister answered. I asked to speak with Opal and the sister said, "But isn't she up there with you?"

PEARL WELMONT, *SHOWING FAMILY PHOTOS*:

These here are from the night before she left. We had a nice dinner out, just the three of us, at this Chinese restaurant we used to love because it had those lazy Susans and red leather booths and the zodiac printed on the place mats, but we could still afford it. Pastor, don't Mama look good? So pretty in that turquoise. Oh, she was so proud of Opal—bragging to the waiters and asking them to take pictures.

PASTOR LAWRENCE WELMONT:

Y'all were celebrating, huh? Even got a bottle on the table.

PEARL WELMONT:

Mama loved her white zinfandel. And she made a big show ordering everything Opal had ever liked off that menu. You see all this food piled up on the table? Beef with broccoli, shrimp egg foo young, those spareribs they baste in the bright red sauce . . . Lord. Just mountains of it, and my sister barely touched anything.

Seems like you can see it on her face, can't you? Gone somewhere else in her head. I guess I just assumed she was on the blue side; I thought maybe it was hitting her that she might miss us. And that made me feel sad, which, you know, I've learned is a real unhealthy situation for me when it comes to food. . . . So I was steady stuffing my face and thinking Opal was feeling sentimental too. Then come to find out she was probably just plotting her escape, and making sure it went off without a hitch. Me and Mama thinking she was with Nev, and Nev thinking she was still with us, and Opal just slipped away into the world. Off on her own, devil-may-care.

EDITOR'S NOTE

Near the end of Bob Hize's palliative care, in the master bedroom of his apartment overlooking Central Park, it could be exhausting for him to eat, to laugh, to talk for too long a sustained period. Still, he seemed to get some pleasure from the tentative trips he and I took to the past, no matter how much they sometimes drained him. "You'll come see me again, another afternoon?" he'd asked after our first conversation, with the clock at his bedside reaching 4 p.m. "Afternoons, that's when I'm best." Part of me wondered if this was true, or if Bob was, in his subtle way, producing our visits to avoid some conflict. I had yet to formally meet his daughter, Melody Hize Jorgensen, but she had emailed to say she was "concerned but resigned" regarding my interview request and her father's desire to grant it. Melody, as it happens, also was relieved from one to four each day by a nurse the family had hired.

The nurse, named Alice, was a five-foot-three wonder, originally from Ocho Rios, Jamaica. She had a quiet voice and a sweet round face and was unafraid, it seemed, of anything—the great loom of death, regrets, meddlesome visitors. . . . She fed Bob thin soups and ice chips, rubbed lotion into his hands and feet, readjusted his skullcap, and forever seemed to be doing laundry. She also told me in no uncertain terms when it was time for me to leave, as she had apparently promised Melody she would do.

As far as I could tell, the only thing Bob ever asked for was music. The rooms in the apartment had been wired for excellent digital sound, with tiny speakers painted the same ecru as the walls and screwed into the corners of the fifteen-foot ceilings—a lavish gift from his children for the retirement that this battle with cancer had forced him to take. Within easy reach on the bedside table lay a sleek remote that controlled the entire wireless system. But in his last months, Bob was craving lo-fi—fussy, fuzzy vinyl. As soon as his prognosis came down, he'd had Melody get back into good working order an ugly old console that had "decorated" the apartment's foyer for years, thanks to a painfully literal interior designer Bob had hired after his divorce in the 1980s. Now the thing had pride of place in the master bedroom, its many wires snaking out the back toward the same power strip that juiced Bob's adjustable bed. As a warm, imperfect sound thrummed from the con- traption, from the speakers hiding inside its rattan-covered swing-out doors, sometimes Bob would be moved to hum along. Sometimes he'd raise his hand from underneath the bedsheets and move it like a conductor along with the music's swell. And every time one record played out, either Alice or I, if she was busy doing something else, would rush to put on another. Always we would ask Bob first what he wanted to hear; always, he'd say, "Surprise me."

One of us would then step out of the bedroom and into a strange and small adjoining space—a walk-in closet transformed into a home for his vinyl collection (pulled out of deep storage at Rivington Records). Inside, this cool little room felt as hushed and reverent as the religious-studies section of a university library, but at the same time, its thrilling options for every proclivity put me in mind of a sex shop's DVD back room. Among Bob's collection you could find Beethoven's sonatas or big-booty bass, Nas or Nusrat Fateh Ali Khan. It took me a minute to crack the code of exactly how it had all been arranged, by an ethnomusicology PhD student at NYU who'd once interned at Rivington, but eventually I got a rough idea of the organizing principles— historical period, genre, subgenre, artist.

For some reason I worried about rushing too abruptly, too aggressively, into the work Bob had done with my father, and so I avoided playing *Poly- chrome* until my conversations with him naturally led there. The afternoon I finally pulled that album from the closet, having exhausted the topics of Bob taking a risk on Rivington and an interest in Nev, I dropped the needle on the vinyl with my heart in my throat. There was static and a pop from the console, and then Jimmy Curtis's driving drumbeat kicked open "Yellow Belly." In his bed, Bob smiled as if he'd been waiting for this. "And here we are," he said. "You've got the original pressing there?"

"Of course," I said, and turned down the volume slightly so my recorder could catch whatever Bob would say next. I walked back across the room to the chair set by his side, and held up the cover for him to check.

"My God, what on earth was I thinking?" he chuckled, and shook his head as he ran his fingers over the image of the gumball machine with Opal and Nev's heads topsy-turvy inside. "I didn't much know what I was doing back then, when it came to the marketing. The look."

"Oh, I think the art's kind of fun. A little bit poppy. Was it Warhol-inspired?"

"You're much too kind," Bob said, his eyes sparkling, amused. "When I showed your dad this cover and asked him what he thought, he barely even looked at it. He said, 'Is my name somewhere on here?' I said, 'Of course, Jimmy, yes, you're credited on every song in the liner notes!' 'And you've got it spelled right, man?' 'I'm positive, yes, that part wasn't too hard.' 'And that check you're writing me, it's gonna clear?' 'I promise you I made sure of that, if nothing else.' He just handed it back to me and said, 'Then I guess it looks pretty good to me.' "

Alice, who'd come into the bedroom bearing Bob's lunch and was setting it up on a rolling tray, laughed along with us.

"We're just talking now about Ms. Shelton's father," Bob said, as Alice pressed a button that sat him up higher. "Remember the brilliant drummer I told you about? I was lucky enough to work with him on this album."

"Is that right?" Alice said, quite affably, and yet I felt vaguely embarrassed. She rolled the tray so that it stretched across Bob's lap, then handed him a plastic spoon. "You want to see if you can manage today?"

She tucked a paper napkin into his pajama top and watched over him as he dipped the white spoon into the broth and dredged up a smidge. His hand hovered a moment in midair, promisingly, but then he got distracted. The liquid splatted onto the tray as he shook his new plastic instrument. I'll never forget it: Bob Hize's air drums.

"Will you just listen to that?" he said, smiling at me as Jimmy charged toward the song's climactic end. "Your dad amazed me, how he was able to make the music sound both tight and loose at the same time. . . . Right on the edge of losing control, but never tipping over. Alice, tell us: Have you heard this record before? Did they ever play *Polychrome* on the radio in Jamaica?"

"Mmm, I don't think so," she said, and gently took the spoon from him. "But something about it sounds familiar." She held the broth to Bob's mouth and put her other hand behind his neck. "Calm now, Mr. Hize," she murmured, and the moment was so tender, so uncomfortably reminiscent of how my mother could be with her own elderly patients, that I had to look away. I opened the album cover atop the bedsheets, underneath which Bob's legs were thinning to twigs, and as he drew in the broth and coughed softly, I made a game of spotting my father's name the twelve times I already knew it appeared.

"That familiar quality Alice mentions," Bob finally said when his coughing quieted, "I'd say it's mainly because of your dad."

"Can you tell me more about that?" I said. "What Jimmy was like during the *Polychrome* sessions?"

Bob closed his eyes as Alice pushed a button that lowered him again. The back of his skullcap raised up as his body slumped down slightly, and she leaned over him a moment to pull it snug again. "Well, you must know he could, and he did, play absolutely everything. Any style, any rhythm, he had a facility with it."

"I didn't hear this record until I was fourteen," I said. "My mother would only play the jazz in the house."

"But what a universe that was, the jazz. Bossa nova, bebop, Afro-Cuban, gypsy . . . The jazz is what gave Jimmy a foundation from which he could riff." Bob closed his eyes as the needle moved on to the next track, "Ginger's Lament." "Listen," he said, and licked his lips. "Wah-*PAAAAAH*-pah, wah-*PAAAAAH*-pah . . . That's quite jazzy, isn't it, very swinging—you hear the way he hangs slightly behind the beat? But the song as a whole, with the other instruments and especially Opal's vocal there, it goes to another place. Arriving somewhere new, but carrying that familiar tinge of something old. That's the key."

From the pocket of her pink scrubs, Alice pulled out a ChapStick. "I see

I'm getting a musical education today," she said, rubbing the balm across his lips. "You'll be okay for a while?" she asked him. "I think it's time for some nice clean sheets."

"Oh, yes, I'm fine, thank you," said Bob—but as Alice was leaving the room, she caught my attention and tapped at her wrist. I glanced at the time. Three forty-seven already.

"I'd love it if you'd share with me another story from the time you knew my father," I said, once Bob and I were alone again. "I mean, not necessarily as a musician, but as a person. Does anything specific spring to mind?"

Bob was quiet a long while. Was he thinking, feeling, twiddling, remixing? "Has anybody ever told you," he finally said, "about that funny noise he used to make—that hissing business between the teeth?"

I sighed, disappointed by such trivia. "A lot of people do seem to remember that, yes."

"We were never really sure if that was him laughing or expressing his approval or disapproval or what, but whatever it was—that *ssss-ssss-ssss*— it was very contagious, and if the hour was getting late in the studio we—"

"Mr. Hize," I said, "please don't worry about being indiscreet. I already know it's one hundred percent true, what was going on between my father and Opal. And I know their affair must have sparked in the studio. The sessions, then, were very . . . intense?"

He smiled up at me ruefully. "Have you talked with Opal about this yet?"

"Only so much," I confessed, "and not at the depth that I'd like to. It's not as if she denies anything; she's very matter-of-fact about it. 'Yes, I understood he was married; no, I didn't think to end it.' Detached, unemotional . . . I've gotten more color about their affair so far from Rosemary Salducci."

"Oh God, Rosemary," Bob moaned. "Always one for the excruciating detail."

"But Opal herself . . . Opal hasn't even told me that she loved him. She'll describe the trim on the sleeve of the dress she wore the first time in the studio, but clams up when I ask what she thought of my father when she met him."

"Well, now. A sleeve doesn't have much complication to it."

"Virgil LaFleur would argue otherwise," I said. "He told me he struggled to piece that particular garment together."

We laughed a moment, as the record moved into "Red Handed." The song is arguably Opal's finest work on the album, her staccato vocal playing hide-and-seek with Jimmy's beat. *I'm not a girl that can be caught / I'm not the girl who can be bought.* . . .

"I had been warned that your father was not easily moved by much," Bob said. "Another rock producer who'd worked with him told me not to take offense over it—told me Jimmy was an excellent drummer but would come in, roll up his sleeves, do his bit just as you'd asked him to do it, and then go. Sphinxlike, stone-faced. I imagine he felt he had to be somewhat guarded among us rock-and-roll types. He was lonely, maybe."

"You think he felt isolated? Being Black in that world?"

"I imagine that's so."

"So when Opal came into the picture . . . "

"She charged in and changed the atmosphere."

"You're saying she opened him up?"

"Not exactly. He wasn't too much of a chatterbox, even then. And it did take a while for it to happen, for him to recognize that her promise was real. But eventually something about her seemed to ease some pressure valve within him. Something about her made him go *ssss-ssss-ssss.*"

chapter seven

"A FLOURISH
OF DRAMA"

★   ★

Opal Robinson arrived in New York City via bus in July 1970—the same
month and year Funkadelic dropped that fierce edict to "Free Your Mind . . .
and Your Ass Will Follow." She lugged to the taxi stand at Port Authority two
duffel bags—one of them bursting with brand-new fabrics, sewing supplies,
and paperbacks; the other stuffed with an assortment of shoes for every season
and cheap synthetic wigs. (As for the fluffy Afro wig that would not fit into
her luggage, she wore that during her travels.) In her jeans pocket was a slip
of paper with the address for her new home in Harlem. She had found the
room listed in the classifieds of the Amsterdam News *and arranged to rent it*
via phone from her station at Michigan Bell, after the other accounts-payable
girls had gone home. She gave the address to the hack, and from the back seat
of his cab, Opal absorbed her new environs. In this city of nearly eight million
people, she was completely anonymous. No one she knew, neither relative nor
acquaintance, could say her exact whereabouts.

OPAL JEWEL:

I'm an old chick now and I like my quiet, but when I first came to New
York I was twenty-one years old. I could feel the energy of that place

jolt through my body as soon as I stepped off the bus. At first you just notice the nastiness: You know, everything was so *extra*—extra hot, extra funky, extra loud. But sitting in the back of that yellow cab, I was like an astronaut in a shell traveling through space, pressed up against the window and taking in the stars. There were businessmen in brown and blue suits looking clean and sharp, Teflon dons on those dirty-ass streets. I saw swarms of moving people, people who knew rules I didn't yet know, and in the swarm you could pick out gray-haired society ladies and Hispanic workmen and Hasids in their outfits, the curls and hats and coats, even in that summer heat. And then we drove alongside Central Park, and I saw a fully grown sister on roller skates. In a plaid sundress and cornrows, hollering at folks to get out the way and rumbling down the sidewalk like it was the most natural thing in the world. And I thought, *Oh my God—my people!* [*Laughs*]

Rosemary Salducci had sent me a sublease for some other place Rivington had found for me, I don't even remember where it was supposed to be, but I was adamant about being in Harlem, so I never signed those papers. I had lived among Black people my whole life, and I didn't know a lot about New York except the things I saw secondhand. Harlem seemed to be a place where Negroes congregated but sometimes of their own volition, and it was a place that inspired so much creativity. So that's where I wanted to stay—somewhere I could start my own personal renaissance.

The place I found ended up being a room on the parlor level of the brownstone you saw. At the time, the house was owned by a widow named Miss Ernestine. Sweet as she wanted to be, and from deep country Georgia, where they'd hang a nigger for whistling in the wrong key. But Miss Ernestine had migrated up north with her husband years before, and when she was ready to go back home we bought it off her for a fair price.

Before we opened it up, there were two other units in the house. Right below was a young family that could barely get by because the daddy was in and out of work, but the two little girls were kept cute and clean in their plaits and dresses, and on the first of the month their mother would come up with a bubbling hot casserole instead of the rent. Miss Ernestine would just sigh and say, "Thank you, baby." I imagine she opened up the second bedroom in her own apartment to make up for that loss.

And at the tip-top of the house, as you know, was my darling, my dearest, Monsieur Virgil LaFleur.

VIRGIL LaFLEUR, OPAL JEWEL'S BEST FRIEND AND LONGTIME STYLIST:*

I had been living up in Harlem for about seven years by the time I first encountered Mad [LaFleur's nickname for Opal, short for "Mademoiselle"]. My apartment was on the third floor, so I could see her arrive from my window—she was dragging those bags up the stoop and looking every bit the tortured hot mess. I suppose I was somewhere in the upper twenties by then. . . . But do take note, *s'il vous plaît*, that I had the physique and nerve of a nineteen-year-old. Let me remember . . . 1970 . . . My God, I would rather not, but all right: Earlier in the year I was an understudy for the role of Othello—[*in a rumbling baritone*] you see, I had Shakespearean training, therefore and thou art . . . 'tis I, the Moor of Venice, jealousy, rage, murder, *murrrr-derrrrr!*—but the actor they cast had the part locked down, and the gentleman was going through the whole run without so much as a sniffle. That winter season all the rest of us, even the director and the girl who played Desdemona, had bad head colds. It was so upsetting that I had a shameful moment once backstage, while Othello *Un* was doing the seven o'clock show. I crept into his dressing room and dropped my used tissue into his coat

---

* LaFleur, exact age undisclosed, showed me around his consignment boutique on New York's Upper East Side. Its walls are decorated with some of Opal Jewel's more elaborate costumes, headdresses, and gowns, displayed in museum-quality shadow boxes; according to placards posted next to each in red ink, they are emphatically "NOT FOR SALE!"

pocket, in the hopes it would fell him. Of course, it only seemed to make him stronger. The lesson being that desperation is most unflattering.

When it came to my thespian career . . . *c'est la vie*. The biggest thing that ever happened to me, in the time before your Opal, was that I played a degenerate named Turpentine in an off-Broadway monstrosity called *Bad Willie's Juju*. Musical comedy, *mais comme c'est tragique*. I was not aware then, but that July day, Mad was like an angel falling into my world. [*Pause*] A raggedy angel. [*Pause*] Emphasis on *raggedy*.

OPAL JEWEL:

Miss Ernestine and I were in the living room—she was showing me around the place, and how to get a clear signal on the television—when here comes Virgil, waltzing down the stairs in silk paisley pajamas, talking 'bout *"Ma cherie, enchantée!"* That's what he said to me, and he took a bow and held out his hand in a funny way, not like a handshake but some other gesture I didn't recognize. I looked at Miss Ernestine and she smiled and said, "Go on, baby, give him your hand," and so I did and he pulled it to his lips and gave it a *mwah*, a little kiss. You could've knocked me over with a feather.

Now, I already was a skeptical person, I guess you could say, and I'd come to New York with the words of the Michigan Bell girls in my head. *Don't look nobody in the eye*, they said, and *don't trust nobody*, because *the city is a web of dark alleys infested with druggies and pickpockets and rapists*. I was expecting to have to fight people off, or at least run away fast enough if they came at me, and instead I'm in this Victorian scene, inside a beautiful old house with a sugar-sweet elderly roommate and Virgil acting the damn gentleman.

VIRGIL LAFLEUR:

She was this shapeless thing before I got hold of her, she'll even confess—could have used a toasted oat as a Hula-Hoop, but this is beside the point. When I say shapeless, *chère*, I mean more that she had no remarkable flair, certainly none by New York standards, no *je ne sais quoi*. She didn't know how to accentuate her attributes, and that led her to force her wild strangeness into whatever limited styles happened to be *en vogue*. That is fine if you are rich and can afford all the things, the finest fabrics and accoutrements, so that the look becomes passable. But this was Harlem in 1970, and when one is not rich one must get creative. One *must* show out.

OPAL JEWEL:

I had never met anybody like him before. Not just gay, because we had a lot of that where I'm from . . . But I mean, so big with himself. He didn't talk; Virgil *purred*, honey. No, I mean literally purred—some of his people were Haitian, so he could speak some pretty French, and the other half might as well have been Eartha Kitt. His fingers were long and elegant, the nails filed and buffed smooth and shiny. It's thinning out now, but he used to have what folks called "good hair"—the kind that just naturally leans back and waves—and his head was giant as a lion's. I could see he was trim and fit under the pajamas, and he had these big hazel eyes and a smooth caramel coloring. He was a *specimen*! And he was the first true friend I ever had.

Virgil was my introduction to New York, and you better believe he loved playing *My Fair Lady*. He knew all kinds of interesting people who worked all kinds of places. Busboys on the Upper East Side, costume assistants on Broadway—if there was a back door, we just had to knock to get a meal, or a spot in the rafters to watch a show. Every day back then was like a new adventure. Cattle calls and house parties; up in the morning with caffeine, down at night with cabernet. Making meals out of whatever scraps we could get from Virgil's actor-slash-dancer-slash-waiter friends—knishes, garlic knots, curries, all kinds of exotic stuff I was tasting for the first time. I thought maybe he had some star quality just waiting to bust out, because everybody seemed to be smitten with him.

But also Virgil sold reefer. Everybody loves the reefer man.

VIRGIL LAFLEUR:

I styled ladies' hair. That's how I paid my bills. I don't know what she's told you.

NEV CHARLES:

I'd hoped Opal arriving early meant we could get a jump on rehearsing vocals for the songs I'd finished writing, but even when she was living a couple miles away she might as well've been on Alpha Centauri. To that point she had not heard very much except the raw version of "Girl in Gold," and I started to worry that even the week we'd originally planned to meet wouldn't be enough. I rang and rang the number Pearl gave me with no response at all. Later, when I got the address, I snuck up there to make inquiries. I say *snuck* because I couldn't let word reach Howie that Opal had pulled this disappearing act.

VIRGIL LAFLEUR:

Mad was coy; she did not reveal details about why she had come to New York, and whenever I tried to inquire? *Attitude maximal.* Our proprietress must have known, but she was also tight-lipped—that is a key characteristic, *bien sûr*, of African Americans from our southern regions. So I did not become aware until early one morning, when we were eating toast and jam in our pajamas, watching the *Today* show on Miss Ernestine's television—I adored Barbara Walters, whenever they allowed her to grace the air—and someone started pounding on the door and calling for Opal. The way she scurried back to her bedroom, I thought perhaps she owed a debt.

NEV CHARLES:

I'd been jotting the songs for the album in this spiral notebook, not just the lyrics but the music itself, plus the actual notation for the guitar parts, which mostly informed the melodies. It was full of edits and scratch-throughs and my hideous handwriting, which I doubt anyone could make out, and it was the most personal and precious thing I owned, although maybe back then that wasn't saying much. But after I went to Harlem looking for her and she wasn't there, in sort of a daze I left the notebook with this Virgil character [*laughs*], who was a stranger to me then, and I trusted him to give it to her because what else could I do? The songs had to be learned—that's the most essential thing, isn't it, when your plan is to put them on *record*?

VIRGIL LAFLEUR:

I opened the door and there he was: the young Neville Charles. They say he's strange-looking, but darling, I was . . . *enchanté*! I adore an accent.

OPAL JEWEL:

Virgil told you I hid? Really? Okay. I don't remember that, but I guess it might be true.

Scared? Aw, wasn't nobody scared. I just wasn't ready. I hadn't fully worked out what I was doing yet.

VIRGIL LAFLEUR:

After Neville left, I went back to Mad's bedroom to give her this mystery notebook—well, perhaps I flipped through a few pages, but it was gibberish to me—and the child had thrown herself across the bed like a true and proper drama queen. She had her face pressed into the pillow but when I called her name she turned toward me and I could see her tears making a mess of it. "Well, come now, *ma petite*, what is the matter?" And at first she said nothing, but then when I put the notebook beside her and she looked at it, the chest heaving commenced. [*Imitating sobs very dramatically*] "Virgil, I'm a *pho-oh-oh-oh-nyyyyy!*" [*Laughs*] I sat beside her on the duvet and was quiet until finally she came out with the whole business. She told me about the contract, how she had played *la diva* and now she feared she could not deliver. She did not know how to read music; she had never sung a note with anyone but the half sister. I asked her how much time remained before she had to make an appearance at Rivington Records. [*Sobs*] "Less than a *weee-eeee-k*!" So I said, "Well, then, we will have our work cut out for us, won't we?"

OPAL JEWEL:

A customer of Virgil's lived near Columbia, a middle-aged white guy with long hair who had all kinds of musical instruments lying around his apartment. He might have had a damn didgeridoo, I don't know. The apartment, by the way, was filthy—dirty clothes piled up in corners, and there was an upright piano that had glasses and cups sitting on the top of it, most of them half-filled with scummy water and cigarette butts. I remember thinking Mama would kill me for leaving water rings on her good furniture. Anyway, Virgil gave him a brick of weed, and this man spent a few hours over the next couple days smoking it up and teaching me the melodies of what was in Nev's notebook. Not how to actually read music, though, which is what I needed. At first he tried to explain how to do it, but he was talking in circles and his head was clouded from the weed, and I got frustrated because time was running out. So I said, "Forget it, man— just sing it like it's supposed to go, and I'll copy it after you."

Nev Charles, meanwhile, was staring down his studio date with no word whatsoever from the young woman he'd chosen as his featured collaborator. In isolation, he vacillated between mild worry and full-blown anxiety.

NEV CHARLES:

I didn't tell Hizey; I was horrified at the thought that he was already pulling together the players and calling me chuffed about the progress of it, and I could hear his hungry little baby wailing in the background, and there I was without this girl singer who was supposed to make the pieces fit. Well, I was lying quite egregiously when he'd ask how she was getting on. "Oh, lovely, she's settled in, we had a working dinner last night, chicken à la king, Mum's old recipe. . . . I'm sorry? Meet her today? Oh no, that's impossible because *insert imaginary reasons*." Besides that, I had given my notebook away to Virgil, so I was trying to reconstruct everything from memory—for that I had to play the role of the perfectionist artist and tell Hizey that I wasn't ready to [*using air quotes*] "share the work." Total bollocks.

BOB HIZE:

I had to have a sense of the music before booking the bassist and the rhythm guitar, but I always knew that I wanted your dad to be behind the drums. Jimmy was probably the busiest and most versatile percussionist in the city at the time. I had seen him play in different groups, everything from jazz to rock to R&B to that Latin-based sound Carlos Santana was popularizing. So no matter what Nev would come back with, your dad would adapt to it and make it better.

What Jimmy would *not* do, at least until Opal came into his life, was deal with interpersonal dramas. He was a very serious man, almost arrogant—the kind of fellow often accused of having a chip on his shoulder. But he was simply deep into his work and protective of his time, and clear that it was not to be wasted. I had enticed him to come in to Rivington by letting drop that we had an extraordinary, dynamic Black girl singing rock-and-roll music—mind you, at this point I had not even met Opal. I was only going by what Nev had said and embellished on that. It really was the nuttiest gamble.

JIMMY CURTIS [EXCERPTED FROM
"CLASS IS IN SESSION," *DOWNBEAT*, JUNE 8, 1967]:*

Sometimes you go into a job and it's like you're the only one who knows how to act. I never had any formal training, not a lot of black cats my

---

* My father, who gave the percussive drive to Opal & Nev's debut album, died in November 1971, beaten to death by members of a biker gang in the chaos of Rivington Showcase. He was 32 years old. Because he features so prominently in the duo's trajectory, this oral history includes his voice and perspective on music via a 1967 published interview with the industry's best session musicians.

age really did. Once I picked up the drumsticks, though, that became my profession, and I treat it as such—professionally. But the ones who get chosen to be the biggest stars . . . To tell you the truth, they have a whole lot else going on besides the music. Listen, man, I walk into situations where I have to play behind speed junkies, needle fiends, winos, wife beaters, beaten wives, egomaniacs, grown men who wear diapers under their getups. All that shit is good for a party, if you get down like that. In the studio, though? Man, just hurry up and cut me my check.

Between the hazy lessons from Virgil's friend and what she could remember from her late-night phone conversations with Nev, Opal learned the notebook tunes well enough for the first recording session. That she still could not read music, however, nagged at her. She worried about adjusting to Nev's improvisations or to other sudden, unfamiliar changes in direction, and feared that the players backing her—all of whom, she rightly assumed, would be men— would dismiss her as dizzy and helpless if her inexperience was exposed. She had pushed her musical abilities as far as they could go; the next step was simply to turn up. How she decided to do so is one of the most colorful stories in rock history.

OPAL JEWEL:

The transformation was partly Virgil's idea and partly mine. I had been practicing the songs for a few days and they were all right, some of them were pretty good, but he kept telling me he wasn't feeling it. [*Imitating Virgil*] "Not moved, *chère*, I am just not moved." I kept singing them different, and I thought better and more interesting, riffing and all that, but he still had this skeptical attitude. Then he seemed to be getting bored with me, or annoyed with this whole project that he probably thought was a go-nowhere deal, and at that point I was willing to try anything to keep my ass off the next bus to Detroit.

VIRGIL LAFLEUR:

Her big day called for a flourish of drama. And perhaps a bit of distraction . . . illusion. Because the secret to understanding Mad is that she is not the most brilliant vocalist. But she is an excellent, magical performer.

I pictured her in a caftan, a gauzy and ethereal garment that would float on her and go [*sighing noise*] whenever she moved. It had to be airy enough to show shadows of her underneath it writhing, dancing, gliding . . . yes! I was dressing her for the stage, for all who interacted with her to be thrilled and intimidated by her magnificence. All the different colors were her vision.

OPAL JEWEL:

Polychrome. That was the theme.

VIRGIL LAFLEUR:

We started with a bright yellow organza, which was *très, très* sheer, so we had to get enough to layer it, and we got a Butterick Fast & Easy pattern that I nearly tore to shreds for it being so difficult. We pieced it together in a circle shape, because when she stretched her arms out she had to look as if she had glorious wings. Then we put it on her and she looked like a raving old *madame*.

OPAL JEWEL:

He started going at it with the scissors, edging it up—he cut the shoulders out, which looked good. Then he took some material in the other colors, the red and the green and blue, and he put strips of it on. Vertical down the front and the back, circle around the cuffs and along the bottom. Then we went in with the makeup—aquamarine eyeshadow and a bright magenta lip. . . . It was wild. But then we tried it with some of the wigs I'd carried with me from Detroit, and no matter which one, the Supremes bouffant or the Afro or that Pocahontas mess, it didn't go. None of them was right.

And I remembered Nev already knew about my condition, so who the hell cared anymore? I was sick of hiding it anyway. I was so frustrated I could have ripped out what hair was left, straight from the root. I asked Virgil, "You know where we can get some big earrings? I'm about to need them."

VIRGIL LAFLEUR:

I located the clippers I used on some of my more hirsute clientele, and voilà! Instant avant-garde. Cheekbones, drama, *élégance*.

OPAL JEWEL:

I looked in the mirror and saw a different person. I couldn't stop staring. I couldn't stop turning every which way, couldn't stop wondering: Who is *this* girl? How does *this* girl sing? Not like a church girl, or like an open-mic act, or even like Rose Stone, much as I loved her. This other girl was something else.

chapter eight

"SKINNY MINNIE IN A WHOLE LOTTA LOOK"

★ ★

On August 14, 1970, the players for the Polychrome *concept album were scheduled to gather at Rivington Records. Each of the ten songs, which Nev had meticulously reconstructed from memory for Hize and the session players just three days in advance, included a color in its title and, true to the artist's signature style, told a vivid story about an offbeat character. To achieve the organic sound Hize heard in his head, the album was to be captured live, with the assembled players recording each song straight through after a few practice takes. In addition to my father on drums, Hize had recruited an impressive roster, musicians who had some experience working together but had never before played on a Rivington album: bassist John Squine, the rare white colleague with whom my father was friendly; keyboardist Solomon Krebble; and second guitarist Steve Pratt, who was brought in to amplify the album's louder numbers (including the brittle, high-octane rocker "Chalk White"). A talented college senior at New York University, Jason Moore, came in as intern-slash-engineer, providing some relief to the stretched budget.*

Brimming with ideas for the evocative album Nev had delivered, Hize arrived to the studio in high spirits, he recalled, and felt a surge of excitement as he watched his lineup of backing musicians arrive and begin tuning up. His heart sank, however, once his front man walked in.

BOB HIZE:

Nev looked horrid and ghostly pale, as if he hadn't slept. Dark circles under the eyes and a patchy scruff that made him look like my daughter, Melody, at feeding time—bits of carrot round the mouth. Worse than that, he was giving off a pungent odor. Flop sweat, I suppose. He shook hands with Squine and Solomon and Steve, solemn, and then he got to your dad, who wouldn't shake his hand and only gave a terse wave with one of his drumsticks from behind the kit. And I thought, *If Jimmy's already unhappy, this is not good.* Nev strapped on his guitar with no small effort, and then Howie popped over in full bellow and clapped him on the back—the "attaboy" kind of thing—and Nev went concave. Literally, concave! I pulled him aside and asked, you know, "What in God's name, Nev? Are you ill?"

That's when Opal made her entrance, as Opal does.

OPAL JEWEL:

Virgil had come with me as far as the doors of the Rivington building but he wouldn't come inside. You know in the movies where little Bobby or Sally nurses a wild animal back to health and then releases it back into the woods? And it's this big, brave moment with the violins going? "Go on, now, this is your home, this is where you belong." [*Laughs*] I swear it was like that. Virgil thought he was in one of those damn movies. And I'm looking back at him like, *All this and you just gon' send me to the wolves?*

I went inside and up to the Rivington floor, and the first person I see is Rosemary sitting at the desk. Pretty, normal Rosemary, with her shiny brown curls and shiny pink lips and those luscious titties she had sitting up so nice. Meanwhile here I come breezing up, Skinny Minnie in a whole lotta look. I should have felt like a circus clown, I guess. Most people would have. But when I opened my mouth to tell her who I was, that I was there for the recording session, my voice came out strong and steady. I guess that's when I knew my normal is to be abnormal.

ROSEMARY SALDUCCI:

Oh, I'll never forget it, the first time I saw her. She looked so gorgeous you wouldn't believe. Like a page from *Vogue* magazine come to life.

BOB HIZE:

She looked like holiday on Mars.

HOWIE KELLY:

She looked like a fucking cockatoo. Is that the one with all the colors? Parakeet, parrot . . . whatever. Crazy nut.

NEV CHARLES:

She finally, finally came to me, and when she did I almost fell into hysterics, not because I was having a laugh but because I was so relieved and astonished and *ecstatic* to lay eyes on her, all those feelings in a rush, at the exact same second. She's the fashion heroine, so she can tell you the correct terminology for whatever it was she wore—or better yet, ask Virgil LaFleur, I'm sure he recalls each stitch and accessory. All I can say is that there was this riot of yellow and cobalt and emerald and red, all cascading down her body, tip to toe. And her shoulders poked out from it so that she looked sharp and majestic and, *sha!*, rather compelling. And so my eyes are dancing all over this getup, and finally I get to her head. . . . Shaved to the skin. Fucking well done! Fucking well done!

BOB HIZE:

Suddenly the flush was back in Nev's face, and before she could say hello he literally ran over to Opal and picked her up and spun her, and the studio was so tight with equipment that her foot hit your dad's bass drum and nearly knocked it over. Of course we were very confused by all this—we had no notion of what had been going on, but Nev's delight was pure and infectious. Even Jimmy seemed mildly interested, rather than annoyed, by the creative insanity that felt possible before any of them had played a note.

JOHN SQUINE, BASSIST, *POLYCHROME*:*

Bob Hize is a brilliant producer. Strategic in the studio, each mic precisely placed. That's not to say he wouldn't let us get loose with the music itself—Nev would improvise on the lyrics, change them up here and there—but every day Hize would dictate the order he wanted us to record in, and there was usually a good reason behind it. Take the *Polychrome* record—I was expecting we were going to go straight through that thing, recording in the order Hize had sent the songs to us originally. Instead he insisted we nail down "Yellow Belly" and "Girl in Gold" the first day, even though those were toward the end of the schedule. Whatever, it didn't bother us much, because we were so good together—we were ready for anything. But then watching Opal, I realized why Hize was doing that. Both those songs had Nev heavy on the lead vocal—Opal had simpler parts, a few "ooh"s on the chorus and only one or two lines to sing. Hize was letting her ease into it. He was giving her time to observe and learn. Because the way she was looking around, concentrating so hard with those painted-on eyebrows knit every time he gave a note, it was clear she didn't know what the hell she was doing. At one point, Jimmy muttered to me under his breath, "I'm gonna give this exactly three days."

BOB HIZE:

She arrived in her full regalia, full of swagger, but this was a room of professionals. We couldn't be tricked. Her lack of experience was clear

---

* Squine was Jimmy Curtis's closest friend among the *Polychrome* musicians. Today a grandfather of twelve at age 72, he stays young at heart by running a summer music camp for kids in upstate New York.

from the start. Not that Nev was loads better—Jason Moore kept tittering that the guitar was out of tune—but at least he knew somewhat how the process was supposed to go.

On the small backing parts Opal had, she sang loud and confident, which was promising, except that she nearly blew poor Jason's ears out in the monitors because she was standing much too close to her microphone. When I gave her a pop filter to attach she turned it over and over in her hands until Solomon had the good sense to help her clip it on. And then again with the microphone—well, this was rather charming, but on "Yellow Belly," one take was good and raucous, and everyone was smiling and nodding as they all built to the end, and at the last bit Opal got overexcited and grabbed at her mic like I suppose she'd seen rock stars do on telly, and sent the whole apparatus crashing down. Your dad and the other players were livid because it was the best take of the day and they thought she'd ruined it—but when Jason and I played it back, the crashing noise was actually quite clever. [*Laughs*] It was like this unexpected crescendo that made sense in the context of the song, which, you know, is this rollicking thing about a draft dodger on the lam. So that's actually the take you hear on *Polychrome*—the crashing of the equipment at the end, and then Nev's hysterical laughter.

OPAL JEWEL:

You can't compare performing on open-mic nights to what this was. This was creating something new that was living and breathing. Here you had these guys, really *good* guys, who could do more than just play instruments—they could play emotions! And adjectives! You get what I'm saying? Like, we'd do a first take and Nev would say it was good, but the way he heard it in his head was more whimsical. Don't you know those guys would switch it up for the next take, pluck or hit something a teeny bit different, so that the sound had more looseness, more silliness, even though it was the same notes? I was like, *Wow*. That was incredible to me. That was magic. It's true that I had a lot to learn about the process, but I got so wrapped up in everything, in being with Nev in the center of this hurricane, that my excitement kicked my nerves right on out the room. Up till then I had spent so much time freaking the hell out that I had not made room for the notion that hey, this might be *fun*.

And then Bob Hize . . . Me and Rivington didn't end up so hot, but Bob was kind to me, especially at the beginning. Patient and tuned in and looking out, all the time. Say *that*.

BOB HIZE, *UPON BEING TOLD OPAL'S ASSESSMENT*:

I don't know if I'm a particularly kind man. Maybe so. I hope I'm judged to be, dying as I am. [*Laughs*] I needed to embrace Opal because . . . well, because I knew—everybody who had two eyes and common sense knew—that Nev was in love with her. It was easier to work with it than against it.

NEV CHARLES:

When we got the first day down, Hizey took Opal and me to eat at a twenty-four-hour diner, and he smoked ciggies while she and I stuffed ourselves—I was ravenously hungry, probably because I hadn't eaten well leading up, but now the old appetite had come roaring back. I remember there was a cranky child in the booth beside ours, out way past his bedtime, and he had been crying in that wound-up way that sleepy babies often do, *neh-neh-nehhhh*, but when our lot sat down he shut right up. Opal *was* quite something to look at, all done up.

So we were noses deep in breakfast for dinner—waffles and sausages and eggs and a ham steak besides, and a few mugs of coffee that ramped up the jitters even more—and then Hizey made his excuses and he dropped bills on the table, enough to cover, and he left us by ourselves. We stayed in that diner until the sun came up. There were so many questions I wanted to ask her, about where she'd been hiding and why, about what she thought of the music, but I thought better of it, figured I should just be grateful that the day's session had gone well, so instead we passed the time dreaming out loud, mostly. The beginnings of any new thing are so lovely.

OPAL JEWEL:

We were eating in a diner when Nev asked me how I wanted my name to appear on the album, how I heard it announced from the stage. Shocking, I know, but that was something I honestly hadn't thought about yet. I'd dreamed about my name in lights, up on a marquee somewhere, sure, but I always saw it as what it was: Opal Robinson. That's the truth. But Opal Robinson was a different person now, separate from this entertainer I was becoming.

NEV CHARLES:

We kicked around a few ideas. Opal Odd was one, which would have made a great future punk name, when you think about it, but at the time it seemed too obvious. . . .

OPAL JEWEL:

I told him I had to keep the Opal. After all those years suffering through other people's nasty slurs for me, I had earned the right to own what my mama meant for me to be called.

NEV CHARLES:

The series of exotic-sounding foreign surnames: Opal Amour . . . Opal Magnifique . . .

OPAL JEWEL:

I dig the French, but I'm a Negro from Detroit, USA. We don't put on airs like that.

NEV CHARLES:

. . . just Opal, nothing else, but then we thought, *Well, there's already Odetta and maybe that's confusing.* . . .

OPAL JEWEL:

The sun was coming up when we hit the right one.

NEV CHARLES:

I drank her in, I mean really looked at her—all her vibrant colors, the sparkle on her eyelids, her dimensions and sharp edges. Her rarity. It put me in mind of a gemstone . . . a jewel. Opal Jewel.

OPAL JEWEL:

"Opal *Jewel*?" [*Wrinkling her nose*] I asked him, "Isn't that kinda redundant? Like saying 'desk furniture'?" And he shrugged and laughed and said nah, it's like an exclamation point. A reiteration. It makes it undeniable that's what you are. So I said it a few times, and it sounded all right.

NEV CHARLES:

She seemed to like it well enough—it raised a tiny smile over the toast crusts, anyway.

The recording of Polychrome *spread across four more weeks at a small studio inside Rivington Records. The sessions were scheduled erratically due to the conflicting (and usually higher-paying) gigs of the other players. At Hize's suggestion, Opal and Nev spent time off during this period rehearsing and getting to know each other better.*

OPAL JEWEL:

We were young and we liked to have adventures, and New York was good for that. Some days we'd take the subway out to Coney Island or up through the Bronx—"for inspiration," Nev would say—and he'd be chit-chattering the whole way and strumming on that guitar, making up stories and lyrics about the people we saw. Or some days that meant he was third-wheeling it with me and Virgil around town. That was about as entertaining.

VIRGIL LAFLEUR:

We would concoct fresh daily ensembles for Opal out of what she had in her closet plus some of Miss Ernestine's old effects, and we would mix in whatever inexpensive accessories or materials we could gather.

Well, I was discovering I had a talent! And I was happy to develop it, so that maybe I could start working with the *Vogue* girls one day.

Oh, Neville was my precious Pup. He'd come with us to the Salvation Army or to the fabric store, playing his guitar in the racks, and I was dying to make him over. He was a perfect model, with that beanpole frame. I could have made him a matinee idol . . . but the most he'd let me do was buy him a hat. My vision was *Midnight Cowboy* meets Valentino.

NEV CHARLES:

We'd practice "Evergreen" or "Girl in Gold" sometimes on the subway platform, on our way to this place or that, and the sound bouncing off the tiles was marvelous. After small children started tossing coins at us I got a cowboy hat for collecting our tips. At the end of the show or when the train came, whichever came first, Opal would dump all the money into this handbag she carried, a snap-shut thing that Virgil had covered with the fur of a stuffed animal, and she'd put on the hat and do a curtsy and we'd split the money and find a doughnut to share. A strange pair indeed, me in my holey jeans and she in her couture du jour. I suspect we both loved it—the stares of the tourists, the old folks shaking their heads, the befuddlement when we opened our mouths to sing. Nobody knew what to make of us, and I was pleased to know that together we were as fresh and different as I had predicted.

As for the album's sidemen: Despite the ups and downs of the first day, the subsequent sessions kept my father, Squine, and Krebble invested enough to continue turning up at Rivington—and turning in some of the most inspired work of their careers.

BOB HIZE:

All the acclaim I've been given, right up through that lovely tribute last spring . . . It's been nice, but I have to confess: It wasn't genius on my part. Much of it was a happy accident. Was Opal what I had envisioned as the complement to Nev? No. But ultimately she was better than my imagination, and weren't we lucky for it?

JOHN SQUINE:

Session two, she came back in another crazy mismatched outfit, so we're assuming it's going to be more of the same BS. But wait a minute now— she's figured out how to adjust the mic! And oh, that's a good little run on the bridge. . . . Okay! Now we're in business. And by the time we got to "Chalk White" and "Ginger's Lament," we were really cooking.

All respect to your mother, but in the time I worked with Jimmy, I don't think I ever saw him as impressed with anybody as he was with Opal Jewel. He wasn't the type to go gaga over anybody, but I think she did a number on him. Not because she was that good at that moment, but because we saw she had the capacity to *be* that good.

BOB HIZE, *ON WHAT HE THINKS MAKES* *OPAL SPECIAL AS AN ARTIST*:

She is extremely attuned to the mood of the music and the lyrics. Wherever they go, she goes. She is not one of those girls who can "sing the phone book," as people like to say. If you stuck some nonsense rhymes in Opal's hands and asked her to sing them a cappella, I promise you it would be unrecognizable because she'd have nothing to play off, nothing to interpret. But if you put her in with a good band on a song that means something and then isolate the vocal, hearing her raw becomes a whole different story—you hear the range and color and theatricality. Even when she was warming up before a session, she didn't like doing it alone. She'd ask John or Sol Krebble to play a few notes to help her out—Sol for her upper and mid-range, John for the lower. Suddenly everyone had to reenergize, because Opal was so responsive to what the other musicians would do. We were playing rock music but in many ways the process did feel like jazz.

As he had with a select number of jazz artists before her, Jimmy took Opal under his wing.

JIMMY CURTIS:

Eventually I did learn how to read music, and then I taught a lot of other cats coming up behind me. I still teach 'em. Because that is my responsibility, from one black artist to another. They like to say, usually about *us*, "Oh, So-and-So just has a natural talent, a natural rhythm, you can't explain it." Ain't that disrespectful? Like, ain't this an art form that we practice too? That we put our brains and sweat and heart and soul behind so we can learn and improve, just like you?

OPAL JEWEL, *WHEN ASKED TO ELABORATE*
ON THE EARLY DAYS OF HER AFFAIR WITH MY FATHER:

What you want me to say? You want me to say he was handsome? Okay, he was handsome. [*Long pause*] It's been a long time now, but whenever the anniversary used to roll around and the newspeople would talk about what happened to him, they'd flash up on the screen this black-and-white "before" picture that somebody rustled up, and he's a teenager and he's leaned up against some building, this strapping young man with a cigarette dangling out the side of his mouth. Even better than looking good, Jimmy sounded good, like nobody else I ever heard. That man had a fearsome talent. He was sharp and nasty on those drums. But anybody with half an ear could tell you that.

And then maybe the most comforting to me at the time, it's the most simple thing, but Jimmy was Black. That's it. As close as Nev and I got over the years, as much feeling and friendship existed between us, there was something instant between your daddy and me that didn't require work or words. Oh, you know what I'm talking about. It's a cultural grounding that we Black folks have, whether you are from Detroit or New York or Los Angeles or Bumblecrack, Mississippi. I remember somewhere in the nineties I went to see Pearl's youngest graduate from Howard [University], and some of the children on campus were wearing shirts that said, IT'S A BLACK THING—YOU WOULDN'T UNDERSTAND. And ooh, honey, the white people get so mad about stuff like that, about anything that excludes them, but I would laugh and laugh. Because it's true!

Anyway, since Jimmy and I were the only two Black folks on the record, and since out in the world there weren't many of us making music like the kind Nev was trying to do, we got to be tight. It was a gravitational thing. I'm not gonna sit here and say I'm proud of it. But it was what it was.

[*On how she began seeing him outside of the studio*] Miss Ernestine wasn't having strange men in her house in the wee hours, so after we finished a session we'd go to Jimmy's spot uptown; it was on my way home anyhow. And he'd let me hear some of the records he'd played on. Nev came along the first few times too, and we'd sit at the kitchen table with Corinne [Dawes Curtis, my mother] or his friends from next door and we'd have a cocktail or some scrambled eggs; he liked his with a slice of American cheese draped across the top. But then Nev stopped coming. Probably he got bored or uncomfortable with being left out of the conversation—we would be drinking and getting loose, arguing loud about Angela [Davis] and George [Jackson] and everything that was going down, and I don't think Nev knew what to say or how to handle it. And then Corinne stopped waiting up because the sessions were going later and later and she had her nursing shift in the morning, a real job, so she'd be asleep upstairs. Folks fell away till it was just your daddy and me . . . tiptoeing in the house, whispering on his living room couch. He'd chain-smoke cigarettes and teach me things. At first it was professional and then it wasn't. [*Shrugs*] Yeah, I knew what I was doing; I was the one who started it. I don't have any excuse except that I was twenty-one and had never been kissed. [*Long pause*] That's all I have to say.

ROSEMARY SALDUCCI:

She didn't have any girlfriends and her sister was far away, so Opal and I became friendly. And I got to realize that as worldly as she seemed, this girl was really innocent. One day she came in to Rivington looking worried and she asked me if I could speak privately with her in the bathroom, and when we got there she told me she'd been using rubbers with her boyfriend but she was having some sort of a problem. Now, I don't know why she came to *me* with this—maybe it says something about my character. [*Laughs*] I said, "Well, what's going on?" and asked her a few more questions. And she said, "Oh, my God, Rosemary, the itching and burning," and, you know, all the classic symptoms of a yeast infection. It was so cute, I'm telling you. I took her to a cheap clinic to confirm it and get her something to fix it up, and because I knew the asshole doctor wouldn't tell her this I said she should clean and dry real good after her boyfriend was done down there, every time. And I said, "Congratulations, honey—you got a keeper!" What? Oh, don't be such a prude, I'm only being honest. I was happy for her, that she had a man who pleased her in that way, because men did not do that a lot in those days! Or at least they claimed not to. All right, all right, I'm done. But if I had known then that Casanova was Jimmy Curtis, a married guy? Well, I would have told her from experience that's a road of heartbreak right there.

JOHN SQUINE:

When we were recording, Opal would come in stronger and stronger every time, and I was wondering, *Who's been working with her?* Then I'd look over and notice that she was turned toward Jimmy, and he was looking at her, and every once in a while, maybe on a particular break, he'd nod as if he was sending her a secret message, and she'd bust out with some improvisation or riff that we hadn't practiced before. I didn't know Jimmy to be a tomcat—we'd worked together a lot and had been on the road, where most of that stuff tends to happen—but it was obvious that something was up.

Of course Nev knew, he had to have known. That's probably why those guys wanted to throttle each other.

Though most of the early sessions went extraordinarily well, the recording of a song called "Black Coffee," which Nev had written for Opal to sing, kicked off a war between him and my father. As originally written, it was a bluesy ballad with a dragging beat. Its narrator—a composite of the people, many of them Black and poor, whom Nev had encountered during his tour in search of Opal—is a young single mother gearing up for another grueling day at her miserable, low-paying factory job ("Drop of milk for the baby, black coffee for me / Or I'll be collapsed by the time it hits three"). At the end of the night, she's switching off the light and preparing for the cycle to repeat ("Alone once again, I settle for sleep / And pray for the baby, and my soul to keep / I dream of the day we'll get what we're due / But for now there's that kettle, screaming on cue").

OPAL JEWEL:

"Black Coffee" was a song that *I could not stand*. I get that Nev meant well with it—these white liberal types always do, don't they? But he was putting all these words in my mouth, literally, and they were so damn morose. Listen, we were on some different stuff in 1970! We were all singing [James Brown's] "Say It Loud—I'm Black and I'm Proud"! That's what we were on—the joy! But "Black Coffee" to me was musty and sad and old-school Negro, and taking the lead on it was a threat to my particular spirit. Like me saying what a drag it is to live in my skin. It wasn't how I wanted to represent myself.

My mistake was, I shoulda pulled Nev aside and told him that to his face.

JIMMY CURTIS, *ANSWERING THE QUESTION "WHAT DOES IT MEAN TO BE SUCCESSFUL AS A SESSION PLAYER?"*:

Well, it sure ain't about the dough. You can scrape together a living, maybe take care of your family if you're lucky to get some touring work on the side. But my personal definition of success is that you don't do a goddamn thing you don't want to. If you ain't feeling it, you ain't gotta do it.

BOB HIZE:

Jimmy almost brought the whole project crashing down because he flat-out refused to play on "Black Coffee." He said that he didn't like what it was about and he said that [*using air quotes*] "we"—implying him and Opal, I suspect—couldn't stand behind it. That "we" . . . It was a goading, a jab, and it worked very well. Nev was atomically upset, so offended that anyone would think he had ill intent or poor judgment, and Jimmy was shouting ten times louder that he didn't care, the song was rubbish. . . . Like rams in the battle, those two. And everyone was turning to me as if to say, "What now?"

HOWIE KELLY:

For the most part, I was staying out of the studio, since that was Hizey's deal—I would just drop in sometimes to make sure there was no funny stuff happening. But during one of the sessions there was a racket in the hallway, yelling so loud I could hear it down in my office! Well, I wasn't about to stand for that, because I got business to do on the phone! I go to find out what the problem is and they're going at it, Nev and your old man, and Hizey and Opal and Rosemary just standing around looking like dummies. And I say over all that noise, [*shouting*] "You wanna yell? Okay! I'll show ya how to yell! Now shut the hell up or you're all on your ass!" Back to my office, slam the door . . . settled.

BOB HIZE:

On the face, the song was as good as the others—about a particular person in a particular situation who just so happened to be Black. But the difficulty was, the difficulty still *is*, that everything having to do with race in America is so bloody complex and deep-rooted, and Nev and I, being the pale Englishmen, we weren't well versed, pardon the pun. We didn't even have an audience yet, we didn't know if our fans were going to be Black or white or purple, which was a big problem in and of itself, but with this song there was the threat of alienating an entire chunk simply by being tone-deaf to the times.

Besides that, "Black Coffee" was reliant on the drummer, and I didn't want to go out and find another. In fact, I had hopes that your dad would stay on through the supporting live gigs. I knew all of them could be brilliant together—I was witness to it at the beginning, before the egos landed.

Opal was quiet, but judging from the fact that she didn't contradict Jimmy when he kept dragging her into it, I could suss out that she was going to side with him. I didn't ask her to say it out loud because I couldn't bear to do that to Nev, and Nev was mindful of his own feelings as well, careful not to press her to choose, because I think he knew he would come out the losing end. The other lads were loyal to your father too; they'd worked with him before and would probably have to work with him again. So the writing was on the wall, wasn't it? I said as gently as I could to Nev, "I'm sorry, but I think we'd better cut it."

NEV CHARLES:

We're going to need a string orchestra for this next bit. . . . Are you ready? Prepare the violins! [*Laughs*] I felt very alone, and in some respects betrayed. I still stand by "Black Coffee," and it found its place, didn't it?*

But when everybody rejected it I was out of sorts, and can you blame me, really, considering *Polychrome* was *my* record and not Jimmy Curtis's? That he was allowed to make such a decision was galling to me, especially with him running around with my featured singer and creating all this drama.

JOHN SQUINE:

Your father did have a temper. You could be telling him an actual fact, like the sky is blue, but if he felt disrespected or that you'd talked down

---

* Nev's lost tune ultimately landed on the soundtrack for the controversial 2001 movie-musical *The Jungle,* a tweak on Upton Sinclair's novel starring an all-Black cast; as performed by actress LaTasha Prather and produced by Nev himself, "Black Coffee" was nominated for Best Original Song at both the Academy Awards and the Golden Globes.

to him in the way that you'd said it, he would glare at you with a straight face: "No, motherfucker, it's red." [*Laughs*]

So it got to the point where Nev walked out the building and we thought he might not come back. Yeah, it was kinda childish, maybe it was jealousy over Opal; I don't know.

NEV CHARLES:

I retreated to the flat on Ninety-Sixth Street and I moped in my pajamas for a couple days; I reconnected with a sweet girl who fed me sandwiches and let me wallow, and I really considered just chucking it all. Maybe heading back to England—that was always an option.

Eventually I sent the girl home and rang my dad for a little support, emotional, financial, but do you know what happened? A stranger picked up on the other end, a stranger who called herself Carol and said she had heard a lot about me, Morris's boy gone off to America, and I said, "Oh, are you the new housemaid?" and she said, "No, I'm a special friend of your father's." A *special friend*! [*Making a disgusted face*] She finally put Dad on the line and I was shocked and appalled, but he sounded chipper, totally inappropriate and relaxed, as if they'd just been up to something, and I said, "But Dad, Mum's birthday is in two weeks!" or whatever, and he said, "I know it, lad, and God rest her soul. But life goes on, and I won't pout through it." Well, I felt proper foolish then, because that's exactly what I had been doing, pouting, and nobody was even dead. Oh, God, unfortunate choice of words . . . I'm sorry, but you understand. So I let "Black Coffee" rest for the moment, I put it in the old percolator [*tapping temple*]. And I went back to finish my record.

chapter nine

"AW, NAH.
NOT FOR US."

★   ★

Polychrome, *credited to Nev Charles featuring Opal Jewel, was released by Rivington Records on November 10, 1970. The rushed date was suggested by Howie Kelly, who hoped to capitalize, just before Veterans Day, on the anti-war sentiment of "Yellow Belly" (the album's first single). In addition to the American pressing, Nev contributed funds from his remaining contractual lump sum to cover a limited UK release. The album included "Red-Handed," the final recorded track and Opal's favorite of the replacement songs Nev dashed off after the nixing of "Black Coffee."*

Having blown his budget on the session players, Hize shortchanged other areas, particularly promotion and marketing. To create the album art, he hired another budget-friendly young student, this one a fine arts senior from Pratt Institute. Naomi Sigrin took photos of a colorful candy machine in a brightly lit campus studio, then captured separate shots of Opal and Nev making various facial expressions. After shrinking prints of the portraits down to size, Sigrin cut out the artists' heads using an X-Acto knife and pasted them over a few of the candies, making it look as if they were trapped inside and available for a nickel. (To Kelly's great relief, Opal did not go bald on the cover—she wore her Afro wig for the shoot, to mimic the roundness of a gumball.)

BOB HIZE:

We let it go and held our breath. We thought it was good but didn't know whether that would matter. Rock music was still depressed at the time— we'd just had the one-two punch of losing Jimi and Janis, remember. And the Beatles packing it in a few months before that. If those bed-rocks were suddenly gone, it seemed like everything in the industry was shaky, was subject to change with no warning. Anything could happen.

What happened was . . . not much. Hize's efforts to generate publicity fell short, and initially the album failed to get much attention at radio stations or with critics. (Most ink at the time went toward George Harrison's post-Beatles solo release, All Things Must Pass, *which dropped later that month.)*

However, Nev's stint at university proved not to have been a total waste. Writer Stewart Fitzsimmons, a City, University of London alum who had attended the journalism school during the period Nev had flitted through, penned a critique that appeared in the British newspaper New Musical Express. *In his assessment Fitzsimmons disclosed that, while they did not per-sonally know each other, he had seen Nev play a pub or three around campus.*

EXCERPT FROM "UNI TO THE USA," *NME,*
WEEK ENDING NOVEMBER 21, 1970
By Stewart Fitzsimmons

Since his days performing for a pint, Charles sings with more gravity. The nasal sound that often pushed his clever character studies toward irksomeness has been replaced with a bolder, richer tone—at times it may remind you of the one McCartney employs when singing of Lady Madonna or his darling headed for Golden Slumbers. Perhaps it's a trick of studio magic, but no doubt a percentage of this change comes honest, from the grit New York City must have shoved underneath his finger-nails. . . .

There is also a new colour in Charles's kit: the Negro col-laborator who joins him on the album's better songs and basks in a solo turn near the end ("Red-Handed"). She calls herself Opal Jewel and, according to the promotional materials *NME* received, was discovered wasting away in an amateur Detroit sister act. On the quiet romance "Evergreen," a canon in two, Charles holds the melody steady while his eccentric partner experiments around him. She dips up, she falls down, she speak-sings. . . . She is not the strongest vocalist by any technical measure, but she won't be accused of being snoozy.

I found *Polychrome* to be its most charming when the amps creep up. Should it get any attention in America, "Yellow Belly" will presumably annoy Mr. Nixon and his fogey contemporaries not only with its political message but also with its loud, ramshackle aesthetic. Similarly, "Chalk White" is an ear-piercer turned to 10. . . .

Overall: worth a listen despite its lack of cohesion and its exceedingly silly packaging.

ROSEMARY SALDUCCI:

Bob had me make about a million copies of that article in the *NME*, and then I had to stuff 'em in envelopes and send 'em out to the same radio stations that he'd already begged so many times before. It wasn't even a rave, but it was pretty much the only review that existed.

HOWIE KELLY:

I'm looking for the record sales, I'm looking for the airplay, I'm looking for something in *Rolling Stone* or the *Voice* or even a publication on the level of your shitty rag. [*Laughs*] Eh, I'm fucking with you. But I'm saying I would've sold my left nut for some real traction on this thing. Hizey comes to me all excited with this one puny review from somewhere twenty thousand miles away, telling me how incredible it is to be in the *NME*. And I say, "*NME*? What's that stand for, Bob? 'No Money Ever'?"

BOB HIZE:

I had thought the *NME* piece would lead to some more interest here in the States, but I barely got a shoulder shrug. I castigated myself over that cover art—I thought, *Oh, God, people can't get past it, they're not bothering to open it up and have a listen, that's why!* Because I couldn't conceive that the music was not compelling. I knew that it was.

PEARL WELMONT:

Opal mailed us a copy of the album and when me and Mama opened it up and saw her face on the cover, that gumball machine, ooh, we screamed and carried on like children! We ran over to Mrs. Dennis's apartment to show her and also to use her record player. It was kinda funny when we let the needle drop, because Lord, that music was not what we were expecting. We skipped a couple of the songs, to tell you the truth, because Mama was getting a headache. But still, we were proud.

NEV CHARLES:

Dad rang to tell me that he had trouble locating the record in Birmingham but Carol, good ol' Carol, she had tracked it down, and she and her friends from the sports club had enjoyed listening to it at their wine-and-cheese Wednesday. So yes, gaze in awe, because I was a smash with the middle-aged-tarts set.

OPAL JEWEL:

Claudia [Hize's then-wife] invited me and Nev to Thanksgiving dinner that year. Normally I would've wanted to spend it with Virgil or Miss Ernestine, but they both went away to see their families, and I didn't have enough money to travel anywhere. Bob and Claudia were so nice to have us, especially since it was their first big holiday with Melody, but sitting at the table across from Nev—it was *sad*. He was depressed about the record and still a little upset with me over "Black Coffee," and I was homesick for the first time since I got to New York. I wanted my mama's sweet potato pie and some macaroni and cheese, you hear me?

I wouldn't have minded going the rounds with Pearl if I could've had that. But there we were in New York, and it was freezing cold and we had put out a turd, and you know good and well white folks can't make no collard greens.

Hize had little budget left, much less a convincing justification, for a support-ing tour. The best he could do was arrange acoustic regional shows and hope that his duo could translate a portion of the energy from the vinyl to a live audience, maybe sell a few albums from the milk crate they lugged to each gig. But he was quickly confronted, once again, with the question that first crossed his mind during the recording sessions: Exactly who was this audience?

BOB HIZE:

We started out at some small rock clubs in the East Village. I had Opal and Nev come along with me so I could make introductions, and most of the white managers would take one look at Opal, even done up as wildly as she could do, and they'd say, "We don't take R&B acts." Which is very funny because these same places would've killed to have a drop-in by the Rolling Stones. Anyway, once you explained to them that it wasn't exactly R&B, some of them might relent, but they'd book us on the bill first or second. There'd scarcely be anybody in the house, maybe Virgil LaFleur and his friends, maybe a few NYU students who weren't valu-able because they were too broke to buy drinks, and then when you rang the managers to see about another booking they'd say, "Oh, but you didn't draw enough people." Round and round in circles, burning through venues.

We didn't have the same problem in Harlem and Brooklyn, not ex-actly, but those broke Opal's heart in a different way.

OPAL JEWEL:

When we were first out and going to the white spots, the people would be so confused. [*Laughs*] Looking up at the stage with goofy-ass smiles and tilted heads, like they were trying to process what it was they were seeing. And after every gig it was guaranteed one of these fools would come up to me and raise a fist and say, "Power to the people," or call me "sister" or something else that would let me know nothing—not the music, not the funny little banter, not even the clothes—was more worthy of comment than my being Black. Don't misunderstand: Anyone who says they're color-blind is a damn lie. But there is plenty of time between what you *see* and what you *say*. And their little comments, their trying to talk Black or whatever, to me that was them going out of their way to announce they were cool with me being there, cool with me participating in what they obviously believed was *their* scene.

Then we'd try the Black spots, and the people weren't confused at all—honey, they'd already made up their minds when they saw Nev and heard that jangle. [*Laughs*] Sellout, Wannabe, Oreo, Two-Face . . . For a while, I had a whole new set of nicknames.

JIMMY CURTIS:

The music itself don't have a color. It's a continuum that starts with the drum and branches out from there. The industry and the money, that's what can mess everything up. I understand where black folks are coming from. Rock and roll wasn't nothing but a step away from the blues, but the whites acted like it was their brand-new bag and then had the nerve to cut most of us out when the money started rolling in. So we were like, *Well, fuck it—that's yours now, and this is mine, and don't nobody have no business crossing lines.* See, this is what I say about America—we always gotta be assigning shit, always labeling it and stuffing it in a box. Always dictating who's allowed to own what. But end of the day, that don't have nothing to do with the music, you dig? The music is fire and passion and soul, and however you express it is how you express it.

I get to play behind everybody and I love that, because can't nobody figure me out. I get a lot of respect. Somebody like Hendrix, though, as visionary as he is, he has a hard time with us skinfolk. They look up at that stage, see all those white longhairs around my exceptional brother and they say, *Aw, nah. Not for us.* Focusing on that when he can make that guitar holler, that's a tragedy. But that's what they assume, you know — *This child is lost.*

BOB HIZE:

Everything dried up faster than you could blink. All prospects dead by the New Year.

OPAL JEWEL:

Of course it was painful, but it was a pain I already knew — I never managed to fit in anywhere but the freak bin. The only reason it got to me is because of how it was affecting Nev. He flapped his gums all the time about being proud to be different, but in his heart of hearts, ooh, that man is cocky. He expected to drop this record and immediately be huge — he wanted the love and the money and a big stamp of approval right across the forehead. Nev used to play at being different, but I don't know if he ever understood what being different *really* means. That the regular people like to beat back what's different, because it scares them half to death.

NEV CHARLES:

I became disillusioned with America, with popular music, with people's snap judgments and their stereotypes and their willful lack of imagination. But I want to make it clear that despite whatever creative differences came later, I never regretted for one instant working with Opal. I absolutely do acknowledge her role in my career, as part of the reason I am where I am. She helped me bring to life music of which I am extremely proud, and I believe that a place that couldn't accept the concept of us together was a place I had no business being. So when we hit those early bumps, there was never a question of me switching partners or styles, or going on my own again — it was whether I wanted to even bother trying at all.

OPAL JEWEL:

Naturally my instinct was just to keep moving, moving, moving like I always had, but my partner had gone quiet on me. So I started going down to Ninety-Sixth Street to see about him, see if he wanted to rehearse or let me try out any new songs he might have.

He didn't want to cut on the heat in his apartment, so he'd come to the door wearing about twelve sweaters and mittens and one of those wool hats with the ball on top. You'd talk and vapor would be pouring out your mouth. He'd have lines on his face from his bedsheets—he'd just be getting up, three o'clock in the afternoon. You'd open his cabinets and all you saw was Campbell's soup. Not vegetable or chicken noodle or anything that would keep his system up, but the cheap cans you dump into casseroles—cream of mushroom, you know . . . cheddar cheese. Just *nasty*.

I figured he'd be too proud to take whatever spare change I had in my pocket, so I started showing up with leftovers from Miss Ernestine's, or sometimes a pint of pepper steak from this cheap Chinese spot near his place. And I'd tell stories about where I got it and he knew it was lies, but he'd pick at it and then he'd say he was tired and he'd see me later.

It didn't worry me much at first because you can get by, being poor—in my case it made me more stubborn, more creative. What had me bothered was when he stopped scribbling down lyrics, stopped fooling around on the guitar. It was like it was getting colder outside and everything inside Nev was freezing up too. I went to Bob and I said, *He's not right.*

BOB HIZE:

I struggled with guilt over Nev, because we had all got his hopes up and it hadn't worked out; maybe I had spent the money incorrectly when I should have thought more about the business, and now Howie would surely want to abandon him. I talked to Claudia, who had a deep fondness for Nev and, for as long as she could stand it, a certain patience with me, and she agreed that we could stretch for a while to accommodate him, make his last months in New York at least comfortable. I came up with a ludicrous reason that I needed him around—he could have the sofa in exchange for music lessons for Melody, even though she was only a year old and obviously didn't yet have motor skills. But that was the ruse we all lived under for a couple months, while he got his pride together—either got a proper job or left to go back to England.

NEV CHARLES:

It was hilarious, really: I had come all the way to America just to turn into George bloody Risehart. I thought about that as Melody banged away on her toy xylophone, thought about my dad and his lady friend, this Carol person, thought about my poor dead mother, and I laughed to keep from falling apart.

As Nev hibernated, Opal blossomed. Artists of all stripes, attracted by her outer wrappings, hovered in her sphere. The New York scene in which she and Virgil immersed themselves could be glittery and confusing, but her social experimentation distracted her from the disappointments of Polychrome and, I imagine, her ongoing affair with my father.

OPAL JEWEL:

Giving up never did anything for anybody. I just figured, Well, this project didn't work out—on to the next. Plus, I still had a way to go on my contract, and I'm nobody's freeloader. So I kept myself busy during the downtime. I started drawing out the shows we were gonna have one day, literally making sketches of the stage designs in Nev's lyrics notebook, and daydreaming with Virgil about the clothes.

VIRGIL LAFLEUR,
OPENING AN OLD PHOTO ALBUM:

The winter look was about layers and textures. We used a lot of plush felt, and once even figured out how to tease a purple blanket into a quilted poncho. I threw a belt on it and voilà!—instant chic.

She still wasn't used to the cold on her bare scalp, so we played with hats—this one is just a pleated turban with a Japanese folding fan hot-glued to the side, see? Ingenuity! Yes, and that one had a salad bowl as the base. We lined the inside with flannel, turned it upside down, and built it up from there. . . . It had a chinstrap but she had to wear it cocked to the side and hold her head just so—it could *not* be a windy day. The lip became plum, the eye bronze. Gorgeous. I took a photograph of her every day for a while. My portfolio.

OPAL JEWEL:

I felt like . . . otherworldly. Like walking art. Whatever I wore was my shell and nothing outside it could touch me. I attracted so much atten-tion just strutting down the street. All that energy—horror, delight, sex, disgust—it would warm me up and then bounce off. Whatever you gave to me, I threw it right back at you, and every day was a performance. Me and Nev couldn't get a decent crowd anywhere, but I imagined that playing to a giant audience, all those people focused on you and cheer-ing, could give you that feeling two thousand times over. So honey, I was in rehearsals for the role of intergalactic showstopper, and everybody in New York City was on notice.

VIRGIL LAFLEUR:

There was usually a party somewhere downtown on a Saturday night, and if your papa had obligations elsewhere Mad would be my date and we would be the hit. She left an impression. If I went out the next week alone people would ask, "Where's your fascinating girl?"

OPAL JEWEL:

An art dealer we met somewhere wanted to give me money to show up at his gallery opening. I said, "What do you want me to do, sing?" and he said, "No, just be as fabulous as you are right this moment." So me and Virgil get there and we walked around and around this gallery, drinking champagne and pretending to look at the paint splatters. Everybody was glamorous and rich and cold, and none of them talked to us much but you could feel them staring out the corners of their eyes. At the end of the night the man gave me fifty bucks and thanked me for coming. I thought, *Well, isn't that interesting.*

VIRGIL LAFLEUR:

Our home address fluttered onto someone's list, and we started receiving invitations. More galleries, concerts, a higher echelon of artists . . .

OPAL JEWEL:

Sometimes it did get boring. I didn't mind the attention, but some of these party-party scenesters could be as phony inside as they were out, and besides that they were half-crazed on speed and their own huge egos. You'd try to hold a conversation with these people about something, anything—politics, music, what you ate for breakfast—and they'd be nodding like they were listening, but their eyes would be spinning out of their heads.

Virgil suggested I start smoking weed, God bless him, so I could relax and make it through the nights. He promised something big was gonna happen. For him that meant meeting Miss Diana—Vreeland, not Ross, although he wouldn't have been mad at that either. For me, it meant getting me and Nev booked for a show at Max's [Kansas City, a restaurant and club near Union Square].

Now *that* was a decent place—a wild, drugged-out place, yeah, but a hot spot for freaks and any artist who loved them. By the time I started making that scene, Andy Warhol had stopped showing up, but his vibe still lingered in that back room he ruled—you know, the feeling that you could be a nobody weirdo one day and then pop out of Max's a glam superstar the next. Everybody who went had a quality about them, a buzz, and the connections were legendary. I wasn't surprised, when Blondie got big, to hear that Debbie Harry had once waited tables at Max's, or that Iggy Pop first met David Bowie there.

The summer before I started going, they'd flipped the upstairs into a venue for parties and concerts. The Velvet Underground had done a residency, the last shows before Lou [Reed] left the band, and after that the upstairs only got hotter. You never knew who might show up. Celebrities, yeah, that was always a given. But also maybe [music executives] Ahmet Ertegun or Clive Davis [who signed Aerosmith after a 1972 show at Max's]—money folks who might be useful to me and Nev if Rivington did decide to drop us.

I was trying to learn how to work the place. My MO was to act the same way Lou sang, or like my favorite, Rose Stone, on "Everyday People"—cool and casual, you know . . . unbothered. I couldn't walk up in there demanding to talk to [Max's concert booker] Sam Hood, or pass out the record and beg for a shot. So I made my way around. I smoked, drank my wine, studied the people and the shows they put on. I made conversation with the ones around me and they thought I was funny, I guess, and maybe I looked extra interesting in the red light [emanating from a backroom sculpture by Dan Flavin]. And then I casually slipped in that oh yeah, I do music, me and my British partner. . . . Ooh, I wanted a shot at that upstairs so bad! "Nev Charles featuring Opal Jewel at Max's Kansas City": I was already drawing up the flyer, honey, I was *visualizing*!

But we never did make it to Max's, because Rivington Showcase happened before we had the chance. Imagine if our first big show had been there instead: Maybe I wouldn't be talking to you today. I'd like to think I would, though. I'd like to think that we couldn't help but get famous, just because we were that good. I'd like to think that folks didn't have to end up destroyed for Opal & Nev to have made a name.

Say that name, "Opal & Nev," and it's likely a picture of chaos that pops to mind—specifically, Marion Jacobie's iconic 1971 shot, of Opal riding Nev's bent back as they escape their calamitous set at Rivington Showcase. After its initial publication, six columns wide inside the *New York Times*, The Photo, as we'll henceforth call it, appeared in both its black-and-white and color versions in *Life*, *Rolling Stone*, and *Aural*. It flashed across the evening news and on chat-show programs, even stood as a finalist for a Pulitzer Prize alongside other visual representations of that uneasy era. The precise contextual details reported around it may have fuzzed over time—who hurled what slurs the night of the concert, and who threw the first punch, and in what exact manner did Opal destroy that flag, anyway? Still, The Photo endures, screaming *helter-skelter* louder than words ever could. These days it's deployed as political provocation and identity statement, recontextualized on posters and T-shirts above hashtags like #BlackLivesMatter, #HeForShe, #TheFutureIsFemale.

Its subjects, though, get notoriously touchy when talking about it. During our hastily arranged interview on his private jet, for example, Nev shooed away, with increasing peevishness, most of my questions about the minutes leading up to the shutter's click. After that, I was determined to better prepare for what could be the most pivotal interviews featured here—including my third face-to-face with Opal, to explore the role she played as an agitator that night; and my first with Chet Bond, whose buddies responded to said agitation by beating the breath out of Jimmy Curtis.

Each interview I dreaded for different reasons. I was still at a loss as to how to crack Opal open about her affair with my father, and I feared she would shut down on me completely if I said the wrong things about how he'd ended up dead. Chet Bond posed the opposite risk—I knew, as soon as I got him on the phone to firm up my travel plans and he drawled his thanks "for letting a regular guy like me share his side of the story," that he would delight in spouting off shamelessly.

But beyond any general trepidation I felt, I swore strategic reasons for putting off both of these interviews. Saving the toughest confrontations for last is an old journalist's hack—a way to ensure you've got at your disposal all the facts, all the different perspectives, before you go poking at explosive subjects. As groundwork for talking to Opal and Chet, then, I asked my team at *Aural* for help. I was seeking a variety of thoughts on The Photo, and what associations it evoked for different people. "Either when you first saw it," I said in our main conference room one day last summer, "or sitting here looking at it right now."

"You're putting a staff meeting on the record?" asked Phil Francisco, *Aural*'s most popular columnist/contrarian and a thirty-plus-year vet of the magazine. His last back-page rant had been about the nuisance of cell-phone recording at concerts; now, he glared at the iPhone I'd set on the tabletop to capture our conversation.

"I know it's a bit unconventional," I said. "I guess the whole project is. But I've got a room of captive rock-and-roll enthusiasts and experts here, so I figured it couldn't hurt to get some honest perspectives before I bring it up with Opal. If anyone's uncomfortable talking to me about it, though, if anybody feels like they can't be honest, it's okay, you don't have to stay. I promise it won't offend me." I felt several sets of eyes nervously slide toward me, but no one stood to go. To my right, Phil leaned back in his custom Aeron chair and tapped his fingers, heavy with silver rings and crawling with tattoos, against the armrests. "So yeah," I said, "what exactly is it about this picture? Ben, any thoughts?"

I'd picked on my managing editor, Ben Hinneman, first—not only because he was typically the most thoughtful, measured voice in the room, but also because at an office trivia night years previously, back when he and I were still colleagues and our jobs were more fun, he'd won an Amazon gift certificate in the bonus round by recalling an extraordinary bit of minutiae: the designer name and size number etched onto the bottom of Opal Jewel's platform shoe, outstretched in the foreground of The Photo like the business end of a battering ram. (And okay, maybe I'd picked on Ben because I was still busting his chops a little: When I'd first confided in him that I was the daughter of James "Jimmy" Curtis III, he'd looked at me and asked, with such guilelessness that I nearly spat out my lunch, "Who?")

"*Welllll*," said Ben, "I'm not sure you're supposed to pinpoint the magic *exactly*. That's the thing, right? It's got mystery on top of drama. I mean, of course we know the basic facts of what happened, but how did the two of them *feel* in the moment? Neither of them really goes into much direct detail about that, and—no knock to your reporting skills, Sunny—I worry that they never will."

"Yeah, I couldn't get too much out of Nev about it," I confessed.

"Probably because giving up too much would ruin the effect," Ben said. "I mean, just look at her face—*wow*, that expression! It's like, so tense but open at the same time. Is it a look of power? Rage? Triumph?"

"Grief?" I asked, because I was genuinely curious to know if he saw it.

"Absolutely, could be. The point is, if they ever said too much about what went into this moment, it wouldn't be as evocative, would it? As it is, you or I can take any number of opinions we have about the Confederate flag, about politics' place in art, about Opal and Nev's careers separately, about, um . . . the victim. . . ." He paused; I nodded for him to continue. "And we can project those ideas onto it."

"I always thought she looked like a star," mused Hannah Cleary, a photo editor. "A punk warrior goddess."

"An *Afro*-Punk warrior goddess," clarified our new social media director, Pooja Banerjee, to a few murmurs of agreement.

My staffers went quiet as they studied The Photo, which I'd blown up and affixed to the same wall of corkboard where we pinned the contents of each issue in production. It was the version that had first run huge in the *Times*—I'd always preferred the black and white. Something in its starkness, I thought, made the details more dramatic:

Opal's Mohawk wig, catching the wind and trailing behind her. The furrowed brow, the tensed mouth open wide, the bulging vein running down the right side of her angled neck. The burst of white light popping off the sequins glued to her lash lines. One leg stretched out to do damage, the other one bent with kneecap scraped raw. A bare foot. Her long black arms, crossed at the wrists like the X she annihilated, draped around a white neck.

"So if Opal's the Afro-Punk warrior goddess," I said, breaking the reverie, "what does that make Nev?"

"*Warrrr Horrrse,*" somebody intoned, in the rumbling British accent we liked to imitate from a Broadway commercial that had once been in unbearably heavy rotation on NY1.

We all snickered for a moment at the office inside joke, but I didn't want to let them off the hook just yet. "Seriously," I prodded, "what do you make of Nev in this photograph?"

The white neck. Lean frame stooped, stumbling forward underneath the weight of her. Black rivulets streaking his cheeks, black blooms of blood staining his button-down. Arms hidden, eyes blank, mouth slack as a fish.

"I think that's what an ally looks like," Pooja said.

"Oh, come *on,*" said Phil, rolling his eyes. "What does that even mean?"

I saw Pooja shrink into herself a little. I held my hand up in Phil's direction to stop him from interrupting. "Go on," I told her.

"I guess . . . I guess it just means he was there in the battle with her. And if you strip away what we know about them now . . . In terms of visual symbolism, isn't it a powerful reversal of narratives? The traditionally privileged and the traditionally marginalized switching roles, just after she's totally canceled a symbol of white supremacy?" Nobody answered. "I mean, there are levels of race and gender stuff happening here," she continued. "It's like ground-zero woke. There's a whole TED Talk about it. It went viral last month. I'll send the link around later."

"Here's what I see," said Phil, leaning back so far now that the Aeron creaked. "He's hauling ass, his *and* hers, after some bad shit went down. End of story—that's it. Oh, and he looks fucking miserable about it. Fucking whipped, man. I mean, I know we were joking earlier, but doesn't Nev Charles strike you as the poor bastard Mick and Keith were thinking of when they wrote 'Beast of Burden'?"

"So you're saying he looks like a victim," I said.

"Kinda, yeah, but mostly I'm saying he looks like a pus—"

"All *right*, Phil."

"Sorry," he said, throwing up his hands, "but I thought we were being honest."

"What I want to understand," said Hannah, "is why you think her strength automatically must mean his weakness."

Phil sighed. "Jesus Christ, Sunny, what is the point of this again?"

"There's no right or wrong answer," I said. "I'm just curious to know what impressions different people take away, because it's obviously gonna be crucial to the book, and it obviously inspires strong feelings, even now. So everything's valid, everything's helpful."

Just then Jonathan Benjus Jr.—*Aural*'s young publisher, our big boss, JBJ for short—slid open the conference room door. "Don't mind me, guys," he said, crouching low as if finding a seat in a darkened theater. In one quick move he hopped atop one of the cabinets lining the back wall of the room and sat cross-legged. "Just thought I'd pop in a minute to see what cool stuff you guys are working on."

JBJ had inherited Aural Media from his father in late 2014, and was a twenty-eight-year-old Harvard Business School graduate who'd made many of us skittish with his first "town hall": He'd gathered us in a rented movie theater, fed us popcorn and Twizzlers, trotted out Vin Diesel to say hello for some unknown reason, and then launched into a slick presentation about the need for more seamless collaboration between our editorial and ad-sales divisions. I'd scarcely known him at the time he called me up to his office to gauge my interest in becoming editor in chief, and my surprise promotion was touted as the first major move JBJ had made as publisher—the scion finally emerging from his father's shadow, the *Wall Street Journal* had trumpeted, alongside a portrait of JBJ sitting at his desk with his *Star Wars* toy collection lining the shelf behind him. Now that I was his direct report, I was still struggling to manage. On one hand, the fact that JBJ rarely wore suits, opting instead for black jeans and vintage concert tees underneath expensive slim-cut blazers, suggested he was a cool, laid-back guy who simply loved everything *Aural*, and hovered out of a desire to feel closer to that rock-and-roll spirit. That he strenuously focus-grouped every cover subject I had proposed so far and emailed me constant examples of "innovations" from other magazines—that is, the kind of lucrative advertising integrations that made me, as an editor, feel incredibly queasy—suggested otherwise. More frustratingly, JBJ's hovering often sucked the air out of the room. My staffers would freeze when he was around, whether he was peering over their computers on late nights or showing up unannounced at meetings like these.

Well, *most* of them froze, anyway.

"Don Jon!" said Phil, rising from his chair. "Take my seat, dude."

"Oh, no, I didn't mean to disrupt," said JBJ. "Sit, Phil, sit! Sunny, continue."

I flipped through my notebook. "Let's move on to what we've got planned for the September issue. . . ."

"Oh, but were you talking about the new Aural History?" JBJ said, looking over his shoulder at The Photo. "Opal & Nev, yeah. Wow. What an incredible shot. Isn't it incredible?"

"We were actually just discussing what specifically it evokes," I said. "It's kind of like a Rorschach test. What do you see in it, Jonathan?" *Humor him a minute*, I was thinking, *and he'll leave you alone.*

"I mean, I'm not really an art guy, but something about it just . . ." JBJ shook his head and let out a long, slow breath. "No pressure, but I cannot wait to read this part of the book."

"I don't mean to burst the bubble," Phil said, creaking again in his chair as he leaned back, "but I was just telling Sunny I don't really get it."

"How do you mean?" JBJ asked.

"End of the day, I just wonder about its significance," he said. "How long did Opal & Nev even last? They put out two semi-okay records and then they were done. This thing"—he gestured toward The Photo—"it's irrelevant to what we're trying to be about, you know? What you've said yourself, Jon, when you talk about our brand promise."

I cleared my throat and tried to speak. "Let's not—"

"Is *Aural* really gonna be about the music?" Phil interrupted, parroting our official mission statement as he glanced back at JBJ. "Because if it is, to me that means no gimmicks. Rock and roll that's classic, that has legs outside a niche of cosplaying idiots who flit in and out of political fashion. Hell, everybody here knows I'm no fan of Nev's solo shit, but a book focused on *that*, I could see. He's gone platinum, he's managed to kick around and tour forever—I gotta admit, that speaks to a certain . . . timelessness. But this brief moment with Opal? Okay, yeah, it might be a piece of his story, but do we need to blow it up bigger than what it really is? I just don't see how we can justify this as the heart of a full Aural History." He held up his hands and turned to me as if pleading innocence. "There, I said it."

"No, no, that's cool," I said, smiling. Burning inside. "I get that not every-body here is as invested in this story as I naturally am." I was going to leave it at that, but I could feel JBJ observing my performance, seeing how I would squash this rebellion. "So here's my thing," I said. "If there have been numer-ous books and films about Stuart Sutcliffe—"

"Well, yeah, because he was the fifth fucking *Beatle*," said Phil.

"—and if people still are fascinated by Edie Sedgwick, and revere the Faces, even though Rod Stewart solo eclipsed them, charts-wise, and . . . Oh, wait. I also seem to remember someone in here pitching me a story about the making of Minor Threat's one and only album. Who *was* that, again?"

"A six-page magazine feature," Phil said, reddening as the rest of the room snickered. "Not an entire book."

"Okay, okay. My point is that our idea of what's important, what's influ-ential, *we* have the authority to open that up," I said. "So I'm glad you brought up the brand promise, Phil, because there's another aspect of it I think we should all be focused on: how *Aural* is evolving. How we need to reflect the spirit of the times and of our audience, and remain inclusive of all aspects of music and the conversations people are having about it."

"Guys, I cannot stress Sunny's point enough," said JBJ, and laced his fingers together. *"Inclusivity."*

"Personally, I'm proud of the fact that all of us in this room are passionate music fans, and that none of us can say we got here the same way," I said. "Pooja, what's your first memory of really loving an artist?"

"Um . . . I guess when I was a kid, I was really into Gorillaz?" she said, and I could feel the older staffers in the room struggling to hold in their titters.

"Right," JBJ said, nodding. "I remember that song . . . 'Clint Eastwood'!"

"They were, like, this intersection of rock and electronica and anime," she said. "All kinds of stuff I was into. It felt ambitious to me . . . like, futuristic."

"Phil?" I said. "What was your formative listening experience?"

"Easy: Zep," he barked. "*Physical Graffiti.*"

"Monster of a record, yeah," I said. "Ben?"

"Me? Oh, I was kind of a geek," he said. "My mom passed on her love for Billy Joel. *The Stranger*, though—not the doo-woppy stuff. I'm not that bad."

"And speaking for myself," I said, "not to get too goopy about it, but I discovered Opal & Nev when I was fourteen, and I will say unequivocally that loving their music is the reason I'm here. I was lonely in school, only Black girl in my class. Lonely at home—no brothers or sisters or, as you know, a dad. And I saw these two misfits, and despite everything—well, maybe *because* of everything—I felt an instant emotional connection to them. I know, I know, partly that was the power of taboo; being drawn to shit that's supposed to be off-limits. . . . But I swear, I looked at her face, that fierce expression she's got, and for the first time I felt like I could have some power too. Like I had a model of a Black woman who was more than just a survivor—she was, like, the bravest, fiercest bitch alive. And then *Things We've Seen* . . . my God: When I heard the rage and wildness pouring out of that record, Opal & Nev sounded exactly like a little piece of me that lived on the inside. Isn't that the kind of story we should aim to be telling—how it is that this rock-and-roll music could reach a sheltered Black girl like me, and make her feel not just seen and heard, but empowered?"

Again, there was a silence in the room. A few of the younger women smiled shyly at me, signaling their support. But among the men—the majority of this staff I had inherited—a palpable discomfort thickened. Even my old friend Ben was studiously enhancing a doodle in his notebook. I looked over at JBJ to see that his mouth had formed a thin, tight line, the same concerned look he got lately when our newsstand numbers came in. Had I been too candid? Simply by relaying my own American story, did they think I was playing a race card? I couldn't put my finger on exactly how I'd lost the room, but somehow I'd done just that. And it was imperative that I get it back.

"Anyway, enough about all that," I said, with what I hoped was a self-deprecating chuckle. "The thing to really know is, Opal & Nev are playing Derringdo 2016."

This was the ace I'd dropped when pitching JBJ, the piece of news that had made him go all-in on publishing this project as our next Aural History. And in this moment it had the same effect, but multiplied.

"Wait," said Phil, cutting through the surprised chatter. "The Friday-night slot? Headlining?"

"Yep," I said. "They're the big reunion show."

"Oh my God, that is *perfect*," said Pooja. "I'm shook!"

"I trust we can keep that between these four walls," JBJ intoned over the noise. "It won't be announced for a little while yet. *Aural*'s got the exclusive. So from the beginning we'll own the story, and when the book comes out, there'll be really strong interest. There's a whole rollout plan Sunny's working on—some really fantastic synergies with Nev's next tour." He smiled and gave me the thumbs-up. "Guys, this is a massive win."

"Well, then," Phil said to me. "You could have just said that in the first place." He mimed zipping his lips, and for a moment I felt victorious, back in the position of authority this asshole continuously tried to steal from me. But that night in the office, after everyone had gone home for the weekend, doubt overwhelmed me. I realized just how much pressure there'd be on nailing this part of the book, about what had gone wrong at Rivington Showcase. Through these interviews I was searching for my father, of course, but for all the Aural History readers, the faithful Mercurials and Phil-level skeptics alike, I had promised to deliver more. To squeeze out the juicy, page-turning details of the riot, and to get at why Opal & Nev—as a singular musical duo, not just as an empty image or the precursor to a solo superstar in Nev—deserved such rigorous attention in its wake. Was I capable of pulling that off? As persuasive and vulnerable as I'd tried to be in that meeting, speaking my truth in front of everyone, it still seemed I was considered dubiously other. And how could I lead the way on anything, if even my soldiers kept questioning me?

chapter ten

"THE MONSTER YOU MADE"

★ ★

In this mess of a story, there is at least one fact no one would dispute: Jimmy Curtis died because the vertebrae in his neck snapped against the edge of a wooden armrest. This is the direct cause confirmed in police reports, medical records, eyewitness accounts.

What is more complicated, more open to conjecture, are the other factors building to the deadly beating he took that night. Not just the business pressures and poor planning and political tensions you've maybe read about before—but also the betrayals, inflated egos, lies, and excesses of ambition these collected confessions attempt to reveal. Everyone I interviewed presented a different take on why the Rivington Showcase riot happened, and certain subjects put up a testy defense when my questions leaned aggressive. In the end, perhaps Bob Hize put it best when accepting his own culpability. "It was all my fault," he told me, "and hers, and his, and theirs, and on and on and on."

But we'll start from the top, where the buck proverbially stopped: with Rivington label head Howie Kelly. Following Polychrome, Rivington's priciest flop to date, Kelly was anxious for a taste of success after spending five years floundering in the industry. His agreement with Bob Hize was nearing *its expiration, but Kelly agreed to extend the deal another six months—on the condition that his producer turn his focus toward the label's other acts.*

HOWIE KELLY:

Hizey would get attached to the creatives—he had Nev living with him, for Christ's sake. You can't get that personal, because sometimes it doesn't work out and you gotta move on. I had the other artists coming to me upset. "He won't take a meeting with me," or, "You promised we'd be recording by now." I liked Bob but it was time for him to snap out of it. So I took it upon myself to bring in new people who were gonna shake shit up.

BOB HIZE:

He didn't have a cohesive vision for what Rivington should be. You can judge that from two perspectives—one, that it's brilliant strategy, because it means you aren't beholden to any particular style and you have a diverse roster; or two, that it's craven, spaghetti-against-the-wall commercialism. Before *Polychrome* I would've agreed with the "craven" camp. But the collapse of that record humbled me and I began to see that maybe Howie had a point. Sometimes survival in this industry requires detaching from personal tastes and going with the flow, as they say. And so we started to develop different kinds of artists we'd signed, to see what might hit.

Waiting their turn to record were the Bond Brothers, a Southern-rock quartet that Kelly had discovered while on vacation in Florida in the late summer of 1970. Chet Bond (vocals), twenty-two; his younger brother, Beau (lead guitar), nineteen; and their neighbors Cole Young (bass) and Donny Pendle (drums), both twenty-one, were born and raised in Live Oak, eighty-five miles outside of Jacksonville, where legendary groups like the Allman Brothers Band and Lynyrd Skynyrd trace their roots. They met Howie Kelly in nearby Atlantic Beach, where they were spending summer weekends building a following at a dive bar called Sharky's.

HOWIE KELLY:

Everybody and their mother has an opinion as to whose fault [Rivington Showcase] was, all right? Everybody likes to toss that blame around like a goddamn hot potato. So as long as everybody's playing that game I'll offer you two cents you can spend, somebody you should call up and grill: the gal who was my goddamn masseuse, that's who! Breaking news: She was the one who told me I needed to take a vacation in the first place, so she's the reason I happened to go down to Florida, okay? If people wanna blame me for bringing on the Bond Brothers, they also need to call up Song . . . Sing . . . fuck if I remember.

This was around the time I had to break up that fight between Nev and your father over that song, so obviously my stress level was through the roof. And this gal said my muscles were like rocks and that Florida might be a good place to loosen 'em up. I should've gone to Miami or the Keys but Bob was spending a lot of dough making *Polychrome*—Jimmy and John Squine and those guys were not cheap—so I settled for Atlantic Beach, not knowing any better. And let me tell you, I came back more stressed than before. My God, the heat . . . The fucking winged cockroaches—one of them slapping against the bathroom mirror in my motel room woke me up . . . and have you ever seen this thing they call a crawfish? There was a whole giant festival dedicated to 'em near where I was staying, and I swear looking at the color of those boiled fuckers you couldn't tell the difference between one of 'em and one of the locals—that's how red the necks were down there. I was hoping for a taste of the Caribbean and instead it's like I'm in coastal fucking Crackerville.

But one night I stopped by the bar, because even after dark that humidity's like a brick to the face, and I wanted somewhere to breathe for a second and hydrate. That's when I discovered [the Bond Brothers] playing their set, and I liked what I saw. They had the stuff to fill a place and they had the girls squealing. That was the kind of energy Rivington needed. What'd I care whether they were Boy Scouts?

CHET BOND, LEAD VOCALIST, THE BOND BROTHERS:*

We came up from nothing. The kind of poor white trash that got shipped off daily to Saigon, except by some miracle we got a pass. One way or another, all of us in the band got out of [drafted service]—Cole on account of he caught something off a bad tattoo, my brother and me because our birthdays got pulled late, just luck of the draw, and Donny because he already had an old lady and a kid. I guess we felt pretty invincible in those days. But you best believe if our numbers came up we woulda been the first standing in line when it was time to go. We wasn't no cowards, you know. We wasn't no special snowflakes. We had friends who'd had their asses shipped over, a lot of poor brothers who didn't never come home, so we had respect.

We started the band back in high school, mostly because after hours the music teacher, a real nice woman, would feed us after class. She had a couple old guitars she'd brought in that her son used to play, and later she gave 'em to Beau as a gift. And then come to find out, we *liked* to play. We weren't half bad either—did some birthday parties, a couple backyard weddings, and then one of Beau's little girls with the stars in her eyes got us some gigs at bars in the area. We couldn't believe it.

Outside of the band we liked to work on cars and bikes. Junk heaps left on the side of the road that my old man would tow home—he drove a tow truck for a mean sonofabitch all his life—and we would juice 'em

---

* Chet Bond is the only member of the Bond Brothers to go on the record for this project. Cole Young died of liver failure in 1989, Donny Pendle declined to be interviewed, and Beau Bond disappeared sometime in 1973, when, Chet recalls, his little brother abruptly cut off contact with family and friends. The owner of an auto-body shop in his hometown of Live Oak, Chet—who says he has been sober since 1997—is active in local politics and in 2016 campaigned in his swing state for Donald J. Trump. The ranch-style house he shares with his wife, Shelly, and their three Pomeranians is well-known in Live Oak for the twelve-foot-tall US flag he flies in the sprawling backyard.

up and race 'em. Asshole grease monkeys outside with the tunes on, you know? We always loved Elvis, like everybody did, and our mamas loved playing country radio but I admired the rougher guys—Merle [Haggard], Johnny Cash. So later when we started getting more serious, dreaming all pie-in-the-sky about getting a record contract, I always thought, *Nashville*. But Howie Kelly was the one to come into Sharky's that night. He was like a walking hundred-dollar bill, and we didn't know no better than to lunge.

BOB HIZE:

Howie decided to sign them without consulting me—his prerogative, I suppose, considering I hadn't yet proven myself. The first time they came to the offices to sign their contract, I was uncomfortable. Long hair wasn't unusual, of course, but they had the denim jackets with the sleeves ripped off and the Confederate flag patches stitched on, and Chet carried a switchblade tucked into the top of his boot. Three of them had these beastly beards and you couldn't see underneath whether they were smiling or snarling at you. I remember them passing around a flask; I remember one of them complaining about the subway and doing a horrid impression of the person who'd served him in the token booth. I wonder now if it was all just a front because they were in fact intimidated by the city and felt foreign themselves in it.

With their contract signed and money to burn, the Bond Brothers went back down south, where they continued cultivating their live act and an impressive fan base.

CHET BOND:

We spent some of the advance on a cherry-red truck that we used for lugging our equipment and a heap of a van we fixed up to have a bed in the back. And while we were working on the songs for the record we went for runs up and down Florida, then over through the panhandle to Alabama, Mississippi. We'd alternate who got to ride in the van and who drove the truck, and sometimes we squeezed a couple fun girls into the van with us.

I had my fans and my particular appeal, but Beau had the looks that made the girls go nuts. Whenever we were outside, even sometimes when we were on a stage in some hole with no air conditioner, he'd have his shirt whipped off, and he could tan real good and the sun played up the natural blond in his hair. He was our mama's favorite too, her little darlin'. . . . We used to beat his ass and call him Little Bobby, for Bobby Sherman—he *hated* that. [*Laughs*] Yeah, I'm telling you, ever since he was a kid, thirteen, fourteen years old, my baby brother had the girls following behind him, and like any red-blooded American boys we really loved the girls.

ROSEMARY SALDUCCI:

They would mail Howie photos of themselves partying with total rando nutjobs or groupies with their tops off and Beau or Chet signing their tits. Disgusting. But Howie was grinning and showing them off around the office and he'd bug Bob: "Do you see? Do you see this money we're losing every day there's no record?" So Bob started to feel like he didn't have much choice but to bring them back up and get them in the studio.

BOB HIZE:

The Bond sessions were a nightmare. They'd be blotto off cheap beer; these raccoon-eyed women they'd have hanging around would bring cases of it to the studio, rolling it in on dollies, and then lay about all night complaining. Chet would get into vicious barking rows with the other guys, and once he hurled a bottle at my head when I cut him off in the middle of a song to make some necessary adjustments—I think the primary reason he missed is because he wore sunglasses indoors and could only estimate my general vicinity. After that, I was interested in getting that album done as quickly as possible. In fact, we blasted through it in six nights, and the mixing was done soon after. Other than the constant threats of violence and idiocy by osmosis, making it was simple, wasn't it? All I had to do was let any thinking and caring and creativity seep away.

I was relieved, but also extremely bitter, when the first single hit.

With a targeted release to both country and rock radio, "Outlaws by Birth," from the Bond Brothers' April 1971 self-titled debut, became the first charting single from Rivington Records. (Hize's postproduction touch on the song: the sound of a revving motorcycle engine that backs up Beau Bond's guitar.) It reached No. 7 on Billboard's *hard-rock chart, and a follow-up, "Dirty Boots," entered at No. 18.*

NEV CHARLES:

I studied this—these were *literally* the lyrics to a Bond Brothers song: [*reciting in a deadpan*] "Good ol' boys cuttin' loose in your town / Bring all the booze, bring all the gals / Rev me up, baby, rev me up / Hop yourself on in my truck / Enough could never be enough." But oh yes, it *could* be enough, couldn't it? Certainly enough for me to want to stick my head in the oven, right, and toss in my own tortured notebooks while I was at it.

The hilarious part is that neither Opal nor I, nor any of the other artists we knew on the label, had even met them yet to know the full extent of their boorishness. Before we knew it, they were suddenly getting radio play. I asked Bob, "*These* are the Bond Brothers you've been complaining about at the dinner table? *These* are the guys you hate but somehow managed to get some attention?" And oh, God, I remember there was a review of their album somewhere, I can't remember the publication, but I sat down to lick my chops—good old Schadenfreude, everybody feels a bit of it; don't tell me you don't root for *Rolling Stone* to go under every day of your life, young lady. . . . But then as I was reading along, *la-di-da*, I realized the review was actually *positive*! The critic wrote something like, "If you take them on their own terms, the Bond Brothers are a fun and mindless novelty." And I thought, *Fun?*

Mindless? When's it ever been passable to be *fun* or *mindless*? How about *fresh* and *clever*, *unique*?

OPAL JEWEL, *SHRUGGING*:

Hell, they could've been singing "A-B-C-1-2-3" and I would've congrat-ulated them on their little hit record and kept it moving. For me it wasn't about the lyrics being dumb—and, I mean, it wasn't like they were *say-ing*, "Nigger nigger nigger." But that image, those symbols, *that's* what's insidious. Folks rally around that stuff, they claim it, they hurt people like you and me in the name of it. So when I laid eyes on that Bond Brothers album cover [a studio shot of the members facing the camera in a line, each wearing a Confederate flag belt buckle on the waist of his jeans] . . . It was like I had built this life I loved in New York only to zoom right back to summertime in Alabama. Me and Pearl, and our own mother worried about what people who waved flags like that could do to little girls like us.

HOWIE KELLY:

No offense to you, because I understand that the African Americans have some misgivings about that particular symbol. But back then, it just didn't seem like all that big of a deal. It seemed like another slice of Americana, right? I mean, what's the biggest movie of all time? *Gone with the* fucking *Wind* [in which Confederate soldiers are the noble he-roes and their flag flies just before intermission]. And then even a few years after [Opal's objections], the same flag was on top of the General Lee [the Dodge Charger popularized on the television show *The Dukes of Hazzard*]! Didn't every little kid in America, Black, white, or yellow, have the toy version of that fucking car? I know mine did!

On top of that, I gotta say: I thought Opal had some kinda gall to make a comment on what other people wore. Opal Jewel! Of all the cuckoo-crazies! No matter what I ever thought, I never tried to be the fashion police with *her*. I believe in free speech and I believe in letting artistes be artistes.

BOB HIZE:

[The Bonds' success] was a mixed bag for me. I got my promotion and the small stake in the label just as Howie had promised, and, more important, Claudia seemed happy. We really needed the money. But the larger part of me was aghast because the Bond Brothers meant nothing to me beyond a gimmick, an appeal to something that made a lot of us nervous. And I was chagrined to face the other artists with whom I'd been working so hard, with little to no result.

VIRGIL LAFLEUR, *WHEN ASKED HIS OPINION OF THE BOND BROTHERS' IMAGE*:

With the possible exception of Wonder Woman, I've never cared for cartoons.

OPAL JEWEL, *CHUCKLING AFTER HEARING LAFLEUR'S QUIP*:

My friend Virgil ain't never lied. That's exactly what the Bond Brothers were. Cartoons . . .

Here's the thing I've learned: When you approach art with the goal of making a quick and dirty buck, that's fine; sometimes it has to be done. But nothing that happens as a result should come as a surprise to you. And with the Bond Brothers that was the whole idea, right? Howie said, *These guys seem like gen-u-wine Bubbas—let's take their Stars and Bars and their bad behavior and their gruff-rough looks, and let's ride this cartoon straight to the bank.* And Bob, he just rolled over and said, *Okay.* And hell, the Bond Brothers themselves, they wanted that money! They rolled over too and said, *All right, yeah, you want a cartoon? We'll give you a cartoon.* But then the cartoon starts to pull away from reality, from the three dimensions that make you a human. . . . And when the laughs run out, you can't suddenly ask in the middle of the show, *What happened?* What you mean, *What happened?* That's the monster you made.

Opal Jewel recalls that as the only Black artist contractually bound to Rivington at this time, she often felt frustrated and alone. Offended by the imagery

*of the Bond Brothers but uncertain what she could do about it, she sought
out Jimmy Curtis for advice despite the fact that he had moved on to other
labels' projects. Born and raised in Beaufort, South Carolina, Curtis likely
understood very well the fear and outrage stirred by the loaded emblems of
the Confederacy and Jim Crow South. By this point, however, the relationship
between Opal and Jimmy was undergoing a shift, as my father had other concerns on his mind.*

OPAL JEWEL:

People seem to forget we were colleagues too, Jimmy and me. We had
similar interests, similar concerns. So yeah, when this foolishness at Rivington was going on, I called him up. It took me a few tries to reach him,
it took like a couple weeks actually, and when I finally got him on the
phone he apologized and said he'd been booking a lot of regular studio
gigs. So I said fine, okay, that's great for you, Jimmy, but a) have you
seen this Bond Brothers mess, and b) would you help me figure what to
do about it, because I'm all alone out here? And he made this big deal
of meeting up to talk. I was getting my ideas together, I was drawing up
language for a petition or something useless like that. But when we got
together, he looked at me with this pitiful expression and said he'd probably want this to be the last time we spent together, because Corinne
had just told him he was going to be a father.

I think I burst out laughing.

VIRGIL LAFLEUR:

I hear you are an exceptional journalist, so let us test your skills of ob-
servation. Of all the many clothing options I selected for Mad at the
height of her fame, what is one thing they share in common? [*Looking
at his Jaeger-LeCoultre gold watch*] I'll wait.

No, no—dig deeper! They've all been fabulous, anyone can grasp
that. But what I am asking you, *chère*, is this: Even at the pinnacle of
the 1980s, why was the look never leather? Why never spandex? Because our Mad requires a sense of freedom and looseness. Oh sure, we

experimented to hit upon the appropriate styles, we made some early mistakes, but it soon became clear what was not going to happen. And so we work the flounce, the flare, the volume, the cutaway . . . items that allow air for her to breathe, yes? Occasionally I take my liberties with her accessories, or else I would shrivel up and die of boredom. But the clothing itself must never cling.

So it is with Mad and her men. Perhaps this will make little sense, as it does not fit the heteronormative narrative, but she veritably blossomed with relief at the news of *petite* impending you. Remember, James was her formative experiment in love—conclusion being that Mad is not a woman who cares very deeply for romantic commitment. She had never wanted to possess James, and more than that, she did not want to be possessed by him. Once they dropped all pretense that they had potential for more, once she knew that she would never be in a position to replace wife and mother and also that she did not prefer to be stuffed down that particular hole, all her guilt regarding their affair went *poof poof*. I understand, though, that your poor papa, like so many of the others after him, had difficulty processing such modern styles.

NEV CHARLES:

Their relationship was none of my concern, but I did hear whispers, and I suppose I did find it disappointing that a woman as progressive as Opal, as bold and feminist and fiercely independent, could be caught up in a situation so sad, so . . . typical. I didn't believe a young woman like her was meant to be skulking around as someone's afterthought! Not to say anything against your father, but I thought Opal deserved better than that sort of treatment. She deserved someone who could love her, really adore her, and publicly at that.

ROSEMARY SALDUCCI:

Oh, they *were* public! I'll never forget the first time I saw them out together, because I was on a date myself—this hot guy with a mustache who was the worst fucking dancer, oh my God. We'd gone to Electric

Circus and Bigfoot had stepped all over my new white boots. I was so disgusted I almost went home, but the guy says, "Lemme buy you a drink to say I'm sorry." So we go to this nice hotel bar somewhere and I'm sitting on the plush upholstery in the lobby, I'm sipping my mai tai and looking around for other options, when the elevator dings and who should walk out? Yeah, Jimmy Curtis and Opal Jewel.

Well, I waved her over—there was no point pretending I was blind. She was wearing this bright orange jumpsuit, for heaven's sake, with feathers stuck all over it! So she comes over to say hello but he just ducks his head low and nearly sprints past us out the revolving door. And Opal, she has this look on her face, because she knows I'm not born yesterday and she's waiting for me to say something. So I try to let her know I'm not judging. I say to her, "Gosh, Jimmy must be doing all right these days if he can swing a room in this place." And I guess she's trying to prove she's not ashamed, not scared of what anybody thinks, so she goes, "Yeah, you know, he's been working more, his wife's having a baby"—and next to me Bigfoot spits out his G&T. [*Laughing*]

Meanwhile, indignation over the Bond Brothers' overnight success had lit a fire under Nev. He stopped moping around the Hizes' apartment and started sketching out ideas for new material with Opal, including one tune featuring a slide guitar (to prove they could beat the Bonds in any given style, he told me). But Opal, he maintains, was increasingly hard to pin down.

NEV CHARLES:

Whenever I think back on this era of my life I feel a tingle up the spine, to tick off everything that happened in the eye-twitch of time that Opal and I worked together. And yet it's also bittersweet because I really do believe so much more could have come out of our partnership, so much more brilliance and art on a par with my solo work, if only we'd managed to swat away the distractions gobbling us, the extraneous people pressing in on us from the outside and keeping us from focusing all energies toward the music. I take my part in our later tensions, of course, as a proper opioid addiction never helps to solve anything. [*Laughs*] But early on . . . Well, let's take your dad, for instance. You must have considered this, and I'm sure your mum has as well—not with any anger or bitterness, just a wee bit of normal human musing: *What if Jimmy Curtis had never been part of the Opal & Nev story?* What if, what if? It's like I'm Gwyneth Paltrow in that alternate-universe movie with the bloody doors on the train!

Well. I know some critics argue we'd have just disappeared off the radar if it weren't for your dad jumping into the ruckus that landed us in the papers the next morning. . . . But if the scenario had been such that Jimmy Curtis had never even known Opal Jewel, then he might be alive to know *you*, right? And I suspect Opal & Nev would've found a way—a saner and less dramatic way, of course, but huzzah, a way! So who knows? If things had gone differently, I might not have needed those opioids in the first place.

chapter eleven

"WE ASKED HIM, 'ARE YOU MENTAL?'"

★　★

Despite whatever misgivings anyone in New York expressed about his marquee act, Howie Kelly was betting big on the Bonds. He planned tour dates for the band in the southern states, along the eastern seaboard, and in central California. And between those dates, at the special invitation of New Guard Pictures, he sent them to the Blue Ridge Mountains to film cameos for a biker B movie called Skulls in Their Wake. *In the film, which remained unreleased until 1974, the Bonds provide background music for a bar fight and join a scene featuring dozens of extras riding through picturesque North Carolina towns.*

CHET BOND:

The flick was shit, one of a thousand outlaw biker movies that they were churning out at that time, but the producers making it had brought in a script consultant for it, some local character who went by Howler and had been in and out of prison. His probation officer showed up to the bar where we were filming to check up on him, but Howler got the jump and slipped me some junk to hide in Beau's guitar case. When he patted down clean and the PO left, Howler was very appreciative, so he offered to take us to an actual biker bar that sat deep in the woods, once the shoot was done. Our attitude was, *Fuck the fake—let's mix it up for real.* We wanted more junk and more thrills, and the lovely ladies Howler promised they'd have on offer. A lot of it was legally sketchy, yeah. You might judge that, us wanting to have a firsthand experience, but ask yourself: How is that any different from Method acting?

We played the fight sequence, take after take after take, so god-damn boring I wanted to rip my hair out, but the studio had rented us chromed-out Harleys for the ride scenes and we borrowed them to get to this place. Well, technically we stole those bikes, I've gotta own that, but we brought them back eventually. We pulled up into a sea of chop-pers, some of them real beauties but none of them sweeter than the ones we had. We went inside and Howler vouched for us, but everybody got real cagey—they assumed we were pussies and poseurs, I guess; they didn't know we'd come up hard-knocks just like them. So me and a cou-ple of my brothers, we pulled out some cash and started settling tabs. Our good-faith show of respect to them. These guys, they didn't really give much of a shit about the music, they weren't easily impressed. But once they figured out we knew a little something about handling the equipment and that we had some cash we were willing to lay out, we were in real good with that chapter of the Danger Fiends. We were doing all kinds of crazy shit that night—God, I think we traded bikes with some of them and went on a midnight ride through the dark, playing chicken with the headlights off. I look back on that now and thank my Lord Jesus that he looks out for fools and babies—it was a miracle we didn't kill our damn selves. Everything was about chasing a high.

We did talk about joining up as recruits, once the shit settled down. We partied with the Fiends chapter in Jacksonville, we gave them a nice donation to their clubhouse and a couple of their charities, we sampled some goods, and the word spread up and down the East Coast that we were bona fide.

Kelly maintains he was unaware of the increasingly blurred line between the Bonds' persona and their real-life criminal associations. At the time, he says,

he was focused on how he might best amplify their success, by using their fame
to boost the label's other, flailing artists—whether or not such creative attach-
ments made any sense.

MARY SHARP, RIVINGTON ARTIST, 1968–72:

I was working on material for my second album when the Bond Brothers were making money. I had been doing all right—not charting like
them, but I had a decent following in New York and was about to pro-
pose a move to LA, where the folkies on my vibe seemed to be evolving
and gelling into something special.

Bob and I were in the studio, rehearsing and revising a couple things
at the upright piano, when Howie brought in Chet Bond, who reeked
of alcohol. It really bothered me that I couldn't look him in the eyes; I
could only see myself looking tiny and scared in the reflection of those
obnoxious aviator sunglasses. And Howie says, "Mary, Mary, why don't
you come up with a duet, and Chet can help you out with it? This is my
hit maker right here!" And I was thinking, *Oh Christ, no!* But I didn't
want to set off this lug of a man, so I tried to say, you know, "Well, I don't
think he'd like my music very much." And Bob, bless his soul, tried to
back me up by suggesting Nev Charles as a better fit if Howie wanted a
duet. He could get Nev writing for me and for some of the other artists,
he said, but Howie rejected that idea right away. I was trying to spout off
another excuse when suddenly Chet picked me up—literally, he lifted
me up off the piano bench. And he threw me across his shoulder and
he started smacking me on the bottom and *growling*, "I like this one,
Howie, I like this one!" I closed my eyes and prayed for it to end. When
the two of them left I was hysterical, trembling, and Bob was trying to
calm me down and saying he would fix it, he would fix it.

BOB HIZE:

Howie's plan was to have a few of the other acts cut new records with
the Bond Brothers as guests, the thinking being that the band was so hot
in the moment they'd raise everyone up by association. I tried to keep

that idea under wraps, but our dear Rosemary could be indiscreet—
nearly all the artists got wind of it.

OPAL JEWEL, *REGARDING HER*
FELLOW RIVINGTON ARTISTS:

Of *course* I told them that the Bonds shouldn't be representing our label
in the first damn place. When their album came out with that terrible
cover, with the Confederate flag all over it, I went to a lot of these folks
and asked them, *Please, back me up in calling bull.* Everybody was too
scared to rock the boat. Once it looked like the Bonds were gonna gob-
ble up space on their records, though? Suddenly these same people were
up in arms. And that right there is very typical of white people—won't
do what's right till they're directly affected. I was willing to let them
off the hook for that, though, if it meant we were finally gonna band
together to say, *Nah, we won't participate in this Bond Brothers business.*

BOB HIZE:

They were calling me up threatening a revolt, but I could feel Howie
clamping down his jaw; he would drop every single one of them from the
roster before he would drop the idea of these Bond Brothers cameos. A
collaboration had to be done in some fashion in order to appease him,
and it was on my shoulders to figure it out. My logic was, *Let's just do it
in one go.* One big show, nothing to be recorded for posterity, nobody's
work compromised, and it will be over. So the idea for Rivington Showcase, I'm ashamed to confess, was actually mine.

When I mentioned to Howie that a splashy showcase like this would
probably attract the attention of the big boys, the Columbias and the
RCAs, and that Rivington could even be acquired, he was sold. To be
honest, I wanted something like an acquisition to happen, because even
owning that small stake—some responsibility but not a lot of deciding
power—was turning out to be a significant source of distress for me. I
thought it might be best for Howie and me to cash out, if we could, and
move on with our lives.

NEV CHARLES:

Hizey called in us talent—us dodgy leftovers, us losers with fuzzy mold round the edges—and we had this meeting where he floated the idea of a showcase headlined by the Bonds, and we asked him, *Are you mental?* I'd say we had a simultaneous panic attack about the Bonds leading some wretched singalong finale—sort of like they do at awards shows these days. . . . Artists who have no business being on a stage together made to sing some corny medley because somebody thought it was a game-changing idea, but really everyone is cringing out of their skin.

BOB HIZE:

I knew it would be a very hard sell, so I kept Howie at a distance during the negotiations. And I went into that meeting with an open mind and some concessions already decided—I promised them that we'd score a big venue for the showcase, that there'd be no duets, and that every-one would get their own short, separate set. One by one, they started to come around. Started to get excited, really.

OPAL JEWEL:

My mama was UAW [United Auto Workers]. So I should've known very well how to spot some scabs.

NEV CHARLES:

You have to understand that in a certain light, the Rivington Showcase was a stay of execution for me. I had just vowed, not three weeks earlier, that I was going to scrounge some under-the-table work to save up for a plane ticket home and maybe some cash besides. I had never had a real job and I wasn't qualified for anything that would keep my hands in good strumming order, so I was preparing to prostrate myself before the gods of hard labor. I fully expected to be washing dishes, scrubbing toilets, laying traps for sewer rats—the bleakest of the bleak options, very dramatic. Ooh, that's a good line, isn't it? "Laying traps for sewer rats . . ."

Anyway, here was this last-ditch opportunity that was shaping up to be intriguing. And Bob was very open to negotiation, very open to making it what we needed it to be so it worked for us all.

OPAL JEWEL:

My good friend Nev Charles was sitting right next to me. And he was quiet while all the rest of them—Mary Sharp and [the Curlicutes'] Cherry Allison, et cetera—started cutting deals for more wardrobe money, extra time, stuff like that. I didn't expect too much from them; I barely even knew them. But for those couple of minutes that Nev held the line, I can honestly say that I had never felt more like his partner. I was squeezing his hand under the table 'cause it was me and him in it together. We would never under any circumstances agree to play with those clowns. And then Bob offered him that [penultimate] time slot [considered the second-best in the lineup in terms of exposure, as invited press would likely all be in their seats], and I heard my friend Nev clear his throat and say, "Well . . ."

BOB HIZE:

I did manage to get Nev on board, but such a prominent slot wasn't going to fly with him alone out there; at the time, he just couldn't hold a crowd of that size. So of course I hoped Opal would perform, and that way *Polychrome* would be properly represented, properly promoted the way it always should have been. But I did give her the option of tapping out, if she felt that strongly opposed.

In the end, Opal Jewel, defeated, chose to make her own ask.

OPAL JEWEL:

I glared at Nev, who couldn't even look me in the face, and I said, "If I'm going to sing, I want that *baaaad* motherfucker Jimmy Curtis on drums."

Now, I could tell you I made that request because your daddy had played on the record and he knew all the songs already. I could tell you that if I was gonna play on the same bill as those dummies, I'd at least score a seriously fat fuck-you check for a Black man. It's not as if those things would be *untrue*; it's not as if I haven't given those reasons before in every other interview I've done about why I chose to go along.

But the extra reason was that I was mad at Nev. And I asked for Jimmy, specifically, to mess with him.

chapter twelve

"SOME KIND OF PEACE"

★   ★

*The optimistically titled Rivington All-Star Showcase was planned for fall
1971 at the Smythe Theater, a grand and ornate venue that had struggled in
recent years due to its inconvenient location on Forty-Fifth Street and Elev-
enth Avenue. The space exuded old-style elegance, with full orchestra seating,
a balcony level, and private boxes draped in burgundy velvet curtains. In an
attempt to revive the Smythe's prospects, the owners had recently expanded
its offerings from traditional theater productions to popular music, and they
welcomed the business of concert promoters. But in the frigid and snowy
months, the theater's distance from a subway station meant that foot traffic,
crucial to any such event, was limited; by the time warmer weather finally
arrived, competing music venues in better locations had emerged as the more
viable options.*

*For Howie Kelly and Bob Hize, these drawbacks worked in their favor,
at least initially. Kelly negotiated a decent rate for renting the space from the
Smythe's desperate and accommodating managers. Hize, de facto PR man,
used the cost savings to arrange private cars for his media contacts, who typically ignored his calls but whose attention, he knew, could be caught with the
promise of gratis luxuries.*

Hize envisioned the showcase to be a small, invitation-only event mainly

*geared toward industry executives, media, and other artist prospects. But he
and Kelly worried about the potential for careening costs, as well as their ability to fill such a large space. They decided to sell tickets for the orchestra seats
to the public, and reserve the balcony and boxes for invited VIPs.*

*As the most popular draw for the paying fans, the Bond Brothers were
set to headline. Mary Sharp, still traumatized from her experience with Chet
Bond, was scheduled to open; she had stipulated that there be as much distance
as possible between her and the main act. The label's other artists would fill
the slots in between and, as necessary, the* Polychrome *studio players (Curtis,
Squine, and Krebble) would provide backup as the house band for the night.
For most of the Rivington artists, including Nev Charles and Opal Jewel, this
was to be the biggest, highest-profile gig they'd ever had, and the preparations
for it were high-stakes and intense.*

NEV CHARLES:

Nobody I knew had ever played the Smythe but I'd heard word of how
majestic it was, and when I popped up to Opal's place to chat about it
one morning Virgil LaFleur was there, as he always was, and he mentioned how good the acoustics were—he'd done some sort of musical
theater there, years before. I went to check it out for myself—one of the
managers was good enough to let me hop on the stage with my guitar—
and when I sang the first lines of "Evergreen" it was the first joy I'd
experienced in a very long time.

OPAL JEWEL:

I was still nervous when we started to plan the thing. All the artists were
supposed to share the same instruments and amps so we could go from
one set to the next without a lag, but Rosemary told me she'd seen pictures of [Bond Brothers drummer] Donny Pendle's brand-new kit and
it was custom-made with the Confederate flag on the skins. After I told
Jimmy that, he made it very clear at the first rehearsal, so that everybody could hear and take note, that pigs would fly before he sat down
behind that particular piece of trash.

*Once Hize guaranteed that Pendle's kit would not be used—he appeased the
Bond Brothers by offering them exclusive occupancy of the theater's only
backstage dressing room for the duration of the concert—rehearsals for the
showcase began at the theater. As Rosemary Salducci tallied an impressive
"yes" list of RSVPs, Opal Jewel confesses, a twinge of excitement began to
temper her trepidation.*

OPAL JEWEL:

Seeing Bob bend over backward to make this work, seeing how everybody else around me was getting giddy . . . I won't lie, it was hard to
keep playing the killjoy. The showcase was obviously going to be a huge
opportunity—you could feel it standing in that beautiful theater, looking up at the rows and rows of seats. And as annoyed as I could be with
Nev sometimes, getting ready for the biggest shot we'd ever had was a
bonding experience. It helped us to reach some kind of peace. He was
back in action being creative again, which, you know, is always an interesting frequency to hover around. We only had one damn album, but
he was constantly revising our setlist, playing mix-and-match like a sug-
ared-up preschooler. [*Laughs*] *"Chalk White" is in; no, "Chalk White" is
out, but a reworking of "Ginger's Lament" is in, and can you please try
the bridge in a different key?* Around and around like that, plucking my
nerves and Jimmy's too. Him and Nev weren't the best of friends, not
by a stretch, but they managed to strike a truce before the showcase
because Jimmy could see it meant something to me. And Nev couldn't
argue the fact that Jimmy was an incredible drummer. We all knew he
brought the right kick to our sound. So yeah, everybody in our little
squad was feeling optimistic. Nev and I both thought, *We might not love
everything about this show, but at least we'll be proud of the set that we
do. . . . And maybe it might make people notice us, so that when we put out
the next thing, they'll be ready.*

*Several of the showcase's other players also recall the rehearsals as a time of
collegiality. Although three of the Bond Brothers blew off the practice sessions*

*(to most everyone's relief), they sent Beau Bond, the quiet guitarist who was
a favorite among the band's female fans, as their representative. Away from
his bandmates, many recall, Beau emerged as a surprisingly sober and sweet
presence among the Rivington artists. Some even began to feel they had mis-
judged him.*

NEV CHARLES:

If you size up a group of people based on the best of them instead of
the worst, your guard does tend to ease down. Getting to know Beau on
his own terms that week had a bit of a lulling effect on our nerves—he
was not the sharpest pencil in the pack to be sure, but at least he was
curious about what the rest of us were doing, and interested in improv-
ing, and not a halfway bad guitar player. When the other acts were on
the stage rehearsing, he and I would sit in the audience sometimes and
watch their sets and have a chat. It seemed to me that Beau's bandmates
took advantage of his looks and talent, but when they were around they
never let him speak much, which was a shame, because he had the most
lovely Southern American accent, more lilt to it than any Dubliner I've
ever met. I asked him once if he considered singing lead himself, because I could hear him doing a love song, something tender with a bit
of a shuffle underneath, something I even said I'd be willing to write
for him, but he'd protest that he didn't have a good voice. I'd ask him,
"Who's told you that?" and he'd just look down or look away, very skittish. I'd tell him, "It's not about the perfection of your voice, it's about
the tone of it, it's about your special signature."

ROSEMARY SALDUCCI:

I had a few girlfriends who wanted access, but I had to warn 'em, "You
might be disappointed by the pillow talk." I'm not saying Beau was
dumb—just that he hadn't been exposed to much. Case in point: During
the rehearsals I was picking up lunch for everyone one day, so I give
him a menu and he says he'll have the corned beef. But when I bring
it back he's opening it up and poking at it, digging around in the bag. I

ask him, "Beau, what's wrong with your sandwich?" and he says to me, completely serious, "I thought it came with corn." So he certainly wasn't a man of the world—certainly wasn't reading, like, the Pentagon Papers every morning. Physically, though? Freakin' adorable. Like a bumpkin Bon Jovi, in the face.

CHERRY ALLISON, LEAD SINGER, THE CURLICUTES:

We had the short skirts and tall boots and sexy dances, and the three of us did this synchronized routine involving bubble gum. And I had the idea for the showcase, *Wouldn't it be fun to have Beau come out and play with us a little bit?* I was thinking a tease-y number, something to excite the girls in the audience, but he was too shy to even try it in rehearsals.

VIRGIL LAFLEUR:

I will assume that as part of your reconnaissance, you have seen *Skulls in Their Wake*, that film the Bond Brothers were in? Vulgar, true, but there is one moment: In the saloon just before the fisticuffs, a dusty light beams in through the wooden slats of the windows, and the camera swoops in to peer at the details of our musicians. Rather artlessly in most instances, as no one has ever needed a visual of [Cole Young's] yellowed fingers plucking at the strings of a bass guitar . . . but there is a lingering on the side of Beau Bond's face. The hair is snatched back, the profile clean and open, only a touch of flaxen sideburn. And most surprising to me at the time that I saw it, there is a sensuality around the mouth and the eyes, in the hang of the lips and the slowness of the blink. For me, young Beau was revealed in those frames as quite a beautiful and blank canvas.

At this point, however, Beau had not endeared himself to the Bonds' biggest critic.

OPAL JEWEL:

During rehearsals I could feel him looking my way, studying me, but he wouldn't ever look me in the eye and he wouldn't talk to me either. I just assumed that was because he hated uppity niggers. [*Shrugs*] What else was I supposed to think? That was the evidence I'd been given, right? Because at their own concerts, on their own album cover, him and his boys trotted out the literal battle flag of the people who fought tooth and nail to continue subjugating mine, so . . . Nah, I wasn't really feeling Beau Bond, and I couldn't have cared less that he seemed cool on me too. I had other things to get together. My look, for one, which I needed to be extra ferocious because I put some of the people I'd met at Max's on my VIP list.

VIRGIL LAFLEUR:

The other shows Mad and Pup had done, if you can call them that, were these dreadful acoustic tragedies where she was essentially on the same level with the audience, maybe sitting on a sad little stool, so there was no proper sense of awe. This [Smythe] stage, though, it presented an opportunity to be epic. The height would force the front rows to gaze up. I thought, *Why not elevate her even more? To the gods!*

The shoe would be key, the most avant-garde that we could find. This was an investment—Opal and I could craft many amazing garments, *chère*, but we were not cobblers. We found them in the West Village, a pair of strappy red leather wedge platforms that made a wonderful clamor with every step. The straps snaked up and around the leg, all the way above the knee, and I mean "snaked" literally because the gold buckle at the top was in the shape of a serpent's head. The platform was wood with curlicues carved into the sides, like the feet of antique furniture, and they tapered down into a narrow sole. I made the wood gleam with a spritz of Lemon Pledge. They were exceptionally high, more than five inches, so if you took a wrong step you might twist your ankle and come tumbling down. This was excellent for dramatic tension. We worked very hard on how she would move.

OPAL JEWEL:

In hindsight, the shoes were a bad idea. They were a cross between leg braces and stilts. . . . Getting in and out of them was a trip.

VIRGIL LAFLEUR:

Everything else was in service to the shoe, allowing it to captivate and command. We borrowed a tutu from a dancer friend who I prayed would not curse me out when I cut it shorter, dyed it black, and added more tulle—maximum flounce was a must. On top we had a simple black T-shirt, and I cut segments from it so that what remained reinforced the snaking effect of the shoe. When I was done it was a midriff: belly button on display, winking to the masses below. We took her Pocahontas wig and used it to construct a Mohawk—it was trimmed to a strip and placed on the center of the head, and the hair ran like an inky waterfall down the back while the sides remained naked. Silver glittery eyes, bloodred mouth, *fini*.

chapter thirteen

"SHE WAS LIKE A BULL AND HE WAS THE GODDAMN TOREADOR"

★　　★

On the late afternoon of November 13, 1971, the minor leaguers on Rivington's roster began gathering at the Smythe, preparing for showtime. The backstage of the theater was shaped like a horseshoe: Artists came out into the spotlight from the wings at stage right; the Bond Brothers' large dressing room (with sofas, vanities, and platters of cold cuts) took up the bulk of stage left; and in a narrow crossover area between the two sides, the opening acts mingled, made use of the two gendered bathrooms, and warmed up for the biggest show most had ever played.

A buzz of excitement and camaraderie had nearly everyone in a froth of nerves and hope. Although he could have stretched out in the dressing room reserved exclusively for him and his bandmates, Beau Bond, in a simple black T-shirt, blue jeans, and a new pair of boots that Rosemary Salducci had scuffed for him in the alley outside the backstage door, shyly hung around with the opening artists as he waited for his brother, Chet, and the others to arrive. The stage-right wings had been set up like an elegant holding pen, draped all around with red-velvet curtains that cut off distractions from the back of the house and also shrouded the artists from the audience. It felt private there, nearly sacred—a space where each artist was meant to corral their butterflies in the moments before hitting the stage. Hize brought everyone together here for a preshow pep talk; Kelly, who had decided to play emcee for the night, popped champagne and told them all to break legs.

In the house the hour before curtain, Hize headed upstairs to greet the arriving VIPs. Among them: Wallace Jopson, a New York Times *editorial assistant for whom Hize had reserved the best private balcony box in the house, in hopes that one or more of Rivington's artists might someday earn a sliver of space amid the listings and reviews. Hize left the seat beside Jopson vacant, so that between welcoming duties he might catch a breath and answer any questions the young journalist had. To calm his own nerves, Hize remembers, he sat his wife, Claudia, upstairs on the aisle, so that in passing he could squeeze her arm for a burst of courage without disturbing his guests.*

Capturing a visual record of the evening was Marion Jacobie, a freelance society photographer whose work had been published by a handful of the invited media outlets. Her press credentials warranted an all-access pass to the Smythe, and before the doors opened she wandered on either side of the house, a fly on the wall as Nev tuned his guitar, as my father set up his kit, as Opal, not yet in her shoes and makeup, sipped champagne and laughed with Virgil LaFleur.

A few minutes after 6 p.m., the scheduled start time, many of the VIPs had arrived by their private cars, but the quorum of Bonds still had not shown up and the orchestra was only sparsely filled. Still, Kelly was eager to start the show—pushing it any later might have meant overage fines and noise violations. In a powder-blue tuxedo, he took the stage to introduce the night's first performer, as well as the Polychrome *players who'd appear throughout the showcase as the house band.*

MARY SHARP:

It was better to go on early, because although you might not have had the largest crowd they were there specifically to see you. When I

came out onstage I was disappointed at first, because I could see that
the bottom section, the paid section, was only about a quarter filled.
But then I squinted past the lights and I could see more people in
the top, people who were respectful and quiet as I sang to them, and
they clapped for me, and they were apparently important people who
might be able to further my career. I could make out Bob in one of the
boxes, and my family, who had come from Vermont. A photographer
was below the stage taking my picture, and I thought, *Hallelujah . . .
press!* When I was done, there was a critic who'd come backstage with
Bob to shake my hand, and she hinted at something on the horizon.
So I felt well supported and appreciated by my label, finally, and I was
very happy that night. When I was done I wished everyone else good
luck and left with my family—they were only in town for the night
so that my little sister didn't miss too much school. We had a lovely
celebration dinner, and my father made a toast. When I woke up the
next morning and saw what had happened splashed across the papers,
I couldn't believe it.

*The 6:40 and 7:20 p.m. sets, by the pop group the Refreshers and singer/song-
writer Campbell Carter, were similarly subdued but successful. Hize recalls
that Carter, especially, had caught Jopson's attention with his lush pop love
songs. After each set, the house players—my father, John Squine, and Solomon
Krebble—would report the mood and the size of the audience to the acts anxiously awaiting their turns.*

JOHN SQUINE:

We had been told the thing was sold out, and the lower level was starting to fill in, but the front rows stayed empty. We kept waiting to spot
the high rollers who'd sprung for the good seats; we were making jokes
about who they might be.

*Finally, a little after 8 p.m., the other Bond Brothers arrived with a gaggle
of intoxicated friends and women, entering through a backstage door. Chet,*

Donny, and Cole appeared to be high on methamphetamine, as well as their top-dog status.

JOHN SQUINE:

The Gathering [a folk collective] and El Ritmo [a Latin-rock fusion five-piece] were on back-to-back, so me and Jimmy and Sol had our first long break of the night. When we got off after Campbell's set and came out of the wings, we could barely move backstage because the Bond Brothers folks were there and they'd brought all these hopped-up hangers-on. You're not supposed to have nonessential people just loitering like that during a show. It was a bad energy, man . . . volatile. I accidentally jostled one of them, trying to squeeze past him to get to the can, and he got in my face and called me a faggot. I wasn't trying to get my head bashed in, there was still a lot of show left, so I apologized — "Easy, brother, it's all right." And the dude laughed and slapped me on the back like we were old friends. That kind of schizo shit is so not cool.

Beyond the drug-fueled madness, Opal Jewel was incensed to see that Chet Bond had come flaunting the one thing Bob Hize had promised would be scrubbed from the evening: a huge Confederate battle flag, attached to a thick golden pole.

OPAL JEWEL:

I was sitting in a corner with Virgil and Nev, at a dinky little folding card table right across from their dressing room. Virgil was keeping me company while Nev was fiddling with his acoustic guitar, practicing and running some last-minute changes — and all of a sudden I saw this blur of red. That was Chet Bond, waving that thing around.

HOWIE KELLY:

She was like a bull and he was the goddamn toreador.

VIRGIL LAFLEUR:

Against my advice, we had given up the only dressing room on the guarantee that there would be no such foolishness, and the savages were not even occupying the space correctly! Not even keeping their business shut inside! Spilling out their ugliness so rudely! Meanwhile, we artists were banished to the nooks and crannies. . . . To a rickety and rusty table with one leg shorter than the others so that my tools and palettes were constantly jostled whenever anyone passed! Such galling disrespect. I said to Mad and to Pup, "You may sit here and stew, my darlings, but I'll take the toilet over this." And so that's what I did: I gathered my essentials and took my leave to the ladies'. Lined up my creams and powders right on the ledge over the sink. I helped all the girls that night do their touchups, and they all looked phenomenal despite the indignity.

OPAL JEWEL:

Most of the show your daddy was in the wings with Johnny and Sol, out of my sight on the other side of the pipe-and-drape [curtain setup]. During that first long break, he came back to have a drink and to check on me, and I could see that muscle in his jaw clench up every time Chet or one of those other idiots got too close in passing. I could feel Jimmy trying to shut off, trying not to lose his shit. He just wanted to be in and out. But me, I had time. So whenever Chet came close I cursed him; I tried to trip him; I would have chased after him, but Virgil had already strapped me into the shoes and running wasn't a good idea. Jimmy had gone back to the wings and I didn't know where Bob was, so I had Nev bring Howie back to me instead, and I pointed out Chet scampering around like the hateful redneck he was. I said, "If you don't make him put that thing away, I will." Howie told me not to worry, Chet wasn't gonna bring the flag out onstage—he was trying to dismiss me. Howie always seemed to think I was bluffing.

CHET BOND:

All right, I've already admitted to the bad behavior. But I want to set the record straight about one thing: We never said *nothing* against the Blacks by rocking the Stars and Bars as part of our show, and anybody who believes that we did is probably a reverse racist for jumping to that conclusion. Two of my cousins have children with Black individuals and we opened our arms to them as part of our family. I even played at one of their weddings, so believe me, Chet Bond is the least racist person you ever met. To us that flag was a symbol of being a badass, a rebel, and proud of our ancestors who fought and died in the Civil War. My daddy didn't have a lot to brag about in his life, you know? What he did have was family stories he told us, stories passed down from his daddy and his daddy before that, about a time when the Bonds wasn't scrounging, when the place where we'd come up had some glory and some fight. So we don't shy away from our heritage—the good, the bad, and the ugly of it. You can't just take it down and bury it and pretend it didn't happen. You wouldn't wanna do that, would you? Well, I dunno, maybe you would, being part of the liberal media. [*Laughs*] I always say with pride that I'm a son of the South—it is what it is, you know? [*Gesturing to my locs*] To me it's the same as . . . *that*. That's a symbolic statement of your personal pride in your Africa culture, right? You think I should have the right to make you cut 'em off because I don't entirely understand the meaning of 'em?

And another thing: *Our* show for *our* fans ain't have a thing to do with *their* show for *theirs*. I wasn't fixin' to run out waving my flag during their part! The way the show was explained to me was that everything was gonna be clear and separate; everybody pretty much got to do what they wanted with their own time. All that violence coulda been avoided if certain persons, and by that I mean *her*, had shown an ounce of respect for that.

OPAL JEWEL:

A few minutes passed and I guess Chet wore himself out—he'd stopped running and waving that flag in everybody's face, but he'd unclipped it from the pole and draped it across his shoulders so it was hanging down his back like a damn superhero cape. They didn't have the decency to shut the damn door of their dressing room, so from where I was sitting I had a clear view of him and his cronies laughing and partying. Dirty feet up on the nice couches, sitting on the makeup tables and drinking, snorting up whatever . . . having their little hootenanny or whatever it was they did back home. And I caught a flash of that flag every time Chet moved. It was impossible for me to ignore a thing like that.

Meanwhile, at the front of the house, another crisis.

ROSEMARY SALDUCCI:

They stuck me in the lobby to do the VIP check-ins, near the box office. So I didn't get to see any of the show itself, but I saw a lot of other shit go down. The outer doors of the theater were open, with a red carpet leading from the outside, so that the big shots riding in the black cars could just roll up and know they were in the right place. They came straight to me and gave me their names and I handed them their tickets and told them to have a good time. Each of the artists got to have four VIPs they could put on the list, and it was nice to see people's families and all that.

After the show started, that area was dead for a while, so I was making conversation with the shrimpy guy who was one of the Smythe's managers. And all of a sudden, there's this racket outside to make your heart stop. I peeked out the doors and saw this gang of motorcycles, I'm talking like a dozen of them, circling the block. And driving each of those bikes was a hairy, filthy guy who had an even filthier chick hanging onto him. I guess they were looking for somewhere to park, but then they just lined those monsters right up on the sidewalk, and a couple of them even rolled up on the red carpet, and I was wigging out because I had rented the thing and knew I was gonna have to pay a fee for the damages.

So these guys were just sitting there for a while, idling, and then one of them climbed off his bike, and he came up to the high school girl who was working the box office and told her to give him the tickets that had been left under Chet Bond's name.

I was throwing the manager looks: *Aren't you gonna say anything to them?* And he very nervously approaches this dirty asshole and he says, "Um, er, ah, excuse me, sir, but are you sure you're in the right place?" That asshole peers down—by this time he's got hold of the fat envelope with the tickets inside—and he pushes it in the manager's face, jabbing at the words written on it: "'Guests of Chet Bond.' That's us." And the asshole walks back outside to gather up his cronies, he does this piercing whistle and a roundup motion in the air, and they all stream inside like goddamn cockroaches. I counted about twenty of those motherfuckers, and when they passed I read what was on the back of the guys' vests: DANGER FIENDS.

HOWIE KELLY:

I'm out on the stage introducing El Ritmo and I see these hoodlums stomping down the aisle like an avalanche, loud as fuck, and then they're jumping into their seats in the front rows. They're hollering at each other over my announcements, very rude, and I tried to crack a little joke, you know, to get their attention and get them to shut up. But they only got louder.

BOB HIZE:

In the balcony I had reporters from the *Voice*, the *Times*, of course, *Billboard*, the radio program directors. . . . And all of them were peering down below to see what on earth was going on. These characters looked as if they hadn't bathed in days, dirt streaking their faces, and they were passing around a flask and yelling obscenities and laughing very rudely through everything. They turned that beautiful theater into their own motorcycle clubhouse, and they were completely disrespectful of the performers onstage. I began to panic and looked to Claudia, who was searching me out as well. I wished for her to reassure me, but her face was very alarmed.

MARION JACOBIE, PHOTOGRAPHER:*

At first I was making the typical pictures. I got the singers doing their thing, some wide angles and detail shots. But all the normal stuff went by the wayside when the Danger Fiends showed up, when I realized that, *Hey, I might be on the front lines of an actual news story here.* I tried to be discreet, standing down by the side of the stage and using my zoom so I could get something authentic from those front rows, but one of the girls spotted what I was up to, and after that all the other ones were calling me over to take their pictures. They wanted their portraits done with their old men, as if they were any other romantic couple, except the men were flipping off the camera and baring their teeth. They wouldn't give me their names. Some of them put their hands over their faces.

The racket they made was beginning to distract and dispirit the performers. Even El Ritmo, a band Hize admired for their focus and precision, lost the thread of a song and had to start it over from the top. Gaffes like these led to more trouble, bigger headaches.

HOWIE KELLY:

While El Ritmo was on I ran out to the lobby to find the guy I had been dealing with at the Smythe. That fucking asshole . . . Rosemary's telling

---

* Marion Jacobie's searing news photograph of Opal & Nev fleeing the scene of Rivington Showcase remains her most famous work. In the aftermath of the riot Jacobie covered my father's funeral, although those photographs, including a graveside shot of my heavily pregnant mother, failed to catch the attention of editors. She worked many years as a portrait and fashion photographer, shooting celebrities and models for *Vanity Fair* and *Vogue*, but never again has she photographed the subjects who made her career. Today Jacobie, 68, runs her own studio in the Chelsea neighborhood of New York City, where she took me on a trip through her archives and suggested her services for the author photo of this book. Jacobie did not seem surprised that I declined her offer. "After all these years trying to get Opal again," she said, "I'm used to the hard no."

me how he just let them waltz right in, and she takes me outside and shows me where they parked their vehicles on my carpet. The manager guy finally turns up and I'm laying into him, you know . . . I'm *furious*. And the guy gets very shifty with me, and he's shrugging his shoulders and telling me that the front rows are paid tickets, so what can he do? I'm incredulous, because these are the priciest seats in the house! And your people just hand 'em to *these* jerkoffs?

I go backstage again to find out what the fuck is happening and it's gotten more out of hand, a scene out of a goddamn druggie nightmare in the dressing room, in the crossover—my girls in the Curlicutes are so freaked out they're hiding in the toilet!

CHERRY ALLISON:

We'd gone to say hello to the Bonds in the dressing room, to wish them good luck—I really couldn't stand Chet and those guys, but we wanted to check ourselves out in the vanities with the good Hollywood lights, since they obviously weren't using the mirrors—and Jesus, that was the worst mistake. A few of their more aggressive friends, these total strangers, they stuck to us like white on rice. Oh, I got my ass slapped and worse about a million times in that room. I had to wriggle my way back out, and even then, some of them were hanging on my tail. We were scheduled deep into the bill so we had a lot of time, too much time to put up with this. I couldn't stand it anymore—when the other girls managed to make their way out, we banged on the bathroom door, and thank God Virgil let us squeeze in and locked it behind us.

When it was time for us to take our places in the wings, your dad was the one who came to get us. He tucked two girls under one arm, me under the other, and I could hear the crowd outside going, "Bond Brothers! Bond Brothers!" I remember I kept pulling at my skirt, wishing it were longer. I said, "Jimmy, what the hell are they doing out there?" and he asked me if I was sure I still wanted to go on. But we were just as ambitious as anybody, and we didn't want to lose a chance because we were scared little girls. I didn't realize then that *everybody* was scared.

HOWIE KELLY:

[Just before announcing the Curlicutes,] I go to find Chet in the dressing room, lounging like the goddamn mad king in the middle of this mess, and I say to him, "Listen, who is that in the front? Are those your pals out there acting like convicts?" And he shoos off whatever dingbat's attached to his lap and comes with me to the wings so he can peek out and see, and he says to me and your father and my girls in the Curlicutes: "Hey, look at that, the Florida chapter made it!" And I say, "Florida chapter? Chapter of *what*?" And this lunatic tells me that yeah, he had personally bought out the first couple rows for his biker buddies who were passing through on a ride, in the hopes they'd stop by. Jesus Christ.

As Chet Bond strolled toward the wings with Howie, most everyone in the back of the house was too distracted or high to notice that the Confederate flag loosely tied around his shoulders had slipped off and fluttered to the floor. Some of the Bond Brothers' crew even unwittingly trampled it as they jogged toward the wings to gawk at the Curlicutes muddling through their act. But sitting at the dinky card table, Opal says, she saw the flag fall, and Nev saw it too.

OPAL JEWEL:

The thing was just lying in a heap on the floor like roadkill, like they didn't even give a damn, really, so as soon as nobody was standing on it, Nev darted in to grab it. There was this big garbage can near the table where we were sitting, and he was about to just drop it in there but the trash didn't have a top and it was nearly full up with bottles and junk—I wanted to make sure nobody could find the thing in case they came looking. So I shook my head at him and beckoned to him with my finger. I had him hand it over, and I hid it up under the card table, on my lap. I guess he probably hoped that would be the end of it because he looked down at me like, *Okay, now? Satisfied?* and I said: "Yeah, okay." And I'm telling you, nobody even missed it till the very end.

Virgil had carried most of his stuff off to the bathroom to get set up, but he'd left some things behind on that table where I was sitting, a few of his brushes and a nail file. One of those stainless-steel jobs, you know, with the abrasive side and the pointed end for pushing back your cuticles and picking out the dirt. I can't even say I was conscious of what I was doing. I would say my hands had a mind of their own, but the general instinct was *destroy, destroy, destroy*. If I'd had some scissors on me I woulda made quick work of it right then, but I didn't have any scissors on me, I had the nail file. So I slipped it down under the table, I was working a ragged little hole in the thing, probably nothing bigger than what a drop of cigarette ash might make. And I made another hole, and another one . . . yeah, sitting right there at the table, doing vocal exercises with Nev while he played his guitar. I probably woulda kept going but then Virgil poked his head out and told me to come see him for a touchup because we were next to go on. I didn't know what to do with the thing at that point. Nev was looking at me with the big eyes, like, *Get rid of it!*, so I balled it up and hugged it to myself and he helped me stand up in my shoes and he shielded me too, till I could make it to Virgil.

NEV CHARLES:

Sorry to disappoint, but I'm afraid I'm not much use after this; I won't be able to help you fill in the gaps, because, as I've told everyone previously — and as I told Lizzie [Harris, Charles's publicist] to reiterate to you before you bothered focusing on these few crazy hours out of my whole crazy life — my mind goes into absolute static when it tiptoes too close to certain moments. I've read a lot about the brain and I'm sure you have as well; I once watched a fascinating six-part documentary on it, BBC Three, I think it was, but the point is, trauma is a trickster! Who did what awful thing, who pitched what insult . . . who can say? I suppose the broken ribs and the tear gas and, of course, what happened to your dad, all of it robbed me of specifics, to the point where when I look at that photograph I have just as little an idea as someone who wasn't even there. [*Reminded of vivid memories he'd already shared with me over the course of our interview covering other traumas in his life, including his mother's death*] Oh yes, I *know*! It's so strange, isn't it, the selective way the mind works?

[*On whether he grabbed the flag off the floor*] Of course I would never say anyone was a liar, just that I can't confirm, can't deny . . . I mean, I suppose it *sounds* like something a person in my position might have done, anything to try to patch up a row, but for me it also sounds unlikely, because, as you know, I'm legendary for going very internal before a performance. When I'm on tour these days, I always have someone who's responsible for snapping a finger in front of my face five minutes to showtime. This trip it's poor Candice. Speaking of Candice . . . [*Calling to the flight attendant*] Candice, darling? Could I bother you for another club soda?

9:15 p.m.: As the Curlicutes continued their set, my sources remember, the energy inside the theater changed toward something even more tense and frightening.

BOB HIZE:

For about thirty seconds, the guys in the front row got quiet, leering, and then it devolved into hooting and wolf whistles. And that apparently upset their women, who started shouting up at Cherry and the girls, calling them sluts and whores.

MARION JACOBIE:

I ran up to the balcony to see what everything looked like from above, and it was a sight. I'm convinced I made a great picture up there during the Curlicutes set—one of the bikers, this fat slob bursting out of his denim, had jumped up out of his seat and was clowning, imitating the girls dancing onstage. He was turning around and shaking his hips, jiggling his gut, making his friends laugh. I was lining up the shot so you could see him from the back, the skull-and-dagger insignia on his vest, and he had one hand in the air and the other on his hip, and then at the top of the frame I had the Curlicutes onstage in their girly getups basically hitting the same pose. Can I tell you something? If I'd been able to save it, I think that might have been my favorite one from the whole night—maybe it would've been the one that got reprinted again and again. Because it was gonna be like this striking, artful illustration of two forces clashing: masculine and feminine, vulgar and beautiful. . . .

BOB HIZE:

Something was thrown and hit Cherry Allison square in the face; you could see her flinch all the way upstairs. At that point I thought, *Dear God, this is getting violent.* Wallace Jopson [the *Times* reporter] had been gregarious all night—obviously he was very junior, just happy to be there and flattered with the royal treatment. But as things progressed he got quiet and began scribbling in his notebook, and he kept whatever he was writing shielded from my view. He got very businesslike, very fast. I went over to my wife and said in her ear, "I think you'd better go on home."

Locked inside the bathroom with Virgil, Opal wasn't aware of any of this. As Virgil perfected her makeup and applied sequins to her lash line, she tried to figure out what to do with this flag she wanted to destroy.

OPAL JEWEL:

The thing was too big to flush down the toilet; I wasn't trying to flood the joint. Virgil offered to hold on to it for me, stuff it inside his cosmetics bag, but I guess I felt like it was my show and my responsibility to handle. We were close to throwing it out the window—in that bathroom there was the kind with the single pane that hinges out, but it was real high up on the wall, and he was looking for something to stand on so he could reach it without breaking his neck. Then I had this dumb thought that made me laugh. It started as a joke, honestly.

VIRGIL LAFLEUR, *FLIPPING THROUGH HIS "PORTFOLIO" OF OPAL'S LOOKS*:

We were quite good at tying and tucking material in fabulous and surprising ways, don't you think? Look at this one [*pointing to an elaborate headwrap*]—you'd never imagine that a flat rectangle of otherwise cheap, garish material could make such a show-stopping piece.

OPAL JEWEL:

I said to Virgil . . . I said I could just put old Dixie the last place a dumb cracker would come looking for it: wrapped around my pitch-black ass. And then he was laughing too, and then we were actually doing it: I was standing there in the bathroom like a deranged ballerina in that big black tutu, twirling damn near on pointe in those shoes while Virgil folded the thing and pulled it between my legs and around my hips and lifted and tucked. Whatever extra material I had on didn't matter—it just gave that tutu even more poof. And we were laughing harder and harder because Virgil had tied it so that the X in the thing was sitting perfect, right on the crack. At the time we thought it was just our funny little secret—I wasn't planning to *do* anything else with it. I was thinking way past the show, to late-night breakfast at the diner when I'd be telling Nev about it, and Jimmy too if I could get him to come out with us, and we'd laugh and laugh, all of us there together, about how we got one over on 'em.

Horrified by what he saw unfolding during the Curlicutes' set, Hize left the balcony and went downstairs to inquire about security measures.

BOB HIZE:

I found the manager [of the Smythe] in the lobby getting browbeaten by Howie and wincing at all the spittle flying his way. I thought it might help if I was the reasonable one—*Sir, if only you could send security down to take the flasks, maybe give a sharp warning. . . .* But the sick expression on the man's face told the story.

ROSEMARY SALDUCCI:

Bob is stuttering, he's so upset he can hardly get his words out, and he says to the manager, "You do have security, don't you? Please tell me that you have proper security." And the manager says, "Um, er, ah, well, we have the ushers. . . ." The ushers, he says! The ushers were children! Skinny little minimum-wage high-school kids with pizza faces! I hated to stick my nose in but I told those guys, "Say the word and I'll call the cops."

It could have ended right there, if they'd only listened to me. But they didn't listen to me—I was just the secretary, the T&A sitting at the front desk. So there you have it. And oh, cookie, what a mess.

HOWIE KELLY:

Well, we were reluctant to call the police, and I'll tell you why: There were some moments where we thought it might be all right, you know? We thought maybe it would just calm down and blow over. And the last thing we wanted was to make the situation more fucked than it was. Of course, everybody these days sees enough videos of the cops to know that once you get them involved, it's never any good.

ROSEMARY SALDUCCI,
LAUGHING ON HEARING KELLY'S DEFENSE:

Oh bull*shit*. That's a convenient explanation, isn't it? You and I both know Howie Kelly wasn't thinking about police brutality in 1971, or ever! And besides that, the idea was to call the cops on the creeps in the front rows, and they weren't exactly the right skin color to make the cops a problem, if you catch my drift.

HOWIE KELLY:

Listen, I had the most amazing idea to fix it. Simple, clean, no cops necessary. I told Bob, "Go back in and keep schmoozing the press, and let me wrap this thing up." I was gonna calm down these Fiend thugs by giving them what they wanted, which was the Bond Brothers' show right away, and then *Thank you and good night, now get the fuck out.*

But there was at least one kink in Kelly's plan: Going straight to the Bond Brothers meant skipping over the penultimate set by Nev Charles featuring Opal Jewel.

OPAL JEWEL:

[In the ladies' bathroom,] Virgil gave me a couple pulls on a joint and a kiss on the cheek [before going up to his VIP seat in the balcony]. And I walked out of the bathroom feeling like myself—like I was in control, like I had a leg up on these fools. Jimmy was still out on the stage playing for Cherry and them, but I could see Nev standing over by the wings—I could always find him by that carroty hair poking high above everything. When I got closer I saw he was arguing with Howie. I asked him, "What's the problem now?" and Nev blurted out, "After all this they're trying to skip us over!"

John Squine, Solomon Krebble, and my father were meant to keep their places onstage at this point, for a seamless transition from the Curlicutes' set into Nev's. But when the Curlicutes finished and skittered off the stage—vulgar cheers, wolf whistles, and Chet's rowdy backstage clique trailing behind them—my father went unscripted: He got up from his kit and came off too.

JOHN SQUINE:

As he passed by me I whispered to Jimmy, "What are you doing? We're supposed to stay on, man!" Sol and I were just standing there, hung out to dry. We wanted the night to be over with as much as anyone else.

OPAL JEWEL:

Suddenly Jimmy stalked out of the wings, and as soon as he laid eyes on me he grabbed my arm and said, like this direct order, like I had no say in the matter, "Ain't no way you stepping foot on that stage." I planted my feet and I said, "Wait a minute now—on whose authority?"

HOWIE KELLY:

Your old man is shouting in Opal's face, and she's shouting right back at him. "You don't tell me what to do," that kind of thing. I coulda told Jimmy that a hardheaded woman like this only digs in her heels deeper when you try to exert any common sense. I shoulda told him that good men need steady ones like your mother, not crazies who don't care if you get done in.

OPAL JEWEL:

Me and Jimmy got into it hard—he was calling me all kinds of "crazy bitch" and I was giving it right back to him. Then Nev started yapping. Telling Jimmy we didn't need him anyway, that he didn't own me, that he didn't have the right. . . . Jimmy ignored him at first, pulled me into the wings so he could talk to me without other people around, but then Nev followed us in and Jimmy got fed up. Called Nev a corny mother-fucker, a phony, a fraud—it was like the fight over "Black Coffee" but worse, me in the middle again. On the other side of the curtain Howie told us to fuck right off—told us he was going to see if the Bonds were ready and that if they were, they were next. And once Howie made that threat, Nev started begging me, saying this was our shot to get the shine we deserved, saying we could do the set just the two of us, acoustic like we were used to doing anyway.

NEV CHARLES:

I always bring an acoustic everywhere to practice, to write, and I must've had mine with me that night. In fact . . . [*pulling the nicked blond-wood guitar out of its case near his seat on the private plane, then strumming and humming, beginning to sing*], "Call me yellow belly / Can't say that I'd care / To fall to my knees in a land far from here. . . . " [*Kissing the guitar's neck*] This one's an ugly and beat-up thing now, lost some of her luster, but she's always been a true friend. And too bad, really, that Opal and I *didn't* go acoustic that night, yeah? Might've calmed everything down quite a lot.

OPAL JEWEL:

I told Nev to stop yammering and go sit down somewhere, because he was making Jimmy crazier and he sure as hell didn't own me either. And he sulked away, same as he had the last time all this stuff came to a head.

JOHN SQUINE, *ON HOW LONG HE AND*
KREBBLE WERE STUCK ON THE STAGE STRUGGLING
TO ENTERTAIN THE AGITATED AUDIENCE:

Oh, I dunno, maybe five, ten minutes? But it felt like forever. There's not a whole lot you can do with just the bass and the keys. . . . Sol played that riff from [The Band's] "The Weight" and I counted in, tried to get those assholes in the front to clap along to something rootsy they might dig, but they weren't fooled, man. Just kept going "Bond Brothers! Bond Brothers!" I arched my head back, trying to see through the curtain: *Are we on, are we off, what the hell's happening?*

Meanwhile Howie Kelly, storming through the crossover toward the dressing room, was determined to round up his headlining act.

HOWIE KELLY:

I pulled the first one of those Bond fuckers I saw—Donny, I think it was—and I told him, "I'm done with these front-row cocksuckers and I'm sure as shit not introducing you, so get your asses on that stage ASAP." I'm so fucking mad you wouldn't believe; I gotta step outside the backstage door to the alley to smoke a cigarette, just to calm myself down before I keel over dead of an aneurysm.

CHET BOND:

Oh, I was raring to go, soon as Donny gave me the word! And it was gonna be good too, 'cause we'd get to play longer—we were gonna have their time plus ours. What wasn't to like? Problem was, just before we were about to head out, come to find out somebody got sticky fingers 'round my personal property.

I bet you don't know where that flag come from, do you? Aw hell, I don't mean where it come from in general—I'm talking 'bout the *specific* flag that woman messed with. You got a guess? Well, I'll tell you then. It was my daddy's, straight from our front yard at home. When he took it down and gave it to me he said, "Son, don't y'all ever forget who you are up there." Now, maybe I got a little worked up that night, what with the shit pumping through my system. But you damn skippy my number one priority was looking for my family heirloom.

HOWIE KELLY:

So I'm outside in the alley expecting to hear the goddamn hit records I paid for, the beginning of the end of this fucking nightmare, but I'm almost three cigarettes in and all I hear is more commotion from the other side of the door. I go back in to see what's the holdup, and the Bonds are *still* not on the stage. They're not even in place in the wings! Chet and a few of his cronies are rummaging through the dressing room, throwing around sofa cushions, tossing garbage cans, turning over chairs and tables, on some rant about how they're not starting the show till he has his colors on. Well, I didn't know what the fuck he was talking about! I'm so pissed I'm shaking! I say to him, "If you numbnuts don't get your asses out there, I swear to fucking Christ . . ." And he says, "I'm not doing a goddamn thing till I recover my property," and his goons are starting to gang up behind him. I'm thinking somebody took *money* from him, drugs even, something of actual value! Meanwhile Squine and the other guy, they're still noodling around onstage but you can barely hear 'em play because now the whole bottom section is going, "Bond Brothers, Bond Brothers. . . ." I'm panicking! I'm thinking about the ticket holders mobbing the box office to get refunds!

And out the corner of my eye I see Nev buzzing around like a mosquito, looking like he'll take anything, like he's just fine if I use him to stall—he just wants the shot. What an ego on that one, thinking he was so good back then he could calm 'em down. And I didn't wanna hear it; by that point I didn't wanna hear anything from anybody. Before he could even open his mouth I barked at him, "You wanna play so bad? Fine! Knock yourself out."

Alone with Jimmy in the wings, Opal says, she never understood that just behind them, on the other side of the curtain that led into the back of the house,

a search was on for the flag concealed underneath her costume. She continued
arguing heatedly with my father about whether she should perform.

OPAL JEWEL:

It didn't make sense to me, giving up our chance—rolling over felt like
letting those idiots out there win. I didn't understand why Jimmy would
ask me to walk away, and besides that, I'd invited a few folks from Max's
for the VIP, including Sam Hood—if they were still up in the balcony
and I was a no-show, I'd be starting back from zero again.

Your daddy was going off on me about my hard head, my cold
heart. But when he finally saw the yelling wasn't gonna work he pulled
me to him and started rubbing my arms. He said, "You don't even
know how bad they treated Cherry." I told him I wasn't nothing like
those girls in the Curlicutes, they did their thing and I did mine, and
Jimmy said, "You think they're gonna treat the nigger better?" That's
when he started making some sense to me, when I started to come
around, started to believe him when he told me to give it some time
and he'd help me get a classier show than this one. He's rubbing my
arms and he's saying to me, "Trust me, baby, it's a bad scene. You don't
want it—just let them have it." [*Long pause*] And I really was two seconds from taking his hand and splitting. Out through that backstage
door and into the night. But then we could hear something else from
the house, rising between the [front rows chanting] "Bond Brothers,
Bond Brothers. . . ."

BOB HIZE:

Up in the balcony someone's family or guest, I'm not sure whose, started
with their own shouting directed to the seats below: "Shut the fuck up!"
So there was this call-and-response between the downstairs and the up:
"Bond Brothers!" *"Shut the fuck up!"* The VIPs who'd been gathering
their things to leave sort of froze, with an amused look, and some of
them were curious enough to sit back down and join in.

VIRGIL LAFLEUR:

New York can be hideous and crude, but the creative classes often display a wonderfully colorful spirit of *résistance* when we've had enough of the nonsense. Even the most delicate among us becomes weary of the tactics of bullies—we lift our pens, our brushes, our voices, our sequined off-the-shoulder floor-length gowns, and then? *Mon dieu*, we make a *gorgeous* noise. That evening in the balcony I unloosed the baritone my theater training had given me with great intention and gusto, so that Mad might hear us behind her curtain and know that her kindred was there.

chapter fourteen

"THE BACKBONE
DROPPED OUT"

★ ★

My father was thirty-two years old on November 13, 1971—ten years older than Opal Jewel. She often sought his counsel on navigating the music industry and recording process, as their relationship crossed from professional admiration to something inappropriately intimate. And yet at the most consequential moment of their complex affair, when he asked her to walk away with him from the Smythe that night, it was the balcony, filled mostly with strangers and loose acquaintances, that swayed her.

OPAL JEWEL:

The weed plus adrenaline had me mellow and alert at the same time, like I could reason and focus on everything at once inside that crazy space with the red curtains all around. But I could see through the crack in the curtain leading out to the stage, and there was my mic set up all pretty and waiting for me; I looked to my right and there was my friend Nev. Bursting into the wings, tall and skinny as an exclamation point, grinning and giving me the thumbs-up with his acoustic guitar strapped across his chest and that black eyeliner he'd scribbled on like war paint. And he ignored Jimmy and said in my ear, with the people in the balcony still pumping me up, "Do you hear that, my Girl in Gold? Are you ready to show them who we are?"

I don't think I even answered him; I didn't need to, because my blood knew that it was time, showtime, and it was coming at me fast. Nev nodded, and I nodded, and the choice was made.

I remember Nev saying cheers to Jimmy, holding his hand out to shake, like, *Bye*—I guess he assumed Jimmy was gonna leave me alone, pull out of the set. But your daddy wouldn't shake Nev's hand. He told him real low to get out of his face with that bullshit, to never say boo to him again or he'd be picking himself up off the floor. I remember Jimmy turned his back to me then; I remember his hair puffing out the edge of his snap cap, his drumsticks in his jeans pocket. . . . I can still see him standing strong on his own two feet, striding through the crack in the curtains past Johnny and Sol, sitting down at his kit.

And then it was just me and Nev standing together in the wings, and without Jimmy there suddenly I got a little nervous. And Nev wasn't much better—he'd gone whiter than he already was, taking off his acoustic guitar [since the shared electric waited for him onstage]. He was telling me it was going to be okay, everything would work out in the end because this was our moment, and *just listen to that crowd*. Said it like he was convincing himself too. I breathed in deep, thought about that noise like a wild wave to ride, and I stepped out just like we'd rehearsed—a few beats behind the band, so I could have a moment to shine before Nev came out. My heartbeat was thudding as loud as my shoes across the floor of that stage, the biggest I'd ever been on. It seemed like all the other sound dropped out while I crossed the distance to my mark, right in front of Jimmy's kit. I planted my foot down on one side of my mic, *boom*. Then the other one, *boom*. I expected to feel the spotlight hot on my skin, but we had come out so quick I guess it took a minute for whatever poor child was at the controls to catch up to what was going on. So without the lights blinding me, I could see very clearly the people in the audience, I could see these bogeymen in the front row with their windburned faces and their hands circling their mouths, I could see one scratching himself like a damn monkey and another one making that filthy gesture with his tongue between two fingers. Sol and Johnny started up with a little intro music, warming up, and then Nev jogged out [downstage left, beside Opal]. Howie was supposed to announce him, you know—"Ladies and gentlemen, Neville Charles!"—but obviously that didn't happen.

Then the lights cut on and the people whited out, and in their place all the noise rushed back in—I could pick out the booing down at my feet, yeah, but up above, in my cheering section, they were loving me in a way I had never been loved before, and when I raised a fist they cheered louder, and that rush of energy just . . . it boosted me into a different frequency. Behind me I heard Jimmy start the count [for "Yellow Belly"]; he kicked in with the beat double time, either trying to rush us off or mess us up, I don't know. But the other guys were too good, and they sped up perfect to match him. We had that proto-punk thing going, you know? Nev's fingers were flying across the strings, struggling to keep up, but right when it was time for him to charge in with the verse he didn't miss. And I thought, hey, Jimmy was wrong—Nev *was* the real deal, a talent worth taking a gamble on. I thought, *This is it, this is it!* My confidence just soaring, *go go go*. I kept pumping my fist up to the balcony, and swiveling my hips side to side and shaking my head with the beat so that my wig was flying around, the ends of it slapping me in the face, strands getting stuck in my lipstick. . . . It was getting real good to me. And then the vibe changed.

You know "Yellow Belly"; you remember how at the bridge everything falls out but the drums and my vocals, that whisper that builds up. "Run, honey, run . . ." Very sparse and dramatic and I was aiming for glory. Well, just before I pulled in my breath to sing, I heard one of them down below shout out to another one, like some big hilarious joke, "Hey, So-and-So, ain't she just the kind of gash you like?" And it was the tiniest pinprick to my spirit—just enough to make me lose some air, make me miss my cue. I was standing there dumb behind my mic while Jimmy lined up a second pass, a third, and I heard Nev say, "All right?"

next to me. I guess I was waiting for the other one's punch line; I guess I've always been the type who wants to know where she stands, wants to hear it to her face. So I was craning my neck and trying to make them out of the blur, trying to find which face to look into. I hate that I gave whoever it was the satisfaction. Because he could see me but I couldn't see him, and right then he said loud and proud, "*That* nigger? Looks like my tailpipe spit her out at the Georgia line." And then the laughing.

Since I was standing there like a waste of space, Nev picked up the slack and went to the last verse [skipping over the bridge], and my moment on the song was over. I got so damn *heated* then—literally, I was sweating from the lights and that thing I could feel wrapped around me and just pure, overwhelming rage—but I took another deep breath to fill myself up again, and I remembered I had my own little gag. A joke that made *me* laugh. So just as Jimmy kicked into the next song I stepped off my mark and got close to the edge of the stage. I didn't need no microphone, I shouted it out: "This one's for you." And I turned around and bent over and flipped up the bottom of my tutu so they could all see, see that X kissing the crack of my Black ass, see exactly what I thought about them and all their hate. My fingers found where Virgil had tucked in the end, near my hip, and I pulled it loose and popped back upright at the same time. For just one second, before I turned back around to face them, I caught eyes with Jimmy and he was shaking his head at me— *Don't you dare, girl*, even though he couldn't have known. Well, nobody could tell Opal Jewel what to do, because she had it under control. Before that girl even blinked she was sneering into the lights, holding that flag high over her head so that everybody in the house could see it good, and she stuck a couple fingers through one of the holes she'd made with Virgil LaFleur's good nail file and she yanked and yanked till the thing ripped apart.

I was standing there with a piece of it in each fist, breathing hard like I'd just whipped somebody in the hundred-meter hurdles. I let go of one piece and then the other, and don't you know it, both happened to float down right at my feet. So yeah, I stomped on 'em good a couple of times—they were in the way and I had to get back behind my mic to do my part. Maybe they were shocked [in the audience], maybe they were booing and hissing, maybe some folks were laughing along, I don't know. While they were collecting their little emotions I was already burning through "Red-Handed," pushing all my power and energy into my diaphragm like Jimmy had taught me to do. I had my eyes squeezed shut so I could focus, so I could see the red, red, red of my own pulse, my own power, and all of a sudden the backbone dropped out. I always call my drummer the backbone, because it's the beat that holds the whole thing together, and once it goes everything else falls apart.

They tell me that Beau Bond stumbled out [onto the stage], and that Jimmy got some good licks in—that it was like your daddy had been tensed for a fight, the way he sprang up from behind the kit quick as lightning and tackled that boy, straddled him and whaled him a couple times across the face with his sticks. All that, I can believe. But they also try to tell me that Beau Bond wouldn't have hurt a fly, that he didn't have a mind or the heart to come after me, that probably he was only trying to dive for his trash before it caused a bigger mess. Maybe so. But how was Jimmy supposed to know that? How was I? Because Beau Bond mighta been the quiet one, but he made it perfectly clear in his silence that *he was with them*. And then here he come charging out like the Redneck Avenger. Like Bubba the Bobo.

By the time I realized what was happening, some more of them had run out from the wings all het up and they pulled Jimmy off that boy like he was nothing but a twig. They started punching and kicking at him till he just rolled down the little set of stairs on the side of the stage [leading down into the auditorium], real methodical, talking about teaching the spook a lesson, and I guess their thug friends were just in it for kicks—they were down there waiting to snatch him up like zoo animals when the raw meat gets dropped in the trap. I was trying to get down to Jimmy but I still couldn't see right, the stage lights were still blazing. Then somebody knocked into me hard and I wasn't braced for it—a bone in my ankle said *nah!* inside the straps of those shoes and I fell off 'em like a bag of bricks. Busted my lip, skinned my knee . . . I was down on my stomach struggling to get up, but the pain in my ankle shot up through my skull, and then somebody had put their body over mine—I guess that was Nev. I heard the people screaming; *I* was screaming. Let me tell you, the noise of that night was bad enough—meat pounding on meat, one of the amps buzzing right by my head. . . . But nothing was worse than the minute the stage lights finally clicked off and all the house lights came up [so that the audience could find their way to the exits]. I don't see how Nev could ever forget one minute of that night, and at the same time I wish to hell I could too.

People were scrambling over chairs, over each other—the theater was almost cleared out except for the devils down in front taking their time to beat the tar out your daddy, and the goons watching. And for the few of us still on the stage, we were high up and could see everything down on the floor—it was like the tables had turned and we were the audience now. They had Jimmy surrounded in a half circle [in the space between the front row and the stage]; they were tossing him from one to the next. I saw a boot connect with the side of his face, and his nose was gushing blood, his eyes were swelling shut, his mouth was a mess. I was screaming at him, "*Get out! Get out!*" and at one point I think he must've heard me. He managed to push up to his feet and I saw him try to run for it, but obviously he was delirious, halfway to gone. He stumbled into one of their old ladies, and when that white girl fell back on her ass with Jimmy bleeding and breathing heavy on top of her, when she started screaming her fool head off . . . Well. That's an old song—you know how it goes.

One of those thugs picked your daddy up so he had his arms pinned, and they let the white girl kick him in the stomach and then spit in his face. I knew that would hurt him more, haunt him more, than any violence they could do. And it was like *nobody* was doing anything to try to save him. I didn't see Johnny, I didn't see Sol, I didn't see my people in the balcony coming down to help, or the cops, or anybody else.

So I hit and scratched at the body that was holding me down till it let me go, and my ankle was obviously good and broke but I crawled toward a mic stand that had fallen down on the stage. I took that mic out the cradle, I whipped it around like a lasso by the cord, and then I let it fly. I caught that bitch right in the back of her head.

She was bleeding from her scalp, all down her face. . . . I always thought it was odd that nobody went to her to see if she was okay, they just let her sit her ass back down on the ground and cry. But they weren't gonna just let it go. That's when they threw Jimmy into the seats, as unbothered as if they were tossing a sack of trash, and the ones who were hanging around and gawking, they scrambled out the way so they wouldn't get hit. They didn't even try to catch him. So Jimmy landed hard. I saw his neck hit and snap back, and his body slide down. I was screaming, hysterical. Hustling to undo the shoe that was on my good foot, because I figured if I could just get up and hop I could reach him. But before I could a couple of them had stepped up on the stage. Coming, I guess, to see about me.

Nev grabbed my good ankle and pulled me back and started up with his fast-talking, telling them they'd done enough, they'd made their point. Those thugs weren't having it, though, they were hovering over us, calling him a faggot, a limey, asking if he was a goddamn nigger lover. And one of them said, "This bitch wants to fight, let her fight." That one kicked Nev in the face and the chest till he was hugging himself and I was exposed. I was scrabbling backward on my hands, one shoe on and one shoe off, looking for something to grab. Somebody tossed a bottle in my direction and it hit an amp and shattered right over my head; the noise made some of the white girls who were supposedly gonna kick my ass scream and run—it sounded like a gun popping off. I tried to get up one more time, tried to balance and push myself up, but I cut my palm clean open on a piece of glass. That's about the time the cops showed up and started doing what they do.

chapter fifteen

"CLICK, CLICK, CLICK"

★   ★

After squealing up to the curb in a five-van cavalry, the NYPD stormed the theater. In the lobby, Rosemary Salducci, Bob Hize, and Howie Kelly were among those roughly shoved aside with shields and threatened over bullhorn with arrest. Helpless, the three of them were spat outside in the resulting surge toward the exits. So was Virgil LaFleur, who'd had a terrifying view of Opal falling on the stage before getting swept down from the balcony. Outside on the ruined red carpet was a full theater's worth of people frantically searching for friends from whom they'd been separated. Screaming, shoving, punching.

ROSEMARY SALDUCCI:

I managed to find Bob, and we clutched each other's hands and made our way to the corner so we could still see what was happening and try to account for all our people. He was whispering prayers, over and over. You gotta understand, we didn't know *who* was gonna make it out. We didn't know who had gone out the back alley, who was still trapped inside, who was hurt. We never even knew what happened to the Bonds till the next day when Chet, that coward, showed up at my desk asking for money to bail out some of their buddies.

Photographer Marion Jacobie was among those still in the theater. As soon as Opal Jewel had stepped onto the stage, Jacobie, anticipating more drama, had raced down toward the front of the auditorium; when the fight broke out, she recalls, one of the Fiends forced her to pull out the film she had in her camera and dump out the contents of her backpack. Jacobie, however, had kept a spare roll in her pocket, and as police stormed the premises she discreetly reloaded her Leica.

MARION JACOBIE:

They sent a bunch of them in riot gear—some genius among them had decided the best way to handle an already hectic situation was to toss tear gas, as if they were fumigating for roaches. It wasn't a lot of it and, as I understand it, it was mild as those things go. But it doesn't take much when you're indoors, so those of us still in that theater were dying. Hacking our guts up, scattering to whatever exits we could for fresh air. I made it out the lobby doors and there were more cops lined up outside, pushing the crowd back with batons and waiting to make arrests. One moved toward me but I fumbled for the press credential around my neck and held it up and he left me alone after I promised to stay out of their way.

OPAL JEWEL:

Everyone else who had been on the stage had run out; it was only me and Nev. I could hear the sirens, the bullhorns. Nev was curled up next to me groaning and gasping—they had knocked the air out of him and banged up a couple of his ribs. I couldn't catch my own breath to speak. I just knew we needed to get out; we needed to get Jimmy out. I nudged Nev with my good foot to get him up, and he rolled over to his hands and knees. I climbed up on his back, wrapped my arms and legs around him, and he half crawled, half dragged me toward that set of steps at the side of the stage. He grabbed onto a rail and stumbled up to his feet and I almost fell off. My ankle was screaming, but I managed to hold on long enough for him to get down the stairs, and then he clasped his arms around his back so that they were holding me up. He started staggering down a side aisle, heading for the front doors. I was trying to tell him, "Stop, stop, get Jimmy!" But either no sound was coming out my mouth or he just wasn't paying me no mind. I was trying to stiffen my body, jerk him back to the place where I saw Jimmy slide down, but Nev just kept stumbling forward.

MARION JACOBIE:

When my vision got a little clearer I found a decent position around the cops that had a good view on the doors if I held my camera high enough, and I rooted myself there even though I probably should have gone to the hospital to get my lungs checked out. The lights of the marquee were still up, plus the lights from the squad cars and ambulances. . . . I kept one arm up, the one that held my camera, and I braced my elbow with my other hand to try to keep it steady. Almost everybody was out by then, and a lot of the time I was bent over in a coughing fit. But every time I saw feet coming out, I clicked the shutter. *Click, click, click.*

OPAL JEWEL:

Must have been seconds after she got her damn picture that Nev collapsed and we were both down on that carpet, gasping to get some air. I saw more hard shoes running toward us and by instinct I curled up in a ball right on top of Nev, but it was just the paramedics. I remember screaming for them to go back and get Jimmy, but nobody would listen. Nobody even seemed to know what I was screaming about. I threw a fit in the back of the ambulance. I didn't want them to fix me till I knew how he was, but when we got to the hospital they just grabbed me up by the arms and wrestled me onto a gurney like a slab of meat, and they rolled me to some back area where I guess folks could be spared the sight of me. They pinned me down and Nurse Ratched came in and gave me a shot.

MARION JACOBIE:

I didn't even know what gold I had. Wallace [Jopson] found me out front of the theater and offered to let me come to the *Times* newsroom with him. It wasn't far, so we just hoofed it [to the Times Square office], but he had to lead me by the hand because I was still coughing and my vision wasn't 100 percent.

We got there and he was making his pitch to the page-one editors, telling them I maybe had some art that could go with the story. I had never worked for the *Times* before, but they let me go into the darkroom with one of the photo guys, and while the roll was developing I could hear the guy say, "Holy shit." Turns out most of it was bad, blurry shots you couldn't make out—but then there was the one. A very good one. We brought the contact sheet to Wallace so he could peek through the loupe, and I said to him, "I'm sorry, my eyes still aren't right, but aren't these the ones who were up on the stage? Isn't that the crazy girl?"

I hung around until the copy boys brought the first papers hot off the press up to the newsroom. At first I was disappointed that my picture hadn't made page one, but it was hard to stay that way once I saw how giant they'd run it inside. So even though I'd been up all night, there was no way I was just gonna go home and go to sleep. I tucked my paper under my arm and walked all the way to Chelsea as the sun came up, and I felt a little surge every time I passed a newsstand and saw the stacks arriving. I stopped somewhere and treated myself to steak and eggs, and showed the waitress my teeny little credit line: "Marion Jacobie, Special to the *New York Times*." When I finally climbed the stairs to my apartment, exhausted, I could already hear my phone ringing off the hook.

OPAL JEWEL, *SHAKING HER HEAD WHEN ASKED WHAT
SHE FEELS WHEN SHE SEES JACOBIE'S EVOCATIVE PHOTOGRAPH,
WHICH I'D SET ON THE TABLE IN FRONT OF US*:

Nice try, but nah. Go ahead and put that away.

I'd hoped that my personal ties to this history would give me a leg up on those who've gone before me in attempting to pierce Opal Jewel's facade, but just as I'd feared while preparing for this interview, she initially refused to ruminate

on The Photo or its significance to her career. She also maintained a remark-
able stoniness when recounting the play-by-play of that night, and the reper-
cussions of her choosing Nev over my father. "You've very politely asked me
what happened, and I've very politely told you," she said to me at one point,
after I'd rephrased the same question a number of times, and I'd (very politely)
backed off.

As for my other sources, many seemed eager to explore the topic of re-
grets. I asked every person who'd been a part of Rivington Showcase to tell me
the single biggest one they carried.

MARY SHARP:

I regret that the world can be so unkind, so ungenerous. That people still
haven't learned how to love, in 1971 or 2016.

HOWIE KELLY:

That the venue turned out to be a turd wrapped in red velvet. This is
what you get when you try to kiss the press's ass with chichi shit, when what
you need to do is put on a no-frills rock-and-roll show with people who
know how to put it on right.

ROSEMARY SALDUCCI:

Maybe I should've asked to be on their little planning committee. [*Rolling eyes*] Sometimes men just aren't good with the details, you know. *I*
woulda thought to ask [the Smythe's managers] about the security. I had
four knucklehead brothers who woulda done the job for cheap.

VIRGIL LAFLEUR:

In those days I worked mostly on feeling and natural instinct, and I was
boundlessly creative . . . but I can admit that I lacked the finer tuning
to detect the line between provocation and recklessness. Of course I
couldn't have imagined what Mad was going to *do* up on that stage with
the impromptu garment we'd made. In hindsight, I might not have been
quite so playful. Fashion can be a serious thing.

Also, I would have carried a good pair of shears. For shredding the offending item, yes, before it could do harm. [*Pause*] For defensive purposes as well.

CHERRY ALLISON:

It sounds crazy now, but back then people tried to tell me we had riled up the guys because of the sexy way we were dressed—even a few *women*, those Phyllis Schlafly types, said we made them more crazy and aggressive. Can you believe it? Well, unfortunately, for a long time *I* did. Of course, it's different today. People will read my story or the stories Rosemary and Mary Sharp probably told you, and they'll say, *My God, Cherry, that's sexual assault!* And they'd be absolutely right. So no, I don't have any regrets. None of it was my fault.

MARION JACOBIE:

When I was going through a tough divorce in the eighties, I made a financial decision to sell the rights [surrounding The Photo] to a picture collection. I get a small royalty every time they license it for books and stuff, but I don't have a say where it goes and I haven't always been happy to see how it's used.

JOHN SQUINE:

I can tell by the questions you're asking that you think me and Sol should've gotten involved in that fight. So let me ask you a question in return, and I don't mean anything offensive by it, but: Do you have any kids? No? Well, at the time I had two babies already, and Sol, he had three. So we backed away, man, and got out early on. But to tell you the truth, if I *weren't* a dad? I probably would've been right in the mix with my bass in my hand, swinging away to help my buddy Jimmy.

What I really regret is being a chickenshit when it came to your mom. Jimmy was my friend, and I should have been there more for his wife. I should have paid her a visit after you were born, instead of sending along a gift like an asshole. But I was feeling guilty because I knew that he'd been fucking up, and I had my own family to protect, and it was just so easy to let things slip. When you talk to her, will you please tell her hello from me? And that I'm sorry?

BOB HIZE:

There are a great many regrets, but I suppose they all fall under the same umbrella: failing to act always from a place of integrity and love. I knew I never should have worked with the Bond Brothers in the first place, but I helped lead the charge, didn't I? And from that one bad decision, all the others flowed.

NEV CHARLES:

I regret being redundant as I must tell you once again, and hopefully for the last, that I do not, cannot, remember much of anything about that window of time, or offer you anything more than the obvious wish that the night had been peaceful. A terrible moment, but I'm hoping we can move to the good that came out.

CHET BOND:

Well, I've been trying to give my apologies. Not everybody's picked up the phone to accept them, so that's part of the reason I decided to talk to you for this book. And I really do thank you for that opportunity. You're the only person who's bothered to meet me on my turf, to hear what Chet Bond had to say. So what I'll tell you is this: The drugs are the regret of my life. I let 'em cook my eggs for almost thirty years, and I know that I caused a lot of pain, that I lost so much. My record deal, [a relationship with] my brother, sometimes even my freedom [following several arrests].

But you know what helped me? Years and years later, hearing how Nev Charles come up from that bottom he hit. Uppers, downers, it don't matter—he and I both know they will fuck your life sideways. And one day I was in an emergency clinic right near where we're sitting—I had knocked a couple teeth out after some addict bullshit in the middle of a Saturday—and they had some dusty old magazines spread out in the waiting room. Wouldn't you know it, there was a copy of yours with Nev Charles on the cover. I picked it up and inside was that story of him after the rehab, talking 'bout his new direction. And I thought, *Well, I'll be a son of a gun.* It still took me a while to get clean, but I figured if that pansy got another shot as a new man, maybe someday I'd get the monkey off my back too.

And it just makes me chuckle thinking 'bout how the Lord works, because I swear I *never* thought I'd listen to a word that guy had to say to me again. [*Snorting when asked to clarify*] That slick sonofabitch . . . He ain't tell you 'bout how he stole his slot back? How he was the one give me the heads up that my flag was gone, and got me all worked up thinking your daddy had took it? If he'd kept his mouth shut, who knows? I probably wouldn't have even missed it till later, till long after the Bond Brothers took the stage and kicked some ass. Musically speaking, I mean.

PART TWO

EDITOR'S NOTE

Motherfucker, WHAT?!?!

Chet Bond's final revelations throbbed in my head as we wrapped up our interview, as he led me back through his house and down the steps of his screened-in front porch in Live Oak, Florida. His Pomeranians, awakened from their spread-eagle naps, yapped at my heels. It was early December, but at the peak of the afternoon the temperature had hit an ungodly eighty-one degrees. The silver Prius I'd rented was molten in the driveway, painful to look at straight on. I guess that Chet noticed me wince. He took off his MAKE AMERICA GREAT AGAIN ball cap and tried to hand it to me.

"You can have it if you want," he said, grinning. "Brutal hot out here."

Stripped of the cap, his hair, I saw, was as long as it had ever been but stringy now, strands of it gathered at the base of his skull in a cigarette-thin ponytail. I dug frantically inside my messenger bag while walking toward the car, searching for the keys. Chet had paused in my path, holding his monstrosity out like a holy offering. It was a bright and triggering red, this thing— similar, I imagine, to the flash of flag that provoked Opal backstage that night. And I felt sick to realize that Chet Bond thought he was some kind of gallant. That he was still, after all these years, either oblivious to the terror he was capable of conjuring or reveling in it.

"Go on, take it," Chet said, "it ain't no thing. I got a whole family-and-friends box of 'em inside the house."

We were beside the Prius now, and I propped the bag against the broiling door, the better to quickly paw through it. "I'm sorry but I can't say I'm a fan of your . . . candidate."

"Well. I figured that, you tooling around in this piece a' shit." He pounded a fist on the Prius's hood. "You liberal types are such suckers. Don't you know that climate change is a lie put out there by the Chinese? All to destroy the American economy. It's about the money, honey, and don't let *her* tell ya different. But you know what?" He poked me in the arm, when I didn't respond. "You know what?"

"Mmm?" *A water bottle, two notebooks, a granola bar, a compact . . . everything but the goddamn keys . . .*

"I'll *tell* you what: Just to show you Chet Bond's not a bad guy, I'll let you borrow a truck my boys just fixed up at the garage. It'll do you right on mileage and you'll have more power for getting around while you're down here. 'Cause believe it or not, at some point today these skies are gonna cloud over just as black and open up into a storm. And then what're you gonna do?" He fiddled with the adjustable strap on the back of the hat; snapping it, unsnapping it. "Get blown off the road, is what."

"I appreciate the offer," I said, "but I'm leaving. For the airport. Right away."

"Oh yeah? All right, then. That's too bad." He paused. "I hope it wasn't something I said."

I caught the smug grin, the twinkle in his eye. The same look he'd had while rattling me moments ago, pontificating from a recliner in his sunken living room. He had explained it to me again and again, with disturbing consistency. How Nev had almost got himself cold-cocked that night, touching Chet on his back that way. How Nev had then said, "Aren't you missing something?" and pointed toward the wings at my father. How Beau had overheard all this and tried to defuse the situation, tried to bring Chet down from his high, telling his brother to keep looking for the flag because none of it sounded right to him. How Chet had reluctantly agreed to cool down, but then heard that draft-dodging song he hated. How he and his buddies ran up to the wings to boo, just in time to catch Opal disrespecting his flag. How he figured Jimmy and Opal were in cahoots, because *birds of a feather, they sure flock together. . . .* How he got so mad in that moment that he kicked his baby brother out on the stage—literally kicked Beau in the ass—to prove there wasn't a Bond alive who was a pussy, who'd sit back for that kind of an insult. . . .

"There's a big holiday concert 'round Jacksonville way," Chet was saying now. "I thought you might like to come with, meet some folks and check it out for your magazine. Truth is, I play in a new band on the weekends. Just a little something to give my old lady a thrill." I heard a nervousness in his laugh. "Y'all still cover country music?"

"Mmm, not so much anymore."

Finally, my hand hit jagged metal, sunk down in a bottom corner of the bag, and I nearly kicked the dogs as I unlocked the door and shut myself inside the hotbox. Chet made a signal for me to roll down the window, which I pretended not to see. I cranked the ignition, smiled tightly, nodded, and hit reverse, backing down his gravel driveway. Skidding away from his lot, I could feel him standing there, watching me, and when I dared a glance in the rearview mirror I saw him waving goodbye in his dead, dry front yard. I saw the dust my tires had kicked up swirling around his flip-flops, and the giant American flag in the back poking up over the tree line. Saw him put the hat back on as the dogs scrabbled around the cuffs of his jeans.

"Jesus Christ," I gasped as I played hot potato with the steering wheel, merged onto US Route 90, and angled the full blast of the AC vents in the direction of my face. I punched the buttons on the satellite radio, searching for NPR, any soothing voice. "Asshole!" I screamed once I was twenty miles safe down the road. *A bigot and a boor. An idiot, a denier of facts and science, an egg-scrambled motherfucking ex-junkie . . .*

But—*oh Jesus, oh Christ!*—what if Chet Bond, king of deplorables, last and least on my interview list, had accidentally turned himself into a star witness? What if this one time, the idiot ex-junkie bigot was the one telling the God's honest truth? Had I really gotten him on tape exposing Nev Charles as a liar and a schemer? As guilty of instigating the Rivington Showcase riot, in pointing the finger at Jimmy, as Opal Jewel or the Bonds themselves had been? Could it be that in the end Nev Charles, *that slick sonofabitch*, had played every single one of us?

Four hours later I had returned the Prius to Enterprise, but still I sat in the airport bar next to my gate, stuck on a weather delay. The heat had finally broken and a vicious storm was raging through, just as Chet had predicted it would. Sheets of hard rain pummeled the arcing picture windows, and the jet bridge connecting the gate to the tin can due to carry me home bounced and wavered like the bellows of a giant accordion.

I pulled out my laptop. I was supposed to be answering emails related to a crisis back at the office—four advertisers had dropped out of the next issue, meaning our page count would have to be chopped down, *again*—but I found myself instead scrolling through a folder of interview transcriptions for the Aural History. There was one portion of an interview with Bob Hize that I'd underlined, a portion that had piqued me. I couldn't say why at the time. Now I read it again with fresh eyes:

> *[Immediately following the riot] I was with Nev [in triage] at the hos-pital, waiting for all his [X-ray] results. Of course I was worried as well about Opal, but I didn't know at the time where they'd carried her off to, and I certainly didn't know she was being targeted in any-one's investigation. And Nev was essentially my boarder, my charge, so it was my responsibility to take note of everything the doctors said, because I was the one who'd have to call and inform his father. [The doctors] thought he might have a concussion and there was the concern over his broken ribs [dangerous for their potential to puncture a lung]. Until they knew for sure, they'd told him to rest, to be as still as possible.*
>
> *We could hear the other patients all around us, we could hear them telling their loved ones the stories of what had happened to them. . . . And right next to us there was a teenage boy whose mother had rushed in hysterical, and he was telling her to calm*

down because at the end of the day he was lucky to walk away with a broken finger—at least they hadn't carried him out on a gurney with the white sheet draped over. And I'd wanted to pull back the curtain separating us and ask that young man, "Did you actually see that? You saw that someone's been killed?" Because we didn't know. But I looked over to Nev and he was trembling all over; even his teeth were chattering. I saw him take a breath as if to speak, but the pain level was obviously high, because he gasped and squeezed his eyes shut. I told him to hush, to sit back like a good lad and relax as the doctors had said that he should.

It was nearing daybreak, and I went in search of a coffee, maybe something with which Nev could write down what he'd been trying to say, and in the café I saw someone had abandoned the morning paper. I picked it up and saw the story, saw your father's name. I found the chapel, sank down to the floor, down to my knees, and I . . . [Pauses, overcome] I want you to know, Ms. Shelton, how sorry I felt. I feel.

To be honest I stalled [before returning to Nev's side]. I wasn't sure how to break that kind of news to him, and I didn't know how he would handle it with his head so foggy. I finally asked a nurse for a pad and pen, and then I gathered myself and went back in. But he'd got the Times already—I guess someone had recognized him in it and thought he'd want to see it. And it was opened in his lap to the page with Marion's huge photograph, and he was staring at it. Staring at his and Opal's faces staring back at him. Well, he was shattered, obviously. I wanted so badly to hug him but I didn't want to hurt him. I said, "Nev, are you all right? Do you have something you want to say, something you want to ask?" and I gave him the pen and the pad. His hand was still shaking but he managed to write it down. He gave me a look of such fear and sorrow as I'll never forget, and he held up the pad and he'd written, "IT'S ME." That broke my heart all over again. I didn't know what to do to comfort him; I just said, "Right, that's you there in the newspaper, Nevs, and it's *unthinkable what's happened. But we're so very glad that you got out. And look how strong you are! Look how brave."*

———

I signaled the bartender to bring me a second bourbon, to dull the damning tape that looped in my head: the private jet I'd taken with Nev, his interminable nap, his well-tuned anecdotes, his rat-a-tat deflections about being a victim of trauma. Rewinding to a couple days before all that: I remembered arranging the interview with his publicist/gatekeeper Lizzie Harris, and her insistence that Nev's schedule was hopeless, that he had one available window and if I wanted it I had to jump on it *now, yes, as in two days from now, that's right, and I'm sorry but what do I care about your other interviews, do you want his participation or not, and really, he'll only do it out of respect for Bob Hize, otherwise this would be a total no-go, understand, so consider yourself lucky, all right, doll, we're set?* I remembered that I'd sent Lizzie an orchid to thank her for the interview, and later an email asking, as I usually do, if I could get in touch with her client regarding any follow-up questions I might have. I remembered I never got any reply to that.

Now, I understood, Lizzie had never intended to send me one.

Clever, clever. I raised my glass of Maker's in salute. Tipped back the pour till the ice cubes knocked against my teeth.

———

"Hey there, Kayleigh, it's Sunny Shelton from *Aural*. Lizzie there?"

"Oh hiiii-eeee! Gosh, you just *missed her."*

"Any idea when she'll be back?"

"She won't be back today—for the rest of the week, actually. She's got a meeting off-site and then she's going up to Chappaqua to pitch in on the campaign for a couple of weeks before Christmas, isn't that so exciting? But I'm sure she'll get back to you as soon as she can!"

"Well, besides bugging you daily, ha ha, I've been leaving voice mails on her cell twice a day, emailing her too, and she's still not getting back to me."

"No?"

"No."

"*Gosh, that's weird.*"

[*Audible sigh*] "Do you have a number where I could reach her in Chappaqua, then?"

"*I mean, um, I'm sorry, but is this, like, an emergency?*"

"Yes, I would say it is like an emergency. As far as emergencies in this business go."

[*Fake laughter; fake laughter*]

"*I mean, I have to ask because she stressed to me that I should only call her with, like, emergencies? And I—*"

"Okay, Kayleigh, let's do this instead: When she calls in for her messages—and I know Lizzie calls in every day for her messages, right?—I want you to say to her these exact words. Do you have a pen?"

"*Yes. Ready!*"

"Great! Tell her I said, 'He's not fooling me with the memory-loss act.' "

"*Mm-hmmm . . .*"

"Then tell her, 'I will'—emphasis on the 'will,' please, can you say it like it's all-caps and underlined, Kayleigh?—'I WILL continue without his participation. But maybe he'd want a chance to comment.' Got it? Can you read it back to me?"

"*'He's not fooling me with the memory-loss act. I WILL continue without his participation. But maybe he'd want a chance to comment. Got it?'*"

"Good, good, except kill the 'got it?' at the end. That bit was for you, not for Lizzie."

"*Ohh . . . got it!*"

[*Fake laughter; fake laughter*]

"*I'll tell her, Sunny, okay thanks by-eeee!*"

[*Ten minutes later, when an undisclosed number lights up my personal cell*]

"Hi, this is Sunny."

"*How dare you harass my girl?*"

"You *have* been getting my messages, then."

"*Screw your messages. Here's a statement from me to you: Neither my client nor I will respond to any kind of trumped-up nonsense.*"

"Really? All due respect, Lizzie, but that's what you want to say? I haven't even told you exactly what the allegations are, or what they relate to."

"You don't have to tell me. I already know whatever you've got is bull- shit. Don't you think I've seen and heard it all? Gold diggers, lawyers, indus- try wannabes, hacks . . . all of them have tried to go the rounds with me and all of them turn out to be liars. Tell me, whose lies are you spreading now?"

"I don't feel, ah, comfortable just yet. Revealing my sources."

"Is it really that serious? You know, I'm not trying to disrespect you, I understand that this probably feels very high-stakes, considering the circum- stances around your dad. But Sunny, come on. We've worked well together a long, long time. I've got more important things to do, and you're better than peddling trash."

"It's not trash, it's—"

"What's this all about, then? Something he did back on the pills? Some- thing crazy he said? Who cares? It's been forty-five years! He's earned the crazy!"

"I know what he did at the showcase."

"I have no idea what you're talking about, doll, and I don't have the time to play Agatha Christie."

"My sources tell me Nev ratted to Chet and Beau Bond that their flag had been snatched, to cause a distraction and get his time slot back—"

"Oh my God, is that all? Chet Bond, she says. Who is he, anyway? That's a whopper of a story you're cooking. I can see the headline now . . . 'Breaking News: Rock Star's a Narcissist.' I'll send Kayleigh over to come clear your desk for that Pulitzer."

"Hold on, wait—I'm not finished. I'm also told that when Chet yoked him up and asked him what he knew, asked him who swiped that flag, Nev pointed the finger at my father."

[*The briefest silence, followed by a disbelieving peal of laughter*]

"So I want to ask Nev for a comment. Is it true, and if so, why would he do that? I mean, I get him trying to slip back onto the schedule, but why go the extra step of setting up my father? Was he that jealous over Opal, over what he thought he was entitled to? Was it some kind of weird revenge? What?"

"You of all people should know how much Nev Charles has done for civil rights causes, for women. . . . You're going to give Chet Bond sway over him?"

"Maybe Chet's a liar; he's most certainly an asshole. But the thing that's bugging me is, he's owned up to his part. He's damn near proud! I can't say the same for your client. He can't *remember*, Lizzie? Really?"

"Yes. Really. I don't know what's wrong with you, but clearly you've lost all perspective. Next thing I know, you'll be one of these idiots saying Hillary and Trump are the same. Have you given to the campaign yet, by the way? Hillary supports expanded coverage for mental health care, and clearly you could use it."

"Let Nev tell me himself that I'm crazy, then. Let him deny this on the record."

"Sunny, listen to me: I'd never advise him to dignify such nonsense with a response."

"Are you sure about that? I mean, imagine what it means if I'm able to confirm this. All these years, my God, Lizzie . . . Your client's been so happy to play the rescuing hero, this great political activist, Opal Jewel's ally, when maybe the truth is he's only a thirsty, selfish opportunist who put a target on a Black man's back."

[*Heavy breathing (mine)*]

"I don't see any problem, then, because it's impossible to confirm a pack of lies. Best of luck while you waste your time."

[*The click of a phone disconnecting (hers)*]

My plan was to tell Opal right away. Tell her what, I wasn't entirely sure, but at least give her notice I'd be quitting this project. Much as I hated to admit it, Lizzie had called my bluff. It would be impossible to verify what amounted to hearsay four decades later, and so soon after I'd been forced to lay off five *Aural* editors due to JBJ-mandated budget cuts; I had neither the time nor the money to track down Beau Bond as a corroborating witness. But how could I continue feeding into the legend of Opal & Nev if I suspected that it was riddled with holes? If I thought even a shred of what Chet had said about Nev was true, how could I stomach putting together the kind of hagiography his team—hell, *my* team—hoped could be sold in merch booths to adoring fans across North America? As Jimmy Curtis's daughter, I couldn't be a part of that. I had no choice but to recuse myself. *I will tell Opal I am done to her face*, I decided as I clicked the purchase button on a 6 a.m. flight to Los Angeles. *I will thank her for this opportunity. I will wish her the best and move on with my life. I will figure out later how I'm supposed to do that.*

———

But then Opal answered her doorbell in Baldwin Hills, wearing a beanie and a denim jacket. She was clutching fresh-cut sprigs of basil, and with a terse hello she led me quickly through the house and past the curtained French doors that opened onto the backyard.

She had relegated me to her garden. Again.

Surely by now, I thought, she knew I'd be curious about the interior of the house. The Harlem brownstone was Virgil LaFleur's style, but this one, presumably, was 100 percent hers. Since the beginning I'd wanted to linger over the decor, analyze the mementos and material things that held personal meaning to her, but the most I'd been able to glimpse, dashing through on my previous visits, was a palette of cream upholstery, throw pillows covered in tangerine-and-aqua kente, a tribal totem standing guard in a corner, the hint of a kitchen as suggested by a citrusy smell wafting from my left, and, to my right, a hallway lined with framed photos I'd been eager to explore. Now it occurred to me that maybe, like Nev, Opal had been in full control of the terms of these talks, parsing out what stingy morsels I was allowed to know. That whatever "opportunity" she had given me was nothing but a farce.

She'd moved the patio table to a patch of direct sun, and, as usual, she'd prepared it with two place settings. I sat down as she rinsed the basil in the trickle of a garden hose. In the center of the table, one platter held a baguette and a large serrated knife propped against its edge, and another was spread across with heirloom tomatoes and burrata, sliced and layered in alternating rounds, peppered and glistening with olive oil. Opal shook the excess water from the basil, sending droplets everywhere, then sat down and began tearing the leaves, making piles on both our plates.

I shivered in a small breeze. "Aren't you kind of chilly out here?"

"I'm good in the sun."

It was clear she wasn't moving an inch. She'd barely spoken since I arrived, and she seemed to be waiting for me to get to the point. I'd been mysterious on the phone with her to arrange this new interview, our fourth so far—an annoyance, I guess, considering the original schedule had called for us to wrap up in three. To get the additional sit-down tacked on, I'd only said that I wanted to close the loop on a few things about the making of *Polychrome*. Now I found myself driven by a growing rage, and barreling in another direction.

"Do you remember where the Smythe used to be?" I asked her.

A small grunt of assent, eyes still on the task.

"You wouldn't recognize it," I said. I told her about a field trip I'd made to the site of the riot, where developers have built an EDM dance club catering mostly to European tourists—sleek and neon-new, the grand old horror erased down to the studs. "To be honest," I said, "I found my visit disconcerting."

"Well," she said. And nothing else.

"Opal. You don't have a single thought about that?"

"About what part?" she said, still tearing that basil.

"About the fact that nobody seems to care at all. I mean, I know that sounds unfair, I know it's not the club's fault, or the fault of the kids who go there. But it's crazy to me that Jimmy was killed on those grounds and now the place is like . . ." I made farting and hiccupping noises, trying to imitate the beats-by-computer. "You know?"

"Not really." She sighed. "I guess it's been ages. Damn near forty-five years. What were you expecting?"

She'd meant the question to be rhetorical, I knew—flippant, at worst. And yet, even as I felt resigned to abandon the Aural History I had been planning, I was also frustrated that I'd gotten nothing out of my work to this point. That Opal had teased me into revisiting this story in the first place, only to throw a fence around her heart at the moments I needed her to give me new insight. How was it, I wondered, that I had come so far to get where I was, and yet here I sat as if twelve again, flailing through familiar games of keep-away? I stared at this woman I'd held up for so long as an illicit fascination. I watched her fussing over her stupid hors d'oeuvres and wondered how she could give more care to that task than this offhand way she was speaking to me. How dare she be so cavalier, knowing the familial wreckage into which I'd been born? Had she been so busy mouthing off to the Man and the pigs that she'd raced past all us collateral damage? Oh, us poor, proverbial "little people": stuck in the past, clinging bitterly to our grief and resentments, to our Establishment-issued pieces of paper. . . . Perhaps she'd forgotten I descended from them, from Jimmy's true survivors. Perhaps it was time I flashed that credential. Reminded her, exactly, who the fuck asked the questions.

"What I'd rather know," I said, struggling to match her cool tone, "is what *you* were expecting."

She glanced up.

"I mean, I'm the one in the dark here, right?" I said. "The one who doesn't understand a damn thing? So enlighten me: What were *you* expecting, choosing to go out there with Nev that night?"

"Didn't we go through this, the last time we talked?"

"Let's go through it again," I said, pulling my phone out of the bag at my feet and turning on the recorder. "Tell me more about your carrying on with Jimmy in the first fucking place. What kind of a future were *you* expecting, Opal Jewel, with somebody else's husband?"

"With somebody's daddy, you're trying to say."

"Yes," I said, "with *mine*."

"SarahLena, it wasn't like . . . You weren't even born yet."

"But I was about to be," I said. "And you knew that, right? Wasn't it enough, to know? Wasn't it enough for you to stop and think about the consequences for him? To have some sense of shame? Did you ever even love him?"

Opal laughed and smacked the table, as if I'd just said the darnedest thing. The knife clattered against the plate.

"There she is!" she hooted to the sky. "Finally, the girl shows some heart!" She stuck out her hand for me to shake, put it back down when I wouldn't. "Okay, fine, come on with it now. What else you got? Drill, baby, drill! Hit all the angles! Give me every damn bit of that master's degree."

"I hope it was expensive," I spat.

"Oh honey, it sure as hell was," she said, laughing again.

"But you don't own me," I said, the words coming hot and furious now. "Nobody does. You understand that, right?"

"Well, *now* I do," she said. "Which means I can relax. So go ahead, shoot."

I fought an urge to pick up a round of cheese and squish it through my fist.

"Girl, calm down, I'm not making fun," Opal said. "It's just that I didn't know what kind of a person you were. You were starting to remind me of all those others."

"What 'others'?"

"Those reporters who used to come sniffing around back in the day after Nev got real big. They were always saying they wanted to tell the story, but they didn't give much of a damn about us. Your daddy was just a tidbit of tragedy to them, a bump for Nev to overcome. And after a certain point in the story, I was too."

"What in the world made you think I would ever be like them?"

"Honestly?"

"Jesus Christ, *yes*. Honestly."

"We've been talking awhile, and until right this minute you never pushed back, never challenged me. You let me off so easy; you didn't say boo. It was like you didn't want to be told any different from what you'd already assumed."

"Wait a minute, what kind of a . . . Were you *testing* me?" I thrust my notebook toward her face and jabbed at it. "I was trying," I said, "to be calm. Professional!"

"Well, this isn't completely about the 'professional,' is it? All of it is personal to me. And it should be to you too, to get every drop of this story right.
That's the advantage you have, SarahLena. You care more than anybody else
who could ever try to tell it. Go on—shoot me a question now."

"I don't have a new question! I've asked them already. Same questions
I've been trying to get answered my whole fucking life."

"Maybe so," she said, "but do you feel the same way when you fix your
mouth to ask them? Now that you actually know me, and don't just have me
pinned up to your wall? Look at me now, Sunny, and tell me what you think."

I glared at her. The smooth, hairless skin over her left eye, raised and
demanding, her lips twisted in a smirk. I remembered a moment from our first
official interview, at this same table, in this same garden—buttering her up
about her work on *Things We've Seen*, telling her how I'd just had her photo
from *Vogue* matted and framed for my office. Wondering what I'd said wrong
when her face seemed to freeze. I breathed in the mulch smell of her garden.
Made sure my voice came out slow and even when I opened my mouth again
to speak.

"What do I think?" I repeated. "I think you and Nev are the most arrogant,
self-centered, manipulative people I've ever met."

She closed her eyes for a few seconds, and it seemed as if I'd hurt her.
But she switched it off quick. "Whew," she sighed, "thank God. My ears were
popping up on that pedestal."

———

That day, Opal finally showed me around her house. I had imagined that
its facade was deceiving, that it would open up at some magical crux into
grandness, but it turned out the garden was the most impressive thing about
it. There were two bedrooms not much bigger than the quilted queen-size
beds set inside them, one and a half baths, and an eat-in kitchen with yellow accents—alternating octagonal tiles on the backsplash, the rim of a wall
clock whose hands had frozen, a shiny teakettle on an old gas stove, a glass
bowl of lemons on a small island. I was surprised by how normal, how humble
it was.

"I was lucky to get this house when I did," she said, running a hand across the Formica counter. "Hell of a year, 1993. But I scraped together every cent I still had to buy this place."

"Why did you come out here, anyway? I thought you said New York was your people. Your place."

"Got too cold, in more ways than one." She pulled a joint from the waist-band of her harem pants, turned a knob on the stove, and lit up in the leaping blue flame. I watched as she exhaled smoke up to the ceiling and kicked off her slip-ons, pointing and flexing one naked foot and then the other against the linoleum. I couldn't help staring at those discarded shoes, at the shadows of her feet imprinted inside them, and the way they listed slightly to the left, worn down at the heels. "Come," she said suddenly, grabbing a coffee mug for her ashes.

I followed her into the hallway, the one with the framed mementoes I'd been wanting to study. She clicked on a light so I could see them better. The arrangement was wild but artful, frames of different sizes, shapes, and fin-ishes clustered together, their outer edges almost but not quite lined up. Opal hung back, toking and ashing, while I took my time going down the line. The paint-splattered cover of her second solo album, *Temper* . . . A letter from the Debbie Allen Dance Academy thanking Opal for her contributions . . . A collec-tion of campaign buttons for Shirley Chisholm . . . Wallet-size school portraits of Pearl's children. One of Opal's nephews, snaggletoothed and wearing a gold cross around his neck, had been doodled over with a Sharpie, cartoon horns sprouting from the sides of his high-top fade. ("That's my little devil Isaiah," Opal said in a startling burst of baby talk. "Pearl's youngest. He's thirty-four now. Got kids of his own.") I stopped to study a grainy but glamorous black-and-white portrait of Stephanie St. Clair, the formidable "Queenie" of Harlem,* and to read the French on a 1974 flyer announcing an engagement

---

* Besides ruling a Harlem policy-banking enterprise through the 1920s and mid-1930s, the West Indian–born St. Clair was an activist who invested her wealth back into her community and educated Black people about their civil

by Opal Jewel, *la chanteuse fascinante*. Underneath those words was an illustration that reminded me of a Toulouse-Lautrec sketch, the lines of a woman with twisting lips and hips, a round bare head, gloves up to her elbows.

"I never knew you did shows while you were in Paris," I said.

"They were tiny little things. In a cramped record shop some friends turned into a cabaret. I wrote some original songs there too, but they never saw the light of day." I heard her give a huff of a laugh.

"See, why haven't you ever talked about that?" I said, moving down the hallway. "It's hard for people to ask about what they don't—"

My breath caught in my throat at that moment, as my eyes fell upon a rectangle hanging from the wall slightly above eye level. There was my father, inside the frame.

Handsome, talented Jimmy Curtis, captured in a four-by-six color snapshot turning orange with age . . . I'd never seen this one among my mother's collection. In it Jimmy sits behind his kit with the sticks in his hand, holding them in the traditional grip—one overhand, blurred in motion at the hi-hat; the other underhand and poised at the snare. He stares intently up at something, or someone, as if tensed for a cue. A trail of sweat courses from his thick hair into the horizontal furrows of his brow. He has a goatee. *A goatee?!?*

"That was the last day of the *Polychrome* sessions," Opal said softly behind me. "I had a bad stomachache that morning before I went down to Rivington—I took a swig of Miss Ernestine's Pepto, and I could still taste the chalk of it on my tongue when it was time for me to sing. That ache I felt, it wasn't nothing but dread. I knew something major was ending, something special that I'd had a part in, and all I wanted was to keep it going. I tried to drag out the last song as long as I could, asking the guys to do just one more

---

and legal rights. A mentor to Ellsworth Raymond "Bumpy" Johnson, she was ruthless about her business and her personal affairs; through schemes and sometimes violence, the glamorous and quick-tempered St. Clair hit back at Mafia rivals, dirty cops, and several unwise men who dared try abuse or betray her. Opal Jewel auditioned to play her in the 1997 film *Hoodlum*; Cicely Tyson was ultimately cast in the small role.

take, again and again. When it got to be one, two o'clock in the morning, Jimmy pulled me aside on a break and said, 'Girl . . .' " Here Opal cleared her throat and paused. "He said, 'Girl, what are you up to?' "

OPAL JEWEL:

So I said, "All right, just one more time, I promise," and I took the camera I'd borrowed from Virgil out of my purse and I handed it over to Bob. I asked him to take this picture of Jimmy. It was the only way I could think to hold on to him in this moment, in this phase. I had already made it up in my mind that whatever grasp we had on each other, it wouldn't last outside of this context.

In some ways I was right about that. After we wrapped up the record we'd still get together, but every time there was a little less magic, a little less need. I had started going to the parties and art shows, having my nights out with Virgil, and that wasn't frivolous; that wasn't *nothing*. That was the start of my spirit expanding, the start of me trying to make my way.

Your father was a lot older than me, though, more traditional. He didn't really get what I was doing with my performance style and why I gave it so much energy. In the time when we were working together, he seemed not to mind it so much; maybe it even tickled him some. But later, if he'd get a hotel room for us and I'd agree to meet him after one of my late nights out at Max's or wherever, he'd look at me and say, "Please take that mess off." I'd have to come out my lashes, my wig, the makeup, the wraps and layers, the bangles and anklets before he would want to touch me. It would make a pile in a corner of the bathroom, or if we had more time and the room was nice, with one of those wingback armchairs, I would set my things tidy on the seat. He'd be sweet to me then—he'd ask me to sing something to him, he'd tell me to go ahead and fall asleep in his arms—but I'd still be staring at that pile, all the dead and disconnected pieces of whatever fabulous creation I'd been that day, and without them . . . A terrible shame ate at me. For being with Jimmy in the first place, yeah, but mostly because I felt disloyal to myself. See, I was too young, too convinced I was ugly, to get that maybe Jimmy wanted me without the armor—but that was impossible, understand? My armor *was* me, my best asset. It kept me protected in this world. A world that either hated me or just didn't know what to do with me.

When Jimmy told me he was expecting a baby, I was truly happy, for him and me both. He had to accept the woman I was, whatever wild ways I chose to show up, because he was the one with the pregnant wife—what say could he have in the life I was building? And me, I felt better about what we were doing, because no matter what escapes we enjoyed, I knew that Jimmy would always go home.

What Jimmy and me became, in the absence of pressure, was better than lovers. We became actual *friends*. And that understanding between us freed him up in a beautiful way. Those last few times we saw each other, he could be an open book. He could talk about everything that was going on in his life. His ambitions, his worries . . . Yes, even you. Because no matter what was happening in his career or his marriage, there was no question that man was over the moon about his baby on the way. He loved you already, I swear that he did.

One time he tagged along with me to a record shop in the Village— sometimes we just liked to flip through the covers and ask to sample whatever was new—and while we were browsing he told me about these dreams he was having, dreams about a little girl running around some-place warm and bright. He knew you'd be a girl. He couldn't see your face, just the back of your head—two big ol' Afro puffs. I asked him did he know what your name was and he said, "I was chasing after her and calling her Seraphina, like she was an angel or something. What you think?" I told him I liked the music and rhythm, but it sounded like it belonged to a little Italian girl. And right then we hit the section for female jazz vocalists, all those beautiful old albums by those beau-tiful Black queens, and just like that [*snaps fingers*] Jimmy knew your name. He laughed in that funny way he did, *ssss-ssss-ssss*, and he said, "Yeah, that's right. It's SarahLena." The Sarah for Vaughan, the Lena for Horne. That's how Jimmy and I could inspire each other, just riffing free and easy. Digging through records in the middle of a Wednesday.

That laid-back vibe snapped the night of the showcase. When we were arguing in the wings, I had it in my mind Jimmy was back to bossing me—telling me who to be, how to act. And that roar in the crowd was going back and forth, this intense wave pitching and sloshing inside the walls of that theater, inside my blood, and . . . I don't know, it's hard to describe in a way that a real pretty, put-together girl like you could ever understand, but that noise was drowning out whatever sense Jimmy was trying to drum into me. On one side of the curtain was this man who I loved very deeply, on multiple levels, yes . . . and who I also knew *would* not, *could* not go to the diner with me after the show. But on the other side of that curtain? Past him blocking my way? Out there was a stage and a crowd and a *chance*.

I looked down to where your daddy was holding and rubbing my arms, saying, "Please, baby, don't." And I can't remember exactly the words that I spoke, or if I even spoke words at all. But I must've told him, in some way, that he had to let me go. And for the moment he did. Pushed a puff of air through his teeth—*tuh!* Snatched his hands away from me as if I'd burned them, stuck them up in the air as if to surrender. He looked at me like he was seeing me for the first time in his life, and the last thing he ever said to me was, "You ain't nothing but a child."

And he was right. *When I was a child, I spoke as a child, I understood as a child* . . . The fact that I didn't listen to Jimmy in that moment was tied to a childishness that I grew out of immediately after that night: an illusion that I was unstoppable, that I was supreme, that I could play as white and as male as any of them who wanted a thing and set out to have it. It was an illusion that led me to do something very foolish and then fall on my ass, with a perfect view of your daddy paying the price.

You asked me about that other damn photo? Well, that's why I don't talk about it. I refuse to discuss and critique it how people like

to, because *it is not a piece of art*. There was no intention on our parts
to end up that way, stuck forever in a moment of great distress. And
people think time gives them the right to switch up the lens, to roman-
ticize a thing and make up meaning from it. But no matter how much
time passes, one year or forty-five, it will always hurt to hear people—
brilliant people, people who I like and support!—describe this moment
of that night as *fascinating* or *political* or *inspiring* or *provocative*.

I know what people will say when they read this—"But Opal Jewel,
you and your people *let* us talk that way! It benefited you, you've crafted
your whole image around it!" Well, I can't speak for the motivations of
all the people I've worked with over the years. As for myself: What I
would say to you is yes, I pushed very hard after that night to steer in
those directions—political and provocative and, I hope, inspiring. But
the reason was because I wanted to take my power and my intention
back. I wanted to succeed in being all those admirable things they said
we were, in ways that I knew to be authentic, clear, deliberate—different
from that clueless, impetuous girl getting hauled out the theater.

As for that simple snapshot of Jimmy up there on the wall? I had
Virgil develop the roll after Jimmy died, and I spent so many days before I went back to work forcing myself to look at it. Searing it into my
mind, and onto my heart.

———

Taking deep breaths in my hotel room that night, Opal's stories still haunting
me, I called Jonathan Benjus Jr. Despite the late hour on the East Coast, he
picked up right away, frazzled. Not only was the new issue coming undone,
he said, but now Lizzie Harris was phoning in threats. She'd called him while
I was in flight to Los Angeles, claiming she'd deny *Aural* all future interview
requests with her other clients if I continued to pursue "ridiculous theories"
regarding Nev Charles. "I was totally fucking blindsided," JBJ said. "Sunny,
you've got me twisting in the wind here."

Just a day earlier, I'd been ready to give up—plotting ways to reassure
my boss that everything soon would get fixed. *No worries*, I would have said,

I was planning to back off the Opal & Nev thing anyway. It's turned out to be a headache and a half. And then I would pitch, from a list I'd prepared, other potential book subjects, synergies, wins. *Ooh, maybe we can do a collection of Phil Francisco columns!,* I would have suggested. *Such high ROI, such low-hanging fruit! A perfect gift for your dad or your uncle!* I would have tap-danced a doozy to make sure that by the time he hung up, Jonathan Benjus Jr. was appeased. Comfortable again in his decision to give me the reins.

But hearing my young boss's panic on the other end of the line, I felt strangely calm. "She's bluffing," I said of Lizzie. "Nev's the biggest client she's got left anyway—as soon as Clinton wins next year, she's defecting to an arts council somewhere."

"Okay, but *what happened*? What's going on?"

Now, maybe I should have given JBJ credit. Maybe I should have at least tried to explain—how I'd realized, once Opal finally opened up to me, that if I chose the right direction for the rest of this book, I could resist the typical narratives: that Black people don't sell, that our stories don't appeal to the so-called mainstream. From this point on, I knew, I wanted to curate this story standing on the premise that the lives and legacies of Black men, like my father, cannot be reduced to the awful shit white men do to them. That the voices of Black women like Opal should not be discounted or diminished in deference to those who have hijacked our shine whenever it suits. *We could aim for something higher here*, I would have said to my boss, in this ideal world. *Something much more exciting and unique than another tired rehash of white-dude rock-and-roll lore*. But I remembered the thin line of his lips in that meeting, and so I didn't bother verbalizing my argument like that. I answered his question with the only one I knew really mattered.

"Do you trust me, Jonathan?" I asked. "As the editor you hired?"

"She's saying Nev won't do promotions for the book anymore, she says it's totally off the table!" he squeaked. "I mean, what the fuck did you do to piss her off? Listen, Sunny, if he's not gonna sell the book on his tour, I don't know what the point of continuing—"

"Do you trust me, I'm asking, or do I need to just go on and quit right now?"

"Wait, what? Sunny, I trust you, but—"

"Jonathan: *Do you trust me or no?*"

I can't say what JBJ thought of me then. I'd like to believe his father handed him the company because the kid had solid judgment. Or maybe he was calculating the damage it would do to the brand to have its much-touted first Black editor resign, disgruntled, after scarcely nine months in the job, eager to spill about the undeserving heir who'd kowtowed at the smallest twitch of a PR strong-arm. . . .

Whatever JBJ was thinking, he gave in: "Okay, I'll trust you—for now."

"Good enough," I said. "Then don't worry about Lizzie Harris. I won't be bothering her or her people with any more questions regarding Nev. I realized today I got all I wanted from him already—you'll see."

"See *what*?"

"That his story is pretty much done," I said. "It's all about Opal Jewel now."

chapter sixteen

"SET HER ON THE RIGHTEOUS PATH"

★　★

OPAL JEWEL:

I woke up in a hospital bed, in a white room with my hand bandaged and my foot propped up in a boot. I didn't know what day it was, what time. . . . The first person I saw was Virgil, in a chair watching over me. My stage costume was folded up on the floor next to him, and the sight of it made the whole night come rushing back. He got up, walked over to the bed, and told me to close my eyes. He started picking the sequins off gently, so gently, and he hummed to me while I lay back against those pillows. When he was done he took my hand and kissed it, and when I opened my eyes again I was ready to know. "They killed him," I said, and Virgil gave me the smallest, saddest nod.

I didn't even have a chance to grieve before the pigs stormed in. One in plainclothes and two goons in blue, and they pushed Virgil right out the room. At first I hoped that they would help us, you know, be of some actual service. Because I thought if I had a minute, I could piece together what the thug looked like—I'm talking about the one who did the most violence, the one they never did catch . . . the one me and Nev had seen grab your daddy by his feet and take part in throwing him. I guess I watched way too much TV, thinking they'd sketch the picture and go out and arrest the bad guy. Justice, you know. Ha.

I told those cops everything I could remember. And you know what they said back to me?

You knew what you were doing, didn't you? You meant to make trouble. And your boyfriend, that Black bastard, he was in on it too, wasn't he?

I laid back in that hospital bed and thought, *Ohh.* [*Tapping temple*] *I remember now.* Because it didn't matter that *I* was violently offended, that *I* had been a victim, that as a human being *I* deserved respect. When the fighting started, all I did was try to defend myself and Jimmy, but that didn't matter either. All that mattered was that there was a hospital full of injured and pissed-off white folks, and thousands of dollars in property damage, and a nigger they thought couldn't take a joke.

At that point, Virgil recalled, Opal shut down—"no tears, no fight, such little lip that it was alarming." He took her home to the Harlem brownstone, where he hoped he could bring her back to herself as her ankle healed and the scandal played out. The district attorney, Virgil soon learned in a phone call from an irate Howie Kelly, could very well bow to pressures to pursue charges against Opal over "the stunt" she had pulled. Inciting to riot, Kelly's lawyers had warned, as they sought to protect Rivington Records from potential lawsuits. And yet Opal had little reaction to any of it—to the news of the trouble she faced or to Virgil's attempts to distract her from it.

VIRGIL LAFLEUR:

"No," she would not like to sketch; "no," she would not take calls or sample the tasty plates Miss Ernestine made her; "no," she did not need my help in bathing herself; "no," she did not even care to listen to her favorite the Family Stone, and if I put it on anyway she would curl up on my chaise with a pillow over her head. I believed that part of her convalescence would entail wrapping a bright and bold energy around her, but she would not wear the clothes I selected for her, the brilliant pieces I adjusted to fit over that cumbersome cast they'd put on her foot. She insisted on staying in an old pair of pajamas, and the bottoms dragged pitifully across the floor when she hobbled up occasionally to go to the bathroom. I reached my wits' end; I did not know, at that point, what I could do.

Many blocks downtown, at Bob Hize's doorman-guarded apartment build-ing, Nev was recovering from injuries too — from facial cuts and contusions, a mild concussion, and fractured ribs. Unlike Opal Jewel, he'd had minimal interaction with police, who cleared him of any wrongdoing after a brief in-terview in which he'd stressed the provocation had never been a planned part of his set. Discharged with a prescription for painkillers into Hize's care, Nev, Virgil told me, called Opal several times to see how she was faring. But as with the other friends and acquaintances nosing around, Opal refused to speak with him.

One person, though, would not be so easily deterred.

PEARL WELMONT:

It was dinnertime [in Detroit] and I'd set up the TV trays in front of Walter Cronkite — I'd gone back to the kitchen to get our plates when I heard Mama hollering. I ran back out to the living room and dropped the dinner all over the floor once I saw [The Photo] flashed up on the screen. Mama said, "Girl, is that your sister looking like a banshee on the *CBS Evening News*?"

I got my address book and called the number she'd given us, and eventually her little friend answered. He had a golden voice, mm-hmmmm — he should've been one of those radio announcers, don't you think? And he said to me [*imitating Virgil*], "Oh, I apologize, but she will not take any calls, she simply refuses to talk." I just couldn't be-lieve that — I looked at that phone receiver in my hand, like, *Who in the world . . . ?* I said, "Um, this is her mother and her sister calling? Please remind her we are not strangers off the street." So then he gave her the phone and that stubborn little girl I remember like yesterday said, "Just tell Mama I'm fine," and hung up!

Oh, *noooo*; no ma'am; nuh-uh. Ooh, I tell you, I prayed for the Lord to give me the strength that day. She can *refuse* all she wants to, but I was the family God gave her. Not her fan, not her employee, not her New York City friends. And when Pastor heard me all worked up, he said, "Do what you feel is right, sweetheart." So I dipped into the money we'd been saving for our wedding and I bought myself a ticket on Pan Am. That was the first time I ever flew, can you believe it? Before Opal Jewel herself had even stepped onto a plane!

VIRGIL LAFLEUR:

We'd had trespassers and troublemakers come up our stoop. Vampires and looky-loos, reporters scheming to get their blood . . . Miss Ernestine had broached the idea of reinforcing the front gate with chicken wire, which was a rather drastic and country-Georgia solution, but I was not of the mind that making our home feel *more* like a prison was best for encouraging Mad to be positive. So we simply ignored the knocks and the ringing of the bell, kept the shutters closed and the chains and dead bolts engaged. But before long Miss Ernestine had had enough—she decamped to stay temporarily with one of her sons—and then there was someone new at the door, pounding and yelling and, my God, singing.

PEARL WELMONT, *SINGING*:

"What a friend we have in Jesus / All our sins and griefs to bear . . ."

VIRGIL LAFLEUR, *LEANING IN*:

I went to peer out the peephole, and . . . [*Jerks back*]

She had a beautiful bosom, *très impressionant*, and it deserved the proper décolletage but was covered in the saddest textile. There was nude pantyhose paired with sensible low-heeled shoes . . . *Abominations*, darling. But—*quelle surprise!*—I heard a voice behind me saying something other than "no." I turned around and Mad was up on her crutches, out of her bed, asking me to let the woman, this half sister, inside! Well. *Perhaps there is hope!* I thought. *Perhaps there is deliverance from this funk she is in!*

Alas.

OPAL JEWEL:

[When Pearl showed up in Harlem] I wasn't even surprised. If I ever did have a moment when I believed in God, believed in some force up high giving folks what they need when they need it, this was it. Because what I needed was somebody separate from this mess, somebody who knew that old version of Opal, the poor, funny-looking freak who didn't grow up with any friends and certainly wasn't born to be in the sights of nobody's camera. Even before I could start my new life in New York, Pearl was good for questioning everything about it—the wild people who were gonna be in it, the late hours we kept, that worldliness we were drawn to. . . . But everything in my life needed a thorough questioning at that point, right? Some amount of judgment, passed by somebody who knew me inside out and wasn't halfway impressed or liable to let me wiggle out my place? Didn't I need to be prepared for worse?

And listen: Sister Pearl had traveled hundreds of miles and the length of our childhoods to *let me have it*, honey. She pulled that Bible out her pocketbook almost as soon as she crossed the threshold—she kept it in this pink leather case that zipped up around the sides and had a loop for carrying it around the wrist, and that case is probably the most stylish, luxurious thing she has ever owned. And she asked me to give her a testimony, so I laid it all out for her, plain and clear, right there in Miss Ernestine's parlor. Oh, I told her everything: the lust, the pride, the wrath—just ticked all seven of those bad boys off.

PEARL WELMONT:

You could see the gleam in her eyes while she told me the things she had done, the fornicating and so on, and wasn't nobody but the devil and his minions who put it there. Drove her to whack off the perfectly good hair she had left on her head, tempted her into committing sins with married men . . . Well, it was a struggle, especially with her ankle in that cast, but I managed to get her down on her knees, yes I did!

VIRGIL LAFLEUR:

As you can imagine, this was quite terrifying but also fascinating to witness. *The Exorcist* was still years away, understand.

PEARL WELMONT:

I snatched her in my arms and rocked her back and forth on the floor while she wriggled and cursed, fighting me. I asked her did she want to surrender to Him and she didn't answer me, but that was okay, I was there on a mission to pray over her if she wasn't ready to let go and let God. I asked the Lord that He forgive Mr. Curtis and welcome him into His kingdom, and prayed for the health and strength of Mrs. Curtis, yes, Lord, and for the innocent child she was carrying. [*Smiling*] That little peanut was you, wasn't it? And I asked that He forgive Opal Rochelle Robinson, enter her heart and push out that dirty old devil and make her clean again. *Let this loss not be in vain, Lord; set her on the righteous path.*

VIRGIL LAFLEUR:

And then suddenly Mad just stopped moving, stopped squalling! Went to deadweight! [I thought,] *Mon dieu, what is this? What is next?*

PEARL WELMONT:

She calmed right down, resting there in my arms. What a powerful thing that was, to bring my baby sister some peace. To witness her humbled before God's grace.

For the next two days, Virgil says, Opal burrowed deeper inside herself. She lay on the parlor sofa, mute and with her eyes closed, as Pearl read her Bible verses and told stories from home. Virgil anxiously watched over his friend while answering the constantly ringing phone with "no comment."

VIRGIL LAFLEUR:

Oh, Sister Pearl, with her endless strictures and verses, the creak of her flopping on Miss Ernestine's gorgeous antique rocking chair . . . Much of the time I could tune it out—I have no argument with faith, understand, so long as it helps one to cope with the slings and arrows of life while keeping its hands outside of my pockets—and yet I could not hide my horror when the prattling turned to philosophies to which I knew Mad would naturally be opposed. Oh, you know, *l'habituel*: concepts of turning the other cheek, the meek inheriting the earth, the virtues of a humble existence back in the Midwest . . .

I finally lost my patience with this. I shouted at Mad, "Speak up, speak up! Who *are* you?"

Opal's meekness was A-OK by Howie Kelly, whose lawyers had advised Rivington's executives and artists to keep their mouths shut in the press. But in this silence, a mystery built around the white boy and Black girl in The Photo. Particularly upsetting was a story published the day before my father's funeral and written around a grainy, distant new image of Opal: her standing on crutches at her bedroom window, looking down at a small but noisy crowd that had gathered outside to confront her.

"WEIRD O. TO INJURED FANS: 'EAT DIRT,'"
NEW YORK POST, NOVEMBER 19, 1971

Guess she just doesn't give a rip!

Mere days after her antics led to the bloody chaos of Altamont East,* hairless harpy Opal "Jewel" Robinson seemed to

---

* Media outlets frequently compared what happened at Rivington Showcase to the violence at 1969's Altamont Free Concert. During the Rolling Stones' set at that Northern California disaster, a high and armed 18-year-old Black man named Meredith Hunter was fatally stabbed and stomped by members of the Hells Angels, who'd been vicious in their role as concert security and who, according to some, had been paid in $500 worth of beer.

have not a care in the world as she ignored the pleas of several injured rock fans seeking payback for their medical bills.

On Thursday, the *Post* accompanied five victims of last weekend's violence to the grand Harlem brownstone where Robinson has been hiding out while authorities consider filing charges against her. Standing at a second-floor window and staring down protestors shouting angrily outside, the militant "artist" refused to speak with the victims about the broken bones and black eyes suffered in the wake of her epic temper tantrum.

Cops have already arrested and charged 13 of the biker scumbags involved in the brawl with multiple criminal counts in connection with the riot, in which drummer James "Jimmy" Curtis was fatally beaten and more than 37 others were hospitalized. But they're mum on whether Robinson will have to face the music for egging on the creeps.

To make the charge of inciting to riot stick, prosecutors would have to prove the chrome-domed crooner intended to stir up violence the night she ripped up the Stars and Bars, a symbol of Southern heritage sacred to headlining act the Bond Brothers and their fans. Legal experts say that's a tall order. But one salt-of-the-earth New Yorker we accompanied thinks Robinson deserves more than a slap on the wrist.

"You can't yell 'Fire!' in a crowded theater—well, if you've got an audience full of riled-up hicks, seems to me it's common sense not to mess with their belongings," said Adriana Lucco, a 67-year-old retired schoolteacher from Bayside. She was protesting on behalf of her teenage grandson Dominick, who had orchestra seats to see the Bond Brothers that night and suffered a shattered wrist in the panic to get out. "He's a knucklehead for being in that crowd in the first place," Lucco admitted of 16-year-old Dom, as she began to weep, "but this didn't have to happen! He's only a boy! How's he gonna get into college now, if he can't play baseball?"

And how's this for adding insult to the victims' injuries: *Polychrome*—aka that dud of a record on which Opal Jewel "sings" backup for Neville Charles, aka that guy she rode to infamy—has experienced a spike in sales, according to King Karol. At the chain's main location on 42nd Street and 6th Avenue, mere blocks away from the Smythe Theater, we're told that the record managed to sell only two copies before Saturday night's riot. Now it's out of stock.

"You just missed some kids looking for it," said Angel Boriquez, an employee who plays customer requests inside the store. "They can't ever remember the name of it, though. They just say, 'What's that record with the crazy black chick and the white guy? Yeah, I gotta hear *that*.'"

In Harlem, Virgil barely had the time or energy to get fully outraged about the inflammatory Post *piece. The good news was that the article had popped Opal out of her stoic silence. The bad: She was now amenable to a suggestion from Howie Kelly that Virgil found unthinkable.*

VIRGIL LAFLEUR:

Howie called us with his attorneys on the line and made an . . . *insinuation* that we should attend James's memorial service the next morning. He said to me that it could be an appropriate place for all of us, including Mad, to be seen by others as quietly paying respects. "Remorseful, but not liable"—that was how one of the lawyers phrased it.

HOWIE KELLY:

What's crazy about that? She was a representative of my label! She rolled up to my good name, and they had her in the paper looking like she didn't care one little bit! And to my mind, if she was sincerely sorry about Jimmy, this was her chance to show it.

VIRGIL LAFLEUR:

A *mistress* attending the *funeral*? How tacky. How *gauche*.

Perhaps it is true your mother was unaware; perhaps those mourn-ers far outside of our circle were still ignorant, but these possibilities were beside the point. Enough of us *did* know the nature of Mad's re-lationship with James, and Mad *herself* knew. Is that not enough reason to show common sense and a degree of grace? To find a different, more private way to grieve?

PEARL WELMONT:

She hadn't had much to say for days, so when she spoke up to tell me she wanted to go to the funeral I took that as a sign of God at work. To my knowledge, that was the first time she'd been moved to step inside a church since Uncle Bill's in Birmingham. I wasn't going to discourage that. Embarrassed, ashamed? . . . Why should I have been? We teach forgiveness in our faith. I would have been proud to sit beside my sister at that service, to show her she was always welcome in a house of the Lord with a cleansed and penitent heart.

On the morning of November 20, 1971, Pearl helped Opal bathe and dress, picking a simple black shift from her own suitcase and cinching it with safety pins where the fit bulged too large. She told Opal she was proud of her, and that she hoped they could fly home to Detroit together once God answered their prayers and cleared Opal of any legal mess. Perhaps Opal could take college courses, Pearl suggested, and get a salaried job back at Michigan Bell.

In the parlor, Virgil sat aghast. For hours he had tried to change Opal's mind about attending Jimmy's funeral, and yet Opal had remained steely, seemingly resigned. He'd cooked up one last-ditch plan to avert what he viewed as a looming disaster, and now, dressed in a suit as if to accompany the sisters to the service, he hoped that it would work.

VIRGIL LAFLEUR:

The church was walking distance from Miss Ernestine's, but with Mad on crutches I argued she would need transportation. I said to this stepsister, "Why don't you walk ahead of us a little early?" The idea was that she would reserve us seats in the rear of the sanctuary so there would not be some regrettable scene when we arrived, and I would do the heavy lifting of getting Mad down the steps and into the taxi. And the stepsister was amenable, I suppose, because I'd had the wisdom and fortitude to hold my tongue when she appointed herself Mad's stylist for the day.

So on she tromped, and when I bundled Mad into a taxi and slipped in after, I simply gave the driver Robert Hize's address.

What I'd had to do, you see, was put myself in Mad's shoes—get the perspective, if you will, from the stage and those towering platform stilts. Once I did that, I realized Mad was likely feeling misunderstood. This stepsister and I were bickering over what Mad should do, how she should be, and yet neither of us had experienced the horror quite the same way, neither of us had the prime view to brutality—but Pup had. Pup had been right there with her, and yet she would not speak to him. I thought, *If only I could cajole them together, if only I could make her see she could have someone to talk to, to share the grief with.* Of course I had no idea what Pup might *say* once we arrived, and yet anything was worth a try.

Oh yes, she shot me a quizzical look. But she did not put up a fight. Just sat back and closed her eyes. [*Nodding*] She knew it was the necessary thing.

OPAL JEWEL:

It sounds crazy that I would even think about stepping foot inside that service. But I think . . . I think what I wanted to do was express that I was sorry to the people who deserved my apology. Jimmy and his wife and his family, first—that's partly what the funeral was about for me, although looking back on it now I can understand it was selfish. A service

is a public thing, and my being there might have caused more pain to the
people who had dibs on loving Jimmy in that way. Out in public, I mean.
But then I needed to say sorry to Nev as well, for dragging him into a
mess he hadn't asked to be a part of.

BOB HIZE:

Nev didn't have the appropriate clothes, so I let him borrow one of my
dark suits. The jacket and pants were too short—he looked like a ghoul,
pale, with the right side of his face still scabbed and swollen, his socks
and shirt cuffs exposed. He hadn't been outside for days, so when we
opened the door of the building, the sunlight was so bright I think he
actually hissed. We'd got a town car to drive us uptown to the church,
but when we got outside there was a taxi idling out front. I said, "Is that
Opal?"

He went running up to her like an overexcited puppy. Claudia said,
"Nev, careful, your ribs!"—because he had been complaining about the
physical pain he was in, driving her mad asking her to fetch this and
fetch that while he obsessed over the papers and gnawed at the skin
around his fingernails. We had been concerned about Nev's state—
perhaps not as worried as we ought to have been, it turns out, especially
when it came to those pills he was taking—but then, one look at Opal
and he seemed to feel miraculously better.

OPAL JEWEL:

I hadn't seen Nev since the night I did what I did, and I didn't think I was
ready to face him yet—I'd been punishing myself, shutting down from
the people who wanted to care about me. When he came bouncing up to
the cab, I assumed it was to bless me out. I mean, he *looked* furious—his
whole face was swollen, beat to hell—and I rolled down my window so I
could get it good. But then he stuck that busted face through my window
and grinned that way he does. He looked so nutty I had to laugh; I had to
rub his stupid red head. I think that was the first time I'd laughed since
Virgil and I were in that bathroom backstage at the Smythe.

He asked me if I was really going to the service. By this time I'd figured what Virgil was doing and I was too tired to fight him, so I said, "Well, I guess not." And Nev said, "Then why are your clothes so sad? Who's dressed you?"—because Pearl had put me in the old bouffant wig and a plain dress with no kind of shape.

I told him, "I'm not sure I can be Opal Jewel anymore."

And Nev said, "But surely you've seen the papers. I don't think we have much of a choice." And he climbed right inside that cab on the other side of me [while the Hizes left separately for the funeral].

So there I was, riding between the two friends I had left in the world, and I kept thinking about this "we" that Nev had used. I was surprised, and touched, I guess, that after everything he still considered the thing to be a "we," as in "we" would ride out this storm, whichever way it would turn, together. Partners. He wasn't blaming me for anything, or making one noise about wanting to cut me loose. Wasn't even looking back to the couldas and shouldas. And I thought to myself, *Well, then—is this it?*

Because crazy enough, mean as I could be to Pearl, my sister had made an impact on me that first night she came. Something she'd said when she had me down on my knees, something about a "righteous path." Rang a tiny bell in that fog I was in, and I thought maybe meditating on what that path was and then following it was the way I could . . . turn my worst flaws into something shining and good. Of course, I didn't interpret those words the way Pearl wanted me to—it's not in me to be anybody's convert, and I couldn't see a loving God in any of this—but maybe she'd planted a seed, you know? To explore what it meant to be righteous by my own definition. If I could have my style of righteousness plus half of my sister's conviction to give me the courage, I thought, I might do all right.

PEARL WELMONT:

I can tell you it was a beautiful service. So many interesting people! I wish I could have told my sister she didn't need to be anxious about anybody studying her, because there were plenty of other folks to look at. People from the community, Black leaders . . . I didn't know it at the time, I wasn't one to be up on the hip new things, but they tell me Mr. Herbie Hancock was there! Wasn't that nice, for him to come? And ooh, you wanna talk about a talented band! Whoever it was that was up there playing [John Squine and Solomon Krebble, along with other studio musicians with whom Jimmy had worked], they did a powerful job sending your father home. I wouldn't have thought you could take that many liberties with "Amazing Grace," but oh, those guys were going a good long time! Somebody caught the ghost that morning!

Meanwhile, Virgil paid the taxi driver to circle Mount Morris Park, and promised the hack a hefty tip "for the service of minding his own business." In the back seat with Opal between them, with the windows rolled up to discourage gawkers, Virgil and Nev each took one of her hands as she wept.

VIRGIL LAFLEUR:

She kept repeating that she was sorry, crying those words louder and louder. . . . I thought at some point Pup might burst into tears himself, hearing her howl in that way; he kept telling her to stop, that he understood, he knew. Heterosexual males can be so uncomfortable with emotion, *non*? But this was the first time Mad had truly unleashed, and it seemed to me it was necessary. It meant her voice was growing strong again, that something inside her had shifted toward the better. So I said, "Let her, Pup. Just let her."

EDITOR'S NOTE

Opal's wanton, unruly, hot-blooded howl . . . It first arrested my attention when I was fourteen years old and voraciously curious about most things—among them, what small rebellions I might pull off under my mother's watchful eye.

If I knew not much else about Corinne Dawes Curtis that year, I understood that when it came to my formal education, my mother would allow some measure of independence. And so one Saturday, I lied to her that I had an AP History project to complete ("worth *half* of my *final grade!*" I'd shrieked). Without further questioning, she dropped me off at the main branch of the Philadelphia public library and said she'd be back in three hours. There, instead of researching the various aspects of the New Deal, I began my first dive into subjects verboten in her household: every plot and character connected to my father's last days.

Though the music section beckoned like some dark and tempting force, I breezed past it at first. To my mind, serious research required diligent reading. I sat at the clanking microfilm monster, attempting to comprehend the outcomes of various court dates connected to my father's fatal beating. Among the facts I pieced together, from articles dated alarmingly close to my DOB: Not one of the Danger Fiends caught trying to flee the Smythe after beating in Jimmy's head got longer than six months' time (all of them cut deals with the district attorney, pleading no contest to charges of rioting plus assault and battery). Beau Bond was not charged at all, because witnesses could not agree whether he was actually threatening anybody, and because Jimmy had been the one to throw the first punch. Rivington Records got off the hook too, after the *New York Times* investigated breaches of the event contract and serious security gaps at the Smythe (whose owners ended up filing for bankruptcy—no money to be had, they claimed).

As for that "bald-headed bitch" my sore-loser cousin had once taunted me about: Following the incendiary *New York Post* story, Opal Jewel found a larger base of support in the activist and artist communities—including a cadre of young Black men in turtlenecks, leather jackets, and berets, taking positions at the top of Miss Ernestine's stoop. The young Panthers had been deployed for their revolutionary sister Opal's protection, and to disabuse outsiders of the notion that they could raise hell in Harlem and not be met with community response. They stood guard for Opal too on the December day she briefly came out onto the stoop, balancing on her crutches and flanked by her odd lot—Virgil, Nev, a newly returned Ernestine Grimes, and a soon-to-depart Pearl Robinson—to make her first public statement to the handful of persistent protesters and rock-tossers who'd continued trying to provoke her. "For those of you threatening me and my family: Let me say that nobody up here is scared of you all," she'd said, as quoted by the *Amsterdam News*. "Not one sissy, not one limey, not one old biddy or holy roller, and certainly not this 'hairless harpy.' So you can pick up your trash, go on back to your homes, and have yourselves a merry Christmas." I never found any newspaper stories reporting on the particulars of how Opal finally dodged the DA's sights (though it's since been hinted to me that then–New York City mayor John Lindsay used his influence, due to his general terror of how trouble with the Harlem Negroes might tank his White House dreams). But I did discover another story in the *Village Voice*, which was apparently so amused and enchanted by Opal's flippant statement that it picked up the quote as part of a write-around profile. It was titled "Black Magic Woman" and featured anecdotes from downtown scenesters gushing over Opal's style, her wit, her strange sex appeal—an appeal that attracted, someone indiscreet had blabbed to the reporter, the "unlucky bastard" killed at the concert.

Absorbing all this, just a girl at that microfilm machine, I gasped. My beautiful, dignified mother so publicly humiliated. . . No wonder she had been stony over the years whenever I asked her to tell me about my father beyond the handful of rosier myths she deemed appropriate; no wonder my uncle David, her usually gregarious older brother, furiously chewed on his toothpick when I came to him with my questions. Jimmy and his little rock-and-roll friends had been grade-A assholes.

There was one more story in the archives, though, that gave me hope Jimmy was more than that. In his interview with *DownBeat*, which I quote in earlier sections of this book, he came across as funny and loose and ahead of his time, discussing his musical style and philosophies. This was the closest I'd ever come to my father's voice, its syntax Southern and profane; I even thought I could hear, for the first time in my life, that mythical hiss between the teeth. Yes, he had acted a philandering fool when it came to his wife, but was that the summation of his existence? What about the talent and swagger that had drawn my mother to a man like him in the first place*—didn't those things deserve celebration? Shouldn't his name be remembered, his work immortalized? Shouldn't someone have paid a steeper price for killing him?

This is where Opal & Nev called to me.

It's a miracle their albums were even in the library's collection, among the Appalachian folk songs and orchestral arrangements of the Beatles' greatest hits, and perhaps that's a testament to the tastes of the bespectacled young woman who managed the collection and wore an APARTHEID NO! button on her distressed-denim jacket. But here they were, these taboo artifacts—not jazz, not R&B, not anything as boxable as that—and a thrill raced up my back to finally have them in my hands. I'd heard Nev Charles's pop songs before, of course—1986 was a huge year for him, with his fifth solo album, the top-ten duet with Annie Lennox, and the kickoff of his third world tour—and I'd caught

---

* Among the rare stories my mother will share about her opposites-attract romance with Jimmy is the one about the night they met, in line at a corner store in Philly (where he was playing a show). At the register he bought her a box of Sugar Babies and told her she was so much sweeter. He whistled "I'm Your Puppet" as he peacocked out the door with her telephone number stuffed down one back pocket. In the other, my mother likes to remember, he carried a single maraca.

snippets of Opal's speaking voice when she'd showed up on television for whatever disaster she was promoting. But I'd never heard these full albums before, never been able to grasp the cardboard of *Polychrome* and trace the letters of my father's name printed in the credits. For at least two weeks, I listened to the A and B sides every day, parked at the record player with the giant headphones perched carefully atop my head so as not to muss my curls in a way my mother would notice. Yes, I wore out that record and admired it too, patting my palms on my thighs in time with my father's rhythms, causing the librarian to smirk at me when I got to the drum fill on "Chalk White."

Wow, I thought. *My dad did this.*

Still, that album didn't hit me with the same force as *Things We've Seen*, the double LP that the label rushed out not long after the showcase. Its front cover featuring their simpler post-riot stage name, "Opal & Nev,"* and the tops of their heads poking up from the bottom—on the left, her bare scalp oiled and glistening; on the right, his hair variegated in hues of red that intensified toward the roots, stiffened with product to mimic a flame. Between them, her raised fist was like an alien baby bursting into frame. This album had more screech, less bottom, and, aside from a simple dedication ("For James Curtis III") in small blue script on the opposite cover, not one hint of my dad. I should not have loved it for exactly those reasons; inexplicably, shamefully, I did.

It's far from a perfect album; I doubt it would crack the top one thousand of most colleagues' personal favorites, and, sales-wise, every Nev Charles solo album afterward annihilates it. But the music, lyrics, and vocals on enough of its songs expressed a passion and a fury, a focus amid the discord, a give-zero-fucks freak-flag bravado that felt, in some ways, like a tribute. Hearing it

---

* Their individual contracts were merged into one broad agreement upon their 1972 re-up with Rivington. New PR exec Lizzie Harris advised the name change, needing less of a mouthful to take to market. On radio and onstage from here on out, Opal's name would always come first. But behind the scenes, the songwriting credits—which would be the most lucrative, in the long run— still belonged to Neville Charles alone.

for the first time triggered what I can only describe as a fear response inside my body. I'm talking heart racing, palms sweating, tiny hairs on the back of my neck doing the wave. *You gon' fight,* this bald-headed bitch and her people seemed to be asking me, daring me, *or you the kind that's partial to flight?* I'd feel similar thrills years later, through spins of N.W.A and Nirvana, through piercings and zip lines and experiments with everything from sex to Thai chili peppers, but there's nothing like the first time you take on a thing that scares the shit out of you and discover the intensity turns you all the way on.

Pandora's box; the slippery slope; you know, my fellow fans, how it can be.

"Did you know you can check the records out?" the anti-apartheid librarian asked me one day, and even though I didn't have my own record player I smuggled home *Things We've Seen* anyway, just to have it physically near me, to be able to reach underneath my bed, past the hanging edge of my comforter, and feel it lying there. I knew every strum and yelp by heart, scribbled lyrics from memory in the pages of my school notebooks among the formulas and equations. Started mixing in original compositions too: preachy poems with metaphors about shepherds and sheep, fantasies about a band of unpopular kids taking over the headmaster's office, a not-half-bad takedown of *Heart of Darkness*. I never showed these to anyone. Certainly not to my mother, whom I feared would burn my notebooks as contraband and send me away to some Bible camp; not even to my only friends at Haviland Day School, two goth girls with whom I'd forged a shy bond based on our mutual outsider status. Still, the ideas and passions of the artist I most admired took root inside me. She was building me fearless and strong, intellectual, creative . . . in other words, into the kind of badass chick my father would love. I didn't know back then that she was my benefactor on this road of self-discovery. And yet, as she'd been for many a weird Black girl before and after, Opal Jewel was already my idol.

chapter seventeen

"TAKE ALL THAT
JUNK AND USE IT"

★ ★

**PARTIAL TRANSCRIPT OF LIZZIE HARRIS* SPEAKING
AT THE 2003 NEW YORKER FESTIVAL, ABOUT HOW
OPAL & NEV BECAME HER FIRST MUSIC-BIZ CLIENTS:**

I mean, weren't they just so great-looking? I know that sounds
crazy in the context, but I looked at Marion's picture of the two
of them and thought, *Wow, how in the world did* this *happen?*

---

* Elizabeth "Lizzie" Harris started her career working in Hollywood, but in 1972
she fast-tracked by moving to New York and exploring unique opportunities
in music. In previous interviews she has said that she spotted "something cin-
ematic" in Opal & Nev, and that, like Bob Hize before her, she approached
Howie Kelly at a do-or-die moment with a risky idea to realign and rebuild
his roster. Her proposal involved a personal cash investment in the label (part
of an inheritance from her late father, a movie studio exec), and after success-
fully steering Rivington through its post-riot crisis, Harris served as the label's
executive vice president of marketing and promotions for twenty-three years.
When Kelly named his son Mark as his successor in 1995, Harris left Rivington Records and launched an independent firm, L. Harris & Associates, which
today specializes in celebrity PR and management and counts Nev Charles as
a banner client. She declined to be formally interviewed for this book.

Opal was dark dark dark and Nev was pale pale pale, and they were being physical with each other in a way that felt intimate, sorta taboo and sexy and dangerous, you know? Like rock and roll is supposed to be. Actually, you know what that picture always reminds me of? Those Benetton ads they were doing in the eighties, where they find all these weird and tribal-looking people who live on completely different landmasses [*audience murmurs in recognition*]—you know, one's from Africa and the other's from Iceland, and then they stick them together in the shot. Or I guess it's more accurate to say the Benetton ads reminded me of that picture. Very influential. First thing I ever saw that was like it.

And then as a sidebar [in the December 1971 "The Year in Pictures" issue of *Life*], the magazine ran a capsule review of *Polychrome*, which was remarkable for the fact that the album had been out for over a year already. But the critic was gushing, talking about its urgency, its uniqueness, his songwriting, her spirit. . . . It was like this total package sitting in their laps, except there was no quote from either of them anywhere, no news about the next project. And I asked myself, "What are they *doing*? This is a gift!"

Long story short: I drafted this wild proposal to come and take over [Rivington Records'] public relations and clean up the mess they had going. I sent it via certified mail from "L. Harris," and I think they assumed I was a man, because of the look on these guys' faces when I showed up at the label, surprise surprise. [*Audience laughter*] But at that point they were on the brink of total ruin and didn't have much to lose—nobody wanted to touch them! The first advice I gave, after telling them to get Opal & Nev in the studio ASAP to make a new record, was "Drop the Bond Brothers," because they were assholes who I thought would drag everybody down and only get into worse trouble later on—I'd heard some disgusting stories having to do with a couple of them demeaning women. They said, "Drop the Bonds, are you crazy?" I told them, "Do that for me, and in three weeks I'll get Opal & Nev on national TV for you."

And three weeks later, right on time, I got them booked on *Cavett*. [*Smiling*]

PARTIAL TRANSCRIPT FROM OPAL & NEV'S FIRST TELEVSION INTERVIEW, *THE DICK CAVETT SHOW*, APRIL 4, 1972, FOLLOWING THEIR DEBUT PERFORMANCE OF "WHO'S THE NIGGER NOW?":*

Dick Cavett, *to Opal, motioning toward the thickly padded hips and posterior underneath her tight red dress:* Have you heard my seats are that uncomfortable?

[*Titters from the audience*]

Opal Jewel: Oh, I just make it a point to be comfortable wherever I go. I call my outfits my armor. This one is my Black woman power suit. You dig it?

Cavett: Well, ahh . . . I'd say the two of you make an eye-catching pair. [*Waving his hand over Opal's wig*] Look at these spikes.

Nev: I'd say we've got extraordinarily good imaginations.

Cavett: And on the note of imagination, the new song you just played for us, the song from this new record . . . [*Holding up the cover of* Things We've Seen] I'm sure the folks at home, ah, will be talking about it.

Nev: Uh-oh, oh no, prepare the space rockets!

---

* For the live performance on Cavett's show, with "nigger" uncensored but the lyric "fuck him up" replaced with "mess him up," Opal Jewel pulls out two red bandannas from her stuffed bra and ties them around Nev Charles's eyes and mouth as he plays the guitar. While he is blindfolded and gagged, Opal pushes Nev into a chair, writhes and stomps behind him, and at various points enacts upon his body a series of caresses, slaps, and hair tugs.

Opal, s*miling:* What about the song would you like to discuss?

Cavett: I just wonder, ah, if people might regard it as violent. They might say that word you use is offensive.

Nev: The character in the song, the racist man is offensive. He's a villain who says it first, and then our heroine gets her revenge and she says it back to him and flips the tables, you see?

Opal, *to Nev:* You're not explaining this right. [*Audience laughs*]

Nev: What? All right, then, you have a go.

Opal: That word does have an offensive history. And yet many evil-hearted people in this country still use it all the time. It was used against a Black American named James Curtis the Third on the night of Rivington Showcase. It was used against us too, just a few minutes before that woman took our picture.

Cavett: I see. Someone called you that, and someone called Nev that as well?

Nev: I was trying to help her out, trying to protect her from being injured, and I'm told that as they assaulted me they called me a very nasty name.

Cavett: You were told?

Nev: I go a bit fuzzy in the head. Tends to be my natural state. [*Audience laughs*]

Opal: He was called a nigger lover, Dick, which I guess was supposed to make me the nigger. And they called our drummer a nigger and beat him to death, as I assume you've read about by now.

Cavett: How do you feel saying that word, Opal? It seems to just roll off your tongue.

Opal: Well, of course I have a problem with the word *nigger*, depending on the context. If you say it or he [*pointing to Nev*] says it, that's you trying to put me in my place, trying to remind me you're on top and I'm on the bottom. It's menacing,

it's a weapon. When I say it, that's just me interpreting and mir-
roring back what's already been spat on me without my say-so.
It's a word that the people in power here dump on people like
me, but they don't realize that sometimes people like me take
all that junk and use it.

Nev: We wanted to create a character who is assumed to be
powerless, but is shown to be very powerful indeed as the song
goes on.

Cavett: Do you think that violence makes someone powerful?

Opal: Of course it does.

Unknown audience member, off camera: Outrageous!

Cavett: Thank you, sir, let's hear them speak.

Opal: Get real—if violence didn't lead to power, there
would be no wars. We'd just be loving each other up. But we
don't do that, do we? We bomb villages full of children across
the world, and—

Nev: In fact, you might've heard a song from our first album
about that. We hope to come back and play it for you sometime
soon, it's—

[*Crosstalk*]

Opal: —use violent words as a way to intimidate other peoples.

Cavett: What would you say to those who argue you're actively advocating for violence in this song? That this is a "kill
whitey" message that goes against the doctrine of Dr. King?

Opal: Dick, I certainly don't have to tell you how my
brother Martin met his end.

Jane Fonda, from her spot down the couch: What I find interesting is that we're focusing now on the violence that's done
against the man in the song. We're not talking at all about the
violence he commits against the woman in the first place, the
casual and awful violence he commits against her body.

Opal: Ain't that the truth, Jane? And the other thing we

need to address is that this is, specifically, a *Black* woman. Historically, the Black woman has been subject to this kind of violence because to a lot of very foolish people in this country, there's nothing lower than us. But guess what? Don't underestimate our spirit, baby, because we'll surprise you every time. [*Winks*]

GLORIA STEINEM, FEMINIST ORGANIZER AND JOURNALIST:

I'd watched Jane's interview earlier in the show and had snapped off the TV, but then I got a call from my friend [the lawyer and Black feminist] Flo Kennedy, and she said, "Are you seeing what I'm seeing on *Cavett*?" When I turned it back on, there was Opal Jewel, blasting through this revenge fantasy against the racist who'd raped this heroine she embodied. It was extraordinary. Not because the content itself was shocking to me—we know that every two minutes a woman is assaulted in this country, and we know that racism still exists—but because we weren't seeing that familiar trope of the damsel in distress. Charles Bronson or Clint Eastwood wasn't going out to avenge this woman. She has agency, she handles herself, and that message was incredibly provocative.

At the time the team and I had just launched *Ms.*, and the next morning I called to arrange an interview with Opal for our next issue. That ended up being a little profile, the first time we worked with her.

**QUENTIN TARANTINO, IN A 2012 PRESS JUNKET
INTERVIEW PROMOTING *DJANGO UNCHAINED*:**

"Who's the Nigger Now?"—how great was that record? Yeah, I watched that clip on YouTube a lot while writing this movie. I mean, you listen to the song alone and you get a full revenge opus, starring a badass vigilante Black chick. You can see it, right? Like, a young, sexy Pam Grier type pulling out the knife all gangsta? "Who's the nigger now, bitch?" [*Making stabbing motions*] And she guts him like a fish right on top of her . . . total bloody mayhem. At one point I was hoping to work the song into the soundtrack, maybe for one of the Broomhilda scenes, but sonically it didn't mesh with the rest of the tunes. Still, *incredible* song.

JANELLE MONÁE, SINGER AND ACTRESS:

I loved the way she played with character, with those alter egos who seemed to take over her body when she was onstage. The older I get and the more I try to evolve as an artist, the more I appreciate what it must have taken emotionally, especially back in those days, for her to channel her anger and pain. And then she'd sit on the couch and do the interview and be cool and smart as hell. That's that Black girl magic right there.

QUESTLOVE, DRUMMER, DJ, ENTREPRENEUR:

In my DJ sets I used to do this thing where I'd go back and forth between James Brown's scream on "The Payback" and Opal Jewel's on "Who's the Nigger Now?" I thought I was pretty clever till the dance floor let me know I was fucking up the vibe. [*Laughs*] No disrespect to Opal, I love her—that song is just not an easy groove.

HENRY ROLLINS, PUNK LEGEND, ACTOR, AUTHOR, ACTIVIST:

Keep in mind that when The Cavett Song happened we were still a while away from the Sex Pistols, the Ramones, my band . . . and here was this revolutionary Black woman screaming her face off and rocking spikes. So in my opinion, anyone who doesn't acknowledge Opal Jewel as a pioneer of punk is a racist and a sexist, and they can do me the favor of fucking right off.

TOM MORELLO, GUITARIST,
RAGE AGAINST THE MACHINE, AUDIOSLAVE:

I was seven years old and up past my bedtime watching Opal & Nev perform on TV, and I had my nose pressed up to the screen even though they were scaring the shit out of me. [*Laughs*] I mean that in the best possible way—in the way something can both excite you and intimidate you and you can't say why because you're only a kid and you don't know what the grown-ups are talking about; you only know that you've never seen or felt anything like it before. Opal was an incredible performer— she scorched my hair completely off. But not for nothing, so was Nev.

Next time you watch it, check out his hands—how easy he is with the guitar the entire time she's losing her mind.

That appearance on Cavett *popped Opal & Nev out of the limited frame of Marion Jacobie's photograph and into three complicated dimensions. When it was released one week later,* Things We've Seen *sold better than even Lizzie Harris had likely expected, especially considering its standout song could not be played on radio ("Better Living on Mercury," featuring Nev's lead vocal, and "Sister Stacked,"* featuring Opal's, were sent as singles instead). The album entered the middle portion of the* Billboard *200 chart and crept slowly up, up, up over the next four weeks, peaking at No. 45 (between Alice Cooper's* Killer *and the self-titled comedy debut by Cheech & Chong). Polychrome got another residual sales boost too, signaling that Opal & Nev had potential to be more than just a fifteen-minute curiosity.*

OPAL JEWEL:

I was never driven by money, but there were some nice moments having to do with it. Got my mama that house in the suburbs she wanted. And Pearl, she was thoroughly pissed about "Sister Stacked," but she wasn't too mad at the dough—I paid for her wedding and the honeymoon too.

This was also around the time I started investing in you. [*On how that arrangement came to be*] Your mama didn't talk to you about that, huh? Well, there's not much to tell, at least on my end. After I got my first big check, I mailed a cut over to Jimmy's old place, along with a handwritten note to Corinne saying, *If you ever need anything, don't hesitate.* I thought she'd rip up the damn check; she actually didn't cash it for months. Then when she finally did, I got a letter back. One typewritten

---

* In keeping with many of the songs on *Things We've Seen*, including "Who's the Nigger Now?," the lyrics to "Sister Stacked" were written by Nev Charles but based on an idea by Opal Jewel. "Sister Stacked" told the story of a big-chested Sunday school teacher led astray by her church's minister.

sentence to say she was taking you to Philly, with the new address underneath. So I sent a fresh check there—I figured she could use help with
the moving expenses. I sent her more every once in a while. That went
on for a few years, and then one day I got a thick envelope with a bunch
of brochures from different private schools. I didn't understand till I saw
they had tuition schedules your mother had taken the time to highlight.
I thought, *Oh, okay, I guess we doing* this *now.* [*Laughs*] But never, *ever*
did your mother ask me directly for money. You know how she is. Real
classy like that.

*With his first taste of success, Nev finally moved out of the Hizes' apartment
in the summer of 1972. He rented a bright blue house in the West Village and
made one of the bedrooms a studio where he and Opal could write and rehearse. It wasn't long, Virgil recalled, before Opal's effects slowly began to mi-
grate downtown.*

**VIRGIL LAFLEUR, *SHOWING ME A PHOTO HE TOOK OF HIS FRIENDS
IN THE KITCHEN OF THE WEST VILLAGE HOUSE, OPAL HOLDING
A JOINT TO NEV'S MOUTH, HER FINGERS GRAZING HIS LIPS:***

They were always finding excuses to touch. Mad has accused me of
being a hopeless romantic, and perhaps there is truth to that. But there
is a reason that I brought her to him, after the sadness with your papa.
They had a special alliance, if you will. And it is my belief that in the best
times they delighted each other, and lifted each other up.

OPAL JEWEL:

I had more space in the West Village house than at Miss Ernestine's. It
was easy to spread out, because neither of us had much furniture. We
had a television and one of those rattan circle chairs with the big orange
pillow inside. We had stacked-up throw pillows in the bedrooms. And
I had a whole bathroom to myself, where I could set up my makeup
palettes and cosmetics however I wanted them. Sometimes if we were
taking a break from working, we'd cook dinner—I had to get creative

because we had never shopped for anything like a colander; we had one big pot. When I made my macaroni and cheese I'd have to drain the noodles by holding the pot lid so the water came out slow and clean when I tipped it over. I never let Nev do that part because he didn't have any patience, he'd be tipping the thing too fast and the noodles would fall out into the sink.

When the weather turned colder we'd sit in that one rattan chair together, wrapped up in a blanket I'd brought from uptown, and we'd eat and drink wine and just talk. People always used to comment on how different the two of us were, but a lot of that was optics. Me and Nev had real soul connections—funny stories about growing up, the hilarious things you do to make your way through this world as an outsider. But behind that there was some heaviness too. Me never knowing my daddy, him losing his mother like he did . . . Anyway, what I'm saying is we both had some loneliness, some confusion, some dark feelings we were working out at the time. Sometimes we worked that stuff out in healthy ways—in the performance, in rehearsals, in talking about the future— and sometimes we looked for relief in places that weren't so healthy. Ah, hell, I'm not talking about *that*. What I mean is, I'd started to notice him gobbling those painkillers, and me, well, I probably overindulged in the things that made *me* feel better—the weed and the wine, the pieces for my wardrobe. With those things and each other, I guess, we were trying to hang on through the craziest ride.

Soon Opal & Nev could pack the same New York City rock clubs that had once turned them away. Their shows—part rock concert, part performance art— attracted everyone from Lou Reed to Lauren Hutton, Candy Darling to Carlos Santana. They also drew a cult of flamboyant unknowns who identified with something in the duo's music, and would come to call themselves "Mercurials."*

---

* After the *Things We've Seen* song "Better Living on Mercury," about two misfits blasting off into outer space.

FROM "THE OPAL & NEV EXPERIENCE,"
AURAL, DECEMBER 1972
By Scott Dorchester

Looking like a holiday gift in a red dress with gold buttons
down the bodice, Opal Jewel first enters the stage hopping on a
pogo stick, barefoot. Her pageboy wig and the flouncy skirt of
her dress catch the air with every jump, expanding and collapsing in what seems like slow motion. She bounces over wires and
around amps, matching the drummer's relentless rhythm. Once
she reaches the mic stand at the center of the stage, she kicks
away the pogo stick so that it flies behind her. In an astonishing
bit of choreography timed to a dramatic pause in the music, Nev
manages to catch it.

"Who's ready?" she shouts into the mic, and launches into
the staccato phrasing of "Red-Handed," backed by Nev's wailing guitar. *I'm not a girl that can be caught / I'm not the girl who
can be bought.* . . . The spotlight follows her as she runs and
jumps and vamps, and when she reaches Nev she illuminates
his corner of the stage momentarily. He leans toward her and
winks, already sweating through his gold slim-cut suit, and then
she's off again.

For fifty blistering minutes, Opal & Nev wear this audience out. They wear *me* out, anyway. Yes, there are welcome
breaks from the bombast, when the music slows into something
more melodic and the spotlight hits Nev. It's just enough time
for Opal to catch her breath and for Nev to introduce snippets
of new songs it seems he's still working out, like a comedian
nervously testing new material—but in almost no time, just as
these tunes begin to settle into their sweet charms, the music
revs again to its relentless pitch.

So it's much to my surprise when the knockout of the night,
both musically and aesthetically, turns out to be the loudest: the
show's encore, "Who's the N_____ Now?" Through my television

screen, it had seemed quick and dirty, designed purely for shock. But the song transforms in front of an appreciative audience who is ready for it—who knows not only every word but also, magically, the rules around who is allowed to sing the operative one. Among those allowed is the compelling young black girl jumping beside me, whose spiked Afro hairdo, an homage to the one Opal wore on *Cavett*, has wilted inside this hot little club. No matter, though; she screams her love as Opal strolls the stage in the spectacular outfit she'd changed into during the break: a black coatdress with an absurdly high collar, and a cocktail hat clinging miraculously to the side of her whistle-clean head. The hat, I notice, is blooming not with flowers or feathers, but with a clutch of plastic black-power fists. And the compelling girl beside me is singing along with her heroine from some guttural place: *When he holds you down, you fuck him up / Slip the knife from its sheath, that's how / When he calls you a nigger, you look up and smile / Say, "Who's the nigger now?"*

OPAL JEWEL:

The more we played around town, the more fans would show up [*outside the West Village house*], like this Pied Piper thing. Late in the mornings I'd go downstairs to get some cereal or whatever, and right outside the glass panels there'd be fans in full costume. They'd dress up like the characters in the songs and just hang out—push flowers through the mail slot, poems and drawings they'd done, flyers for protests and rallies they were going to. It could get intense sometimes. Like the night we found this group of young girls who'd managed to sneak into the back garden—we couldn't see how they'd got back there. Nev was freaked and ready to call the pigs. I said, "Calm down, they're only young girls with crushes." And he said, "Young girls with crushes—sounds a lot like the Manson Family to me." [*Laughs*]

But you had to learn how to separate the threat from the love, or else you'd go crazy. And to me, the fans like that weren't ever the ones who were scary. If I could see you with my own two eyes, I wasn't afraid of you. What was scary to me was all the things we *couldn't* see, *couldn't* control. Paranoia was usually more Nev's speed, but the thought did cross my mind that whatever we were doing, the feds could be watching, listening in. A loudmouthed Black woman and her foreign-national friend, are you kidding?

Yet Opal & Nev, at least early on, seemed to welcome any opportunity to amplify their fame. And as with The Photo, the national media were fascinated by their image.

VIRGIL LAFLEUR:

Word of us did reach Grace Mirabella, and Mad was invited to participate in a shoot. Perhaps this was not as fashion-forward or as exciting as the era helmed by the incomparable Ms. Vreeland, but still, this was American *Vogue*! The end product was a full-page portrait of Mad in a color-block frock [designed by up-and-coming Black designer Stephen Burrows]. I still disagree that this dress was The One—I'd found the shell for that magnificent coat she wore in her shows at a vintage store and improved it with the collar—but at least they let us use the wig. I'd trimmed it so that every strand behaved like an arrow pointing toward the angles of her face. . . . [*Sighs*] Mad did ask that the photographer take some portraits of us together, me posed at her pumps with my barber's shears. I never knew what happened to those.

OPAL JEWEL:

Vietnam, *Roe v. Wade*, and ooh, those bullets that George Wallace caught* . . . The press loved coming to me with all kinds of questions

---

* The Alabama governor and infamous segregationist had run as a third-party presidential candidate in 1968, winning five Southern states and 10 million votes. He was running for the Democratic nomination in '72 when he was shot

back in those days, because they knew I would tell it like it is. A reporter once called me a quote machine, and I took that as a compliment. Because it was unusual for somebody like me, not only a young woman but a young *Black* woman, to get a voice in the conversation.

PARTIAL TRANSRCRIPT FROM "THE INCENDIARY OPAL & NEV," *60 MINUTES*, JANUARY 21, 1973

Nev Charles, *smoking a cigarette and seated next to Opal Jewel in the kitchen of the West Village house:* It's dangerous, yeah, to make art that has people stepping back and thinking critically about the world and the institutions and the orders that we've allowed to have control over us. Someone's always going to be upset; someone's always going to feel implicated. Do you know that people, farmers guilty over the poor ways they treated their workers, they burned even the work of John Steinbeck? Steinbeck! Imagine! *The Grapes of* bloody *Wrath*! So yeah, some people out there do hate us and hate our records. But I suppose that's the price, you know, of telling upsetting truths, as writers and artists are meant to do.

Mike Wallace, *off camera:* Talk about that price you're paying.

Nev Charles: Oh, well. [*To Opal*] I hear clicks on the phone sometimes; do you?

Opal Jewel: Death threats. We get death threats mailed to our label, to this house.

Mike Wallace: Do you feel afraid that violence and danger follow you?

Opal Jewel: I'm Black and living in the United States of

---

on May 15 while campaigning in Maryland. The shooting paralyzed Wallace from the waist down and killed his presidential hopes. "Did you expect me to squeeze out some tears?" Opal Jewel asked a reporter for the Associated Press, before riffing on Wallace's most notorious quote: "Sorry to say I'm fresh out now, fresh out tomorrow, fresh out forever."

America. Violence and danger surround me always. At least Hoover's going cold in the grave.* That's one goon down.

Mike Wallace, *smiling tensely:* Are you nervous about the sentiment you might be stirring, saying incendiary things like that? Or that the content of some of this music you perform is fueling more animosity toward you?

Opal Jewel: There's too much work to do in this revolution and too many people to wake up. Too much to fight. Nobody has time to get waylaid by fear.

Mike Wallace: But I looked at the schedule for this tour you're planning, and I have to ask you, Opal—why not put Southern cities on it, the places that might benefit from hearing your messages and music the most? Why no Memphis, no Dallas, no Birmingham, Alabama?

Nev Charles: We've got a tour manager now who handles the bookings.

Mike Wallace: And if you aren't afraid, then why, in the cities where you do perform, are you using members of the Black Panther Party—

Opal Jewel: Hold up, hold up, I got—

Mike Wallace: —as personal security?

Opal Jewel: —I got a better question for you. Why are you so deeply invested in proving I'm scared? Does a Black person showing they're scared make *you* feel safer? I suggest you sit back and interrogate *that*.

---

* After decades of targeting Black activists, influential celebrities, suspected communists, and his own critics through illegal methods (like violent raids and wiretapping), FBI director J. Edgar Hoover died of a heart attack on May 2, 1972.

Of all the aspects of Opal's story that have made my love for her so fraught, the one that gets me queasiest is the speed of her blastoff. Within five head-spinning months of my father's burial, Opal had done her part in recording and boosting the fiery *Things We've Seen*. She had barreled on to some nebulous new relationship with Nev (if she'll never admit to an actual romance with him, it's clear she at least flirted with the idea). Beside him, she had sparred with her critics on prime-time television, the flash in her eyes betraying her eagerness to land a good jab. *Unapologetic*, my younger, impressionable self had labeled Opal's brash grab of the moment. I knew others, especially a few in my family, had a different word for her trajectory: *shameless*.

Because no matter how much Opal & Nev presented themselves as politically aware auteurs in the wake of Jimmy's death, the fact remained that their art—in its thematic content and well-timed release, in the direct correlation between its outrageousness and their upticking level of fame—had exploited Black pain. On the days I fix my most skeptical lens on their origin story, I can't help but question Opal's version, in which an ideological righteousness prods her ever forward. To hear Opal tell it, she was almost helpless to its sway. Watching the old clips on YouTube, though, reevaluating her stride into the spotlight as something of a gallivant, I start to think that maybe, after having a taste of the cool crowd's favor, the Opal Jewel of '72 simply loved the thrill of chasing new highs. Maybe, in that sense, she and Nev weren't such an odd pairing after all.

I decided to broach the subject of Opal's real raison d'être with Virgil LaFleur. Had I expressed such dubiousness about his best friend and muse in our earlier interviews, Virgil surely would have eviscerated me with a cut of his eyes or an exasperated sigh. But since my reboot with Opal in her Baldwin Hills home, where she finally laid down some of her armor, he had been surprisingly patient with my probing follow-up questions and more revealing in his responses. He'd lowered his own guard about moments of her life that weren't so light and fabulous—moments in which a messier, more nuanced picture crept in to replace the impervious image of Opal Jewel that he'd helped to buttress over the years. When we talked about how he'd watched over her at Miss Ernestine's after the riot, he seemed almost eager to discuss that time of sorrow and searching—in other words, to defend her more questionable decisions by reminding us that she was young once, and sometimes vulnerable, and always human.

Now Virgil indulged me in the office of his consignment shop, while seated behind a desk and repairing the hem on a beaded cocktail dress the day's last customer had brought in. "I abandoned the theater some years ago," he said, coaxing needle and thread through delicate fabric, "but one thing I learned about the stage, *chère*, is that artistic motivation may come in many forms. For the matinee, you might envision starving children to eke from you the required waterworks—is it wrong, then, that for the seven o'clock you sniff a sweet onion to pull the same trick?"

"Not *wrong*," I said. "But does it make the work less genuine, somehow? Less pure?"

"And what does it matter, if the audience still feels the power, the emotion inherent in the performance?"

"I'm not saying she should have worn black for two years," I said, "or disappeared altogether as some kind of penance. But you don't think how they capitalized on the riot was a little . . . distasteful?"

Virgil smirked. "Listen to you, speaking of taste." He snipped the thread and spread the top of the dress across his desk. The beads made a light shushing sound against the wood as he examined every row of them under a banker's lamp. "Yes," he said, "after the horror with James, Mad felt a call to make stronger political statements—and as a result the world is more enlightened, more aware. And yes, Mad felt moved to forge a viable career"—he glanced up at me over the tops of his tortoiseshell reading glasses—"and now here you sit with the fine education that has apparently trained you to question her heart." His eyes fell back to his work. *"Quelle ironie."*

I didn't know what to say to that.

"Anyway," Virgil continued as I sat there gawping, "such speculation is useless, Ms. Shelton. Many things can be true at once, and we must find inspiration in the materials we have. Materials of all different moods and textures. And speaking of materials . . ." He snapped off the lamp and glanced at his watch. "Accompany me to the showroom a moment?"

I followed Virgil as he crossed the floor of his shop toward the front door and flipped the OPEN sign to CLOSED. From a peg on the wall he unhooked a carved wooden cane he walked with sometimes, "merely for panache," and used it to pull down the steel shutters over the storefront windows. We were completely closed in.

"Safe from the looky-loos," he said cheerfully, and after unlocking a storage closet behind the register and rummaging inside, he wheeled back toward me a clothing rack. All the items were arranged on velvet hangers, evenly spaced and cloaked in black suit bags.

"What's all this?" I asked, though my heart was racing madly.

"A preview," he whispered, "for this Derringdo event."

Inside I saw not finished garments, but a series of foam boards, each clipped to its hanger and displaying samples and doodads. One held dozens of tiny fabric squares in different textures and finishes of black, arranged in a neat grid, with the columns separated by lines of piping in neon hues. Another board featured buttons and zippers pinned through their tiny holes like scientific specimens, and a third was a collage of color images from runway shows, some still bearing the watermarks of the photo agencies from which they'd been sourced.

"These are only the inspirations, to give you a taste of the feel and our process," Virgil said. "The pieces are being constructed as we speak. Twenty-two of the best seamstresses in the city, working off my sketches and Mad's exact measurements . . . I must admit, we have never enjoyed such luxury. When this Derringdo comes? She will be ready."

"Is that human hair?" I asked, when he got to the board with curly, kinky, and straight tracks clinging to Velcro strips.

"Wigs are under consideration, yes." He unclipped that board from its hanger and eased it out of the suit bag, and the subtle tints in the hair caught the overhead light. "Why do you ask? Do you think wigs are impractical? Too hot for the lights of this festival stage?"

"Oh, I'm not qualified to have an opinion," I said. "I hardly know what I'm looking at."

"Nevertheless . . . surely you have some thought?"

I realized then that Virgil was anxious.

"My thought is that you'd never have Opal look anything but her best," I said. "I can't wait to see how her costumes come together."

"What are you saying, 'costumes'? This will be *couture*. Do use the correct terminology." But Virgil was giving me a rare smile. I could tell he was pleased by my response. "Perhaps you would like to come back in the following weeks, to see the completed visions for the full tour? This will of course require your signing a nondisclosure agreement. . . ."

"Wait—a tour?" I said. "She's decided the tour with Nev is a go?"

"I get the sense she's leaning toward it, yes." Virgil frowned, reacting, I guess, to a note in my voice. "And why would she not?"

Derringdo was one thing to stomach—an elaborate one-off show that Opal no doubt had committed to contractually. There was no getting out of that now, I knew, and in some sense I thought she was owed this moment, this gig that would be the biggest by far she'd ever played. But signing on for a full set of arena dates? For an ongoing partnership with Nev? My guts twisted as I imagined it. And yet I wasn't ready to share the reason for my trepidation. Telling Virgil what Chet alleged would mean telling Opal too, and I had no facts to stand on.

"It's just that she seems at peace with her life as it is," I said haltingly. "She's got her little slice of heaven out there in Los Angeles, and I don't understand why she'd want to give that up."

"Oh, Mad might take a restorative break every now and again," Virgil said, "but when the time becomes right and her heart is aligned, she will always heed the performer inside."

"*Two decades* is a break? I thought she was retired. Bordering on recluse."

"You underestimated her, then," he said. "Not an uncommon thing."

"But why not ease into it, if she's interested in a comeback tour? It could be some smaller club shows, just by herself. Cabarets, like the ones in Paris! That way she could have everything exactly the way that she wants it. Doesn't she deserve that?"

"What she deserves," said Virgil, stiffening, "is the due she has never been given. And what are these words coming out of your mouth? 'Smaller,' *chère*? Why would one go smaller when bigger beckons?"

I understood then how much was at stake for Virgil too, with this comeback of Opal's. He'd say to me in a later interview that as much as he had loved working with her through the years, as proud as he was to have been there for her whenever she'd needed him—"and she needed me often, and desperately"—he still did wonder how his career might have turned out had he taken other paths, or worked with other clients. "It is not an infrequent conversation between Han [Ishi] and me," he would confess with the tiniest sigh, and I would be touched by the image that sprang to my mind: Virgil wrapped in the arms of his loving artist husband, counting the chances that had passed him by.

But that evening, in the shop that had been his plan B, Virgil shook his head at me and chuckled at my meager ideas as he zipped away his designs. He had been blessed with this late-breaking shot to show out, to see his patience and loyalty pay off in a grand and far-reaching spotlight. Imagine: Opal Jewel elevated again! Regal night after night in LaFleur originals! But underneath his breezy demeanor, I still sensed that anxiety . . . perhaps an earnest question. Plans had gone left before; they could go left again. What cruelty lurked to cut them down now?

chapter eighteen

"I DON'T THINK I'M SUPPOSED TO BE ANYONE'S MOTHER"

★ ★

Opal & Nev had grabbed the nation's attention; the next logical step was to take their show on the road. Rivington's triumvirate of executives had put in motion plans for their avant-garde duo's first tour: forty-six gigs at midsize clubs across North America. Though they might have been able to fill larger venues, Opal & Nev were booked according to a counterintuitively risk-averse strategy—sell out every show fast to keep them a hot ticket rolling from date to date. How the duo would be received outside of New York City, especially considering Opal's wild mouth and reputation for engaging all foes, remained to be seen.

HOWIE KELLY:

After the *60 Minutes* thing, some very upset people down in Alabama put themselves in the papers by rolling over a couple barrels of *Things We've Seen.* Of course they had to *buy* the records in bulk from me in order to destroy them, but, you know . . . [*Laughs*]

[*On whether he had concerns over Opal & Nev's safety*] After everything they put me through, *I* was supposed to worry about *them*? C'mon.

Besides, anybody who ever worked in this business knows that touring is where the real nut is. No way out of that.

ROSEMARY SALDUCCI:

We got some crazy shit in the mail, most of it for Opal. She'd come into the office every week in giant sunglasses and I'd pull a milk crate of 'em out and she'd read all the ugliest ones. She'd jot down notes about them and then take out a lighter and set them on fire. [*On whether Opal ever did, in fact, seem afraid*] If she did, she didn't let on. It seemed like she just wanted to know what there was to be aware of out there.

OPAL JEWEL:

Of course I got scared now and then; I'm human. My thing about doing the tour was, we can either do it dumb and blind, or we can do it in a way that factors in common sense. Who do you think arranged for added security that *I* could trust on the tour? Me. Who took note of all the cities those letters came from and made sure we got routed around them one hundred miles? Yeah. Also me.

ROSEMARY SALDUCCI, *READING FROM A LETTER SHE SAVED FROM THESE DAYS:*

"A message for Neville Charles, aka Race Traitor,

"You and your ugly nigger cunt"—pardon me, hon, but I'm sure you appreciate me not sugarcoating this—"You and your ugly nigger cunt deserve each other. I hope that monkey cuts off your balls and shoves them down your throat. If she doesn't, you can bet that I will, you fucking piece of shit."

And it's signed "Your Worst Nightmare." How about that.

[*On whether she remembers Nev's reaction*] Oh, I never showed *him* this garbage. He was already popping too many pills.

What would turn out to be Opal & Nev's only concert tour launched on March 3, 1973, at Philadelphia's Electric Factory. The ragtag personnel, split between two Volkswagen Transporters, included opening act Estella "Star" Acadia, a waiflike singer/songwriter with a husky voice and a distinctive shroud of long dark hair; a touring band; Virgil LaFleur, who handled Opal & Nev's wardrobe and documented a handful of the shows using his 35mm; tour manager Stanley Coombs, who was hired by Rivington and drove one of the vans; and, taking turns driving the second, Percy Purdie and his younger brother Artis, Black Panthers who assisted Coombs (in lugging equipment) and venue managers (in securing the shows and Opal's dressing rooms).

Virgil's snapshots, annotated with datelines in the scrapbook he showed me, build a curious portrait of these days on the road. Every mundane aspect and object catches his attention—the mile markers, a menu touting the "Best Deli-Fare in Delaware," that regal coatdress he'd fashioned for Opal hanging off the back of a door, and the jumble inside her jewelry box (including a pair of silver thunderbolt earrings gleaming on top). Eventually, Virgil's eye settles down and the objects fall away, until we are left with more people, more action, more of what you'd expect to see on this tour: a group of Mercurials dressed like Opal & Nev on Cavett *and huddled together for warmth on a patch of sidewalk while waiting for a venue to open. Coombs and the touring bassist fooling with a wall of amps as a club employee looks on. The Purdie brothers chatting with three unsmiling comrades in berets, outside a door with Opal's name on it. Opal gazing at herself while gluing on lashes inside a small dressing room, with half of a shirtless Nev caught in the mirror's reflection behind her. A view of a roiling crowd from above, mostly pale arms raised up toward the camera. An obese white girl dressed in a nun's habit—her rapturous face shining with sweat, her arm thrown around the shoulders of an androgynous brown teenager in red lipstick and a sequined gold dress. A shot of the band taken from behind during a show, with the exhaust from a fog machine curling cinematically around their silhouettes.*

ARTIS PURDIE:*

Their sound wasn't my speed—I was more of a soul cat. Give me some Stevie, some Marvin, some Bill Withers, I'm good. I went ahead and took the gig because Opal was a friend of some folks in the Party, and because I thought it was gonna be the easiest cash I ever made. It was little white college kids and shit who loved that kind of screeching noise. I figured, *What the fuck are* they *gonna do?* My brother and I laughed looking at the capacity of the venues—emptied out, they didn't look much bigger than school cafeterias. We thought, *No problem, we got this.*

Then we'd roll up at showtime and *maaaaan* . . . [*Shakes head, laughing*] These kids would come running up to the bus looking like Halloween on drugs. And as soon as me and Percy got out to lead Opal inside, the regular security guys at the venues would take off grinning: "They're all yours, *brothas.*" Peckerwoods.

OPAL JEWEL:

The young fans we had at the shows in New York were different from the ones most everywhere else. That's because if you spend any time in New York, if you grew up there or you had the chance to break away there, you're constantly plugging into those crazy energies around you. Knowing that one day you can let go of your mama's hand or the hateful voices around you—whatever it is that's holding you back—and slip real slick into another world when it's time to become who you turn out to be. And if you prove yourself to have half a brain, a good eye or an ear, and some talent to smash those elements together? Hey now! You could be king of your thing, understand what I'm saying?

---

* After his time on the road with Opal & Nev, Artis Purdie moved to Oakland, California, to help support Black Panther Party official Elaine Brown's city council run in 1973. He still lives in Oakland today, and manages a community center offering after-school tutoring and activities for teenagers.

But in some of these places we played on the tour, there were people who I think never had a fair chance, never sensed their options. Who saw life shoving them one way, no detours allowed. Any kid who wasn't white, of course, but also the fat kids, the gay kids, the artsy, nobody-understands-me kids, the kids with physical disabilities and speech impediments, skin conditions, emotional issues, abuse issues, you name it. Some older folks too—you'd be very surprised who related to us. Saw our misfit circus rolling into town and figured, for a night or two, they could join up and be stars. And for those kinds of fans, as Opal & Nev we were more than just rock stars they loved. We were like freedom to them.

ARTIS PURDIE:

The Mercurials were some overzealous motherfuckers. First of all, you had to separate the ones who actually had paid for tickets from the ones who just liked to follow us around to every show. Then you had to pat down the ticket holders before letting them in, because you never knew what somebody might be carrying, especially if they had a costume or a wig on, and if they *didn't* have a costume or a wig on, we learned you still had to be careful—we had a few people, some of these rich, bored white boys with nothing better to do, and they were just there to fuck with the crazy niggers and the freaks on parade. Opal was worried about the South, you know, but Boston? *Listen:* Boston was *bad*. We had the racists throwing all kinds of shit at us and at the fans waiting to get in—I'm talking literal dog shit. And rocks, and sticks, and eggs . . . Some religious group came to march with their signs because Opal had just said something about abortion rights, and you know those Catholics up there don't play with that. And then in New Hampshire we had somebody who thought it was real funny to toss poppers on the floor during the show—you remember those firecrackers, *pop pop*!? Well, somehow this clown got them past us, and in a small space they sounded like a real gun going off. Percy had to run and snatch Opal off the stage, and after that *everybody* got patted down.

On the other hand, a lot of our time was spent checking out gifts the fans would bring for Opal or Nev. . . . Cans upon cans of strawberry Quik. Jars of sequins and glitter for her, cans of hair spray for him, because he was doing that flame thing with his hair. All kinds of cartoons and sketches people had drawn of the two of them, tracing the album covers . . . It was wild, how much love the two of them got.

VIRGIL LAFLEUR:

Can you understand what Mad has meant to so many people? Listen to the question, *chère*. I did not ask "*Do* you understand?" as a theoretical matter. I asked, "*Can* you?" as an emotional one. Is it possible, considering your position as James's bereaved child, that you may be struggling to see beyond that tragic moment in order to appreciate her larger story? That of a woman who, in the sum of her life, has been a champion for those who are marginalized, bullied, discriminated against? Why do you think she is resonating now? There are sadly legions of these people who need her essence today.

ARTIS PURDIE:

I picked a knife off this very young Black girl who showed up in DC one night trying to get into the show. Not a fake knife like some of them would make to go with their costumes, papier-mâché or whatever, but a bona fide goddamn *switchblade*. And the girl was acting hard, but she couldn't have been older than sixteen—had a squeaky voice and pimples up and down her face, and she'd obviously run off from wherever she lived. When I opened the blade I could see it had somebody's dried blood on it. I asked her, "Little sis, what you want me to do with this?" And she asked me to take it as a gift to Opal, to show her how she'd sliced some pervert in the thigh after he'd tried to push up on her. Now, I wasn't supposed to let that girl inside the club because it was eighteen and up and she didn't have any ID on her, much less a ticket or any money. But I snuck her on back to Opal's dressing room so she could have a bite to eat and somewhere to rest. I figured there must be some way we could help her out.

OPAL JEWEL, *NODDING*:

I remember her—I remember so many who came to us with stories like that. That little fighter . . . after the show I found her on one of the sofas in my greenroom curled up underneath her jacket, probably sleeping for the first time in who knows how long. Crumbs all over her mouth from the little finger sandwiches and whatnot we had. I guess she'd seen us on TV somewhere and got it in her mind to come all the way up from Richmond, Virginia, to meet me. I ended up rustling through my bag to give her a few toiletries, and I didn't have a lot of cash on me but whatever I had I gave it to her, plus a few pieces of knickknack jewelry. I made her promise she'd get herself a bus ticket to go anyplace where there was somebody who loved her. I asked her, "You have someplace like that, don't you?" and she said that she did, but you never really knew. She thanked me for the money, and I told her to be thankful for her own skin, her own wits, her own steel, because she was stronger than she knew. It about killed me sending her back out onto the street that night. Pulling out of the alley and watching her just stand there, getting smaller . . .

Of course you wish you could do something more for every single one of them. Maybe something different, if you'd had the good sense to know what that was. But at the time the best I could do was be Opal Jewel, because that seemed to mean a lot to them.

PEARL WELMONT:

She would call home from the road—she claimed it was to check in on Mama, but I think she wanted to hear my advice on how to help these people who'd come to her in search of something. One time she said to me, "Oh, Pearl, you just don't get it—what am I supposed to say to some sad white child who wants us to autograph the leg where she used to cut herself?" I told her, "Well, don't sign your name to that. Pray with her, and sign 'Child of God.'"

The pressures on Opal weren't only external. By the time the tour moved west, her partner's addiction to pain medication, which he'd begun gobbling after the Rivington Showcase, had escalated dramatically.

OPAL JEWEL:

When Nev would take one too many of those damn pain pills, he would get to bobbing and weaving up on the stage, in the middle of the set. Messing up the songs to the point where it would be embarrassing. Then he started to miss the big catch [of the pogo stick], and that was our signature moment. I would try to aim it so it landed by an amp behind me, but one time that thing nearly beaned our bass player right in the head. We couldn't keep on like that, so I took it upon myself to tweak the show—me and the guys in the band. I don't know, maybe Nev thought I was trying to hog more attention for myself, but that wasn't it; it was because we were scared half the time he was gonna keel over. So it became, you know, [*waving*] "Over here! Look at me, look at me!" I did more costume changes, right there on the stage—we had a Chinese screen set up, and I made up some choreography playing with the shadows I'd cast against it, so even when I wasn't in the spotlight I could keep the attention away from Nev. He didn't have to do much except focus on his playing. And by that point we had played the songs so much, been through the setlist so many nights, that it became like breathing.

Of course I felt responsible to help him. I can't count all the times I went through Nev's shit and tossed out whatever I could find. He'd say, "Oh yeah, yeah, it's for the best, dump it all out for me, Jewel." Then the next day one of us would have to slap him awake again. Come to find out that after the shows, when I was talking to the people who looked up to us and wondering where in the hell *he* was, he and Star would be off somewhere scoring. Sometimes they didn't even have to go out. *Huh.* He'd get some poor little lost Mercurial to bring him a fix, and if he threw a tantrum big enough, Stanley would.

STANLEY COOMBS, *THINGS WE'VE SEEN*
TOUR MANAGER:

My primary job was to smooth things over, to get them what they needed. That meant chewing out the people at the venues if they didn't have the proper setup for Opal to feel comfortable. And other times, for Nev, that meant calling up this particular doctor in New York who would then call a pharmacy in whatever city we happened to be gigging. It was pretty obvious to me early on that Nev was an addict, but he put on this show about how he was in so much pain from his injuries at the riot that he couldn't work, and he was insinuating that he would be un-happy with me for not taking care of him. He was very good at getting whatever it was that he wanted, by hook or by crook.

OPAL JEWEL:

He was convinced that someone was gonna come up on the stage and as-sassinate him—that was the word he used, *assassinate*, like he was a damn Kennedy. The tiniest things would spook him, so when we did have a few of the more serious hiccups [like the firecrackers set off in the crowd] . . . Maybe that chaos brought back a memory of the showcase or whatever, but he would go entirely off the rails. Had a bunch of routines and super-stitions. Wouldn't stand near windows when the Mercurials were outside singing, that was one. And those pills . . . They stole so much of his light.

In the places we stayed, Nev and I usually had connected rooms on the same floor, and early on in the tour, if I had insomnia or if something was bothering me, I would go over to his and we'd watch whatever we could find on TV. Not have to talk, you know? But then we had this disaster of a show in Phoenix where everything was off. I'd intended to have it out with him that night, to let him know I'd had enough.

I was beating on the door and he wasn't answering. I could hear the TV blasting, though. I got scared because Nev had been so zonked out during that gig—I thought he might have messed around and hurt him-self bad this time. I woke up Artis Purdie and we found a bellboy—we paid that bellboy two hundred dollars to open up the door and to keep his mouth shut. And when Artis and I went in the room there they were, him and Star. Butt-ass naked, passed out on the bed.

STAR ACADIA, "I WAS HOOKED ON HEROIN . . .
AND SEX WITH NEV CHARLES!," COVER STORY,
NATIONAL ENQUIRER, FEBRUARY 22, 1983:

I was crying out for help, literally, in my songs, and I had greedy in-dustry people telling me it was my misery that they found artistic and marketable. At the time, I was struggling with an eating dis-order, still suppressing memories from my abusive childhood. . . . I could see Nev had a problem too, and I thought maybe he was my soul mate. Life on the road could be frightening sometimes, and we both were feeling estranged from the group—I was the opening act everybody ignored, and Nev, I could tell, was frus-trated that he was becoming a smaller part of what he'd started to call "the Opal Jewel Show." It was inevitable that the two of us paired off and shared the things we did together. . . .

I pulled him aside once, took his hand and pulled him into a bathroom without a word, and I lifted the hem of my long skirt to show him how I got my fix. I never used my arms—I had a spot on my foot, a fat vein right by the ankle that was bruised and purple—and I kept my kit in one of those children's diaries that have a lock and a key. I'd cut out the pages and in the hol-low I kept a baby's silver spoon, a lighter, the works. He would never use anything requiring a needle. Maybe he looked down on me because sometimes I did. Maybe that's why he kept me around—so he could feel superior, with his powders and pills. They'd turn out to be just as bad, though. For a while drugging was our secret, but soon our addictions got glaringly obvious.

OPAL JEWEL:

Artis hauled up Nev and told me to get Star, and we dragged them to the bathtub. Turned the cold water on full blast till they snapped out of it. I got Star's hair wet and I pushed it back from her face so I could finally get a good look at her, and honey, the truth had come to the light. Black circles up under her eyes and a green undertone . . . I honestly thought she was dead already.

ARTIS PURDIE:

That night was when I knew I didn't want to be on this tour anymore. If we couldn't have done more to help a teenage Black girl in some kind of trouble—taken her to some sisters I knew in that area, or taken her with *us*, even, to look after for a while—then what in the hell was all this screeching about? I had to ask myself, you know, as a Black man, as a man of my community: *Who is it exactly I'm keeping safe here?*

Disillusioned, the Purdie brothers quit in mid-May 1973, leaving the band without personal security for the remaining two months of the tour. And flipping through Virgil's scrapbook covering these dates, it's clear a mood has shifted. Several days go unremarked, and instead of photos from the concerts, Virgil captures the rare day off. Here is where Opal comes more into focus, and she is a satellite spinning away. **Seattle, 5/22:** *In simple jeans, a trench coat, and headwrap, she strolls through Pike Place Market in the drizzle.* **San Francisco, 5/29:** *She laughs at a small round table inside someone's kitchenette, raising her glass of red in a toast.* **Santa Monica, California, 6/3:** *A blurry photo of her and Virgil together at the beach, his trouser legs rolled up as he lifts her in a shoreline pas de deux.* **On the outskirts of Las Vegas, 6/16:** *Opal curls up in the front seat of one of the vans, reading a paperback copy of* Another Country. **Taos, New Mexico, 6/27:** *At a roadside market, she bends over a tray of turquoise necklaces, and a dark-haired little girl stares at her from the comfort of an old woman's lap.* **Minneapolis, 7/12:** *She sits up in a motel-room bed with her head bare, and with a platter of scrambled eggs and bacon laid atop the sheets next to her covered legs. Here is her small, tired smile; here is her headscarf draped over the bedside lamp, casting the room in a yellowish glow.*

OPAL JEWEL:

[After the Purdies left] Virgil and I took one of the two vans for ourselves—we crammed all the equipment in with us so the others wouldn't complain. Virgil did most of the driving and taught me how too, and we just made sure we got to the venues by the time they were expecting us. I'd never believed that performing could be like a job, but it did start to feel that way. The power that performing gave me, it started to go the opposite way; I'd be dead by the end of every night. So it wasn't a bad thing to have a mental separation: *Three days for the tour, one day for me.* That's how we limped our way back across the country, back home to New York. Knocking down the days like that.

VIRGIL LAFLEUR:

She had seen one man she cared for killed, and felt somewhat responsible for it. Why would she want to be witness to another slowly killing himself?

On August 7, 1973, the Things We've Seen *tour returned to New York for a finale show at the club Villageast. When Opal & Nev's industry friends and labelmates gathered to celebrate the duo at an after-party, they found that the two of them were barely speaking.*

ROSEMARY SALDUCCI:

Opal put on a spectacular show nearly all by herself, and once she came off that stage it was clear she was about to fall to pieces.

While they were gone I'd been keeping an eye on the West Village house, dropping by to pick up the mail. Opal had a lot of invitations, to some fashion events and parties, so I offered to come over the next day and help her sort through them. I thought it would be a good distraction, a way to ease back into life before they went into the studio again. But she said she didn't care about the parties. She told me the only thing she wanted was to get her shit out of there and go back to Harlem and sleep for ten days. I said, "Really, is Nev all that bad?" And she said,

"Rosemary, there's a reason I don't want children. I don't think I'm supposed to be anyone's mother."

BOB HIZE:

I asked Opal, "Why didn't you ring? Why didn't you tell me things had sunk to this point?" I suppose she'd thought she could keep them together on her own, but then she'd got in over her head. I told her, "This is what the tour manager is for, love, so that you don't have to carry this kind of weight—you could have told us and we'd have fired and replaced Stanley, just like that." I did cut all ties with him, on the spot at that show, and from that point on I promised Opal to do what I could to help get Nev clean and back in working shape. But I always wondered if the reason Opal didn't confide in me in the first place was because of the botch we'd made of the showcase. She just didn't trust us to take care of her. I'm hard-pressed to blame her for feeling that way.

chapter nineteen

"THAT WAS ANOTHER VIBE"

★ ★

Opal Jewel had made a mission of barreling forward. After the nightmarish tour with Nev, however, she sometimes longed to go back—to remember the moments in the fledgling days of their partnership that had led her to believe she was living a dream. The magic of arriving a newbie in New York City, or stepping into the studio the very first time . . . Would she ever experience such wonder again? Off the road and resettled in Harlem, her career stuck on pause while Bob prodded Nev toward rehab, Opal felt besieged by worry and restlessness. By instinct she craved new adventures and horizons, interesting new people with whom to share them. As luck would have it, in the fall of 1973, a trailblazing contemporary from another field floated an opportunity for Opal to savor a taste of the youth she'd been missing.

OPAL JEWEL:

Ever since I'd worn his dress in *Vogue*, [fashion designer] Stephen Burrows and I had been cool with each other. Both of us were flies swimming in buttermilk, you know, and even though he wasn't the type to get pinned down on politics, Stephen had made some artistic choices I respected—the color and *life* in his clothes, and especially the girls he'd pick to wear them. Those choices signaled to me he wasn't confused about who he was, or what it was he had to contribute.

He'd invited me before to his presentations around the city, or to drop by his boutique at Bendel's. Things were crazy in those days and I never got the chancc. But when he called to invite me as his guest to the show at Versailles, I told him, "You finally caught me at a good time."

Scheduled for the end of November, just days after the second anniversary of Rivington Showcase, the Grand Divertissement à Versailles—nicknamed the "Battle of Versailles" by Women's Wear Daily—*was a benefit fashion show pitting five French designers against five representing the United States: Anne Klein, Bill Blass, Halston, Oscar de la Renta, and rising star Burrows. Proceeds from the event would fund the restoration of the pre-Revolution royal residence.*

OPAL JEWEL:

I gave less than three damns about fixing up a crumbling old palace, but *Paris*? Now *that* was worth investing my time. I had always been curious about going—what intelligent Negro wasn't? James Baldwin was in France, being Black and gay in every sense, and some of the jazz cats had visited and wouldn't shut up about this sense of freedom they felt just walking the streets. I wanted to see for myself what was up. So I told Stephen I would come sit in his box, as long as he could cough up a second ticket. I had a friend I owed a favor or two. [*Laughs*]

VIRGIL LAFLEUR:

A *favor*? Among the biggest miracles I've ever worked is preparing us for the Paris debut. Do you understand the shopping required? The fittings and alterations? By the time we boarded the aircraft, I was ready to collapse with my glass of champagne.

OPAL JEWEL:

Pearl beat me to the flying, okay, but me, I sprung for first-class. Different universe. The flight attendants were *stunners*, honey, with their hair in these spirally updos with the hats pinned on, and they wore chic fitted dresses and white kid gloves. They woke us up for breakfast and before the pilot put the plane nice and pretty at the gate I had a warm croissant with truffle ham and Brie softer than anywhere you'll find on the ground. And they let us off first! *Us*, the Negroes! Even took down our bags from the overhead bins so we didn't have to strain ourselves. That was the moment I understood exactly what my money could buy, exactly how it could be enjoyed. The difference it could make.

The weather on the ground in Paris, though, cast a pall that early morning. Opal remembers trying to sightsee from the back of a taxi, just as she had during her first moments in New York, but this time the experience proved underwhelming. Where was the Eiffel Tower? she wondered, peering into the gloom. Figures scuttled across Pont d'Austerlitz, their heads lowered against the bluster, scarves pulled over their faces.

At their hotel in the Latin Quarter, she and Virgil spent most of the day sleeping off jet lag.

OPAL JEWEL:

It was the light glowing through the slats in the shutters that woke me up. I was so delirious I thought it was still afternoon, that the sun had decided to come on out. I didn't yet know that Paris vibe, of the streets and squares blooming alive at night. Times Square can feel so tacky and loud, you know, but the light over there has a softness, a warmth. I'd brought my photo of Jimmy, because he used to dream about playing the clubs in Europe, and I remember holding him up to the window and wishing he could really see it.

To attend one of the pre-Battle parties that Monday night, held at Maxim's, Opal threw a feathered green bolero over an oxblood pantsuit with halter top. In the taxi over, she and Virgil rode in reverent silence as they absorbed the beauty surrounding them. In the narrow alleys of the Latin Quarter, cafés and bars exuded that golden glow Opal had admired from the hotel's window. At

Pont Neuf they crossed the Seine, its surface glassy and prismatic in the wake of the bateaux traversing its length. And at some point, finally, there she rose: the Eiffel Tower, casting out beams of light that pierced the mist.

Arriving at Maxim's and checking their coats, they joined a cocktail hour stuffed with luminaries of a different sort, both pop-culture figures and aristocracy: In addition to the designer Halston, the party's honoree, there was Liza Minnelli, who was fresh off her Oscar win for Cabaret *and would open the Americans' presentation at Versailles in two nights; Wallis Simpson, the Duchess of Windsor; Pat Cleveland, the ethnically ambiguous model beloved for her whirling moves on the runway . . .*

OPAL JEWEL:

. . . plus a whole bunch of pinched French birds and their geezers—I couldn't tell you who or what any of them were, except filthy rich, and they sure as hell didn't know Opal Jewel. Me in that scene was already surreal, and then Stephen tried to up the ante.

In a quieter corner of the party, Burrows confided in Opal and Virgil that the American team had struggled that day through rehearsals at Versailles. The inclement weather had exacerbated the palace's quirks—for all its opulence, the interior was dank and freezing—and one of the designers' favorite models had fallen out sick. They desperately needed a last-minute replacement; would Opal be willing, Burrows asked, to sub in?

OPAL JEWEL:

I guess when Stephen saw my shoulder blades cut through all that old money, he figured I was skinny enough and sufficiently *fierce*. Or whatever word they use when *pretty* ain't it. [*Laughs*] Anyway, I told him I'd help the team out if he wanted—not so much because the idea excited me, but because I could relax once I knew what the hell I was doing, kicking around with this crowd. Once I knew I had a show to put on.

VIRGIL LAFLEUR:

Perhaps it was past experience as the unlucky understudy that sparked my own skepticism, but when it comes to the things she wants, Mad tends toward unwavering focus. For the rest of the party, I caught her studying Ms. Cleveland. Noting the placement of her feet, the way she raised a cocktail . . . I told Mad, "Mingle, *chère*, enjoy this first night *à Paris*! *If* it works out, we'll take tomorrow to hone." When tomorrow did come, the tune had changed.

Tuesday morning, Burrows called Opal at her hotel, full of awkward apologies: He had been forced to rescind his offer.

OPAL JEWEL:

I said, "Don't try to tell me the girl got better"—because I understood she had pneumonia, and I don't care what antibiotics you got, nobody gets up and twirls that quick. So Stephen had to confess that he'd jumped the gun [with his casting proposal]. When he'd passed the idea by the other designers on the team, apparently they hadn't loved it. I said, *Hmmm.*

At first I let it roll off my back. We spent the next day and a half traipsing around as tourists. Strolling down the Champs-Élysées, cheesing in front of the Eiffel Tower, eating our weight in macarons. I would have been fine to skip the Versailles show completely, but when the night came I took a deep breath and pulled on the sparkle Virgil laid out. "*C'est parfait*," he said when I finished dressing, which made me laugh—when I looked in the mirror, I thought, *Yeah, I look just like a Dairy Queen cup.* A white Scott Barrie dress with a matching fur muff, and a red fascinator propped like the cherry on top. That was the most formal ensemble I'd ever worn, and I guess I felt a little silly in it.

I remember pulling up to the palace and seeing the powdered wigs [of the footmen] lined up outside. And inside the theater, my little red hat nearly fell off for me looking up at the giant chandeliers and paintings on the walls, the rows of seats rising sky-high, the chichi froufrous cheek-kissing each other. . . Then the curtain opened, and the French trotted out.

You talk about an *effort* . . . whew. They had backdrops that looked like Monet himself had been resurrected to paint them, and a damn Cinderella carriage, and the models walking pigeon-toed in all kinds of formations, and at some point Nureyev himself even came out to try jeté-ing some life back into the thing. The best part was when it was nearly over—the finale number with Josephine Baker. Honey, Madame finally gave us something to *see* in her nude bodysuit! Sixty-some years old and still oozing sex!* But when the curtain fell on that first presentation? Overall, we were *bored*. It was over-rehearsed, the whole eternity of it, and during the intermission I sipped my champagne and laughed to Virgil, *Thank God I'm not on the bill for this mess.*

Then we trudged back to our seats for the Americans' turn, and they proceeded to light my Black ass on fire.

Following Minnelli's exuberant "Bonjour, Paris!" the American designers proved, in a simple and head-snapping half hour, that they had come to shake up the fashion establishment. Especially seismic was Burrows's presentation, during which the models, nearly all of them Black, literally danced in their modern silhouettes and bright colors.

OPAL JEWEL:

The sisters had that *je ne sais quoi*, darling! Grooving and gliding across the stage, heating up that chilly old cave! They were joyful and bold, relevant, *it*. Before that night, everybody had looked to the French as the

---

* American-born entertainer and activist Josephine Baker had been living in Europe since the 1920s, when she thrilled and scandalized audiences with her provocative dances and costumes. For her Versailles performance of "Mon Pays et Paris" ("My Country and Paris"), the iconic Black expat, at the time 67, wore a dramatic headdress with feathers and a sheer sequined catsuit that gave the illusion of nudity.

end-all-and-be-all, but here were these Black American girls showing up to say, *Nah, baby, it's* us.

And as proud as I felt, as hard as I cheered, I couldn't help but wonder: *Now what was the reason they didn't want me?* I was only twenty-four years old, after all, exact same age and frame as a lot of those girls—hell, if you squinted and cocked your head to the side you might've thought I was Bethann [Hardison, Burrows's house model], because she barely had any hair either, and Stephen had dressed her in that bright shade of yellow that I just love, that tone that pops off dark skin like ours. Better than that, I had a name many artists knew and claimed to respect. But I guess the American team decided the reputation attached to my name was too spiky for their sleek little show. And they edited down their collections last-minute [to make up for the missing model] rather than take the risk of working with me.

Now, I know I came off militant, hard—whatever it is you want to call it. That doesn't mean I didn't yearn sometimes to be other things too. That image I carried at such a young age, those labels they'd used to define me back home . . . They felt like traps dropping down on my head.

VIRGIL LAFLEUR:

I experienced a rush of emotion, watching that show. Seeing what could be possible *pour un homme noir*. In fact, at a party following the Americans' coup, I discussed with several of the designers the opportunity to visit their ateliers in New York. My plan was to cobble together a rotating apprenticeship, or, barring that, to enroll in school. As a stylist I had an eye, *évidemment*, but now was the time to generate my own collection.

The night before we were due to depart—I was already packing, dreaming about the opportunities ahead—Mad came to my room and proposed an extended stay in Paris. "To do what?" I asked, but she had no clear answer, no clear time frame, only a vague anguish about returning home. And yet there was an assumption that I would stay and support such aimless drifting, simply because she wanted me to.

OPAL JEWEL:

"It is not my mission to drag in your shadow"—that's what my best friend said to me, and when he told me he had things to do back in New York, his own paths to chart, I realized what a burden my unhappiness could be. Actually, let me call it *grief*, because that's the thing I was struggling to carry. Not just grief over Jimmy, but for the pieces of myself getting ripped away. My options and pathways closing up, the tighter my public persona took hold. That night I sank very low in Virgil's hotel room, curled up in tears on top of the bed. He promised that no matter what, I'd be all right. When I saw he wasn't about to stop packing, I had no choice but to try to believe him.

The American contingent who'd come for the Battle of Versailles soon jetted away, leaving Opal alone in Paris. She didn't know the language or any other soul.

OPAL JEWEL:

It was still the low season, so I stayed in the Latin Quarter, just moved to a quieter hotel on a side street. When I went out in the daytime I wore plain-Jane clothes and a hat with a brim to shade my eyes. Anonymity was the point—I didn't want anybody thinking they knew who I was. My only clear goal was to learn Paris the way that Virgil had taught me New York: to sink into it, bit by bit. You gotta get deep in the districts, you gotta try to talk to the people, you gotta eat the food and drink the wine.

I started picking up some words here and there, and venturing further out from the city center. I learned how to say "Where is the metro?" and basic directions, turn right, turn left, straight ahead, follow the river. I went to the eighteenth [arrondissement] and climbed and climbed, up to the outskirts of Sacré-Cœur and back down into the maze of streets around it. And then I turned a corner and I was in Goutte d'Or, where the African people lived and worked. At the Eiffel Tower I'd seen so many of the men pushing trinkets on the tourists, hustling like they had to, and it made me think of the hustlers back home in Harlem . . . but in

Goutte d'Or the women were holding it down too, honey. Beautiful and colorful and dignified, some of them dark as night like me and tending to their business and their babies. I guess I looked like one of them, because in the markets and shops they would start talking to me immediately in French or Arabic and then be surprised when I hit them with the English.

Every evening after I finished walking around like a street urchin I'd come back to a restaurant next door to my hotel, this tiny, tucked-away bistro struggling to attract customers. There was a tall, skinny waiter there who spoke English, reminded me of Nev but with a mustache, and he'd bring me the English-language menu. I'd order something off it and then he'd say my order back in this exaggerated French, very uppity, while he scribbled it down. I wouldn't normally put up with that kind of bougie, but in a way . . . This is crazy, but his snobbishness was almost refreshing, because I think he was reacting to me as an American, and not as Black. I'd never gotten talked down to in that particular way before! [*Laughs*] Oh, I'm not saying the French aren't racist—the Africans will tell you about that special kind of xenophobia they got over there—but for me, at that time, I did feel different in my skin.

After a while I got brave enough to check out the nightlife. Once my friend at the bistro fed me ratatouille, *confit de canard*, whatever was warm and delicious that day, I'd go up to my room and change clothes. Put on something a little more interesting and head back out for a nip. Sometimes right in the neighborhood, but usually to the Right Bank, to a club or a bar on the rue Saint-Anne. The men would flock, gay *and* straight—they liked to dance and practice their English. I liked ordering a Kir Royale and I hardly ever paid. Then one night I'm sitting at a bar and I hear somebody yell out, in this obnoxious, loud American accent, "Jesus Christ, you're Opal Jewel!" Jig was up then.

Opal was spotted by Michelle Mackey, a white American expat and former Yale drama student who had come to Paris in 1967 as part of a study-abroad program and never left. One of her lovers, a Parisian named Guillaume Dumont, owned a record shop in the fourth arrondissement and collected under-the-radar imports: White Light/White Heat *by the Velvet Underground,* High Time *by the MC5,* Space Is the Place *by Sun Ra,* Things We've Seen *by Opal & Nev. But Mackey, attuned to the feminist and Black Power movements back in the States, also recognized Opal as a political figure whose controversial quotes she occasionally read in the European editions of American newspapers.*

OPAL JEWEL:

Michelle was a force of life. Six foot four, lean, skinny inches, and bossier than me. She was full of contradictions—she dressed very chic, in these subdued and sophisticated black outfits with her hair pulled back, but in other ways she was so in-your-face she made me look like Miss Manners. I admired that about her, her comfort in herself, and how she was free to switch from this thing to that. Most of the time she was conversing with other folks in French, and I'm not the best judge but to me it seemed like you would never know she hadn't been born and raised right there, and not in Minnesota. Girl loved her red wine and cigarettes. Everything had her red lipstick print on it.

MICHELLE MACKEY, *SPEAKING THROUGH A VOICE PROSTHESIS CONNECTED TO THE STOMA RESULTING FROM A 2001 LARYNGECTOMY**:

I had lots of friends. Many artists. I took Opal to meet them. They loved her.

OPAL JEWEL:

By that time I'd got a little lonely, so I let that crazy white girl grab my arm and drag me all over—to cafés and clubs that had live music, chill

---

* Michelle Mackey and Guillaume Dumont married in 1975, guaranteeing Mackey French citizenship. The record shop they owned in Paris is now a café (they sold it in the late 1980s), though Dumont still sells rare vinyl imports on eBay. They travel to New York annually to shop, and stopped by *Aural*'s offices during one such trip.

house parties that went till four, five o'clock in the morning. Then we'd walk along the Seine and watch the sun come up, watch all the people in love and tearing themselves away from each other. Guillaume was Michelle's main boyfriend; she lived with him in a flat above the record shop. But everywhere we went there were other men, and sometimes women. They'd be snuggled up with Michelle one minute and crying and screaming at her the next. [*Laughs*] No matter if they were mad at her, though, they were always cool with me.

GUILLAUME DUMONT:

She was a liberated Black American woman, very fascinating, very beautiful, very not-giving-a-fuck. Pure ebony skin, soul and rock and roll together in her body and her attitude, and she carried herself like a man in regard to confidence. I had the record and I liked it before I knew her, but after knowing her it was strange to hear it and to recognize what she could have been fully capable of doing if she had felt even more free. I told her, I said, "America is shit, so you must stay with us in Paris and let me be your manager. We will put you in the clubs."

OPAL JEWEL:

Michelle and Guillaume had this idea to give me a small show inside Guillaume's record shop. They made flyers and everything—the chanteuse one you saw in my hallway.

MICHELLE MACKEY:

I took a stack to every party. Left them in cafés and bookstores. Took them to other places . . . where I knew expats hung out. I told her, "You'll see."

OPAL JEWEL:

I really thought I was humoring Michelle, being nice—I hadn't thought anybody was gonna come, because not a lot of people knew Opal Jewel in Paris. At the time, that was a good thing; it meant I could do whatever I wanted. I threw something together real quick—I scratched out a setlist with a couple Opal & Nev songs, a couple pop covers, and I rehearsed maybe twice with a jazzy trio Michelle and Guillaume had asked to play behind me. I didn't even consider being nervous. When the night rolled around I was in their flat above the record shop, and I wrapped my head up big and tall in some fabric I bought in Goutte d'Or, put on a silky jumpsuit with wide legs I had found, loaded up on my regular old jewelry. Then when I went down I saw . . . *Goddamn!* The people were taking up all the seats and standing in the aisles between the displays of the records and holding open the front door so the people who couldn't get in could hear. I found Michelle mingling up near the front, pouring wine, and I looked at her like, *What?!?*

GUILLAUME DUMONT:

I had pushed some of the displays out of the way to put a small podium with microphones at the front for her and the guys. She went up there and maybe she was thinking what to do, how to adjust, but she began talking in the cabaret style, telling funny things about her mother, her sister, her friend in New York—she had us captivated. Even the few who could barely understand English were smiling. So she did some little songs and finished in twenty minutes, but the people wanted more, and that is when the real improvisation came out.

What she did was from somewhere beyond. Composing on the spot, in front of everyone! She would turn to the drummer and say, "Play '*Tss-tap-a-boom, tss-tap-a-boom, tss-tap-tap-tappity-tap-a-boom*'" and he would do it. Then to the bass player she would say: "Now you play, '*Dah dah dah, dah-la-la, dah dah.*'" To the guitarist she only nodded, she let him run crazy over that rhythm she made, and when everyone was together and the groove was going she came in. Like scat-singing, this way she would take one silly lyric and stretch it. This one stuck with me: "You got the keys, rev the machine." And she took one line like that and chewed it, you know, and twisted it around with her voice to sound like the brass instrument or the electric guitar. . . . The ukulele, you know what I am saying [*laughing*]—anything that would make it a little off-beat, a little edgy.

Then she began to undo her headwrap, slowly slowly, turning around and twisting her body to the ground. By the time her bald head was exposed at the end of the song, the people were cheering. They were as electrified as if she had stripped totally naked. She was so dangerous, wild . . . sexy.

OPAL JEWEL:

Before, I was playing to maybe two thousand Mercurials a night, but there in that hot little record shop where I was *really* an alien? That was another vibe. It was exhilarating, the chance to just play. The question did occur to me: *Could I actually make my life in this place?*

Mackey and Dumont easily talked their new friend into doing a series of intimate after-hours shows at the record shop, extending Opal's time in Paris into the summer of '74. In lieu of payment, she accepted lodging in the guest room of their upstairs flat. No matter how deeply Opal sank into Paris, however, home maintained a decent hold.

OPAL JEWEL:

Besides my sister, Virgil was the only person I'd told how to reach me. It was always nice to read a letter from him. He'd give me the news and gossip I was missing, and he'd stick in sketches of original designs he was working on in his new classes at FIT. I was proud to know he was stretching and growing, and flattered that he missed me—the figures he sketched looked like me, anyway. But the problem was, most of the time his letter would come as part of a bigger package, mixed in with other mail he was forwarding from Harlem. There were a bunch of nasty notices from Howie Kelly, full of underscores and capital letters, warning me what I better not do while under my Rivington contract. And then the letters from Nev . . . Those I sent back to Virgil unopened. [*Long pause*] Just looking at the return address overwhelmed me. Most times I was furious, to be reminded of that miserable tour and how he'd nearly wasted our shot. Once in a while, though, I felt guilty for running off on him when maybe he needed me most.

NEV CHARLES, IN A LETTER SENT TO OPAL FROM REHAB (*COURTESY OF VIRGIL LAFLEUR*):*

Opal my Jewel,

Talk to me. You must, you must. You must come back and see me.

   I miss my guitar, I miss working. I miss the times before at our big blue house. In here I can only bang about on things, bluntly. Cot, desk, metal chairs in a circle: Everything is hard and rhythmic, but you just might like it, Opal; you always did prefer the percussion, and I never could tell what you might do with it, and maybe that is what was so exciting about you always: I never could tell. Maybe you'd sound like a warrior, meeting force with force, or like an angel, dribbling honey over top. Do you remember "Black Coffee"? Do you realize I wrote that just for you? Not the lyrics— I know that you hated those—but the heavy sound, the big drums, and the bass. I'd hoped you'd love it. I hate I never told you.

   There's a fellow with me in here, Raymond Jr., and he tells me his life stories—beautiful, detailed stories about his childhood, his sisters in pigtails, Kansas City–style barbecue, a grandmother who sold Popsicles and crisps from her house and watched over them and whose death set him wrong. And how his little sisters won't come to see him ever, but he still writes to all of them once a

---

* Nev's first stint in rehab began in January 1974, after he crashed a brand-new cherry-red Alfa Romeo on the Brooklyn-Queens Expressway with Star Acadia in the passenger's seat. They had been on the way to the airport for a trip to the Galapagos Islands, as he would later recount in an interview with *Aural*: "We got distracted, took some substances that gave us a sneak preview of the colors and lizards, and ended up with my sports car essentially curved around us." By some miracle, neither was seriously injured.

week. His stories make me wonder where you are and what you'd say about him, what we might say together about such a delight-ful and charming person stuck on a bad jag. What we might say about humanity and persistence and mistakes and forgiveness. But is that all a bit too tender for your taste? I'm not sure any-more and I can't possibly hear you, half a world away.

    And that's just it: You must speak to me, please, or I won't remember where I am. Where we are, who we've been. They'll let me out, but I'll fall right back in.

    Waiting, and so very sorry . . .

Once again, I am:
Your Nev

The longer Opal lingered in Paris, though, the more its pleasures wooed her. Moving in with Mackey and Dumont gave her access to an even wider circle of artists and intellectuals, many of them American expats. Late-night rehears-als at the flat would turn into marathon jam sessions/meet-and-greets. Friends and neighbors, attracted by the music floating down to the street, would come and go; every time Opal would wake from a stolen catnap, she'd find another roast chicken, more wine, a new set of people who'd come to say hello. She made many new friends, took several lovers.

OPAL JEWEL:

I stopped worrying and started relaxing. I don't know how to describe it better than that. Most days my only ambitions were to wake up, make love if I felt like it, dip a croissant in honey. I didn't wear a stitch of makeup and my clothes calmed down. Michelle and Guillaume's place was my refuge, a cozy cave full of records and books where you could plop down in the nooks. I read a lot: [Toni Morrison's] *The Bluest Eye*, Toni Cade Bambara, Maya Angelou, all the great Black women authors who the expats I'd met were wild about. And I started to think that writing—not improvising, but intentional *writing*—was a craft that wasn't off-limits to me. It was something my Black friends especially encouraged me to do, to give myself more options once I got free of Rivington's grip.

The question was, What was I going to write? My goal at the time was to do anything that felt unexpected. I had a notebook and a purple ink pen, and some days I'd walk to the Jardin du Luxembourg and sit on one of the benches in the shade at the Medici Fountain. I'd take deep breaths through my nose and my mouth, trying to smell the air and taste it and describe it. I was writing these flowery poems—literally flowery!—about the beauty of the roses, and the singing birds, and the marble statues, and the silky ribbons in the hair of the little girls playing nearby. Oh, they were trash. [*Laughs*] I never had a thought to put them on record. I was just in a phase, experimenting. Pulling far away from the image that had exhausted me back home. And I had put some of this nature poetry to music, acoustic numbers, because these were my peaceful and pretty thoughts, you know, and I wanted to prove, to myself and everyone else, that I could be peaceful and pretty if I wanted to, damn it.

Normally at the shop I performed covers or the Opal & Nev songs or whatever, but one time I decided to debut a couple new things I'd actually written. I made the mistake of announcing it beforehand to a few of my new friends. The show was extra packed that night, everybody waiting to see what Opal Jewel had to say about Watergate* or Patty Hearst† or whatever craziness was going on. You can imagine how my little nature poems went over.

---

* The unfolding Watergate crisis dominated the headlines in America through the summer of 1974, with citizens absorbing bombshell revelations about President Nixon's attempts to cover up his administration's involvement in a burglary of the Democratic National Convention headquarters.

† On February 4, 1974, the daughter of media baron William Randolph Hearst was kidnapped from her apartment in Berkeley, California, by the leftist terrorist organization the Symbionese Liberation Army. A little more than two months after her abduction, Patty Hearst, calling herself Tania, was caught on surveillance camera participating in the SLA's robbery of a bank.

GUILLAUME DUMONT:

Eh, it was maybe not so genius. Who cares? She wants to try something, let her try, let her get it out of her body! But you Americans with your boxes and demands, with your *pick pick pick* . . .

MICHELLE MACKEY:

She sang nursery rhymes on a stool. [*Shrugs*] I loved her, but . . . it was very confused.

OPAL JEWEL:

After that show I went to a restaurant with Michelle and Guillaume and a few other folks, including this guy I had started seeing, a writer who thought he was my mentor, I guess. The Negro made pouty comments beside me all night. He was devastated, like I'd actively done something to embarrass him in front of the intelligentsia. I got tipsy from the sherry that came with dessert, and he leaned over and asked me the *one last time* that makes a chick lose her mind: "You didn't have *anything* to say tonight, other than that?"

Honey, I stood up and grabbed the first thing I saw . . .

MICHELLE MACKEY:

A square of tiramisu. Poor guy ate it, all right.

OPAL JEWEL:

. . . and I threw it in his face, and I screamed at him, without even thinking, "Leave me alone, *I'm on vacation*!" [*Laughs*] I was so mad, so resentful of anybody else's expectations of what kind of artist I needed to be, that I kept on scribbling those terrible songs and subjecting my audience to them. And that's the irony, right? Even then, singing all that flowery goo-ga, my stubbornness over it was pure Opal Jewel. I finally woke up one night and saw I'd disappointed most of my fans, trying to run away from what I did best. The expats who'd supported me lost patience, lost interest, stopped showing up, and the shit was so wrong that

I couldn't blame them. The only people who did come anymore were a handful of the French folks who barely even knew any English—no matter what I was saying, they stayed glazed and grinning.

Then it actually happened: Nixon was out. Michelle and I were listening to his [August 8, 1974, resignation] speech on the BBC [World News radio], and my heart was thudding. We were screaming and jumping up and down, three o'clock in the morning. The people back home had been protesting, and the protesting put pressure on the representatives [in Congress], and the representatives put pressure on ol' Tricky Dick to get his butt up out the White House. I know a lot of people say it was a dark day for America, but isn't that democracy working? Wasn't that a glimmer of hope that truth could check power, and isn't hope the entire point? The reason any of us raise our fists and run our mouths? The reason we dare to imagine a "better" exists?

I said to Michelle, sort of dreamy, "Is it crazy to wish I was home right now?" I'd been feeling homesick for a while, but until that moment I'd been too sheepish to say it. Of course, everybody's high mellowed out before long—what was it, a month [until President Gerald Ford pardoned Richard Nixon]? But that was enough hope to convince me it was my time to go back.

By the time I left Paris I was low on funds; on the flight back to New York I was smashed up against a window in coach. But I was feeling good, thinking about where Opal Jewel was supposed to go from here. And what lingered as inspiration for me, funny enough, was Madame Josephine half-naked on that stage at Versailles. The woman had led an empowered and ever-changing life, a life of personal and political resistance, and still, at showtime, she served the people what they loved to eat. That was her box to manage, I guess, and she worked within it the best she could.

chapter twenty

"TO LEAVE OLD TRIGGERS IN THE PAST"

★　★

In total, Opal Jewel's Paris "vacation" stretched nearly nine months, from late November 1973 to mid-August 1974. Though the fallout from Watergate led US news during that time, much also happened on the cultural landscape. On the Bowery that December, a scrappy new club called CBGB & OMFUG first opened its doors; the following summer, up in the Bronx, a DJ who went by the name Kool Herc siphoned power from a park lamppost and hosted the first open-air hip-hop concert. Cancer killed Candy Darling, a Warhol super-star whom Opal used to spot frequently at Max's, in March; it claimed Duke Ellington in May.

A lot had changed within Opal's New York circle too. Rivington's executives, who'd been eager to cut another Opal & Nev record once Nev completed rehab, had grown impatient with her dawdling in Paris, and had begun to invest in other projects by recently signed proto-punk acts (including Land of the Free and a reimagined Curlicutes). Harlem also felt chilly upon her return.

OPAL JEWEL:

By the time I got back to New York, even Miss Ernestine was looking at me sideways. With my other expenses, I was late on paying her rent, so she'd offered my room to another tenant.

VIRGIL LAFLEUR:

Mad communicated so little during her time away that I had no idea whether she would return at all, and I worried that was due to the way we'd left things in Paris. Once I returned home, I set my sights on moving on. Why should I have allowed my talents to wither? Besides my new classes, I'd had word of a soap opera actress with a spark, with an interesting enough nose to transition to prospects less dreadful, and I could have helped that girl with her audition wardrobe. Then *poof*, suddenly Mad reappeared, wanting everything back as it had been. Knocking at my door with her luggage, pulling from one of her bags a sad gift of French lavender soaps that she thought would smooth the chafing between us.

I was of course happy for her to return, but I told her in no uncertain terms that if she and I were to continue a professional collaboration, she could no longer take my loyalty for granted. She would need to respect my time and autonomy. Not only has she done so ever since, she has gone out of her way to be generous—she introduced me to Han*, she helped me open this shop . . . she fought for me whenever she could to be her stylist, when I know it was at times inconvenient to make such demands. These are the things I try to remember when I find myself in a ponderous mood over any of my dreams deferred.

And I remember her word to me that night she returned: that she was truly ready to transition back to work. I gave her sheets and a pillow

---

* With Opal Jewel officiating the private civil service, Virgil LaFleur wed his longtime partner, the Japanese conceptual artist Han Ishi, in 2011, shortly after gay marriage was legalized in New York. They had met twenty-seven years earlier, when Ishi directed the only music video made to promote Opal's second solo album, *Temper*.

for my chaise, as well as the rest of her accumulated mail, and I said to her, "That is good news—but you'd do well to check there's still work to be had."

Many of the letters were from Mercurials, screened and forwarded to Harlem by Rosemary Salducci. Something about Opal made certain fans, especially young women, pour out their life stories to her, stories of loneliness, depression, rage. They sent her photographs of themselves and asked her when she'd be making new music, when she'd be coming through their towns. Faced with such overwhelming devotion, Opal told me, she struggled with guilt—a feeling exacerbated when she found, at the bottom of the pile of fan mail, all the letters that Nev had written her, still unopened and bound with a rubber band.

Opal's musical partner had spent the better part of their break in two different rehab facilities, relapsing hard between stays. Before he stopped writing Opal altogether, his letters hit a peak of despair. When was she coming back? he'd wanted to know, and she had never answered him.

OPAL JEWEL:

[After reading Nev's letters] I went around to the West Village to see how he was doing. It was real early in the morning—I didn't want any scene. But when I walked up to the house there was a small work crew of guys putting up a gate, closing off the little patch of sidewalk around the stoop where the Mercurials would leave their flowers and gifts. One of the guys on the crew seemed to recognize me so I smiled at him and asked, "Does my friend still live here?" And the guy said, Oh yes, yes, Miss Opal, and let me pass through so I could ring the bell.

Nev came to the door looking fresh and clean. Better than I'd seen him look in a couple of years—red hair shining like the pelt on a damn Irish setter. [*Laughs*] I joked with him, "Nev, they got you some Blue Magic in that place or something?" But when I went to touch him through the crack in the door, he flinched. Like he was scared of me, like he didn't know me anymore. And I said, "*Oh*".

I nearly walked away but he called me back and took the chain off, so I followed him inside. I could see the house was different—he'd gotten some furniture and dishes, and there were paintings on the walls. Floral patterns everywhere, and vacuumed carpets too. Clearly a woman's touch. Maybe the girl was asleep upstairs; I didn't know and it wasn't my place to ask. I was only glad to see him looking healthy, and I didn't care much how he got there.

He had a blender in the kitchen, and I watched him reach into a flower box on the windowsill and pluck a handful of green blades out of it, and he tossed them in along with some berries and ice. I said, "What in the world . . . ?" He closed the lid and put that thing on pulse for maybe ten good minutes, pressing and pressing the button so it crunched and whirred while I tried to talk to him, tried to explain that after the tour I'd needed a break to figure myself out, same as he'd needed one to get himself clean. When he finally finished with the noise I said, "Okay, Nev, I can see that you're mad. I've been mad before too. So what do you say we lean into that? What do you say we make our new record?" And he's just guzzling down this green wheatgrass concoction from a glass, glaring at me out the corner of his eye, that Adam's apple glugging up and down. [*Laughs*] When he finally finished drinking, I said, "All right?" And he said, "I don't know. I'm meant to be taking things one day at a time."

I told him, "Okay, then, I'll give you your space." What else could I do? I let him go behind that gate he was building and I went back to my piece of the city. I waited for him to call and say he was ready, and in the meantime, I started writing some stuff myself. I lived out the rest of that fall wrapped up in my blanket on Virgil's sofa, steadily sketching out concepts. I had a million beginnings of songs I was nervous but excited to share, hard-charging riffs right in line with the energy and meaning of where we'd been going. I thought when we did get together with Bob, me and Nev, we'd collaborate the same way we had on *Things We've Seen*. Blazing back and forth, punching up the lyrics, making the music bolder, more arresting. We both liked playing with characters, so I dreamed up some that gave both of us shine, characters I knew our fans would love, and then Virgil helped me with some costume and performance ideas to go along with them. I was feeling real good about what I was bringing to the table, hopefully making up for that time I'd needed off.

And then when Nev finally called . . . Forget being on the same page. We weren't even in the same damn library.

PARTIAL TRANSCRIPT FROM "ROSY TIMES FOR NEV CHARLES," *CBS SUNDAY MORNING*, JULY 13, 2008

Serena Altschul: A lot of people would say you came out [of rehab] not just sober, but a different artist altogether. Did recovery make Nev Charles softer, you think?

Nev Charles, *chuckling, shifting on his piano bench:* Maybe so, maybe so. Softer in some places, stronger in others. The only thing I can say is that when my interior organs stopped smashing against my bones, when I bargained that I would rather die than go through this nightmare again, I promised myself that my life would change in some very key ways. It had to . . . simplify. I was in this small town in Vermont, no distractions whatsoever, forced to just be in this deafening quiet. But the founder of the facility happened to be a lover of classical music, had apparently taken some lessons himself and felt there was a therapeutic benefit. There was a piano, of all things, in the common area, so us boozers and junkies could listen to him pick through Bach on a Sunday. Now, the piano and I had never got on very well before—I was [*bleeped expletive*] and still honestly think that I am—but a piano was the only instrument I had access to at the time. I was miles away from my guitars or anything else I had come to rely on, organic or synthetic. I was furious over that at first, because I wanted to rock like I used to, I wanted what I played to match what I felt inside my head. But every day that I passed by that piano in the common room before breakfast time, the opening line of the Serenity Prayer began to loom—*God, grant me the serenity to accept the things I cannot change* . . . The prayer also happened to be propped in a framed cross-stitch that sat on the lid, so there's that. [*Laughs*]

Serena Altschul: And the things you couldn't change were—

Nev Charles: Yeah, yeah, my passion for music. I started to think, *Right, clearly I can't have the exact situation I want at the moment, but that doesn't mean that I can't have music full stop, does it?* After that, I started looking at that piano like a comfort, like a doorway opening and leading me back to the beauty of basics. Lovely melodies, lovely love songs. "Rosy." I started playing my old stuff during free time and nobody seemed to mind; in fact, they rather liked the songs and seemed surprised that I had that kind of a range. Then that segued into writing again, scribbling in the little journals they'd given us to mark our progress, drawing from the settings and people around me. The lyrics I wrote still had an edge, obviously, but the stories I felt most comfortable and confident telling were more personal, intimate ones. Sometimes even silly, if I needed a smile.

Serena Altschul: And that direction was opposed to the music you'd been doing.

Nev Charles: Of course I still felt very strongly about the goings-on in the world around me and very proud of the music, for instance, that Opal Jewel and I had made together. But I was less interested in being big and loud, and more inspired by the smaller, more nuanced, more artful scale. It seemed like a good time to evolve, to leave old triggers in the past.

OPAL JEWEL:

He played for me what he'd been writing on his piano, and it was cool. [*Shrugs*] It just wasn't Opal & Nev. Wasn't how I thought we'd land, not after everything we'd been through, and I couldn't picture how to fit the artist I'd decided to embrace into these songs he'd supposedly written for us. They were like the start of a quirky side project, like doodles— same as my nature poems in Paris had been. Some of them made me tap my feet, but I didn't hear them and think, *This is the kind of work I need to be doing*. I was glad Nev was better, but I already knew this wasn't going to work for the Opal part of Opal & Nev. What would she look like, singing on some funny little valentines?

BOB HIZE:

What Nev had been working on was a series of wonderfully strange and beautiful torch songs—at least they sounded like torch songs; they had the same feel in the music and vocals, even if the lyrics were obtuse. At first we were confused but then got cautiously excited, because these were like Rivington's versions of what was doing exceedingly well at the time on pop charts and on radio: Billy Joel, Elton John, even dear Jim Croce.* But it was hard to reconcile that kind of direction with the one Opal had in mind, which was more of a doubling down. Bursts of guitar, even faster drums, call-and-response choruses that would be incredible in the rock clubs they were used to playing, or, you know, at the anti-nuke protest. Adding on to that, she had grown so much over the past couple of years—between keeping them together on the road and essentially headlining her own act in Paris, she had become quite a leader herself, a front woman. As their producer I had to throw up my hands and say, "Bloody hell, you two, what is it that we're doing here?"

OPAL JEWEL:

Wasn't nobody trying to kill Nev's creativity, Nev's music, and especially not his sobriety. I told him I was willing to toss out all the songs I'd written and start from scratch if he'd agreed to do it too, to work together on building something fresh that might work out for us both. But Nev

---

* On September 20, 1973, the folk and rock singer/songwriter was killed in a plane crash while on tour. Several of his songs from the posthumous album *I Got a Name*, released that December, lingered on the charts through 1974, with the title track used in films and commercials.

was attached to his songs, and I respected that. I wasn't ever *angry* with him, and I tried my best to not resent that, as a white male artist, Nev would always get the benefit of the doubt whichever way he went. I did get frustrated by the process, though. One time I blurted out, "We just need to go solo, then." I didn't wholly mean that, but once I put the idea out there I couldn't take it back.

The idea of solo albums intrigued the Rivington executives but also made them skittish. Opal & Nev had gotten famous symbiotically—Opal's performance sparked by Nev's songs, Nev's songs catching fire through Opal's performance. Disentangled from each other, both artists might flop. And yet Opal & Nev risked falling into oblivion altogether if they dawdled any longer bickering over artistic direction. Harris, the company's publicist, proposed a compromise.

BOB HIZE:

The plan was to do a double album. We were going to call it *Hers & His*, and the idea was that each of them would have a piece of it they could develop to the fullest, something they could both be happy with, each side standing on its own. Opal would sing background for Nev's side, and he'd play some guitar for hers, to keep some ties between them. Lizzie even had an idea for the visuals—black-and-white portraits, Opal on one side and Nev on the other, with their hands clasped in color on the inside when you opened up the record. The way Lizzie sold it, it sounded very fair, like a way they could be together but also independent.

OPAL JEWEL:

Let's have a history lesson, now—rewind all the way back to "separate but equal." Makes sense in theory, right, so how come it's a lie? *Because what you end up with is never equal.* Especially if you got a perceived Negro problem on one side and white folks in charge on the other.

I had a bad feeling about it, but I went ahead and said okay. I did have some requests, though: equal time with Bob in the studio, equal budget for my other musicians, anything that would make my portion of the production as good as I could get it. And simply because I asked for what I deserved, folks seemed to think I was a terrorist.

HOWIE KELLY:

I thought, *How ungrateful is this girl?* He had his problems, sure, but is that any wonder, dealing with her? He'd pulled her ass out of the ghetto in Detroit, and then he saved her life in the riot *she* caused, and *then* he even wrote her some hit songs to sing! We'd made her famous in the greatest country on earth! Suddenly none of it's good enough for her? Suddenly she wants to be the number one boss?

ROSEMARY SALDUCCI:

I got to be friendly with a secretary who worked for one of the bigger labels, and one day we're laughing over drinks, sharing horror stories from the job, and she asks me, "Is it true Opal demanded her own office space at Rivington?" I said, "No, that's ridiculous—where'd you get that?" And then she tells me all this stuff she's heard about what a nightmare Opal Jewel supposedly is. How she randomly barks at people she doesn't like, and burns smelly roots in the studio . . . I'm looking at this girl like, *Are you serious with this?* But that's how they used to talk about Opal in these industry circles. It was terrible, and I'm sure it had some bearing on how everything went down.

Two weeks before the recording of the Hers & His *project was due to begin, Opal remembers, she was summoned to Rivington for a meeting.*

OPAL JEWEL:

I'm thinking maybe they want a last-minute change to the album, a couple duets or something. I strolled on over to the studio and opened the door that led to the control room, and on the other side of the glass I could see them sitting around the piano. Nev was on the bench and had his back to me but I could see the other three glance up. Lizzie looked away real quick, and Bob had a handkerchief pressed up against his mouth, like he was two seconds away from throwing up. I'll give Howie some credit, though: He held his head up the whole time I was frozen there staring at them on the other side of that glass, and he grinned and waved for me to come on in. I just stood there a few seconds bracing myself. *Whatever happens, girl, don't you lose your mind. . . .*

BOB HIZE:

I'd been outvoted in the matter, and so I'd told Howie and Lizzie they'd have to break it to Opal. Looking back on her reaction, I do wish I had done it myself. That might have been more kind.

OPAL JEWEL:

I took a seat next to Nev on that piano bench and nudged him. I asked him straight up, "What's wrong, what's going on?" but he was just staring down at the keys. Then Howie started running his yap. "I don't know why everybody's so glum—we got good news, Opal! You're getting exactly what you asked for." I said, "Hurry up and hit me with it." And that's when Lizzie told me she'd slipped some radio biggety-bigs in LA demos of Nev's new music—demos I didn't even know he'd been recording, by the way, behind that strong new gate of his—and the buzz was already so good that Rivington was ready to bank on him solo, if that's what he wanted too. Well, I could read between those lines. I knew that meant Nev was gonna fly and my little piece of the project was gonna catch dust up on the shelf.

I said to Nev, "So that's it? You're cool with us ending like this?" He said something under his breath then, and it was driving me crazy, him being so mealymouthed and still not looking me in my face. I shoved him off the bench and yelled at him, "Say what you gotta say to me, Nev! Say it with your chest!" Bob and Lizzie ran to get between us and Howie grabbed me by my wrists and pinned them behind me. I'm screaming at Howie to let me go, and Bob's asking me to please calm down, calm down, and that's when Nev got up off the floor. He dusted off the butt of his blue jeans while Howie held my arms, and he pointed a long skinny finger down in my face: "You're the one who left *me* behind. You're the one who started it!" That's what Nev shouted at me, all choked up, like we were six-year-olds on the playground.

ROSEMARY SALDUCCI:

I really do think Opal broke Nev a little. Well, she didn't do that *intentionally*, of course, but I bet she could've easily fixed the situation if she'd swallowed her pride and sweet-talked him some, just enough so he felt like she wouldn't go running off on him again. "You're absolutely right, it was selfish of me to be gone so long, let's please start over, I'm sorry." [*Rolling eyes*] I mean, you and I both know it's bullshit, the way men pout when the women they love hurt their precious feelings, but who knows? Maybe a little ass-kissing might've gone a long way here. [*Whispering*] I'm just saying, look at all the bubbleheads he's paying alimony.*

OPAL JEWEL:

Wasn't no *fixing* it, not in that moment, not in that studio. Because I could tell it was about more than me being MIA after Nev melted down. It was everything he couldn't admit had been aggravating him when I *was* around. The bigger love I got on the road, the more attention I got in the press . . . things that I couldn't really help and that his ego couldn't handle, at least not sober. Now, I could *empathize* with the fact that sometimes he felt insecure, overshadowed, jealous even. But *apologize*? We were supposed to be past that! I had already expressed to him, anyway, that I was sorry for my part in the riot, for what it was that had brought us the heat in the first place. And as part of that apology I'd made it clear that he didn't owe me anything from that point

---

* Nev Charles has been divorced three times. None of his ex-wives—including his first, Wendy Meiers, an aspiring dietitian who was living with Nev at the time Opal visited after returning from Paris—would comment for this book.

forward—he could've walked away from my mess. But Nev said no. Said he wanted to be partners. So now that we were deep in the thing, what was I supposed to do? Feel bad for being me? For expressing my style and my opinions and trying to make the most with the tools that I had? For swimming extra hard to keep us afloat the whole time he was determined to drown? Well, I wasn't about to say I was sorry for any of that, and I wasn't about to promise Nev either that going forward I could dull myself down to build him back up. Not even if apologies and promises would have saved us.

The fight fell clean out of me. Even Howie must've sensed we were done, because he let go of my wrists. Oh, I was very much at peace. Matter of fact, I took Nev's hand, the one he'd stuck in my face with so much anger, so much *hurt*, and I laced his fingers in mine like we were supposed to do on the inside cover of our new album. I closed my eyes and pulled from my heart all the good times the two of us had together, that powerful work I knew could never be tainted, and I sent up a prayer that Pearl would've hallelujah'ed: for Nev to have all the love and success his heart could handle out there on his own. Yeah, I prayed the same thing for my career too. But you know what they say 'bout how God answers prayers. [*With a pained smile*] Likes to meet you halfway.

EDITOR'S NOTE

Bob Hize never got Opal & Nev in the studio again. And though he dreamed of a miraculous recovery that would allow him to attend their Derringdo show, or at least stay lucid enough through a livestream of it, he died on April 28, 2016. Six mean weeks shy of the big reunion.

On the late morning his friends and former colleagues gathered in his memory, I saw Melody Hize Jorgensen in the hallway that led to his apartment's front door. Bob's only girl was going out as I was coming in, wearing sweatpants and a rumpled tank top. Her expression was pained but accommodating, unfailingly polite. The same look I'd seen cross her father's face when I'd ask him about some minutiae he couldn't remember, or when, on a bad day, he was struggling to fight off sleep.

I told Melody who I was, offering her my sympathies and the handful of white roses I'd brought. She smiled tightly, nodded, and took the bouquet. "Thank you for coming," she said, her voice wrung dry. How many times had she repeated that script? Down by the pocket of her sweatpants, between the fingers of her other hand, she twiddled a silver cylinder.

"I can take the flowers inside, if you need to step out," I said.

She opened her mouth as if to object, but then stopped herself, released a quick breath. "I'd really appreciate that." She handed the roses back to me and followed my gaze to her e-cigarette. Held it up with another tight smile. "Nasty habit, I know. I've been trying to quit, like my dad begged me to. I never had his willpower, I guess."

"You don't have to explain," I said. "I imagine it's a stressful day."

The elevator dinged; more guests stepped off.

"Please, help yourself to refreshments," Melody said to all of us strangers before going down the emergency stairs.

Squeezing inside Bob's apartment, I could see how Melody might have felt overwhelmed. The living room seemed much smaller than the space I remembered from my earlier visits. Guests chatting in groups nodded hello from their saucers of charcuterie, muffins, and fresh-cut fruit. A translucent shade had been pulled down over the picture window, obscuring the expansive view of the park that had made me gasp the first time I'd seen it. But the sun burned incredibly strong that day. The room was toasty and aromatic. Aftershave. Coffee. Flowers like the ones I'd brought, on the precipice of wilting.

I traced the source of that last cloying scent to Bob's baby grand, sitting atop its Persian rug. Despite the attempt to dull the sunlight, the piano still gleamed the glossiest black. The guests gave it a respectful berth—the bench neatly tucked under, the heavy lid closed. On top: Among the blooms of strewn flowers, different varieties but every one white, sat the ornate urn of Bob's ashes and a gold-framed eight-by-ten picture of him as a much younger man. He was standing in shirtsleeves and belted slacks, in front of a soundboard and two giant speakers. A clock on the wall read three. His joyful face was turned toward the camera; his arms were raised high, as if he'd been caught celebrating a touchdown of a take.

I placed my offering of white roses on top of the pile, then glanced around the room for where to sit, what to do, some kind of mooring. Near the long table where the food had been set, I recognized two figures from the back, hovering over the platters and chafing dishes—a stooped elderly man hanging on to the elbow of a big-haired woman. I got in line behind them.

"You want melon?" Rosemary Salducci brayed at Howie Kelly, plastic tongs in one hand and his saucer in the other.

"Hah?"

"Melon, Howie, melon! Cantaloupe!"

"Yeah, yeah," he said, and turned around with his face scrunched when I touched his arm.

"Nice to see you again," I said, "although I'm sorry about the circumstance."

"He can't hear you, sweetheart," Rosemary said to me over Howie's head, at a more normal volume. "Something's going on with his hearing aid today. That son of his, slow to fix the simplest things . . ." She leaned down to his ear and brayed again: "That's Sunny. Jimmy Curtis's daughter, from *Aural* magazine."

"Hell, Rosie, I know who she is!" Howie nodded at me, brow still furrowed, then turned back to Rosemary. "She came to get my life story a few months back."

Rosemary indicated a stack of wooden folding chairs and told me to set one up near the window, next to the chairs on which she and Howie had draped their jackets. Rosemary preferred to sit near the sunny window, she said, because Howie's blood was extremely thin; if she sat them anywhere else, he'd complain the whole damn time that he was freezing. It just so happened that the placement gave Rosemary (and me, by extension) an excellent vantage point from which to gawk. While her former boss sat oblivious on the other side of her, cramming into his mouth the prosciutto and salami she had piled on his saucer, Rosemary pointed out to me various guests—a sound engineer; Bob's younger son, Andrew, chatting with Howie's heir, Mark; a security guard who had worked at the label sometime in the 1980s, past the time of most of the hate mail.

We watched as an elegant and trim ash-blond woman, somewhere in her seventies, opened the front door. She wore a dove-gray blouse and black slacks, and a strand of pearls close to her neck. She seemed startled by the number of us here.

"And of course you know who *that* is," Rosemary said to me, nodding toward the woman.

"I don't, actually."

"Oh? That's Claudia," she said. "Bob's wife. *Ex*-wife. Poor thing. Been running around on errands all morning, because Melody's been . . ." A flutter of her hand, a soft cuckoo whistle. "And the boys, you know . . . Well. Can't count on boys in times like these."

I remembered Bob telling me so vividly, so lovingly about Claudia. About her worrying to her sister on the phone after he'd made his risky deal with

Howie: *Oh, what has he done, what has he done?* Sitting on the aisle up in the balcony of the Smythe, shooting her husband a worried look as the night tipped toward chaos.

"It makes me so sad they ever split up," Rosemary was saying, "but Bob could be a workaholic, I saw it. Maybe she got tired of sharing him with all these people. So many fires, so much drama. Never enough time." She shook her head again. "Howie," she shouted, turning to him. "Did you give your condolences to Claudia yet?"

Howie set his saucer on the deep windowsill and grimaced, bracing his white Reeboks against the hardwood floor. "My goddamn knees—gimme a hand, will ya?" he asked Rosemary, and she helped prop him up, got him on his way.

As Rosemary chattered, I saw Cherry Allison of the Curlicutes walk in, and Land of the Free's Holiday Contagious, of the pruning face and squeaking black leather, peacocking behind her. Then Alice arrived—Bob's efficient nurse, who'd been the one to call me with the news of his death. She was dressed in an olive-green pantsuit with light makeup and a short-cropped wig. This was the first time I'd seen her not wearing her scrubs. I waved her over to take the seat Howie had vacated, and introduced her to Rosemary.

"Where is Mr. Hize's music today?" Alice asked after we exchanged cheek kisses, and I realized this was another thing that felt different about this space: There was no record playing, no warm thrum coming from the console.

I plotted my path to the walk-in closet that held Bob's extensive collection. "You think it'd be okay if I picked something out?"

"I think," said Alice, pointing up to the ceiling, "that Mr. Hize would want to hear something good."

So I excused myself to Bob's magic music shop, and shut myself inside it once more.

Classical seemed most appropriate for a somber event, but was it too stiff, too typical for remembering a slyly unconventional man like Bob? I remembered his delightful mimickry of my father's style: "Wah-*PAAAAAH*-pah, wah-*PAAAAAH*-pah . . ." I found the swing section and picked out a couple

records, started compiling the playlist in my head. To the stack I added Toots
& the Maytals, to make Alice smile. Two early albums by Sam Cooke, whose
arrangements Bob always said he greatly admired as a young producer, plus
My Generation by the Who . . . As always, I agonized over my choices.

I don't know how long I was in there, squinting at the records' spines,
but at some point on the other side of the door, DJ S. Sunny Shelton got
preempted. First by an increase in chatter and an unmistakable laugh slicing
through it, and then by a clap that stole my breath. Soon there was a cheer
from the guests, and then music. Not from the console, but a familiar, jaunty
piano tune. I put down the records I'd been gathering.

I couldn't see Nev Charles at all when I slipped back into the room. He
was obscured by the mourners standing now in a crowd around him as he
commandeered Bob's baby grand and teased out the intro to his solo hit "The
Lane Where I Lived." The mourners were smiling and craning their necks,
standing on tiptoe. Holding up their phones high, recording.

"Obviously I was thinking of home when I wrote this," I could hear Nev
say from the center of the circle. "I remember when I first sang it for Hizey,
he asked me, 'Do you ever think of going back, for longer than a visit? Maybe
it would do you good.' And I joked with him, 'No, I'm just fine importing the
occasional Cadbury Crunchie.' But what I really wish I had told him was that
he was like my bit of home here. My older, wiser brother . . ."

As Nev played, I tiptoed around the outer periphery of the circle, my
head hung low. The two halves of myself were at war with each other. I felt a
twinge in my stomach, as SarahLena screamed: *I'm going to be sick if I don't
get out of here.* I felt a twinge in my stomach, as Sunny thrilled at her shot:
You've got a chance to corner him now! Both halves compelled me to the
hallway outside. Out there, SarahLena could swallow her nausea; out there,
Sunny could stake out a position between the elevator and the emergency
stairwell, waiting for the moment Nev tried to take his leave.

"Asters bloom in the lane where I lived / Her heart burst open too," he
sang, and a few around him joined in the verse. The backs of their heads were
a blur. The only person apart from the circle was Claudia—she was flitting
about the room, dumping guests' used plastic plates and utensils into a black

garbage bag. For a moment as I tiptoed past her, I caught a storminess in her face. Then she smiled and mouthed a "Thank you for coming."

I eased out of the front door and let it fall closed quietly behind me. I shut my eyes and swallowed hard; the voices on the other side now were thankfully muffled. But then I realized I wasn't alone. I heard the hollow echoing of hard-bottomed shoes. I opened my eyes and looked down the hallway.

There was Opal, pacing the floor.

"Oh," she said, and stopped. "*You're* here."

I hadn't seen her in more than a month, not since our last interview about her breakup with Nev. Now, catching my breath from the heart attack she nearly gave me, I saw she was beautifully dressed, if a bit overdone. She'd covered her head with a yellow cloche hat featuring a bow detail, and wore a silky navy jumpsuit with a cream blazer draped loosely around her shoulders. Red sequin-crusted peep-toe shoes, sparkly as Dorothy's ruby slippers.

"I thought you were still in LA," I said.

"I was. Nev was there too. We were planning out the show when Rosemary called to say this thing here was going on." She glanced toward the door. "We didn't know if we were gonna make it in time, but . . . Nev's got a private jet, you know. Got a girl serving him snacks and everything. And folks used to call *me* a showoff."

"But why . . . You came this far to hang out in the hall?"

"I just need a minute," she said, defensive. "I've never been good at these kinds of . . . events. And I'm guessing on the other side of that door is a lotta folks I ain't seen in a long, long time." She began pacing again, inhaling deeply. "To tell you the truth, I was practicing a few relaxation breaths, to keep myself from wrapping my hands around Howie's neck."

I laughed. She didn't.

"And you?" she said. "You working?"

"No. Well, maybe? But not originally . . ."

"Huh?"

"I mean, really I'm here because Bob and I got to be friendly," I said. "During our interviews."

"Sounds about right," she said. "Bob *was* the type could get along with any-ol'-body. Even after that ugliness with my contract, you know, he would check up on me now and then. Ask me how my music was coming. He'd say, 'Let's have a crack in the studio, Opal. We can figure out the logistics later.' And I'd say, 'Bob, y'all's lawyers know you got me on this phone?' "

"He wasn't much of a suit, was he?"

"I knew he wasn't 'cause he never did give up on me. One time I was real low, real fed up with how my cookie was crumbling, and still he was talking 'bout working together. Said, 'I know you think this industry is full of nothing but money-grubbing devils, but at least let me be the devil you know.' " She stopped and gave a small, bitter huff. "Lots of folks think I should have listened to him. Instead of giving up altogether. Probably lots of folks think it's too late and too foolish for me to come back now." She shook her head; the pacing resumed. "I guess *you'd* probably be one of them."

"What? Why would you say that?"

"Because," she said, her footsteps echoing, "I talked to Virgil."

Chet's allegations burned deep in my throat. For more than four months now I'd been swallowing them, through all my subsequent interactions with Opal. Hoping against hope I could somehow debunk them, before they had a chance to do more damage.

"The rehearsals for Derringdo were going so well that I figured I better call my principal stylist," Opal continued. "Give him a budget to go on and finish the full tour wardrobe. I thought he would be over the moon about it; he'd been pushing me before to say yes. But then he said that for some reason, *you* told him I shouldn't do it."

"No, wait," I said, "Virgil misunderstood me. What I meant was—"

"Why would you say that? You think I'm too rusty? You think I'm gonna make a fool of myself? Of Nev?"

"Please, Opal, would you just stop a minute?"

But still she kept going. "Why would you smile in my face and talk trash behind my back? You know I can't stand that."

"I do know," I said, and stood in her path. I held her shoulders gently. "So let me try to explain, right now, why I'm not sure you should do a tour with *him*." I gestured toward the door.

And as we stood in that hallway, as Nev finished his hit and the people inside applauded, I finally let loose for her the awful, still-unconfirmed allegations. Could her old partner have once been so thirsty, so jealous, so entitled? I asked. Could it be that Nev had sicced a gang of thugs on my father, the Black man who'd dared try to stop his show? Could it be that he'd shirked his share of that weight while calculating his way to the top?

With her head tilted up, I could see Opal's face clearly underneath the cloche hat. Looking into her huge watering eyes, the two of us bound on the lonelier side of the door, I thought of a story that Nev, of all people, had shared about Opal. About the time he'd lingered in the heat of her mother's kitchen in Detroit, after Opal had whipped off her wig and exposed her secret self to him. *That vulnerability . . . It'll knock you flat.*

Not until this moment did I understand the real reason I had avoided telling Opal any of the allegations sooner. I was putting at risk the one thing that had made her seem, to those enthralled by her image, so confident, so iconic, so much wilder and braver than the rest of us quivering mortals: her faith in the things that she knew for sure. Her performance of conviction had been her greatest gift. Now I could see a terrifying uncertainty tug at her face as she tried to process what I was saying to her. Yes, Nev had disappointed her deeply before; and yes, I sensed, she knew he was keen to boost his flagging career by reengaging her now. But perhaps to make sense of their history and what they ever had been to each other—perhaps to justify this reunion to herself—she'd preserved the version of him that existed in her fondest, most hopeful memory. The goofy, searching redheaded boy who'd ferried her out of the theater, who'd consoled her as she howled in the back of a taxi . . . That boy who'd first seen the gold in her, who'd given her his hand and said, *Out of everyone, you*. It was him she'd believed in at the core; it was him she'd deliberately chosen back. And it was him she was trusting so many years later, for another shot at the lasting love and respect that had always seemed to slip through her fingers once they fell apart.

The door opened and Opal twitched out of my grip. Rosemary poked her head in the crack. "There you are," she said to Opal. "Come in, come in— Nev's waiting on you for 'Evergreen.' " She swung the door open wider and saw me there too. "Oh, sorry, Sunny, am I interrupting? We just thought it'd be nice to hear, it was one of Bob's favorites. . . ."

"Mind your business, Rosemary," said Opal, but her eyes were still trained on mine. Something in them had suddenly hardened when the doorknob turned, when the voices from inside interfered. She squinted and nodded her head: decided. "I see what this is," she said to me. "But you know why I let you in on this project, right? Because I felt *sorry* for you."

"Wait, what's going on?" said Rosemary. She eased halfway into the hallway, keeping the door cracked open with one leg.

"I read that article about your big promotion," Opal said. "A Black girl with the whole business on her back! I read that and you know what? I wanted to help you win. I gave you the story like I never shared it, I owned up to my part in everything. And now you repay me by twisting the knife? You gon' save yourself tryna cut *me* down? Nah, baby. Nah."

"But what if it's true?" I said. "If there's even a chance that it is, could you really stand beside him on a stage night after night? Could you really mean a word that you say?"

"Jesus, what if *what's* true?" said Rosemary. "Come inside, girls, and let's hash out whatever this is."

But Opal wasn't done with me yet. She readjusted the blazer draped over her shoulders. "Miss S. Sunny Shelton. Miss Tough Stuff. I'd thought you were better than to be so desperate, but I guess you're the same as the rest of these scroungers."

"I know you're afraid," I said. "I know this would change the story, change what you've *believed*, and that's a scary thing to reckon with. But you're going to have to reckon with it. None of this will feel right if you don't."

On the other side of the door Nev was starting up "Evergreen." Soon he would be approaching the part of the duet where Opal comes in. I watched her watching the door, frozen. Then Lizzie Harris was snatching it open and standing next to Rosemary, with a big bright smile that dropped as soon as she saw me. She looked back over her shoulder, sang out to someone she'd be back in a jiff, then came out into the hallway to turn the full force of her fury on me.

"You are *unbelievable*," she hissed in my direction. "What are you now, an ambulance chaser? TM-fucking-Z? Shame on you, Sunny." Lizzie reached for Opal's arm and tugged slightly, trying to coax her over the threshold, but Opal snatched it away.

"Don't you ever put your hands on me," Opal said, real low. "You don't know me like that. You never did."

"Okay, let's all calm down," said Rosemary. "Let's not forget where we are."

"Opal, I don't know what she's told you," murmured Lizzie, duly chastened and crossing her arms, "but she doesn't have a shred of proof. Whatever she's saying is out-and-out lies. And I can promise you this: She will be sued if she continues to spread them."

"Lizzie's right," I said to Opal, "I don't have confirmation. And I know this timing is not ideal. But you're the one who told me that this assignment is beyond professional, right? That it's got to be personal too? So I'm asking you now, I ask you as a professional *and* as Jimmy's daughter, to tell me whether you think it's possible."

"Did Sunny happen to tell you," Lizzie interrupted, cocking her frosted helmet of blond hair, "that Chet Bond is her source for this shit?"

"Chet Bond," muttered Rosemary. "Bad egg, hon."

"Tell me that's not true," Opal said to me. "Tell me you got more sense than this."

I took a deep breath. "I didn't *want* to believe what he said, but I couldn't ignore—"

"Okay, come on, Opal," said Lizzie. "Enough indulging this nonsense."

But Opal wasn't moving, and my heart surged with hope that she might hear me out.

"Listen," I said, "end of the day, this isn't about the Bonds or Nev or even Bob, God rest his soul. This is about who *you* are now, what *you* choose to do. Who you could still have the power to be, on your own terms this time . . ."

At the end of the hallway the elevator dinged. Melody Hize Jorgensen, back from her smoke break, stepped off the car.

"Oh, thank God," said Lizzie, and squeezed past me and Opal to draw Bob's daughter into her arms. "Melody, sweetheart, I'm so sorry for your

THE FINAL REVIVAL OF OPAL & NEV

loss. And the last thing I want to do, today of all days, is trouble you with a problem, but . . ." She glanced at me as if highly offended. "Did you invite the media here today? Because I believe this woman is trespassing." She pulled away from Melody just long enough to lean over and hit the call button for the elevator.

"Trespassing?" I said, and it was so ridiculous I had to laugh. "Come on, now. Melody, your dad told me he wanted me invited, when the time came. You can ask Alice—she was there when he said it."

"I don't know what's going on here," Melody said, looking down at the floor as Lizzie rubbed small circles on her back, "but please leave all of us in peace. Please respect our privacy. . . ."

The elevator car arrived back on the floor.

"Opal?" I said, one last try.

But by then she had turned her face away, and all I could see was that bow on her hat.

chapter twenty-one

"THAT'S HOW THEY GET YOU"

★　★

"MELTDOWN FOR *AURAL* EDITOR?" FROM KEITH J. KELLY'S MEDIA INK COLUMN, *NEW YORK POST*, MAY 4, 2016

The editor in chief of *Aural* magazine caused an embarrassing scene last week at a private memorial for legendary record producer Bob Hize, sources tell Media Ink.

S. Sunny Shelton, who was promoted to the top editor job with much fanfare last year, was said to be harassing mourners at the gathering, where Nev Charles made a surprise appearance to pay his respects. It's unclear how Shelton wrangled her way inside, considering the gathering was closed to news media, but sources say that during Charles's impromptu performance in tribute to Hize, Shelton pestered guests with increasingly aggressive and incoherent questions. She was eventually asked to leave the premises.

An insider at *Aural* tells Media Ink that Shelton has not responded well to the immense pressures she faces as editor in chief in a brutal climate for print. Year over year, *Aural* is down sharply in advertising revenue, and although digital traffic has seen some gains driven by a growing social media audience, they have not been enough to turn around the brand's fortunes. Meanwhile Shelton's choices as editor in chief, especially covers that have leaned more Solange than Springsteen, have prompted some on staff to question her judgment. "We just don't know if her heart is here," said one insider. "She seems more interested in a personal agenda. It's disappointing."

Calls to Shelton and Aural Media were not returned by press time.

That column was published on a Wednesday. Deep into Thursday, nobody in the office would meet my eye.

Friday morning, I was asked into a small conference room with Jonathan Benjus Jr. and *Aural*'s head of human resources. They sat together on one side of the table, the HR woman's hand atop a manila folder in front of her.

"So . . ." said JBJ, tugging at a stiff new necktie.

"So," I said, and waited for the rest.

Late Sunday afternoon, still wallowing in bed, I reached for my phone, sitting on my nightstand atop HR's manila folder. I opened Facebook. All night I had been trying to come up with a status update: *One door closes and blah blah blah.* But before I could begin composing, I noticed the feed was full of throwback family photos, pastel flowers, special filters. . . . I nearly fumbled the phone in my panic to dial home.

"Happy Mother's Day!" I blurted, before Corinne Dawes Curtis could say hello.

"Well. I was wondering when I was going to hear from my child. *If* I was going to hear from her."

"Of course I was going to call you, Mommy."

But in fact, my mother and I had not spoken very much, or very warmly, since I first went to Philly to confess I was working on this book. She made it clear that icy weekend that she sees no value in investigating bygone trespasses, and especially not in rewarding, with even more attention, those she believes have trespassed against her. By the way she'd clutched her teacup close to her chest as we agreed to disagree about what of the past entails whose business, I gleaned that she still feels protective of her heart, and trusts no one, not even her own daughter, to understand that Jimmy's indiscretions did not somehow reflect her shortcomings as his wife.

"You're going to do what you're going to do," my mother had finally said of my plans, sipping that Irish Breakfast across our old cherrywood dining room table. Our relationship since that visit had suffered, though, staggering along on a series of brief but agonizing phone calls on obligatory occasions: my birthday ("Well, then, another year"), extreme weather events ("Sarah-Lena, you'd be a fool to go out in that blizzard without the right boots on"), guilt-inducing health updates ("Doctor says it's nothing to worry about. Probably just, you know, my *stress*").

"Did Mr. Peter take you to brunch today?" I asked her now, forcing myself to sound as chipper as possible. I could hear her TV on in the background—her favorite dummies, the ones hunting for houses on HGTV.

"You do know it's nearly three o'clock, right?" she said. "Why are you still in bed?"

"I'm not," I lied.

"Then why can I still hear the sleep in your voice?"

I sat up.

"You want to talk about it?"

"Talk about what, Mommy?"

"I saw that story about you on the internet," she said. "And I hate that you had to learn this the hard way, but I warned you those people were low-down snakes."

I groaned and buried myself under the duvet. "You saw the Keith Kelly column? How?"

"Mr. Peter has the thing set up on my computer so I can know what people are saying about you."

"You had your *boyfriend* set up a *Google Alert* on my name?"

"Well, you barely call me, never tell me anything. . . ."

"Whenever I try to tell you things about my life, Mommy, you don't want to hear them."

"Okay, whatever, we set up the Googly thing," my mother snapped. "How else am I supposed to know what's going on with you?"

"Life gets busy, that's all," I said. "But I guess that won't be a problem anymore. I'll have all the time in the world now to call."

"Why? What are you saying? Is that magazine trying to fire you?"

Struggling to keep my voice even, I explained that I had been offered a package to leave. That my career as a top editor was likely over.

"Oh, my goodness," she said, and I could picture her perched on the settee in the living room. In my mind she was made up pretty as ever—pursing her lips, glossed-over pink; shaking her silvery curls at her dear Mr. Peter across the room. "See, now, baby, that's how they get you. Make you look like the crazy one when you can't work a miracle for them, and then they put you out the first chance they get. You saw how these white folks did Melissa Harris-Perry."

"I swear I didn't have any kind of meltdown, I—"

"Of *course* you didn't, SarahLena," she said, so tenderly that my chest tightened with love for her. "I know my child at least that much."

We were both quiet on the phone for a while. I could still hear the house hunters on her television: *It's safe to say we can cross* that *property off the list!* I considered letting her get back to her show, but then my mother cleared her throat.

"Well, at least you've got that book you can sell," she said.

Wait a minute, what—had I heard her right? "Actually," I said, approaching the trap slowly, "*Aural* owns the rights to the book. I can't see why they'd just let me have them." I felt teary again, defeated. "That's a silver lining, right? The book you always hated is probably dead."

"*Dead*?" said my mother—and yes, by God, that was real indignation in her voice! "Let me get this straight: I fight you on this book, I tell you it will *kill* me to have my business out there like that, and you say, 'I have to do it, Mommy; I *need* to do it.' Okay, then, Mommy just has to get over it. But with these folks you're folding already? You don't even try to work something out?"

"The whole severance package would have to be redone—they'd probably make me give back some money, who knows how much. . . . It's complicated."

"You think it was *simple*, the kind of negotiations I had to make back in the day?" She barked out a laugh, incredulous.

"I don't know," I said. "You've never shared your story with me."

My mother sighed. "You might be the nosiest person in the world, Sarah-Lena, but you're certainly not slick."

"*What?* What did I say that's not true?"

"If you feel so entitled to question me, then quote me on this part right here: Every moment I had to deal with that girl, every dime I ever accepted from her, all of it was *complicated* for me. You don't even know the half. But I had a purpose bigger than me, bigger than Jimmy, bigger than the marriage we got so wrong. I had *you*—your education, your comfort, your future to focus on getting right. And even if my own world was broken, even if I resented that girl with every cell of my skin, I kept my mouth shut and I let her help give you the best of it all. I put my pride aside for twenty-some years because *that*, SarahLena, is what it means to be strong. To sacrifice, to persevere . . . those things you probably give *her* the credit for."

My mother's burst of ire awed me dumb. Suddenly, I couldn't picture her at all.

"Now. Maybe you're more like your father than what's been comfortable for me. Maybe that's made our relationship harder sometimes. But what I know is this: You are also *my* smart, tenacious, driven daughter. And you wouldn't have hurt me, you wouldn't have been so hardheaded all these months, over something that wasn't important to you. Are you telling me now I'm wrong about that?"

"What are you saying? You *want* me to do the book now?"

"Oh, don't get confused: I still do not care to read Opal's hot noise," my mother said. "But this is my advice, if you care to listen: Come out of this loss setting up something bigger. Something that makes you proud outside of yourself. For me, that was you. Maybe for you, it's this work. Whatever it is, I'll try not to judge. But baby girl, you gotta decide."

The next week, I slid that manila envelope back to JBJ. Inside were the proposed terms of my counteroffer: I'd return a portion of *Aural*'s peace-out package in exchange for all recordings, documents, excerpt permissions, and publishing rights connected to my baby, my manuscript-in-progress. Giving any money back sucked, and as my mother had warned me, this negotiation was probably most expensive on my ego: By how swiftly JBJ agreed to my proposal, by the bemused look that played across his face as I signed the redrawn papers, I could glean what little value he believed this book would have, with Nev no longer participating.

And so the two decades I'd invested in *Aural* ended in yet another conference room, with a carrot cake, plastic flutes of sparkling wine, a fake magazine cover the creative director designed (my face superimposed over Ronnie Spector's!), and the presentation of a shaky iPhone video featuring staffers in their cubicles wishing me well. By the time a press release announcing my amicable departure got blasted out to a media email list, I was pleasantly buzzed at the after-party, spontaneously convened at a spot the editors would sometimes visit late at night after sending each new issue to print. We'd dubbed the place "Affair Bar" for its dim lighting, high-backed booths, and persistent rumors that *Aural*'s former ad sales director used to bring his assistant there for the small plates at lunch. I'd stopped going once I got promoted to editor in chief, figuring it would be inappropriate or just too awkward to continue fraternizing with the staff like that, but I remembered the pang I felt every month or so, watching my former colleagues tumble out together into the night. Now we were clinking shot glasses like the old days, and somebody shouted a toast above the music: "Fuck them all, from all of us!" Everyone laughed, crowded together in booths. For me, it was bittersweet. I wasn't a *them* anymore, but I no longer felt like part of the *us*. Now I was out here on my own.

PART THREE

chapter twenty-two

"HE DOES WHAT
HE DOES,
I DO WHAT I DO"

★ ★

EXCERPTED FROM "JUST SAY O.?,"
***AURAL*, JUNE 1984**

The twelve tracks on *Temper* are Opal Jewel's first new recordings since 1976's strident *Weird O.*, and her second stab at escaping the shadow of the arresting work she once did with Nev Charles. Not that she hasn't been busy in the intervening years: She's made a steady enough career by grinding through a few dates at European rock clubs and discos, guest-lecturing on university campuses, even producing a well-intentioned if only modestly successful vanity project, an off-Broadway play about the friendship between the writers Lorraine Hansberry and James Baldwin. But all that time, she says, something she needed was missing—the jolt she gets in the recording studio, creating her propulsive kind of rock and roll.

This comeback album took Opal nearly two years to make: three months writing it, eighteen more wrestling it free from Rivington Records and transitioning it over to Sire. Then another few weeks in the studio, updating it on the fly with what she felt was stronger, more timely material. But, she says, never mind those hitches and delays: They're in her rearview mirror now, and with what some might say is a foolish faith, Opal Jewel has her foot pressed hard against the accelerator. She's zoomed past the peskiest questions—Will this album sell any better? Is it even any *good*?—and she's steering her engines straight for the sky.

During our interview inside a midtown Manhattan café, where she's drawing stares for her naked head and outrageously colorful outfit (more on that later), Opal insists she learned a lot from the harsh reception of *Weird O*. Those lessons, she claims, have prepared her to seize a new moment. "On those songs I went too far one way, maybe a little too hard, and I do get that people sometimes want to feel the music easier in their bones," she says. "At the same time, I can't ever lose sight of who I am—can't ever get too lightweight, too meaningless. So with this record I aimed for that sweet spot in between."

Has she learned anything from the massive success of her friend and former partner?

"I'd be an idiot not to take notes from Nev," she says. "I'm proud of him. He's doing well."

Does she like the music he's making, though?

"He's doing very well," she repeats.

So well, in fact, that with *Brummie Bard*, last year's collection of story-songs, he's been nominated for three Grammys, including Song of the Year for "The Lane Where I Lived." This music is a far cry from the headline-making, direct-assault racket he used to make with Opal, but she says she doesn't begrudge Nev's quick breakthrough to the mainstream. Nor does she feel the need to trash Charles's chart-climbers as everything wrong with popular music, as Public Image Ltd.'s John Lydon once did in a ribald interview with Tom Snyder. "Please quote me verbatim on 'his because I'm so sick of saying it: *I'm not in competition with Nev*," she says, enunciating every word. She shrugs. "He does what he does, I do what I do. And if he gives a few of those millions he's making to good causes, that's all the better."

If this new album hits big, I ask Opal, what causes would she help to sponsor?

"How much time you got?" she says in a scoffing tone, but her feet jiggle against the rungs of her stool with excitement. As usual, Opal Jewel prefers the scattershot approach—she's got a thousand gripes and a list of demands to match each one. Ticking them down: She still wants dangerous bigots properly prosecuted, of course—her lifelong tribute to her slain collaborator and lover, the drummer James Curtis III. But she also wants addiction treatment facilities installed in urban areas hit by the scourge of crack cocaine. Women's bodies to be their own, to do with as they please (cocks or fingers or tongues inside them; unwanted fetuses out). She wants public support for the arts, and for government watchdog groups. AIDS to be properly acknowledged, researched, and over.

On this last front, the overalls she's wearing make a powerful statement. The set designer on that off-Broadway play she produced custom-made them for her, first painting the canvas material in overlapping black, red, and green markings, like an alternative camouflage. Screen-printed atop that backdrop, on the front of the overalls and the back, are two different headshots of the same young black man, each one bordered with safety pins. He is—he was—an aspiring dancer named Christopher Givens, the set designer's homosexual lover. In the "before" photo on the front, Mr. Givens is smiling and healthy, eyes twinkling. In the "after" on the back, he is nearly unrecognizable. His face haggard and slack, skin ruined with lesions. Eyes dead dull.

"The front was taken in '81," Opal says. She turns around and keeps her back to me for the next several moments as she speaks, so that Mr. Givens's visage haunts. "And this one on the back was taken just a year later. Now thousands of people are dead, thousands more are sick with this thing. And your all-American Gipper, he closes his eyes."

Of the *Temper* song titled "Ron Is Gone"—one of the later additions to the album, Opal confirms—the reference is, in fact, to President Reagan. Though the lyrics feel reliably provocative, her vocals on the track go soft and dreamy, perhaps her appeal to those who've sniped that her voice is too loud and unpleasant for today's pop radio: "We'd come out to drink the night / He and he, she by she / Whichever way we'd care to arrive / We are well again / Elegant / Dignified / Free."

What does she mean by all of this, in the context of that title?

Still Opal keeps her back turned to me. "It's my little fantasy," she says, "of what might be, or what might've been for Christopher and all the other friends and artists we've lost, if the people who didn't give a damn disappeared."

So, if Reagan wasn't president, there'd be a cure?

"It's impossible for me to answer a question like that." Her tone has turned cool and wary. "I just know things are getting worse with him in."

Who will she back to fix what's broken, then? Walter Mondale? Jesse Jackson?

She whips back around on her stool, incredulous. Mr. Givens now seems to laugh at me too.

"Oh, honey," she says. "How we gon' get anywhere, with you dreaming so small?"

CAPSULE REVIEW OF OPAL JEWEL'S
FINAL ALBUM, *AURAL*, MARCH 1988
Stew (Uprising Records)

Opal Jewel has yet another new label but the same old devils on *Stew*, her self-produced third solo rant. As the title suggests, she's dumped various styles into the pot, everything from reggae to rap (even trading verses on "Did I Stutter?" with a charitable KRS-One). But it seems that time has continued to dull her palette: Instead of serving up a richly layered conceptual treat, she's oversalted the finished product with preachy lyrics and the tired feminist shtick that wore out two albums ago. Hard to imagine even the most nostalgic Mercurial dipping a spoon into this. ★ ⅃ —*Phil Francisco*

PARTIAL TRANSCRIPT FROM "INSIDE OPAL JEWEL'S CLOSET," MTV'S *HOUSE OF STYLE*, FEBRUARY 17, 1990

Todd Oldham: Now all these explosions of color I just adore, but it's a little different vibe from the character you're playing in *Any Witch Way.* Can you tell us about her style?

Opal Jewel: Augustina is like the grand dame of the coven—347 years young and a classic, honey. Maybe a little too much old-lady lace for my speed, but that's all right, the all-black suits me fine.

———

To be clear: *Any Witch Way,* costarring Opal Jewel and released in theaters two years after her last album flopped, is a *terrible* movie. The plot is stupid, the F/X subpar. Opal's costumes, clearly not Virgil-vetted, comprise a dingy heap of voluminous rags; next to her fellow witchy time travelers (Swoosie Kurtz and Penelope Ann Miller, both outfitted in wispy pastels), she looks sexless and old. Anyone who's ever seen this "comedy" could argue it is among the more desperate moments of Opal Jewel's career, a marker on her downward trajectory into a decades-long silence. For her Black fans, though, the cringe factor is acute. I still remember the first time I saw it, on VHS with my first girlfriend in college, and how, whenever Opal jerked her neck to the side or pooched out her lips, we threw our hands up over our eyes. Watching her image flattened for laughs, stretched toward the most obvious stereotypes about sassy Black women, felt to us like a horror show.

And yet, as with Opal's later albums, there is something worth noting in her committed performance. Following my most recent viewing—in my apartment on a Monday afternoon, as I pondered the frightening decline of my own career—I concede that her character, Augustina, one of three guiding witches posing as substitute teachers at a white-bread Midwest high school, has by far the best lines. In the moments I got terribly annoyed with the main character (played by Christina Applegate), Augustina rose to the occasion as my avatar. "Lemme get this straight," she snipes to her kindlier witch sisters after their blond protegée gets tripped at the homecoming dance by her crush's girlfriend. "I'm conjured back here after hundreds of years, and this dummy *still* can't work a protective spell?" And Swoosie Kurtz and Penelope Ann Miller try to hold the incorrigible Augustina back, try to keep her off the dance floor, but she charges from her station behind the punch bowl, whooshing away the crowd of bopping white teenagers with a flick of her fingers, and the camera zooms on her disgusted face as she peers down at the floor and barks the only line from this movie you probably know. . . .

Damn it, Becky! Get it together!

I first saw the GIF pop up this past January, posted by an old friend on Twitter. The looping clip has since been repurposed for various outrages involving white women, but on that day the attached caption, punctuated after the ellipses with the laugh-cry emoji, was "Serena Williams Be Like . . ."—presumably a commentary on the news that endorsement queen Maria Sharapova had been trounced, for the eighteenth straight time, by her imagined rival during the quarterfinals of the Australian Open.

I laughed at this viral gold for a good ten minutes (I'm only human, after all, and on top of that a Serena fanatic). Then I marveled that it existed, period. Even I had not remembered this moment from the movie until I saw it all over my social feeds. I could imagine that some anonymous internet genius had been reading the headlines about Bree Newsome* and the history of Confederate iconography; I could see them digging toward the same place I'd once been—the bottom of an Opal Jewel rabbit hole. But this fresh convert was a millennial kid, with access to much better technology than me: They'd unearthed this B-minus-minus of movies, in a high-definition format to boot, and then had the patience to make a perfectly edited GIF of it, cutting the clip right at the moment when Opal, having delivered her epic lines, slices her eyes to the side. Whoever it was understood the culture and the language and this current moment of Black exasperation, and was nodding to the eerie relevance of Opal Jewel in them. Whoever it was knew that this bit would land.

In Opal's garden in March, during the last interview before our standoff at Bob's memorial, we talked about what new audience might be ready for her. I pulled up the GIF on my phone and played it for her—she said she had never seen it before. I studied her as she watched it; I expected her to cackle, same as everyone else. Instead her top lip curled as she studied the device. She adjusted its distance from her face as if trying to snap the screen into focus, then started tapping at it, shaking it.

"The damn thing is skipping," she said, and thrust it back at me.

"Oh, no no," I said, taking it from her and squatting beside her chair. "It's supposed to do that. It's a GIF. It loops. Like a highlight. See?"

We watched it together a few times, and I couldn't help but laugh again.

She smiled but shook her head at me. "I guess I'm old, because I don't get it. Is it supposed to be funny?"

---

* On June 27, 2015, days after nine Black Americans were massacred inside Charleston, South Carolina's Emanuel AME Church by a white supremacist they had invited to worship with them, activist Newsome scaled a thirty-foot pole outside the South Carolina State House and removed the Confederate flag that still flew there. Her arrest spawned press coverage and reopened the debate over Confederate symbols, which the murderer, Dylann Roof, had proudly displayed in photographs. Many news stories mentioned previous controversies involving the flag—including Opal Jewel's riot-sparking destruction of one at Rivington Showcase.

I smiled back. "It is. Have you heard about 'Becky'?"

"Yes, that's the girl in the movie. That was the character's name."

"Right, right, but . . ." I briefly considered trying to explain "Becky" and memes and virality, but suddenly felt very silly. I slipped the phone back into my pocket and sat down. "Well, it's a whole thing, but people really do love it."

"I guess that's what Virgil's been trying to tell me. That folks for some reason love this movie now."

"Um, they love that scene, at least."

"Huh." She seemed to consider. "I guess you can see I don't fool too much with the internet."

"Why's that?"

She leaned back in her chair until the front legs lifted. She stretched and spoke through a giant yawn: "People are real sometimey. They didn't have anything good to say about me when it came out." The chair plopped back down to the ground. "Wouldn't buy my records and then called me a sellout when I took this role, when I tried to get paid."

We were both quiet awhile, listening to the crickets sing. She picked up a joint perched in the teeth of an ashtray, lit it, and pulled, watching me with extreme focus, waiting for me to say something else.

"As an Opal Jewel fan," I said, "those were difficult days to stomach."

"I'm well aware," she said, exhaling and breaking her stare. "But were *you* aware that BS little movie helped keep me out of the hole? Besides my other debts, my mama was sick. She'd just had a stroke, and a bad one at that. Needed round-the-clock care. The music y'all loved wasn't cutting the checks anymore."

"For what it's worth? I actually think *Temper* is very underrated. *Stew* too."

"Huh," she said. "You and the fifteen other people who think that should start a club. Had to cancel that *Stew* tour halfway through, you know. Had to cut my losses."

I couldn't help but think of Nev then, and his wins through the eighties—the gold and platinum pop records; the awards-show performances; the massive stadium tours; the lucrative songwriting credits for other artists, when he wasn't promoting a new solo project himself.

"Did Nev ever offer to help you out?" I asked Opal that evening. "Seems he could have easily invited you on a couple of his tours, If he'd wanted."

"Why, so I could drag him down too?" She laughed. "Nah. And if he had offered I would've turned him down. All I ever wanted for Opal & Nev, at the time we broke up, was for what we used to do together to live on its own as a meaningful thing, and as a true collaboration—not one of us giving some kind of charity to the other. So for me, when I was going through tough times, broke times, I didn't want to taint that good work. If the moment wasn't right for my solo stuff to fly, if I miscalculated, then it was just better to leave music alone and go on and do something totally different. Something forgettable and quick, like that movie. Take the money and run. Move on."

"And wow—now people are revisiting and loving these moments you say are forgettable."

"Like I said, I don't get it, but that's life. Real funny how a bunch of somebodies seem to love me again. Want me running my mouth on their talk shows and panels and stuff. Want me to get back on their stage." Her eyes lit up. "Guess that's just time working like the thing on your phone. What's that you called it?"

"You mean the GIF?"

"A GIF, yeah. Looping around and around . . . " She took another drag off the joint. "You see this orange idiot whipping up so much ugly at these rallies of his? You see all these brothers and sisters shot down like dogs and nobody pays? That sure ain't brand-new. That's nothing but a throwback to the bad old days—and folks was on my TV the last election, talking about 'post-racial.' " She exhaled and shook her head. "But there's a flip side to that record—you'll see. The kind of feedback that makes your face screw up." She pretended to hear something, cocking her head like a bird. "Hey, wait a minute, what's *this* loop? What's *this* noise?" She rocked her torso back and forth, shoulders dipping up and down, as if poising herself to jump into a double-dutch. Suddenly she pounded her feet on the grass, dropped her head back, and raised both fists in triumph, the joint sticking up between the knuckles of one like a smoking middle finger. "That's that Opal & Nev speed, baby, coming around again!"

chapter twenty-three

"YOU HEAR ME?"

★　★

For the first time in God knows how many years, I traveled to Derringdo alone.
A civilian.

The general admission tickets I'd bought with my personal credit card
gave me no special privileges. After an eight-hour drive that should have
taken six—in a standard-shift white pickup that was the only weekend rental
available so last-minute in Brooklyn—I parked a little after noon in a cheap,
sun-exposed lot miles away from the festival site in Lancaster, New Hampshire. There was no helpful Derringdo staffer holding up a sign to meet me,
no assigned golf cart to tool me around. Instead I followed the masses toward a fleet of belching shuttle buses, then waited on line for forty minutes
to board.

But as soon as I disembarked, I began to feel better about experiencing
the festival sans VIP pass. The day of Opal & Nev's show was bright and
beautiful, the sky a clean blue above the huge wooden Derringdo arch. The
last time I'd been here, we media colleagues had made small talk about
the vodka sponsor that year, and what variety of mini-quiche might be on
the breakfast buffet. But all around me now the mood was less snarky, more
merry. The stages had officially opened, and the echoes of bass and drum
wafted to where we newcomers stood waiting. In line directly in front of me,
a young woman with a gold bauble glittering in a mass of wavy brown hair

burst into a can't-help-it "Woooo!" and up ahead, a similar call rang back. Everyone was laughing and excited. Giddy, goofy. A guy wearing a T-shirt that said ASK ME ABOUT BERNIE SANDERS jogged up and down the line, offering strangers a handful of his homemade Chex Mix before security made him toss it out. *Where are you from?* people asked each other. *Who did you come to see?* They traded phones and posed for photos, hugging the legs of the great carved arch as we passed under it toward the will call booths. Someone pressed their cheek hard against the wood, and came away with a reddened imprint of a Fender Stratocaster.

Friday had always been my favorite day of this festival. For the past twelve years, that night's headlining main stage slot had been reserved for the return of the nostalgic alternative act you didn't even know you missed. New Order, Big Audio Dynamite, the *Celebrity Skin* iteration of Hole. . . . Some years the festival organizers kept the Friday headliners a total secret; other years, like this one, they dropped big hints to gin up the buzz. "Nev Charles and a *Very Special Guest!*" the shareable graphic had teased for weeks, in an enlarged font sitting atop a jumble of other names, and everyone on Twitter was rolling their eyes at the obviousness of who that guest could be. Still, even after *Aural* exclusively confirmed the news, part of me wished that Opal, ever mercurial, would decide to drop out of Derringdo at the last minute. That she'd consider what I'd said outside Bob Hize's apartment, maybe comb back over her own memories for answers to the questions I'd asked. But as the line inched toward the official festival entrance, the fact of it was inescapable: I saw her face next to Nev's on signage tied to the guideposts. A new black-and-white shot of the two of them standing back-to-back, heads turned and looking into the camera with aloof expressions.

I noticed the young white woman with the gold hair bauble glancing over her shoulder at me with several shy smiles. "I like your dreads," she finally said, and I thanked her. We chatted a bit; she was from Northern California and traveling with friends, all of them celebrating their recent high school graduation. I told her I was trying to finish a book about Opal & Nev. I asked: Did she want to be in it?

**ALISON "AL" ELIZABETH DAUGHTRY, 18; SAN JOSE,
CALIFORNIA; BROWN UNIVERSITY INCOMING FRESHMAN,
CLASS OF 2020, *ON WHAT EXCITED SOMEONE SO
YOUNG ABOUT AN OPAL & NEV REUNION*:**

It's really cool. I mean, I know he's a legend and a great pop songwriter, but I actually didn't know much deep about her until I went on my campus visits. Brown threw this welcome weekend where they had the student organizations set up in an auditorium to hand out information, and this girl I saw at the Black Lives Matter booth had on a T-shirt with that old photo of them on it. I was thinking to myself, *Hey, that's "Damn it, Becky, get it together!" Why is she riding on top of Nev Charles?* [*Covering her face with her hands*] I know, I know! I thought it was totally random or, like, a joke? But anyway, I liked the shirt a lot so I googled it on my phone trying to find it. And then when the results came up I was like, *Whaaaaaat?* I called my aunt because she loves Nev so much, and I go, "Did you know Nev Charles started out totally punk?" and she was like, *Derrrr.*

———

Inside the gates, after a shockingly thorough security process that stripped me of my DERRINGDO 2009 swag parasol and the bobby pins that held up my hair, I took a moment to get my bearings. The map for Derringdo '16 showed five different stages, four satellites and one main. A Ferris wheel rose up in the background, a north star by which festivalgoers could figure out, with help from a few signs, where they were versus where they needed to be. The four satellite stages were genre-specific—EDM, hip-hop, indie rock, hardcore/punk—but the main stage at the festival's heart featured a delegation of representatives. It was most efficient to stick close to the center, inching toward the stage and deeper into the crowd during the opening sets.

But first: sustenance. I found among the food trucks nearest the main stage one that sold falafel, and the woman stuffing my pita, I noticed, was wearing a button on her uniform with Opal Jewel's face on it.

JESSICA RAMIREZ, 26; BOSTON; COOK, MOST RECENTLY AT TGI FRIDAYS:

My older brothers are into punk, and I got close with one of their ex-girlfriends who was into that scene too. She made me a playlist of classic stuff she thought I might dig. "Red-Handed" was on it and, I think, the only song with vocals by a girl on the whole thing. I fell in love with it and just went deeper from there. Me volunteering to work the festival is the only way I could get in   the tickets are way too fucking expensive.

I dunno, it kinda freaks me out how everybody claims to love them now. I was watching this Drew Barrymore thing on Netflix and one of their songs was playing in the background, and that was completely weird. Like, I'm happy that people are finally recognizing how much better Opal & Nev were than his lame solo shit, but at the same time it's like, *Nooooo, please don't ruin my thing.*

———

Munching and wandering through the crowd before Foals, I spotted the Bernie Sanders supporter who'd been jogging down the line at the entrance and handing out the Chex Mix. As his shirt directed, I asked him first about his candidate ("It's not over yet! We're gonna get big money out of politics!") before getting his take on the night's other supposed revolutionaries.

CHRIS DELANO, 34; DENVER; MEDICAL DISPENSARY MANAGER:

It's incredible that Opal is back, you know? And I'm so happy to see more people like yourself here to support her. [*When asked to explain what he meant by this*] Oh. It's, like, I don't know . . . Like, she was always so keyed into the politics having to do with your, um, with the African American community, right? And I just wonder, like, why wasn't her music ever at the top of, like, the urban charts? It's a shame that people, that sometimes they prefer the mindless stuff that goes against their own interests, but anyway, yeah, I'm just glad that they're back.

I chatted with a few other festivalgoers who'd showed up at the main stage to see Halsey and Kygo. Most of them didn't seem to know a whole lot about Opal & Nev, but expressed general enthusiasm about their show anyway. Lots of "cool"; too much "awesome." But just before SZA, when the area around me got more noticeably Black, I did speak with one fan who had a lot more to say.

RYANNE SIWANDEE, 27; NEW YORK; ACTRESS, PLAYWRIGHT, BLOGGER, FREELANCE MAKEUP ARTIST, AND HANDBAG DESIGNER:

Honestly, I would have loved it more if Opal were headlining solo. Which is a fantasy, I know, living in capitalism and systemic white supremacy. But I feel like her aesthetic and the power of her work have been co-opted for so long, and the least a music festival of this size could do is give a trailblazing elder her flowers.

Yeah, a lot of her shit is challenging to listen to. I can't say every song on *Weird O.* is a bop—but that shit is vibrating high on some other frequency, right? When you talk about challenging to absorb, so is Bob Dylan's whiny ass, in my opinion, and that fucking *Ulysses* book I had to read in college. Nigga, *what*? But aren't we supposed to be better and smarter because of the challenging art that makes us uncomfortable? Isn't the culture better for it? Or does that only apply when heterosexual cisgender white men do the challenging? [*As her companions snap their fingers behind her*] You see what I'm saying, sis?

That's not to knock Nev Charles and whatever way they work together. Maybe it's true they make each other better when it comes to the music. But Nev Charles has had his moment and he sure don't need another fan. All I'm saying is, it would be nice if a Black woman got this big a moment to claim as her own. I doubt she'll ever get another.

Dusk fell over the fairgrounds, an orange band clinging to the horizon like a layer of stone fruit sunk to the bottom of a casserole. Deep purple pressed down until night had suddenly, fully descended, at least ten degrees cooler on this late-spring night. The done-up girls let down their hair, if they had it, and readjusted their decorative flowers. They reached in their bags for sweaters or else nestled goose-bumped skin into the warmth of friends and partners. I caught eyes with a young woman in a romper, pulled through the horde by a bullish guy in a backward baseball cap, and as they passed she tried to smile an "excuse me" through chattering teeth.

The Ferris wheel, though still lit up neon, had shut down for the night, and all but a couple of the satellite stages had run through their allotted hours. Every minute or so the crowd that was gathered around the main stage grew in number and then constricted, heaving forward and into a tighter weave, so that even the festivalgoers stubbornly trying to squat on their picnic blankets were forced to stand or else get sneakers and sandals to their spines.

I found myself pushed closer to the stage than I'd intended. Had I stretched a hand between the limbs of the people standing in front of me, I might have touched the metal barricade marking the narrow space where credentialed photographers were allowed to shoot the first three songs of every set. That meant close enough to make out the tattoos of the stagehands who tuned the instruments, and to hear them murmuring, "Check, check," underneath the music a DJ somewhere was playing to keep the crowd hyped. Every so often behind me, a round of rhythmic clapping would start up, the audience signaling their excitement for the show to start. I wasn't about to clap, but despite myself, my pulse had quickened.

The stagehands jogged off and the backing band—Nev's regular touring guys, from Vegas to Kyoto, Gotham Hall to the Hollywood Bowl—marched out to claim their places. I took special note of the drummer: a bald, baby-faced Black guy with a belly, a thick beard, and a pair of glasses like the ones toddlers and NBA players wear, with the rubber strap to hold them in place. Workmanlike, he struck the skins and the cymbal, then settled calmly onto his stool, waiting for the bassist and lead guitarist to get through their adjustments. Soon the DJ's mix faded; the lights clicked off completely. A low vibrating noise, like what you might hear in a popcorn movie before the UFO lands, rolled over the crowd, which commenced to "wooo!" even louder. I put my head down to dig out, from the pocket of my jeans, my pair of rubber earplugs, and I stuffed them in not a moment too soon: I heard a click, the sound of a light popped back on, then that wild human roar that insists, *Entertain us*.

I looked up again at the stage. A figure stood alone at the center, backlit so that he and the guitar slung around his shoulder made a perfect rock-idol silhouette. On the three jumbotron screens, one at each side of the stage and one hovering huge in the middle, he was epically tall, trench coat collar popped, and the tip-top of him—his hair—was molded into a familiar sideways swoop and curl. The flame, from *Things We've Seen*.

For a good minute he stood statuesque through the screaming, as acrid swirls of theatrical fog climbed his body. On either side of me people held up their phones, recording or snapping photos of him, while in front, the professionals slipped into the pit and aimed their lenses up too. That's when I recognized, with a start, Pooja from *Aural*—my last and best hire. How she'd finagled it I'll never know, but the girl had gotten a photo/video credential. I spotted her in that pit darting between guys twice her size, an unselfconscious grin making her look even younger as she leaned slightly backward to get all of Nev Charles to fit within the screen limits of her smartphone.

Finally, movement from the figure on the stage: a tilting of the guitar's neck, a pop-chart jangle, a funny herky-jerky dance. "Daphne, Don't," right off the bat. A bright white spotlight hit center stage, at the exact moment that the drummer kicked in, and Nev, on the huge high-def screens, was revealed in three bright dimensions. This was the crowd-goes-wild moment, but by instinct I felt an urge to look away. In the bright light, to me, Nev looked ridiculous, his face too aged for such stiff, unnaturally colored hair, the long black trench coming off like *Matrix* cosplay. How long had it been since he'd had to try this hard?

And yet everyone around me seemed to be game. The fans up at the front, mostly very young white women, hopped and sang along to the solo Nev hit I imagined most of them had learned from their mothers, from repeat plays during the eighties block on their satellite radios, a soundtrack for the ride to Saturday's soccer. I was old enough, though, to remember when it first came out, and how undeniable it was—how a group of popular older girls at Haviland Day choreographed an aerobics routine to it for a stupid gym-class assignment, how the *doo-doo-doo, oh, don't!* part of the chorus compelled me to tap my foot discreetly while glowering high up in the bleachers.

I had to admit Nev was in good voice this night, and the crackerjack band was reenergized and album-quality. The brother behind the drums got damn near jolly in the pocket, swinging like Ringo. As they jammed toward the bridge Nev loosened up too, hiked a foot on an amp and leaned into the crowd, holding the microphone out for a massive sing-along. On the jumbotron screens, his smile was ecstatic, and I wondered suddenly when he'd gotten veneers. These weren't the same teeth from '76.

"Hello, Derring-duh-doo-doo-doo!" he sang, three fist pumps accompanied by three hits of snare, and then the bass and guitar fell out and the drummer switched into the rabbity pace of "Shot in the Arm," an entirely different Nev fave from *Recovery* (1978). *Heart race / Gun chase / Round the bend with you* . . . Taking his place back behind the microphone stand, Nev deadpanned the lyrics again and again over that breathless-fast beat. He was teasing us, holding off the guitar riff that opened into the rest of the song. He pointed at the audience and nodded encouragement, and as they picked up the chant he shrugged out of the trench to reveal a simple white button-down with sleeves pre-rolled, skinny blue jeans, Chelsea boots. As soon as the coat dropped, an assistant darted from stage right to retrieve it. *Here we go*, I thought. Time was collapsing and this was the bridge, from pure pop into a harder, trickier sound; my mouth went dry riding over it. I stood on tiptoe and searched for Pooja in the pit, rooting for her to be ready, but when I spotted her she was huddled among the other photographers, her cameraphone trained on the side of the stage where the assistant had entered. "No, no," I would have told her, if it were still my place. "Opal would never come in that easy."

Finally, the guitar riff rang out and the crowd gave a roar as Nev and the band launched into the full song. But we weren't satisfied, not quite yet. Not with the promise of Opal still such a tease.

Something—someone—knocked into me from behind; the crowd was rearranging, reconfiguring, jostling me out of the place where I'd been standing. I turned to see three Black women holding hands and coming up fast, snaking their way through the crowd to claim a better spot. The navigator wore a fisherman's hat over long green braids, a three-strand nose-to-ear gold chain, and an X-Ray Spex T-shirt cut into a midriff. The friends she steered had painted their faces with white marks in different, artful patterns: dotting one eyelid and down the bridge of the nose, striping the cheekbones and center of the chin. I stepped aside as much as I could to make room for them, these kindred Black girls a generation removed, and turned back around to face the stage. I expected to feel the brush of them as they passed, even hoped to maybe ask one of them for an interview later, but as "Shot in the Arm" boiled back down to a quick beat and Nev's vocal, the only thing I felt was another rough shove.

"Wow . . . Don't you know how to say 'excuse me'?"

The reprimand came from directly behind me, the *ess* sounds particularly harsh. I glanced over my shoulder to see the Black girlfriends had squeezed next to a short white woman in pigtails and a bikini top whose crossed-arm stance and sour face told me she was the one who'd called them rude.

"I *did* say 'excuse me,' but you didn't move," the navigator muttered.

"And in case you weren't aware?" said the friend with the dots, a little louder. "You don't own the grass here, love. We paid exactly a fortune for these tickets, just like you."

There was a little more sniping, but once it quieted I went back to minding my business. Almost as soon as I turned back around, I felt a tap on my shoulder. It was the offended white woman, signaling for me to bend down to her.

"I'm so sorry for knocking into you just now," she said in my ear, her hand lingering on my shoulder. "Some people . . ." She rolled her eyes in the direction of the young Black women, who at this point were completely unbothered, their attention focused on the jumbotron screens.

"Not a problem," I said, and gave a tight smile.

Again I turned around, hoping that this was the end of it. Because we were getting closer, closer now to the moment nobody wanted to miss. Up onstage Nev was prancing, dragging the mic stand around, sweaty and beatific. "Bloody hell, you maniacs!" he shouted. He pulled the fabric of his shirt in and out and approached the drummer. "These old tunes are a decent workout, yeah, Jordan?"

In response, Jordan grinned and switched to an even more complicated rhythm, heavy on the kick. On the jumbotron screens Nev's brows shot skyward, and he tossed back his head and laughed. "Looks like my friends are in rare form tonight," he said, strolling back toward the audience.

"Come on, Opaaaaaaa!" someone far back in the crowd screamed.

"Well, then," Nev said. "Speaking of friends, and rare forms . . ."

The low, vibrating noise sounded again underneath Jordan's relentless new rhythm, and a spotlight hit the floor near the front of the stage. The three Black Opal Jewel fans were jumping up and down now, hugging each other. The bass and lead guitar came in, and suddenly we had landed inside "Chalk White." Opal's vocals invaded us, it seemed, from everywhere at once. *Hi, hello / I need to know / You hear me . . .* Some clever producer was twiddling with a recording of her, so that her voice was isolated and zipping to the left, the right, the front, the back . . . But where would Opal herself come from? Ludicrously I looked up to the night sky, as if she were going to drop in on a ride from a meteor. The Derringdo cameraman filming the show for the jumbotrons panned over the front of the audience, made us the butt of the joke: We could see ourselves now on the screens, swiveling around, anxious and confused. I picked out the green-haired leader among the three Black girls, and she suddenly pointed straight ahead at something that, I could see when I turned back toward the stage, had shifted on the floor. Her friends, seeing this too, started thrashing up and down, one of them grasping the sides of her head and screaming to anyone around her, "Oh my God, this bitch! This *biiiiitch!*"

"Hey!" yelped the touchy white woman behind me. "Could you please watch your arms?"

But nobody had time for saying "sorry," because inch by inch Opal Jewel was emerging, sprouting through a trapdoor in the stage. Her first live performance in twenty-five years . . . The photographers in the pit scrambled to get it on record, and the clever Derringdo cameraman trained his lens in that direction too.

First came the headpiece: a towering pile of shimmering black, with an African violet blooming 3D from a crack in the front. At the heart of the huge purple petals, a shoot tipped with yellow—the pistil, it's called—reached out toward us, pulsing. And then came Opal's ageless face, that enviable ebony skin. . . . Her eyes were closed, finished with a fringe of babydoll lashes. Her lips, plump and lacquered purple, with a vertical line of bright yellow dribbling from the bow at the top through the V of her chin. Her neck was outrageously long, her shoulders bare—collarbones popping, arms toned and akimbo in an at-ease position. She rose and she rose: With her carriage so peaceful, with the remnants of fog still swamping the stage and coiling around the giant violet, she looked as if she were being pulled from a nap at a cryogenic day spa.

"Wait, is she out here *naked*?" one of the Black friends asked in awe as a faint shadow of cleavage came into view.

Hi, hello / I need to know / You hear me. . . .

But of course she was dressed—Virgil LaFleur had seen to that. Soon we saw the twin rounds of a strapless black bodice, pleated origami-style. A bright yellow line ran from cleavage to crotch, mimicking the detail that split Opal's lips, and a shiny thin belt of the same electric hue intersected this line at her trim little waist. From there, the legs of the jumpsuit split off, tapering into cuffs just above her bare feet. The platform was not done elevating her yet—it lifted past floor level, rising like a round layer of cake with Opal the avant figure on top. A mural of raised fists in every color decorated the sides of the platform, and when it reached about five feet above stage level, it began to slowly rotate, counterclockwise. From his position at the base of the platform, the jumbotron guy let us admire Opal from every angle in close-up. We saw the yellow zipper detail on the back of the jumpsuit; the impeccable tailoring that gave her halfway the shape she'd always envied; the sparkly violet mic at rest in her hands. On display in her LaFleur original,

Opal Jewel was indeed everything: classic and modern, petite and immense, formal and casual, bold and restrained. Virgil must have been, *should* have been very proud.

When one full revolution was complete, Opal facing us once again, the platform stopped turning and her eyes popped open. The rest of her face remained impassive, but as the vocal recording continued to flit from speaker to speaker she turned her head to follow it, coolly considering the screaming sea of us—the largest live audience she had ever commanded. Twenty thousand paying festivalgoers out on this chilly spring night, waiting to see what Opal Jewel would do—at least 150 times the number who'd once cheered a weird-looking Black girl on the stage of the Smythe, despite not even knowing her name. Now, decades after she'd been infamous and loudmouthed and then relegated to the cultish margins, the edgy B story to Nev Charles's A, here was the kind of critical mass she'd always dreamed she could galvanize. And the crowd was not only here in the flesh, but also swarming virtual, sending a steady flow of hearts and thumbs-up floating across the Derringdo livestream. I don't know to what extent Opal understood the enormity of that, claiming as she did to distrust fame and the potential fickleness of this "moment" she was having—and yet I couldn't ignore how well rehearsed she seemed to be in seizing it. She stomped a bare foot along with the beat, pulled her arms from around her back, and dipped into a miraculously controlled and sexy squat.

Hi, hello / I need to know—

Suddenly the sound dropped out—her recorded voice, the drums, and eventually the crowd's screams. All of us reverent inside the same swell of anticipation. Then Opal Jewel brought the mic to her mouth, took a breath, and screamed:

"YOU HEAR ME!"

The next twenty or so minutes . . . Christ, I don't know. It's hard to pick out distinct notes, but I'll try to piece them together in some sort of string that makes temporal sense: Somehow, a set of stairs appeared by the platform and Opal was stomping down them. Somehow, Nev was holding his hand out to her, bowing down toward the African violet, taking theatrical sniffs.

Somehow the two of them were playing off each other, wriggling back-to-back, lunging front-to-front, trading lyrics and growls and coos and winks. Somehow she fucked up his flame, yanked the moussed stiffness out of his hair with her fingers so he looked younger, wilder, oddly handsome again. Somehow he was playing the hell out of his guitar, and made me forget the Doritos commercial, or his head popping out of that apple pie, or 2013's snoozy Las Vegas residency. Somehow they were twenty-something again, conducting the energy of a young, hungry audience.

But what lingers most from Opal & Nev's first and last reunion show was, ironically, their breather—the moment the music settled down, for a medley of "Ginger's Lament" and "Ron Is Gone." Pooja and the other photographers had long since been hustled out, back to the media room backstage to upload their digital content, and Opal sat at the lip of the stage in the spotlight, her legs dangling into the emptied-out space. A softer, bluish gel lit Nev at stage left—he had switched to acoustic guitar and harmonies, and standing behind his mic, he was her only accompaniment. These selections required Opal to sing, to show a more nuanced and tender side, and I noticed a new quality and texture to her voice. It was richer and deeper . . . markedly older. Was her voice where she'd been keeping the wisdom and wear of sixty-seven years? I wondered. But soon my attention was pulled to the images flickering across the huge center screen that seemed to hang in midair behind the band. It had switched off from the live feed to display a series of photos, a slideshow of Bob Hize at work, including the joyful candid shot I'd seen atop his baby grand. That one held steady a moment, inspiring scattered, respectful applause from the Mercurials who happened to recognize him, and then the screen rotated through a longer memorial montage. There was a snapshot from Opal's last Chinese feast in Detroit, and the image on the screen zoomed in on her mother, Ruby Robinson, with her proud grin and her glass of white zinfandel. A black-and-white of Nev in his Boys from Birmingham tough-guy getup and guitar, standing in front of his mismatched parents, Morris and Helen Charles. Opal and Virgil in eighties attire flanking their good friend Christopher Givens, hollow-cheeked and smiling weakly from a recliner, a blanket over his lap and a Christmas tree dripping gold tinsel behind him. The melancholy but beautiful photo of Star Acadia from her one and only album cover, released twelve years before her heroin addiction finally claimed her life.

Oh, God . . . I knew what had to be coming.

And there it was, the photo of Jimmy from Opal's house in Baldwin Hills. Ironic, how it seemed even more intimate in this context . . . With it blown up so giant, so unexpectedly crisp, from where I was standing I could raise a finger in the air and trace that trickle of sweat on his forehead. With my thumb I could rub the worry lines between his brows, like my mother would do to me when I was a child, in our living room reading or sunk deep in thought.

There was more polite applause from the audience, and Opal hit a climactic note while Nev's guitar wore down slow and deliberate. I could see a stagehand waiting to give Nev back his electric, and I realized the medley was nearing its end. *No, no, wait!* I panicked, desperate for the photo of Jimmy to stay as long as possible.

"If you don't know the beautiful man in this picture," Opal was saying now to her audience, "he was our drummer, and his name was James Curtis the Third. Say . . . his . . . name!"

"James Curtis the Third!" the crowd roared back.

"Yes, yes," said Opal. "Almost forty-five years ago now we lost him to the same rot that eats away at this country today. Me and Nev, we were lucky to get out alive, but I'm not exaggerating when I say it was the worst night of our young, dumb lives . . ."

I scrabbled inside my tote bag for my phone, praying I had enough juice left to record.

"Some days I think I have a handle on it, you know?" she said. "Like it's in the past and I dealt with it the best way I knew how." She shook her head and laughed, *Tuh.* "But then I see Black people are still murdered with impunity, I hear us having to scream in the year 2016 that Black lives have value, I see the news trying to blame us in our own stories of injustice, and then I'm snatched right back, struggling to understand what doesn't make sense."

Opal was rising to her feet now, and I hadn't found my phone, and the center screen that held the image of Jimmy switched to a blank bright white. Immediately the rest of the band kicked in, charging back into a high and hard, familiar energy . . . The breather was over, then, and we were moving on. To "Who's the Nigger Now?"

Of course. Of *course*.

"Now, I debated whether we should even do this old song," Opal was saying over the music, pacing the stage as the crowd exploded around me. "But you know what? I think it's still relevant. Because the more things change, the more they stay the same—that's what Jimmy would say. What's the same right now is I'm *still* pissed off . . . and white people, be warned: You *still* can't say 'nigger.' "

I heard laughter and screams, including Nev's crazed cackle amplified, as Opal launched into the verse. Behind me there were waves upon waves of people, an intimidating current to push against. I endured most of the song with my eyes closed and my teeth clenched. Trying to mentally transport myself, to swallow what felt like seasickness mixed with unbridled, unbidden nostalgia.

Later, via several snatches of shaky amateur footage posted to YouTube, I saw the start of the intermittent light that would force me back into my body. Not a strobe from the stage, but distracting flashes moving quick through the right perimeter of the crowd and toward the center, where I was standing. At one point a flash hit me directly in the face and I was knocked nearly off my feet by a violent charge. When I opened my eyes I saw three Derringdo security guards, one of them flicking the beam of his powerful flashlight on and off right into my face.

"Her?" another one said, meaning me. After a couple seconds of blinding light I saw the short, offended white woman from earlier, now in hysterical tears and rubbing a red mark on her forehead. She'd sustained some kind of injury, it seemed, but it was unclear whether the redness was from an accidental elbow or a balled fist or simply from her constant rubbing. She shook her head and indicated to the guards another place in the crowd. Where she pointed I could see the back of the young Black woman with the fisherman hat and green braids, bouncing joyously, obliviously, atop the railing of the metal barricade. I'd later learn that her name was Jamilah Reid, and that she and the friends who'd come with her were in a punk band called the Uppity

Negresses, and that they had pooled their money and driven overnight from Baltimore, just to see their idol Opal Jewel. They had plans to drive back as soon the show was over; one of them had to work the next afternoon. In the meantime they were making the most of this time that they had. And Jamilah Reid had made it *right there*, as close to Opal as any of us general-admission folks could get. As she told media outlets the next day, she was thrilled when Opal saw her—though we must not have been too hard to spot, us Black folks rocking out at the front of this Derringdo crowd—and the two of them had locked eyes and souls, Jamilah said, scream-singing and pumping their fists at each other. *I heard he wore that hood, and flew that flag / I poured gasoline on a dirty old rag / I found where he lived, I set it ablaze / I was going to have my say. . . .*

When the Derringdo guards reached her, Jamilah recounted to reporters the following day, she told them she hadn't assaulted anybody—she'd only been excited, only wanted to get closer to the stage. Wasn't everybody excited; wasn't this a rock-and-roll show? Wasn't everybody pushing and shoving for space, and didn't accidents happen? Couldn't she get the benefit of the doubt? Still, one of the guards had grabbed Jamilah under her arms and pulled her down, because no matter what, she was standing on the metal barricade, and *that* was clearly against the rules. Her friends had grabbed her waist, trying to hold on to her, and they only let go when her X-Ray Spex shirt nearly ripped off in the struggle and the guards refused to stop pulling.

I was standing not far from where this unfolded in real time, but because of all the people blocking the view I got only snatches of what happened. "Jesus Christ!" someone tall near me shouted, then, "What the fuck, dude?" and, "Oh, come on!" I saw a different light around me now, the light of several cameraphones pointing up, trying to catch whatever was going on. There were so many bodies in the way. When I looked up at the side screens, though, I saw that Opal was frowning. She had stopped singing, and the pistil of her African violet was pointing down. Whatever was happening, Opal could see it.

"Hold up, hold up, guys," she said into the mic, but the band charged on behind her. Just as she squatted to her knees and cocked her head, saying something indistinguishable into the audience, perhaps to the security guys, the jumbotron camera careened away and then the image of Nev, behind his standing mic at stage left, filled up all the screens.

I saw it that night but you can see it for yourself, if you slow down the replay of the livestream: When you hear Opal again shout into the mic, "Stop, stop," Nev glances over her way, then turns toward his touring band and shakes his head, *Don't*. It seemed that he'd heard Opal very clearly, then, that he'd gotten at least a hint of something objectionable happening below. But when the most exciting and urgent gig he'd enjoyed in years was on the verge of being inconveniently interrupted, he'd ignored her. He'd simply gone on with the show.

On the amateur videos that would hit the internet later, the shaky ones that showed the Derringdo security guards dragging Jamilah Reid backward out of the crowd and toward some on-site holding station, you can hear several outraged people. They're nearly drowned out by the music from the band and Nev's vocals, but you can hear them, ever so slightly, and some of those who posted to YouTube include subtitles to help you make out their words. They stand back and they get out of the way when the guards come through, but they shout things like "Where are you taking her?" and "What are you *doing*?" "Taping you is completely legal," says a fan, when one of the three guards breaks off from the other two and orders him to shut off his phone. On another video, there's a fuzzy, overly zoomed-in picture of Opal Jewel on her knees gesturing with her hands, shouting something indecipherable.

But here in real time, the vast majority of the Derringdo audience—that is, those outside the cluster of direct eyewitnesses—had no clue what was going on, why Opal Jewel had stopped singing so abruptly. There were a few seconds of confusion, with "Who's the Nigger Now?" trailing off clumsily before Nev guided the band into "The Lane Where I Lived." That weird hiccupy moment smoothed right on out, and the set was back on track. Nev sang and he played; he kept his eyes closed, as if deeply focused and moved by the music.

Though the spotlight had skipped away from her, and the jumbotron camera too, I stood on tiptoe and watched Opal in miniature, watching Nev. For a moment she just stood there at the center of the stage, her hands loose at her sides. Then she lifted her sparkly mic to her mouth and tried to say something into it, but suddenly it wasn't working. She tapped it and tapped it, but when no sound came out, she dropped it.

When I saw Opal heading for Nev, it seemed to me to be happening in slow motion; those with their attention trained on him via the big screens, though, tell me she invaded quick and sudden from the right. In any case, what happened next is recorded and indisputable: As he opens his eyes at the last moment, sees her coming at him, and visibly flinches, Opal reaches up with both her hands, grasps both sides of his face, and pulls him down to her in a hard, deep kiss.

For a moment Nev was frozen in shock—he finally, finally stopped playing his guitar. Then the crowd whooped and he waved his arms comically behind him, as if Opal were really socking it to him, as if the two of them were cartoon characters with songbirds and hearts flying around their heads. When she let him go, she knelt to pick up the headwrap, which had slipped off during the course of all this, revealing her shiny bald head. And then she was gone, down a set of steps at the back of the stage.

Running off, like so many times before. The most predictable part of her show.

In her wake, Nev swayed on his feet behind his microphone, putting on like a stumbling drunk. A mess of purple and yellow smeared the bottom of his reddening face. "Ladies and gentlemen . . ." He began to laugh in a wheezing, unfamiliar way; he could barely get words out as the audience "woo!"-ed and laughed along at his flustered state. The camera caught the drummer and bassist, who'd also stopped playing and were laughing too, shaking their heads. "Oh, God," Nev said, struggling to get himself together. "Isn't she something, friends? Opal Jewel, everyone!"

"Wait, that's *it*?" I heard someone shout.

"She's coming back, right?" a man-bunned guy standing beside me asked, as if I could possibly know.

Three Nev songs later, when it became clear Opal wasn't, in fact, *coming back*, the energy of the show began to wane. Without her there to sing the Mercurial favorites with him, without even a backup singer who might have filled Opal's shoes, Nev and his band leaned fully into his regular solo repertoire. But he'd already spun through the biggest hits that weren't ballads, that had the right tempo and tone for this crowd. There was a moment of restlessness, and then people started to leave, to talk to each other about taking off early and beating the traffic. With the sea of festivalgoers receding behind me, I was free to go now too. *That's it*, I told myself, *that's enough*. I turned away from the stage, looking for the guideposts that would lead me back to the shuttle buses.

I was trudging in that direction, with the Britpoppy melodies from Nev's nineties phase trailing behind me, when a vibration tickled my hip. I stopped and sighed: My phone had been inside my jacket pocket this whole time. When I pulled it out, it was lit with a news alert from Aural.com—like a true masochist, I still hadn't unsubscribed. Goggling at the headline, freezing in the stream of fans heading toward the exit, I opened the story and read.

BREAKING: "OPAL CALLS REUNION WITH NEV 'A MISTAKE,'" AURAL.COM, JUNE 10, 2016
By Pooja Banerjee

Protesting alleged abuses against a Black fan in the audience of the Derringdo Festival on Friday night, Opal Jewel walked off the stage in the middle of her highly anticipated set with Nev Charles and took hopes for a larger reunion tour with her.

"I will not in good conscience perform in environments that are unsafe for my fans," she said, after she stunned reporters by crashing the backstage press tent immediately after her sudden, dramatic exit. "It became obvious to me tonight that trying to do this was a mistake, because my former partner doesn't feel—maybe has never felt—the same way that I do. And I won't have that. I'm too old and too close to the grave, you hear me?"

When asked to clarify her assertions, Jewel, 67, claimed that Charles saw the same thing she did as their performance of "Who's the N***** Now?" reached its peak—a young Black woman allegedly being dragged roughly by festival security off a barricade and out of the audience. When she signaled to Charles to stop the show and try de-escalating the altercation, she claims, he blatantly refused to do so.

"[Stylist] Virgil [LaFleur] and I were in the greenroom all damn day watching the other acts on these same screens," she told reporters, motioning to the monitors behind her on which Charles was still playing to a dwindling audience, "and dozens of white boys were hanging off those barricades at various points. And nobody did nothing to them. So why'd the Black girl get dragged, then? I'm not gonna stand for that, not with my name attached. Not right in front of my face. These Derringdo folks need to apologize to that girl on behalf of their thugs, and Nev Charles should be ashamed for closing his eyes."

When asked whether rumors of a reunion tour with Nev were true, Opal Jewel confirmed that they had been in talks about it. "But all that's done now," she said. The big kiss she planted on Charles before leaving, she said, was merely her way of sealing that fact. "That," she said, "was goodbye."

This is a developing story. More to come . . .

———

Aural's Instagram account featured a snippet from the quickie news conference. The backs of several reporters' heads undulated in the foreground, and Opal's head was like a dot surfing them at the top of the screen. I couldn't hear any of what she was saying, even with the phone on speaker and pressed to my ear. The shuttle buses were closer now than the stage, so I broke into a light jog toward them, anxious to get back to the rented white pickup. At least there I could watch for myself in quiet.

On the ten-minute bus ride, the news of Opal's protest, zipping through social media, proved to be an uneasy topic. Two strangers commiserated about tweeting @Derringdo with their complaints. "I mean, I get it, but it's about professionalism," said one woman behind me. "You have to finish the show people paid to see first, and *then* you can bring up whatever issues."

"I don't know what anybody expected," said someone else from the front, and the rest of the bus fell silent. "Opal's not about the bullshit."

"Well, that's fine, but she needs to give me a refund," grumbled another passenger.

But the comment was loud enough for Opal's defender at front to hear. "So your entertainment is more important than somebody's actual life, sir? Did you even hear what she said on the stage? Fuck outta here."

As the two of them parried in an escalating argument about who needed to get the fuck off the bus, as the other passengers gazed in silent titillation, my phone buzzed again—this time an incoming call. Virgil.

"Ms. Shelton, *where are you*?" His voice full of comforting, familiar rebuke.

Opal had been expecting to see me backstage in the media tent, he said. Now they were at "a twenty-four-hour waffle establishment" a few miles down the freeway. "Mad has just ordered half of the menu," he reported. "I'm assuming this means you have time to arrive."

———

The diner swarmed with a post-Derringdo crowd, and I had to look hard to find her. She was huddled in a back booth, squeezed into a corner next to Virgil and half-eclipsed by his heft. Looking like a teenager, anonymous and androgynous: swallowed by a black hoodie, wearing a black baseball cap with an X in white stitching. The only trace of the show I saw was a faint streak of purple lipstick on a balled-up napkin.

By the time I slid into the booth opposite them, Opal had demolished two plates. Dregs of syrup and crushed pecans clung to one, and to the other, a half-moon of congealed grits. She was working on a third now, bacon burnt crispy and a mound of hash browns. Virgil also wore black, a button-down shirt with the sleeves fashionably rolled up his meaty forearms. A tiny bowl of what the diner touted as a "fruit plate" sat in front of him, and I watched him pick out the grapes in favor of the discs of banana. None of us spoke for a while.

Opal reached for her red plastic cup of ice water and sucked down nearly three-quarters of it. She sat back, finally sated. "I forgot what this felt like," she said. "Being so hungry after the show, and then eating too much."

"How'd you get here so quick?" I whispered. "I'd imagine the Derringdo people are hunting you."

Virgil and Opal glanced at each other and Opal's shoulders began shaking with laughter. Virgil's face twitched around the corners of his mouth with the effort to keep in his own.

"What am I missing?"

"As soon as I saw Mad on the monitors leaving the stage," started Virgil, clearing his throat, "I gathered her comfort clothing from the dressing room and I—"

"He stole a golf cart," blurted Opal, tears beginning to roll down her cheeks now, and finally Virgil let out a low laugh, a *huh-huh-huh* I'd never heard come out of him before. "Oh Jesus, oh God, okay . . ." Opal inhaled and exhaled, dabbed at her tears with a napkin. "He was waiting for me outside the media tent, like the damn getaway driver. We tore off through the woods till we found a main road, then Uber did the rest. Presto change-o in the back." She looked around and lifted the bottom of the hoodie up quick, as if flashing me, and I saw the neon piping of the jumpsuit underneath. They fell against each other in a new round of laughter. Their deliriousness irked me.

"As if you're not in enough trouble already."

"Then I guess it really *is* like old times," said Opal. Both of them settled down after that. When the waitress came to clear away a few plates, Opal ducked her head low and turned toward the window.

On the table, Virgil's phone buzzed and lit up with a photo of Han Ishi. "Speaking of being in trouble . . ."

"Take it, baby," said Opal. "Go smooth-talk that handsome man of yours."

Virgil got out of the booth with a grimace, and we watched him limp out the door of the diner to take the call.

"He forgot his cane in the greenroom." Opal surveyed the remaining food on the table, then glanced up at me. "You want some French fries?"

"No, I don't want any fucking fries," I said.

"Go on, I see you looking at 'em. Don't worry, they're paid for. I'm not one to dine and dash." She nudged the plate toward me and I wriggled one fry from the pile, dragging it through a streak of mustard. "And I didn't take their money, at least not all of it, if that's what you're so worked up about," she said. "The festival people, I mean. They only pay half up front and don't pay the rest till the whole thing's done. I'm sure they'll dock me the golf cart and more. Satisfied?"

I ate the fry silently, savagely.

"Why weren't you in the media tent, anyway?" she asked. "I went in there looking for you, but then the other ones jacked me up with their questions. . . . You know how my mouth can be, once it gets going."

"I wasn't in the tent, Opal, because I didn't have the credentials this year," I said. "Didn't you hear? I no longer work for *Aural*, as of that gathering for Bob." I swallowed the lump of potato. "You remember, right? That time you helped to make me look nuts?"

When I reached out to snatch another fry, she put her hand atop mine.

"I'm sorry about that," she said. "That's part of what I had wanted to tell you. If, you know, you'd been in the tent."

I stared down at the table, at my gnawed, naked nails underneath hers, tapered and violet. "You're sorry about my job, or . . . ?"

"I'm sorry for disrespecting you and your work," she said, "and you can take that any number of ways that you want." She squeezed my hand once, then took hers away.

Outside Virgil was talking animatedly into the phone, under the parking lot lights. Around us, a cacophony: the clattering of silverware, sizzles of sausage, bursts of laughter, country pop. In the window's reflection I noticed Opal Jewel was now staring up at something across the restaurant; I turned around to see what it was. On a television hung above the diner's register, CNN was playing on mute: the clip of Nev glancing over and shutting his eyes, spliced with cameraphone footage of Jamilah Reid's body being dragged through the crowd.

"Even if I didn't believe that ugly thing you told me," I heard Opal say, "I shouldn't have stuck my head in the sand."

When I turned back around to finally look at her, I saw an invitation in her face. By now my phone was nearly dead, but inside my bag was a pen, my notebook. I pulled them out.

"So after what you saw him do tonight," I said, "you believe that old story about Nev might be true?"

She met my eyes. "I don't know," she said, and then, slumping back as if exhausted: "But not knowing is scary enough for me."

I wrote down what she'd said exactly as she'd said it. I slid the notebook across to her side of the booth. "This is your statement, for the record?"

Peering down at it, tugging at the bill of her Malcolm X hat, she said, "That is my statement, for the record."

There in my scraggly cursive was the kind of clear, honest response I had tried and failed to eke from Opal in the hallway that day. Could I call this moment closure, then? Victory? I stared at the page and gripped my pen.

"And what else?" Opal's voice was very soft now. "Ask me whatever you want."

I sighed, struggling to put my lingering dissatisfaction into words. "I guess I'm still curious. . . ."

"About?"

"Just, you waited so long for this shot. I saw how bad you wanted it, how much you loved being up on that stage, how *good* you still are—God, as mad as I've been, even I couldn't help rooting for you. You must have felt that, right? The energy, the love? That legacy I know you've been dreaming about, just waiting for you to bring it on home?"

"Yeah," she said, grinning, "I felt it all."

"So there you were: Opal Jewel, right at the threshold of what could be a whole new adventure. And after making it that far, after getting that glimpse of the future, you just walked away? I mean, I admire what you did tonight, but it damn sure wasn't wise. Do you understand what you've done to yourself? There's a chance you might never work again; Derringdo might sue you—shit, who knows, *Nev* might even sue you—and then you could lose what you already have. And I want to know . . . Not *why* you did it, because you've told the world that, but *how*. How could you bear to put everything at risk?"

"Oh, come on," Opal scoffed. "You're a smart girl. No—you're a *brilliant woman*. You have the pieces. Put them together, SarahLena."

I considered admonishing her again—reminding her that my professional name was Sunny, that good journalists avoid working off assumptions. Instead, I found myself offering an answer.

"My dad," I said. "Because my dad was up on that stage with you."

From her hoodie's kangaroo pocket, Opal pulled out the picture of Jimmy behind his drums. "And how could I not take a risk standing up for that girl," she murmured, handing it over as I set down my pen, "when Jimmy did the same for me?"

I cradled the image in my palms. The print was old, spotted, creased at the corners—the original. It had been carried from New York to Paris, Los Angeles to the fairgrounds in New Hampshire. It had survived tears, framing, unframing, elevation. . . .

"I'll make a copy of it," I breathed, "I'll be sure to return it."

"No," said Opal. "It belongs with you."

"But don't you want . . . ?"

"Don't you worry about me," she said. "*I'll* be fine." She shrugged and shook her head. "It'll *all* be fine."

So I said, "Okay," and shut my mouth.

Virgil came limping back, dropping heavily into the booth. Han wasn't coming, he said, and was certainly not driving them back to New York this time of night. He and Virgil had booked a B&B for the long weekend, with plans to tour wineries and Robert Frost's farmhouse, and Han intended to stick to the itinerary. "With or without me, he claims," said Virgil, darkly.

"Well, *with* you, obviously," said Opal. "Go on and call a car. I can find my way back to the city."

"Oh, stop with the martyr-y shit," I said, and slipped the photo of my father safe inside the notebook. "You'll ride back with me."

And so Opal dropped a few twenties on the table, bid Virgil adieu, and climbed into the cab of the horrible white pickup, heading toward New York. She dozed for most of the drive, hood up, while I steered us down the highway and searched for a radio station that would hold for more than a few miles.

How she could be sleeping, how I could be singing . . . Perhaps this was odd in the context of that night, both of us having blown up our careers. We couldn't have foreseen that in the fall, we would restart with new allies: for me, blessed shepherds for this book,* and for Opal, a host of young artists and activists who would help her to build the kind of platforms she had never imagined.† We were unaware too of the grim hangover that loomed ahead, the aftermath of a November blitz that would blast us back inside the most heinous loops of American history. Yes: On this trip through the dark, we were completely ignorant of specifics, on which side of progress or regress we'd land. But Opal had offered her assurance and I had received it, and this felt to me like a mutual leap of faith: If one of us could be brave in facing whatever came next, then so would the other.

Somewhere near Hartford I found an oldies station with a strong signal, and when a good tune came on I turned it up loud. "Everyday People," Sly &

---

* Following the conversation Opal ignited at Derringdo, culminating in an apology from the festival's organizers and a short-lived "Nev Charles is canceled!" online outrage, Aural Media expressed renewed interest in publishing this book. Though my former employer's bid was flattering, ultimately I accepted an offer from Sojourner Books, an imprint dedicated to stories of African American history and culture. My sincere gratitude to the Sojourner team, for believing in this project and embracing its risks.

† At publication time, Opal had been invited to speak at the Essence and Aspen Ideas festivals, and to preside over a planned tribute to her career at Afropunk 2018. She hired Jamilah Reid to run her new verified Twitter and Instagram accounts, @RealOpalJewel, where, on Inauguration Day, she directed Jamilah to post a photo of orange-feathered chickens roosting.

the Family Stone. Opal stirred in the passenger seat, as I'd hoped that she would. In the headlights of a passing car I caught her drowsy smile, and by the time Rose's part on the chorus came back around she was sitting all the way up, pulling some weird shoulder shimmy.

"What is *that*?" I teased, but Opal was caught up now. Doing her thing, rocking it wild.

Acknowledgments

First, my foundation: the Faulk and Walton families have filled my life with love, laughter, and a rich sense of legacy. Thanks to my mama, Phyllis Faulk Walton, who blesses me daily with her wisdom and grace, and who is among the funniest storytellers I know. Thanks to my daddy, Charles Walton, who taught me not only the beauty of dreams but also how to make them real.

PJ Mark believed in this novel from the first draft and encouraged me, in his gentle way, to be as bold as the Opal I wanted to see in the world. Dawn Davis brought the manuscript home with incisive edits that gave this story more focus and propulsion. I thank them, as well as Marysue Rucci, Chelcee Johns, Ian Bonaparte, Brianna Scharfenberg, Leila Siddiqui, David Litman, Kayley Hoffman, Polly Watson, Cassie Browne, Hellie Ogden, and everyone at Janklow & Nesbit, 37 Ink, Simon & Schuster, and Quercus Books who helped deliver this baby.

My 2015 fellowship at MacDowell gave me the confidence and courage to leap, at nearly forty, into the writing life. Thanks to all the gifted artists I met there, especially Emily Hass and Corinne Manning, for taking a wide-eyed rookie under your wings. I am also grateful to the Tin House Summer Workshop for providing invaluable support toward the completion of this novel; and to my professional mentors, including my friend Bill Shapiro and my former colleagues at *Essence*, for what they taught me about stepping up and into purpose.

I treasure the two years I spent at the Iowa Writers' Workshop, thanks to the Meta Rosenberg and Whited fellowships. I got so much better as a writer there, under the tutelage of an all-killer-no-filler lineup of women workshop leaders who read and critiqued pieces of this book. Sugi Ganeshananthan challenged me to complicate the narrative, leading to the birth of Sunny. Amber Dermont encouraged me to lean into the story's wilder aspects. With her No. 2 pencil and ear for rhythm, Margot Livesey sharpened my sentences and the colors of young Nev's world. And when I struggled with structure and direction, Ayana Mathis, with insights regarding both craft and content, helped me break through to the other side.

I came out of Iowa with an enviable community, a brilliant crew deft with the pen. To Afabwaje Kurian, De'Shawn Charles Winslow, Christina Cooke, Monica West, Jade R. Jones, Regina Porter, William Pei Shih, Melissa Mogollon, Eliana Ramage, Dr. Tameka Cage Conley, Grayson Morley, Magogodi Makhene, Jamel Brinkley, Sarah Thankam Mathews, Siyanda Mohutsiwa, and Jianan Qian: I am in awe of your talents and grateful for your friendship, even as we've scattered to the winds. Thanks as well to Sam Chang and the staff at Dey House—Connie Brothers, Deb West, and Jan Zenisek—for the support and care you showed us all.

Thanks to the Aiken and Santagati families for opening your arms to me, and to my bonus mom, Sybil Walton, for her love.

From Florida to Oregon, DC to New York, my chosen family has held me up. For their steady friendship and counsel over the years (in most cases more than twenty!), I am especially grateful to Hermione Malone, Abby West, Kenyatta Matthews, Kamilah Forbes, Ronda Thompson, Janice Morris, Ta-Nehisi Coates, Rashida Clendening, Nandi Smythe, Jackie Weatherspoon, Elton Bradman, Rachel Bachman, Sarah Fuchs, and Chana Garcia (who is desperately missed).

Finally, for everything beautiful he brings to my life, I thank my husband, Anthony Santagati—my heart and my home, right down the line.